THE

REBEL
HEART

Henry Gresham and
the Earl of Essex

Also by Martin Stephen

The Desperate Remedy
The Conscience of the King
The Galleons' Grave

THE
REBEL
HEART

Henry Gresham and
the Earl of Essex

Martin Stephen

sphere

SPHERE

First published in Great Britain in 2006 by Sphere

Copyright © Martin Stephen 2006

The moral right of the author has been asserted.

*With the exception of historical figures, all characters in this publication
are fictitious and any resemblance to real persons, living or dead
is purely coincidental.*

A CIP catalogue record for this book
is available from the British Library.

ISBN-13: 978-0-316-72670-2
ISBN-10: 0-316-72670-2

Typeset in Goudy by M Rules
Printed and bound in Great Britain by
Clays Ltd, St Ives plc

Sphere
An imprint of
Little, Brown Book Group
Brettenham House
Lancaster Place
London WC2E 7EN

A member of the Hachette Livre Group of Companies

www.littlebrown.co.uk

ACKNOWLEDGEMENTS

My thanks go to Sonia Land of Sheil Land Associates, who ought to give agents a good name, and Ursula Mackenzie and Joanne Dickinson of Time Warner, who should do the same for publishers. Thanks to Tara Lawrence, my editor for the first two Henry Gresham novels, who was and is superb, Joanne Dickinson and Viv Redman. I am grateful to Maeve Jeffrey and Ian Stephen for technical information, and to Cambridge University Library for research facilities. I am totally indebted to Jenny for proofreading, and for the same service to Neill, Simon and Henry. My thanks to them for so much support and understanding for this, the fourth Henry Gresham novel.

There are two key historical works on Robert Devereux, Second Earl of Essex without which this book could not have been written. The first is the classic *Elizabeth and Essex: A Tragic History* by Lytton Strachey, and the second is Robert Lacey's *Robert, Earl of Essex: An Elizabethan Icarus*. The latter, published in 1971, is one of the best works of history I have ever read, and I apologise if at times I have inadvertently copied Lacey's brilliant style, as well as his command of historical facts.

Martin Stephen
Congham Manor, Norfolk
April 2006

For Neill, Simon and Henry

PROLOGUE

February, 1598
London

It should be more difficult to kill a Queen. The final simplicity of the act diminished it, reduced it to something mundane.

The King of Spain, the King of France, the King of Scotland, all gathering like vultures over the throne of England; its aged, childless Queen surely soon to die. So what if that death were hastened? What difference in a few months? Or a year? To kill an old woman was not to go against nature, merely to speed it up a little.

The winter had been bitter, and a biting, cutting wind hacked through London, as if determined to scour the flesh off human backs. The Queen was an extraordinary sixty-five years old, and felt the cold more and more. The order had gone out to stoke up the fires. The chimneys in the Palace were badly swept, and the sharp tang of woodsmoke mixed with the smooth perfumes and acrid sweat of overdressed men. The wonderful symmetry of the dark, arched beams paraded the length of the Great Hall, impervious to the squabbling beneath.

The blustering wind caused the fires to blow back, and every so often wafted a stench of shit from some forgotten drain, or from a curtained alcove where a drunken courtier had dropped his load. Corruption. Foul bodies. They were all there, the colour of their

1

finery lighting up the sombre hangings of the Presence Chamber at Greenwich Palace: the fat clergy and the dandified nobles, the wrinkled and the fresh-faced, united in their greed and craving for power; the parasites who fed off the dying flesh of this tired, decaying old Court, gathered like crows over rotting meat.

Three men stood out, each with his court in miniature assembled round him: Sir Robert Cecil; Sir Walter Raleigh. And the Earl of Essex. His was the largest group, the noisiest, the centre of this firmament. Tall, acknowledging his own arrogance and impossibly good-looking, Robert Devereux, 2nd Earl of Essex, was laughing gaily as if he did not have a care in the world, a carefree young man surrounded by the youngest men at Court. As he laughed, so did others, even some who thought they hated him. It was impossible not to be drawn in, infected by his gaiety. Alone of the assembled Bishops and courtiers, nobles and servants, his eyes did not continually flick to the door, guarded by a gold-chained and velvet-clad gentleman. Was the Queen even now making her move to chapel?

Routine. Every Sunday at Greenwich the Queen exited from her private chambers and walked across the Presence Chamber over fresh hay strewn on the floor, with tiny, fragrant strands caught in the bottom of the fine tapestries hung on the walls. The door would be flung open; the procession would start. First a gaggle of gentlemen, Barons, Earls and Knights of the Garter, all richly dressed and bareheaded, puffed up with privilege and false pride, security the last thing on their minds. Then the Lord High Chancellor, bearing the seal of office in a great red purse, flanked by a man carrying the royal sceptre and another the sword of state in its red scabbard, studded with golden fleur-de-lis.

Ritual, ceremony, routine: the false gods by which false monarchs impose their power on poor and flawed mortals. Then would come the true false god: Queen Elizabeth I of England.

She knew how to make an entrance. The ladies-in-waiting were as comely and beautiful as she was ragged with age, their high chins and firm steps seeming to accentuate the line of their bodies beneath the white, virginal court dresses they wore. It took fifty

2

men to guard the Queen on the short journey from her apartments to the chapel, each one armed with a gilt halberd, sparkling in the sunlight that drenched in through the high windows.

All this pomp and pageantry for an old, old woman in a red wig, her teeth black, with small black eyes, a hook nose and a thin mouth. At least she had not gone to fat in her dotage, but the make-up lay thick on her pasty face, threatening to run on a hot day.

He lurked at the back of the crowd, almost leaning against the tapestried wall in his desperate desire to seem calm. Yet it was wrong to be calm. No one here was calm, when fortunes could be made by a word from the Queen, or whole careers vanish in an instant by the absence of a glance. To be nervous was to be normal in this strange circus of dreams. He had to time this perfectly. Yet now the moment had come he *was* calm, almost unnaturally so. The greatest desire of those present was to speak to the Queen, kneel before her and pray that they might be one of the privileged few she invited to stand, or perhaps even one of the extraordinarily lucky men for whom she took off her glove and invited to kiss her jewelled, liver-spotted hand. It was known that she rarely noted anyone before she had progressed the first five or six yards, so the courtiers would rush for the middle ground. When the door crashed open, the crowd would surge forward, the noise would rise to the rafters, the petitioners would move through them or go round the side to take up their positions on either side of the Queen. Bustle, movement, noise: the courtiers half expecting to be brushed aside by the guards. Twenty seconds to burst through to where the Queen stood by the newly opened door, soaking up the attention, before she started to walk. The Lord High Chancellor would be way ahead of her by then, her ladies-in-waiting still gathered behind her in the private apartments and the guards not yet formed up.

That was the moment when a man with faith could kill a Queen.

The pistol had been loaded, primed and checked ruthlessly. It was hidden in the servant's tunic which he would rip open as he lunged forward. Its fastenings were loosened, hanging by only one or two threads in preparation. The head. It had to be the head. God knew what corsetry and whalebone the old lady had on under her gown and mantle to turn aside a blade. With his left hand he would tear open his mantle and bring out the pistol, put it to her head and pull the trigger, while with his right hand he would grab the dagger also hidden under his clothing. If, God forbid, the pistol misfired he would plunge the dagger into her right eye, the one nearest to him.

He would die; he knew that. He prayed he would have time to do it by his own hand. If not, and before they laid him on the rack, he would bite his own tongue off and bleed to death.

Obsessed with his mission, he hardly noticed the thin, slight figure standing a little distance behind him, a man in his mid-thirties with a thin scar running from his chin to just below his right ear. He was drab in appearance, nondescript, looking like one of the lawyers who sometimes acted as clerks to the great men in Court, and who occasionally, as a treat, were allowed into one of the Anterooms so they could tell their families they had seen the Queen. He was the only person hanging back at the rear of the crowd. The assassin dismissed him. He looked to pose no physical threat, and by the time he realised what was happening the Queen would be dead.

He tensed. Was that a scuffling behind the great door? Yes! It was opening, scraping on the floor as a small stone in the freshly strewn hay caught under its bottom edge. The advance party moved forward, the sceptre seeming to capture the light and hurl it back. Then he saw Gloriana, dressed in white with a black silk mantle, gazing imperiously, almost petulantly, at the assembled horde. Please, dear God! Allow this act in your name! Now!

A great silence descended inside his head. His tunic came undone with effortless ease. He saw a button fly off and bounce one, two, three times on the stone floor. His hand grasped the familiar smoothness of the pistol's butt. He took his first step forward, the weapon already halfway out.

The thin, nondescript man leapt forward, clutched the assassin. It was as if two iron pincers closed round his upper body, the pain and shock so sudden that he lost all his breath. His arms pinioned, the pistol hung from his immobilised hand, half jammed in his

4

doublet. Instinctively he tried to twist round, to face whoever had attacked him, his movements forced by frenzy. The slight man did not loosen his grip but turned with him. Off balance, the hugging couple collapsed on to the wall where there was a gap between two tapestries.

And vanished.

The tiny, open service door was hidden behind the hangings. The two fell awkwardly through the tapestries, tumbled down the stairs in almost comic silence, the only real noise the clatter of the pistol as it slipped from the man's hand and followed them, bouncing on the stairs.

The assassin was stunned for a moment. The thin man had only a few seconds. Guards, someone must have seen the squabble, would be charging down the stairs in seconds. Like a lithe snake, the man stood up and, placing his boot full on the assassin's neck, pushed with all his strength. In almost the same movement he pulled out his dagger and plunged it through the assassin's eye, feeling it grate on the back of the skull as a fountain of blood and tissue leapt out to stain the lace on his sleeve. Three, four guards were at the top of the stairs now, clumping down them.

Had only the sharp-eyed guards seen the fracas? He hoped so. It would make life so much easier.

The thin man leant back against the cold stone wall.

'He had a pistol,' he said by way of explanation to the guards. 'Meant for the Queen, I think. His anger was indescribable. I had to kill him before he blew my head off. Now, take me to the Master-at-Arms.'

Uncertainly, unsure of whether they had a saviour or a suspect, the guards surrounded the thin man, escorted him away. Two of them held up the grotesque body of the dead man, his eye socket a blackened hole, leaving a trail of blood behind him as his feet dragged over the slabs, flap-flapping.

Damn him! the thin man was thinking. Damn the dead man! How dare he act before his time, before the due orders had been given!

PART 1

The Road to Scotland

CHAPTER 1

Last Week of May, 1598
London

'My master demands your presence,' the man had said. Few people walked into the palatial house of Sir Henry Gresham and made demands, if they valued their skins.

But of course this was the messenger to Sir Robert Cecil, the Queen's Chief Secretary. It was late afternoon, and all over the country men would be tramping back from the fields, their limbs aching, to the damp hovels with bare-arsed and mud-stained children. In London, those with respectable jobs were setting up the shutters, and the light was in the eyes of those who plied their trade by night.

'This evening. At the Palace.' The messenger's boots were dripping mud on the floor, and his chin was thrust back arrogantly. Mannion, Gresham's body servant, chose that moment to slip out of the room.

Cecil liked to summon Gresham at night and conduct his business in secret. That much was normal. So was the size of the messenger. Cecil's messengers were always huge, surly men who seemed to sneer rather than speak their message from their master. Perhaps Cecil, part hunchback as he was, chose his servants to compensate for his own ugliness.

9

'Your master is a servant to the Queen and to God, as are we all. Neither he, nor you, are God,' said Gresham coldly. He could feel the sharp sense of fear beating at his heart, yet knew not a sign of it would show outwardly. 'You've failed to address me correctly,' he carried on. 'You've failed to use any of the words a child would have been beaten for neglecting – such key words as "please" or "if it please you". You have the opportunity to repeat your request, in language more suited to that of a servant addressing a gentleman. If you fail to take advantage of my generosity, I'll have you beaten. Like a child.'

The tone was flat, cold and intensely threatening. The man blanched, but his arrogance went very deep. He was servant to a man who created the law, not one who obeyed it.

'You would beat the servant of Robert Cecil? The Queen's Chief Secretary? I think not.' His lip was curled in scorn. The initial fear he had felt at Gresham's icy tone was leaving him as quickly as it had come.

'I would not dirty my hands,' said Gresham very quietly, glancing up and looking into the eyes of the servant. Cecil's man could not hold the gaze, looked away. There was a strange intensity in the startling blue of Gresham's eyes so at odds with his dark hair. The look was chilling in its inhumanity. Yes, the servant thought, this is a man who is capable of doing terrible things. 'They would.' Gresham nodded at someone behind the man, who turned to see Mannion grinning at him from the door. Three lusty porters stood beside him, the first with the flattened nose that bespoke a lifetime of drunken brawls. All three carried stout wooden cudgels.

'Now,' said Gresham, 'you wished to make a *request* of me?'

Conflicting emotions flickered across the man's face. He chose the path of least pain. He turned again and looked at Mannion. Mannion smiled at him. That was enough.

'Sir Henry . . .' he faltered, clearly hating it, clearing his throat. 'My master commands—'

Gresham raised an eyebrow.

'My master requests . . .'

Gresham would go, of course. He always did. Like a mouse who could not resist the cheese in the trap. Why did he insist on playing these silly games?

It was late enough to be dark. The streets were treacherous with mud and slime. A horse at night had no way of knowing if the puddle on the road was one inch or two feet deep, until it trod in it and threw its rider. The tide was on their side, so Gresham opted to go upstream to Whitehall, rowed by four men in Gresham livery all of whom grinned at him and seemed pleased to have been hauled out of their beds.

The torches fore and aft in the boat guttered and threw an oily reflection on the black water. Gresham sat at the stern, pensive yet excited, feeling the surge of the water as the oars bit deep. He heard the sucking smack-smack of the blades, his ears attuned to the sound of other oars, other boats. The river was dangerous at night, as were the streets, even for a short journey. There were crossbows and boat axes on board, and it was part of the household routine to check them every day. The lights of the Palace glittered on the waters, fewer and fewer of its windows flaring into the night nowadays as the Court seemed to die a little each week alongside its Queen.

Robert Cecil's room was richly panelled, with a line of stone-mullioned windows down the left-hand side, full of very old, diamond-shaped panes of glass. The light did not so much pass as ripple through them. There were three ornate hangings on the right-hand wall, concealing a series of doors. Or, as it was Cecil, more likely stone seats where men could sit unseen and take notes of the conversation. In browns, greens and russet reds, the hangings illustrated scenes from the Bible. Apparently Cecil had a sense of humour: one of them showed the massacre of the innocents. He had made no attempt to cover the bare, stone floor, and the fire in the huge, stone fireplace decorated with Henry VIII's coat of arms had only a few meagre spluttering logs in it. At least it gave out more heat than its master.

Cecil was dressed in an unfashionably long gown with fur-trimmed collar, and the huge ruff that helped to hide his one shoulder that was higher than the other. Older than Gresham, he always looked half-starved; small and hard black eyes in his pale face, emotionless except for an occasional flash of the extraordinary intelligence that had got him so far. He sat in a high-backed chair at the head of a long table. Table, chairs and panelling looked to have been cut almost from the same tree, their surfaces polished to perfection, hard, glittering. The guest of the moment was clearly meant to sit at the other end of the table, on what was little more than a stool. The fifteen or so other, high-back chairs that Gresham knew could be ranged on either side of the table had been put away somewhere, presumably to make Gresham feel discomfited. Instead he picked up the stool, and walked with it up the length of the table, plonked it down and sat beside Cecil. On his right-hand side, of course. It was done purely to annoy, and it succeeded. A little tic of displeasure flickered on Cecil's cheek.

Power. That was Cecil's game, his lust, his love and his meaning of life. The Queen was dying childless, and lasting power would go to the person who gambled correctly on her successor. The dark, swirling, treacherous currents of Court were more and more hurling Cecil against the Earl of Essex; a power struggle threatening to explode at any moment.

When Gresham appeared Cecil had made a vague gesture as if he might stand up, but had failed to do so. He raised his chin and looked down his nose at Gresham, but before he could speak Gresham cut in.

'Well, my Lord,' he said, 'who *are* you seeking to make the next King or Queen of England?'

There was a distinct colour change on Cecil's face. Good. The advantage would not last; Cecil always recovered well. And Gresham had caught him this glancing blow right at the start of the fight. It meant nothing, but he might as well enjoy the moment

12

while it lasted. Gresham had toyed with asking how the mission to King Henry of France had gone, knowing that its failure would rankle with Cecil, but had decided being outrageous was the better hit.

'It's all the talk of the town, actually,' Gresham said, as if he were discussing the result of a cock fight rather than speaking pure treason. 'Some people believe the King of Scotland is your choice, others the Spanish Infanta. But perhaps you have another favourite up your sleeve? Perhaps you intend to bury your feud with the Earl of Essex and acknowledge him as your master? Or will you use your undoubted charms on the ravishing Arbella?'

There may have been no child born to Elizabeth, but there were enough people with enough royal blood in them to allow the French ambassador to draw up a list of twenty-seven possible contenders for the Crown when Elizabeth died.

'You are aware that the statements you have just made could lose you your head? Perhaps as you appear to have lost your senses the difference would not be noted,' said Cecil. The voice was cold, hard as frost on gravel.

'But who is there to hear us, my Lord?' asked Gresham innocently. 'I know your honour would not permit you to have us overheard.' Well, there was no sideways glance to the hangings, at least. They probably were alone.

'If things are said often enough,' said Cecil through lips that seemed to get thinner with every word, 'they *are* overheard. And reported. And luck mixed with an over measure of bravado are likely to prove false gods.'

'I bow to your knowledge of falsity,' said Gresham. 'In that area you're certainly my better.'

'This is nonsense,' said Cecil, implying boredom with the exchange. 'The plain truth is that it is you who are the fool. You come here at my bidding, despite the several and various dangers that you know such a summons involves, of your own free will. Only a foolish man would come.'

'Even the Devil can speak true at times,' sighed Gresham. 'And

13

does your Lordship, who knows all things, know why this should be so?'

'You think,' said Cecil, with a voice like a surgeon's knife, 'that you come driven by a thirst for danger, a craving for excitement.'

'And isn't that true?' asked Gresham more idly than he felt. The conversation was taking a strange turn, like so many of those he had had with this spider of a man.

'Perhaps in part,' said Cecil. 'But I think there is a greater reason. I think it is because you want to die.'

Damn the man! Damn him to hell! Gresham fought to keep his heart steady, to stop the colour rising in his face.

'I am quite used to your acting as my executioner, at least at one or more remove, my Lord,' said Gresham, no trace of his feelings in his voice. 'I think I prefer your unbridled malice to your concern. At least the former is more familiar.'

'*Concern?*' For the first time something approaching a laugh came into Cecil's tone. A laugh an undertaker might give at being overpaid for the funeral. 'I have no concern for you. I despise you and all you stand for, you and the other overgrown children who gallivant fecklessly through life. Yet I note and understand you, so I may use you for the betterment of this nation. You are too proud to take your own life, Henry Gresham. Yet you are ashamed of that life, and push yourself nearer to death on every mission you undertake in the hope that some other will do what you are too much of a coward to do and take the life which you increasingly despise.'

Gresham gazed into the malevolent glare of Cecil's eyes and did not flinch.

'I do have one advantage over you, my Lord,' he said. 'I know myself. You may indeed know more of me than I might wish. But of yourself, you know too little.'

Cecil was almost mocking now, sure of his advantage.

'I know the death of a young man, the rather foul death, was your responsibility. And that the burden of guilt you quite rightly bear is dissolving into your soul like acid.'

14

It had to come to that, of course. Gresham could feel hot, biting tears trying to rise up in his eyes, to scour them. He must resist.

'I'll make my own peace with the world, and with my soul,' he said, 'and if I do it by fighting that same world and fighting my own soul, it's really no concern of yours. It's a battle that a mind like yours can never comprehend. But you, my Lord, you'll truly go to hell, unlike those of us who already think ourselves in it.'

'You have taken on spiritual duties now?' sneered Cecil. 'How odd, for someone who attends church so rarely.' Another, minor dig, of course. Failure to attend Protestant worship was a punishable offence. Ironically, the taint of closet Catholicism had clung to Gresham ever since the Armada episode. That was despite his nearly losing his life fighting for the Protestants in the Low Countries. 'And why should I prepare for hell? I who have murdered no man, and have no young man – or should I say *lover* – on my conscience?'

'Because you are in love with power,' said Gresham. 'And the lust after power is the greatest evil of humankind. You cloak your lust with words such as "duty" or "loyalty", yet it is all a hypocritical fraud. You are consumed by your lust, your need to control, your need to dominate. You will plot, lie, deceive and kill – though never by your own hand, of course, always through others – all to keep the power that increasingly replaces the blood in your veins. And you do it for self. Not for God, Queen, nor King. For you.'

It was Cecil who could find no instant answer this time. Finally he spoke, 'And do you not enjoy the power you have, Henry Gresham?' he asked quietly. 'The power of your physical strength, the power of your mind, the power money gives you to ignore the fashion or to follow it as you will, and to be yourself?'

'I'm sure I do,' said Gresham, 'but unlike you, I don't actually enjoy myself much, or even really approve of myself. Or of life, as it happens. I survive. That's all. In our world, survival is the only virtue of which I can be certain.'

Cecil allowed another pause.

'Even if this fallacy of my . . . obsession with power was true, do you not contribute to it by doing what I ask? How can you criticise my supposed wielding of power when you help me, albeit in a minor way, to preserve it?'

'Because Machiavelli was right,' said Gresham. 'Rulers need to be evil. We need the power-mad, such as yourself. How often in this country has a good King led his people to defeat and suffering? The saintly Edward the Confessor? While he was confessing, I wonder how many of his subjects he condemned to death, rape and pillage through his innocence, his lack of worldly wisdom? The by-product of your lust for power and the way it has perverted your soul is that you work for stability, for peace, because stability and peace preserve your power. You do the right things for completely the wrong reasons.'

'The wrong reasons? The Spanish have no cause to love you, Henry Gresham. Would you wish to serve under a Spanish monarch? You know of course that only last month thirty-eight fly-boats and five thousand Spanish troops sailed up the Channel, and were only stopped when my Lord of Cumberland sank eighteen of them in Calais?'

True, thought Gresham, but they had never been intended for England. They were Spanish reinforcements for the war in the Netherlands.

Cecil was not to be stopped. 'And you know we face disaster in Ireland, with Tyrone attacking the Blackwater even as we speak? With the Lord Deputy of Ireland dead and no one in his place? We are besieged by enemies, without and within. You suggest that at this time there should be no power in the land?'

I do not question your belief that the power in the land should be you, thought Gresham. Out loud he said, 'I question one thing, my Lord.'

'What might that be?'

Had he got to Cecil? This time it was difficult to tell.

'You mention your wielding of power. I was under the impression you were fighting for power. The power to defeat Spain. The power,

16

even, to defeat Ireland. But to wield external power you have to secure your foundations. Inner power. That long and, to be frank, exceedingly tedious feud between yourself and the Earl of Essex does seem to be coming to a head, with the Queen as she is. I assume that's why you asked to see me? Some dirty work to give you an advantage over Essex? Who, as you know full well, is a companion of mine?'

Cecil gazed flatly at Gresham, then surprised him by standing up, slowly and as if in some pain, and going over to the sideboard parked in isolation between two of the windows. A fine Venetian decanter and two matching glasses stood on it. Cecil turned to look at Gresham, motioning to the decanter. Gresham shrugged non-committally, and Cecil poured a single glass, bringing it over to Gresham.

Good God! This was an unusual day! The wine was actually quite drinkable. Cecil usually only offered cat's piss to visitors.

'My congratulations on the wine, my Lord,' said Gresham.

'Someone important was here before you,' said Cecil.

Ouch, thought Gresham. That put me firmly in my place. It never did to underestimate Cecil. Or to cease attacking him, for that matter.

The obvious thing was for Gresham to ask who the important person had been. The amusing thing therefore was not to ask. As he had hoped, Cecil was eventually forced to provide the answer.

'The important person was one of my family's oldest friends. He brought me news. Disturbing news.'

'Good God!' said Gresham. 'Don't tell me someone told the Queen how much Burghley House cost your father?' Lord Burghley may have done noble service to the Queen, but he had also done noble service to himself, a service fully witnessed in the size of the mansion he had erected to his own glory.

Cecil's eyes actually closed for a brief moment, in the manner of someone having to restrain the strongest of all possible urges, but he carried on calmly enough.

'Robert Devereux, second Earl of Essex, and Henry Wriothesley, fourth Earl of Southampton. Your puerile insults have at least one germ of truth. Both are . . . crucial. And both have links to my father, Lord Burghley.'

What man referred to his father by his title, thought Gresham?

'Both men were taken into your father's care as boys,' said Gresham. A spy who hoped to survive needed a secure grasp of facts, living as he did amid so many fictions. 'They became his wards when their fathers died. As one of the richest and most influential people in the country, he was flooded with requests to take on the aristocratic children whose parents had been stupid enough to die. He made an exception to his normal rule in their case. Indeed, you must have met them as children yourself. Rather, after you were a child yourself – if ever you had a childhood.'

'Yes, I had a childhood,' said Cecil. For a brief moment, the tiniest of flickers, something fell from his eyes, and a huge sadness came into their hard, undecipherable depths. 'You were taunted because you had no father. I was taunted because of who my father was. And, of course, because I was a cripple.'

Gresham had learnt that there were times when silence was the best answer.

Eventually, Cecil carried on. Brisk. Businesslike.

'And yes, I did meet them in my father's houses. And saw them for what they were. Children reveal themselves even more easily than adults.'

'And what was it you saw?'

'Two young minds unfettered, controlled by no sense of duty, no sense of loyalty, no sense of a higher good. Controlled rather by their own vainglory, their own sense of self. Two minds controlled by their bodies, driven by physicality, devoted solely to the pursuit of their own gratification,' Cecil replied, unable to control the curl of his lip that spoke of his disgust.

'Sounds wonderful fun to me,' said Gresham. 'You should have tried it. I find Essex highly amusing.'

'I know of your relationship. It is an advantage to me in what I wish, not a disadvantage.'

18

'Ignoring my friendship with Essex for a moment, what do two children pulling the wings off flies in wanton cruelty have to do with a man hoping to take control of the new kingdom as he and his family have controlled the old kingdom? And how is your dear father, by the way?'

'My father continues to be unwell,' said Cecil briefly. 'And as for the two children, they *have* nothing to do with that man,' said Cecil, the grammatician in him revealing itself. 'They *may* have an unfortunate amount to do with that man in the future.'

'Why so?' said Gresham. 'Two wanton souls bent on destruction, as you see them, are surely only of concern to themselves and the few who truly love them.'

'Such "wanton souls", as you describe them, rarely satisfy themselves with self-destruction. They are only happy when they carry others along with them.' Cecil's tone was full of loathing.

'Which, for someone whose vision of the world is dominated by his place in it, must mean that you perceive in these two a threat to yourself,' said Gresham.

Cecil carried on as if he had not heard him.

'Essex is the leader of the pair, always has been, even in their childhood. Southampton is rotten to the core, a vehicle merely of his own pleasure. It was always so.'

'But what have they done in their adulthood,' asked Gresham boring in now to the core of the issue, 'to arouse your very evident concern?'

'It is not what they have done. It is the perception of what they are doing.'

Gresham jammed his goblet down on the table.

'Clearly, you need me. And if I'd wanted an oracle I could have sailed to Delphos. Tell me.'

Cecil looked distastefully at Gresham.

'It is rumoured that both men are involved in satanic rituals. Black magic. Rituals that involve child sacrifice.'

Gresham paused for thought. So this was where the rumours came from.

'So what if they are?'

'The rumour does not stop there. It is said that they learnt such satanic observances in the household of my father. Not just in the house of my father. From his second son. From myself.'

Cecil took another sip from his wine. This was indeed an historic night.

'They say, apparently, that my father was so disappointed with his first son that he entered into a pact with Satan.' Burghley's first son was a buffoon. 'That in exchange for his soul, his sons and heirs would hold power in England.'

It is a rare moment in the life of a human being to feel that one is looking straight into the soul of a fellow man. For a moment, Gresham felt he saw into the heart of Robert Cecil.

'The rumours say that the Devil granted my father his wish. That he gave power in England to him and to his children. That he marked me with the Devil's mark, hunched my back, commanded my nurse to drop me in childhood to remind my father that Satan's gifts come at greater than the asking price, to remind him of who the True Lord was. And that, being born unto the Devil, I recruited the boys in my father's care to that same false faith.'

There was a long silence. The frightening thing was that Gresham was entirely inclined to believe the whole story. He had never believed that hell was warm. Fire could burn, true enough, as he had cause to know. Yet warmth, light and heat were also the source of life. No, hell was cold. Burningly, bitterly cold, the cold of death, of exhaustion. And throughout his life he had sensed that cold in Robert Cecil, ice to Gresham's fire.

'I can see,' said Gresham, 'that such a story might be politically embarrassing. And, by the way, I've seen no hint of any such behaviour in Essex. As for that whingeing little turd, Southampton, I can't speak for him.'

Cecil looked at him, almost pityingly.

'I do not need a vote from the populace to carry on in my role,' he said scathingly, telling a lesser man the obvious truth. 'I do not care what stories go round the taverns, or even the Church. And I am close enough to the Queen to defend myself should she hear these rumours.'

'So what part do I play in all this?' asked Gresham. 'If what you want is for me to sell my soul to Satan and use my newly acquired powers of access to visit him and plead your case, I'm afraid the answer is no. You see, I'm not sure he really exists. At least, not as an outside figure. If he is there at all, he is there as part of everyone. Rather a central figure, actually, in anyone claiming humanity.'

Gresham did not shiver. He had trained himself better than that. Nevertheless, the fact remained that a cold wind blew down the room as he spoke, fluttering even the heavy hangings and causing the fire to billow and smoke to come out into the room.

'I do not require you to visit that gentleman. I *do* require you to take a secret message to another,' said Cecil.

'Who?' said Gresham, suddenly bored with the game. He sensed this was why he had been brought here.

'King James of Scotland,' said Cecil, calmly. 'To deny these rumours. To show him they are false.'

Damn it! Gresham knew he must have registered his shock on his face! Cecil had just announced his own death sentence. No wonder he had placed no listeners behind the hangings. Cecil wished to communicate with the King of Scotland, the most likely heir to Elizabeth's throne. If it were known he was writing secretly to James his comfortable lodgings would be exchanged instantly for the lowest and darkest dungeon in the Tower.

And that would be a kindness compared with what would happen to the messenger entrusted with such an embassy. Elizabeth had just sent off a foul and abusive letter to James, reprimanding him for making it known in Europe that he would be the next King of England.

'My Lord,' said Gresham, his manner now composed, 'can I with my poor muddled wits try to make some sense of this? You've just admitted to me, someone who's admitted that they hate you, that you wish to communicate secretly with the King of Scotland. Such an admission is sufficient to lose you your job and probably your

21

life, and to condemn me, were I fool enough to act as your messenger, to a very painful and probably very sordid death. So you've given me on the one hand a chance to destroy you, and on the other a death warrant for myself.'

'I have told you the truth. As in so many cases, the truth does not justify itself. It is justified by its surroundings. If you left this room and said I wanted to communicate with James of Scotland, no one would believe you – you, who are implicated in every plot, and rapidly becoming an *éminence noir* in all who seek to replace our present Queen. Instead, they would believe you to be the person working for King James, and damn you accordingly for trying to bring the Queen's minister into disrepute. You know the truth of what I need. For once, that truth will remain with you. People might believe I am secretly in correspondence with James of Scotland. They will not believe it if their source of information is you.'

Gresham sighed. 'What you're saying is that I'm your only safe messenger. Anyone else you asked could use the information against you. I'm the only person no one would believe if I betrayed you. No one believes or trusts in me. I'm damaged goods. What a brilliant idea! How on earth would anyone believe that you would trust a damning message to someone who clearly hated you so much and was inherently untrustworthy?'

Cecil was silent.

Gresham spoke again. 'You're making me your messenger because no one believes you'd be stupid enough to do so. You've instant deniability. I can perfectly see what's in it for you. I'm rather less clear as to what's in it for me.'

'The survival of your friends,' said Cecil.

Gresham's heart missed a beat. He said nothing, always the greatest challenge to an interrogator. Cecil fell into the trap. People always did.

'You have only three true friends. I discount Essex – a drinking companion and a mere amusement. You care truly for only three people: that man-mountain of a servant you seem to have afforded the role of a father; Lord Willoughby, your friend and ally since you were at school; and that peasant girl you picked up on your way home from the wars.'

Cecil paused for effect.

A tornado was raging in Gresham's head. He of all people should know the cost of loving another person. As the dying screams of someone he had loved had torn into his soul, just as the red-hot metal had torn into his friend's body, he had vowed never again to expose himself to this terrible pain. Jane, his ward, he could live without. Yet life without Mannion or George . . .

'So,' said Gresham, in the quietest possible voice, 'it's actually come to this, has it? No politics, no manoeuvring for position, no wheels within wheels. A simple, straightforward threat. Serve me, and work against a lesser friend, or be the agent of the destruction of those who are my real friends.' There was almost pity in Gresham's voice, behind the hatred. 'You must be truly desperate.'

Cecil said nothing. This time Gresham chose to fill the gap.

'George. It must be George,' he said. 'I don't care a rat's arse for the girl, and knowing how and where Mannion spends his spare time it's always a gamble whether he'll ever come home.'

Cecil remained silent.

'George told me someone was buying up the bills he had taken out on some of his land to feed his peasants through the famine years. Would that person be you, my Lord? And would it perhaps be the case that poor, soft old George over-extended himself to keep his miserable tenants alive, and mortgaged nearly all his estate, rather than the small portion he has always owned up to?'

'Lord Willoughby inherited an estate that was already two-thirds promised to the moneylenders,' said Cecil, in a calm, passionless voice. 'His father was a pleasant man, and wholly incompetent at managing his estates.' There was a shout from beyond the thick wooden door, a servant calling. Cecil's eyes flickered briefly towards it, as if expecting to see the door burst open and reveal a rampant Mannion. Gresham's eyes never left Cecil's.

'So you could ruin my friend at a moment's notice? Cast him, and his wife, and their screaming brood out onto the streets?'

Gresham hunched forward a little, the academic starting to study the question in depth. It was as if he was playing a game. 'But surely that's not threat enough? You know I've enough money for the both of us, if needs be. No, there must be something else.'

'There is,' said Cecil smugly. 'I needed evidence to show that Willoughby was so desperate for money he would do anything to get it. As for you, it is known, has been known for thirteen years, that you sailed aboard the Armada, were actually seen on its flagship, standing alongside its commander. Since then, you have been tainted by Spain. Indeed, many saw your military involvement in the Low Countries simply as a way to wash from your reputation your link with Spain. I will be clear with you, Henry Gresham.'

'Well,' said Gresham, 'that would be novel.'

Cecil ignored the flippancy.

'I have prepared papers over many months past to incriminate you, your ward, your idiot servant and your clumsy friend in a plot to place the Spanish Infanta on the throne of England. I have also arranged for various equally incriminating items to be placed in the household of three people, each of them on the fringe of every shady business in London, each regular travellers to the continent, and each foreign. One is a Jew, which will, of course, help greatly in any accusations of guilt against him.'

Gresham remembered the pathetic figure of Dr Lopez, the Queen's physician, who when an old and harmless man had been hung, drawn and quartered on a trumped-up treason charge. The Earl of Essex had led the prosecution, and the fact that Lopez was a Jew had helped Essex greatly in securing the conviction. It had not been Essex's finest hour. Gresham had no doubt that if Essex were forced to choose between his own profit and the death or mutilation of someone else, selfishness would win. That was how blue blood stayed blue. It also made Essex, if anything, just a little more exciting. Like a warming fire that could at the same time burn a man alive.

'I have also bribed a minor official of the Court of Spain to testify that you have indeed been acting on behalf of the Infanta for these six months past.'

'And why should such a man put his own life at threat?' asked Gresham.

'Because he is dying, and he cares little if he dies a few months early if my money supports his family,' answered Cecil, as if betrayal, lies and perjury were the bread of his daily life. Which, come to think of it, Gresham pondered, they probably were.

'So you are telling me, my Lord,' said Gresham, 'that if I do not agree to be your messenger you will destroy me and my few friends by implicating us in a Spanish plot against the Queen.'

'Precisely,' said Cecil. 'And it will work, because of your past history and the cloud of suspicion that hovers around you in the Court and beyond.'

'A cloud of suspicion no doubt fostered greatly by you in recent weeks and months?' asked Gresham.

'Of course,' said Cecil, as if surprised by the question. 'Hanging, drawing and quartering is the preferred punishment for traitors. You will not be offered the axe – you are not sufficiently noble. Nor will Lord Willoughby, nor your lesser friends. A pity to see the beautiful body of your ward so treated.'

There were two sources of anger eating at Gresham's soul. The first was at himself. He had let himself be manoeuvred by his old enemy into this position of extreme vulnerability. The second was not useful now. It was a mere distraction to survival: it was anger against Cecil. It would have its day. But not now. Not yet.

'You must need me very much as your messenger,' said Gresham, 'to go to all this trouble.' The only way he could unsettle Cecil was to appear unnaturally calm.

'I need you as my messenger,' said Cecil, 'not merely because if you are caught with my message you will be disbelieved. I need you because my enemies will seek to find and kill my messenger. For that reason he must go alone or with a small party. I do not need a puffed-up servant paying lip service to loyalty until the first sight of an implement of torture; or a minor noble desperate for

25

advancement and caving in to the highest bidder. I need someone skilled enough not to be caught in the first place, someone ruthless enough to fight off opposition and, in the final count, someone with enough to lose to keep his mouth shut if the worst happens. I need a killer who will kill not to protect me but to survive.'

Gresham gave a mock bow. 'I'm flattered you rate my skills so highly. But all you do is raise my curiosity about the nature of this message. It doesn't startle me that you'll ruin me or anyone else to ensure your survival. It startles me that something so threatening to your existence has happened as to make you take the risk of employing me, and by so doing revealing your desperation.' He sat back in his chair and smiled at Cecil. 'You see, I won't accept your mission unless I know exactly what the threat is to you, and what the message I carry actually says.'

Cecil smiled a thin, victorious smile.

'You have no threat to bring against me,' he said, with the slightest trace of smugness.

'Do I not?' said Gresham with the same infuriating smile.

There was a blur of movement, and Cecil found his neck being rammed forcibly against the carved wood of his chair, an arm choking the breath out of him and the blade of a dagger actually piercing the loose, wrinkled skin around his scrawny neck.

'You never were a spy, my Lord!' whispered Gresham in Cecil's ear. 'With one brief tightening of my arm here you are dead, or with one brief stab of this dagger up through your warped back.' As if to emphasise the point, Gresham tightened the grip of his arm for a moment. A single strand of dribble left the corner of Cecil's mouth, ran over his chin and landed on the fine velvet of Gresham's dark doublet. 'I leave you here, seated, stiffening in your chair. I have at least five minutes to make my exit, time enough for a poor spy such as me. You see, your message was so damning to us both that you could not afford a servant to listen to it. And your followers, when you are discovered? There is the shock of finding you dead, the confusion, the chaos. I've no doubt you will have left instructions for the revelation of the plot I am

26

meant to have sponsored. Men such as you seek their revenge even in death.'

Cecil appeared to be suffocating. Gresham allowed a tiny relaxation in his grip, whispering close in the man's ear as he might to a lover. 'Yet a dead man is never obeyed as rapidly as one who is living, a man whose patronage is at an end is never obeyed as is a man who still has favours to hand out. And me? One hour. One single hour. That's all I need to vanish, to disappear where you and yours will never find me. I've money put aside to satisfy ten men's wildest dreams. I've horses for me, my servant and anyone else I care to take, even a trunk packed for just this very moment. I've a ship whose only job is to wait for me, to take me overseas if my world collapses around me. And every horse, every sailor has been planned for a time when there's no time, when speed means the difference between life or death.'

This time it was Gresham who paused for effect. He was surprised by the thinness of Cecil's body as he grasped it. The man was all skin and bone.

'So tell me your message. Or face my putting *my* plan into action, not yours.'

Cecil vomited. A pity, thought Gresham, allowing Cecil's head to crane forward so that no sick lodged in his throat and suffocated him. You lost respect if you wet or filled your pants, or threw up the contents of your stomach in front of another man. And you hated the man who saw or caused it even more. Or perhaps Cecil could not hate Gresham any more than he did?

'*Let me go!*' Cecil croaked. The arm relaxed, but as Cecil sucked in air and allowed his head to sink forward he saw the dagger poised in front of his eyeball. He started back, and the blade followed, its point almost touching his eye.

'Tell me now,' said Gresham, 'what your message is, or you lose an eye shortly before you lose your life.'

'The Earl of Essex has written to King James of Scotland,' said Cecil. Gresham sensed he had taken a decision. He relaxed his hold, moved the dagger and saw Cecil sag forward, retching.

27

Gresham was still by his side. Both men knew what would happen if Cecil cried out for help.

'Saying what?' said Gresham.

Cecil's breathing was returning now, and he was gaining control of himself.

'King James has heard the rumours associating Essex, Southampton and his crew with satanism and with sodomy. James loathes satanism before all other human evils. He prosecutes accused witches personally, testifies to the evil of Devil-worship. He is also a sodomite, and denies that sin with all the passion of a man who wants to throw the first stone.' The breathing was almost back to normal. 'Essex has told James that he, Essex, and the other ward, Southampton, were asked to bow to satanism and to sodomy in their youth. By me. And told him how they have denied it, and how I, the son of their guardian, is the anti-Christ.'

Gresham leant back, and the dagger went silently into its hidden sheath.

'And James will believe it?' he said.

'The King of Scotland is most likely to succeed our present Queen. I have told him for years past to beware of Raleigh. I warned him of the wrong man.'

Well! That was a message for Gresham to bear to the man who had saved his life, to Sir Walter Raleigh.

'I underestimated Essex, saw him as a popinjay, a plaything for the Queen. He has stolen a march on me, poisoned the likely heir to the throne against me. Unless I can reach James in time, the poison will bite. Instead of simply reading what he has been sent, the King of Scotland will start to believe it.'

'So you wish me to betray Essex?' asked Gresham.

'No,' said Cecil. 'I wish you to protect those you care for most, and put right a wrong. I also expect you to see that the greatest disaster that could befall this country would be to have the Earl of Essex as its King, or in a position of real power in its governance.'

'You're at your weakest with a man such as Essex. You are correct: he would make an appalling King. But Essex thinks with his

28

heart. Much of the time he thinks wrongly. But at least his decisions are based on blood flowing through his veins.'

'Essex will not defeat me,' said Cecil.

'No?' said Gresham. 'Yet you don't see what Essex has. You are the cold intellect who is never wrong. You command through fear. Essex is the passionate fool, who is usually wrong – but who commands through love.'

'Love does not decide the fate of nations. Love creates scandals, not power. It is fear that rules.' Cecil was now fully back in control of himself.

'To a point, my Lord. Yet you forget one thing. Any prison only operates because the inmates cooperate with the jailers. There are always fewer jailers than there are prisoners. True, there are locked doors. But those doors have to be opened sometimes: food has to be given; access with lawyers has to be afforded. If every prisoner decides to rise up against his jailers, the jailers die. You rule by fear. The prisoners cooperate through fear. But give them a leader they love, and they have an antidote to their fear.'

'Sentimental nonsense!' spluttered Cecil.

'Is it?' said Gresham. 'This country is ruled by fear. London Bridge displays the heads of traitors on pikes over its main gateway. The people are invited to see traitors hung, drawn and quartered. But what if they find someone they love as they love Essex? At what stage does love conquer fear? They cheer Essex in the streets. They scrawl "Toad" on your walls. You don't understand popularity, because you've never experienced it. Indeed, you scorn it because you don't understand it. But rebellion happens, and it happens in the moments when love and passion break through fear and repression.'

'So you tell me that you love the Earl of Essex?' Gresham heard the scorn and fear that Cecil put into the naming of his enemy and his title. 'That you will betray me and my message to Essex, and the power of love will triumph?'

'No,' said Gresham, 'and your question reveals not only how little you understand men such as Essex, but how little you understand

29

men such as myself. Essex can command the mob. He has the power of love – blind, unthinking, living only for the moment. Yet he's a fool, for all his intelligence. A rather special fool. A brave, handsome, rather dashing and rather glorious and all-too-human fool, but a fool nevertheless. Essex is passion, romance and glamour. Essex is in love with himself. And he yearns for the simplicity, as he sees it, of a soldier's life. All this means he is bound for destruction, because nations do not run on passion, romance and glamour. I could love Essex as I hate you. That doesn't mean to say I could ever serve him.'

'I do not care how you justify taking my message to King James. I care only that you do so.'

Gresham's mind was churning. Cecil's wife was probably the only person who had loved him, and she had died eighteen months earlier, leaving his two children motherless. It would be simplicity itself to have them killed. There were men in every tavern in Southwark who would jump at the chance. Should he threaten Cecil with this?

No!

He had been out-thought by his old enemy, and such a threat would be simple vainglory. He could have killed Cecil tonight and got away with it. He knew it and Cecil knew it. That was the important thing: Cecil knew it. The advantage Cecil had over Gresham had been ripped away from him for a moment, a moment that Cecil had not planned for. That was enough. The seed had been sown: the idea that Gresham could never be entirely controlled. No harm in leaving a seed of doubt, though. As for Gresham, those who struggled frantically in the net caught it even more firmly around them. The man who got out was the man who took his time, found his knife and ever so gently made his escape.

And Essex? Gresham had always refused to be drawn into Essex's political ambition. Affording Cecil a right of reply would not kill Essex.

'My best regards to your dear children,' said Gresham. 'I'm delighted you've two friends at least.'

30

No more. No less. It was enough. Was there a brief flicker of alarm in Cecil's eyes?

Gresham moved forward. How satisfying to note Cecil drawing back, as if in fear. Gresham drew out his handkerchief, a fashionable linen flag so vast as to substitute for a tent on campaign. Carefully, he wiped Cecil's vomit from the table, and threw the cloth into the fire, where it sizzled and spat before turning to black ash.

'Send me your instructions,' said Gresham. 'You're right, of course. I'll do what I can to avoid hurting my friends, not least of all because of what happened to another young man who claimed that dubious privilege of me. But pray I survive your mission. I'm also quite good at laying traps.'

And with that, he left.

CHAPTER 2

First Week of June, 1598
London

W*hy?*
It was the simplest question of all, and for months it had been sounding like a death knell inside Henry Gresham's head.

Why create this wondrous piece of work, this extraordinary triumph of a creature called man, and bless it with sensitivity, creativity and imagination? Why go to all this trouble, and then allow that sensitivity to be corrupted and turn into a beast who could enjoy the screams of the man on the rack? Why plant creativity when all too often it soured into the creativity of murder, ambition and politics? Why bless man with imagination and the capacity to learn so much when, in a few brief years, it all ended up as rotting matter – the flesh of the dead pig as indistinguishable on the spoil heap as the flesh of sensitive, creative and imaginative man?

Many less fortunate than Gresham might have commented, had they been privy to his thoughts, that to be one of the richest men in the kingdom, to be still young and handsome and to be acknowledged as one of the best swordsmen in the country, was not a bad position from which to be unhappy. Yet even that, the reprimand Gresham was honest enough to administer to himself, was having less and less effect on the black melancholia of his mood.

Cecil's summons had lifted his mood, but the sudden realisation that, through his own stupidity, he was now fighting for other lives than his own had plunged him even further down a black pit of depression. A strange melancholy, a sapping misery that rose like a fog over a fenland field, drained away all happiness, light and colour. He fought it, as he had fought any threat to his survival all his life. Yet each day the grey mist advanced a little further into his soul, like a tide that would not be held back. And what would happen when it reached the core of his soul?

It was early morning in the Library of The House, the great mansion in the Strand erected by Sir Thomas Gresham and largely neglected by his bastard son. The day looked to be set fair, a brisk wind whipping up the Thames, but only the occasional, scudding white cloud marking the deep blue of the sky. Outside, most of London seemed to be thronging the street, wasps around the jam pot of the rich houses lying conveniently between the City and Whitehall, all with easy access to the river. With the return of the warm weather, the flies had returned. There seemed to be a plague of them this year, and their angry buzzing filled the houses of the great noblemen and the hovels of lesser men with impartial infestation.

There were worse places to be unhappy in. The early morning sun streamed in through the latticed windows, which stretched almost from floor to ceiling, giving a sweeping view out across the Thames. The blustery wind creamed the occasional white blur on top of the wrinkled surface of the water. Any boat that had one was under sail, the wind ideal for pushing up against the tide. Blue sky, blue water and white sails. It was so pretty. Yet the blue water held the filth of the thousands who crowded London, the seething mass of humanity that filled its streets with noise, discord and the rank sweat of assembled humanity. If God had not decided to make the River Thames tidal, sweeping the filth out to sea every day, London would have died of its own stench in a week.

That bloody girl, Jane, had got her claws into the Library, though God knew what business it was of hers, thought Gresham. Or when she found the time, given the amount of that precious commodity she spent in self-imposed exile locked in her room. She had spent the past two days there, the result of some perceived insult from her guardian. He was damned if he could remember what it had been. The Library held one of the largest collections of books in London, and the girl's interfering meant that some half of the books were now free from their coating of dust. Well, at least it kept her out of his way.

Mannion stood by the door, his huge bulk silent, watchful. Gresham was toying with a paper Jane had handed him, in silence for once. She had found it in a book she had been cleaning. It was a half-written letter from Sir Thomas Gresham to a business acquaintance, a Jew working from Paris. It was meaningless in itself, a business communication that presumably had put even more money into Thomas Gresham's vast pockets. Gresham was surprised at the shock he felt on seeing the handwriting after so many years, as cold and crabbed as the writer.

Father. What a strange, evocative word. A word with so many different meanings.

A great clattering in the courtyard and a great noise announced the arrival of Gresham's closest friend, and a promise that the edge of his loneliness at least might be dulled. George Willoughby – now Lord George Willoughby since the death of his father – had been out of sorts himself recently, worn down by the cares of the badly run estate his father had left him, but he was still a welcome diversion. Or had been, until Cecil had made it clear that George's friendship with Gresham might leave him surveying his own guts on a scaffold. There was always a great noise, wherever George went, and things to be bumped into. George never saw doors, and walked into them before opening them. The Library door decided to resist him – it was of stout English oak and had been there far longer than George – with the result that there was much bashing at handles and bad language before it swung open.

'Bloody door!' said George. 'Surprised a man of your wealth can't have a decent handle fitted!'

34

In more cheerful and youthful days this would have been said with a booming laugh. Now it was said with a rather morose glumness, perhaps even a tinge of jealousy. George's pride had refused Gresham's offers of money, however tactfully they had been presented. Still, there was enough good cheer left in the man for him to smile at Gresham. 'How *very* good to see you!'

George was married to Alice; this had been a condition set by George's father for his inheriting the estate. She was the daughter of his father's favourite hunting companion and had supplied him rather joylessly with two children, conceived on a thoroughly businesslike basis. His increasingly frequent visits to London from his vast inherited estate and its debts were an escape for him. Like so many people, he was drawn to the Court in the hope of picking up some crumbs of patronage. Unfortunately, his scrabbling for patronage left him less and less time to see Gresham.

The two men embraced fondly, the one tall, muscled and lithe, the other bulky and running now ever so slightly to fat, one eyebrow pulled permanently down in a droop. George's craggy face had been marked by the smallpox, and his nose looked as if a fat priest had knelt on it at his christening. It had not rained for a week in the country, and every movement that George made seemed to prompt a fine spurt of dust from his clothes. His boots were grey, as if he had just walked through the cold ashes of a fire. George turned to Mannion.

'He won't tell you to fetch the wine. I will. And an extra flagon for you. He won't order that, either.'

Mannion, who was standing at the back of the room, grinned. George was drinking too much, Gresham reflected, on the increasingly infrequent times he visited him.

'It's wasted on him,' grumbled Gresham. 'You might as well pour decent wine into a cesspit. Feed the great lump Thames water with some alcohol in it and he wouldn't notice.' Grudgingly he nodded to Mannion. Baiting him by keeping him waiting for a drink was one of the few things to lighten Gresham's dreary life at present. Mannion nodded to George, and left to get the wine. He moved surprisingly lightly for someone so thick set and visibly muscled. He was older than Gresham, that much was clear, but by how much? Difficult to tell. Mannion's craggy face gave away few secrets, least of all his real age.

George seemed incapable of being jolly for long.

'I know you delight in ignoring all my warnings,' he said as soon as he had his fist closed comfortably round his goblet, 'but will you take one now?'

'I know,' said Gresham, 'Mannion drinks too much and any minute he's likely to run amuck and rape all the women in London. I've tried to warn as many as possible myself, but there are just too many of them.'

'Will you be serious?' said George, annoyed.

'I am,' said Gresham in a serious voice. 'I found out the truth. He's already done it. There isn't a woman in London he hasn't bedded.'

'Ain't raped none, though,' said Mannion. His speed of return suggested the wine was stored nearby. His preferred drinking vessel was a tankard. A large tankard. 'Wouldn't do that, would I? No need. They keeps running at me.'

'Look,' said George, and this time something in his tone made even Gresham look at him, 'the both of you. This is serious. I keep my ear to the ground at Court, you know, though I doubt any of them know my name.'

No fortune could be made and no fortune sustained unless it fed at regular intervals from the Court, the trough from which all sustenance was sucked. All patronage and wealth had as its source the monarch. George had devoted a lifetime to who was in and who was out, who rising and who falling, loving to chart the extraordinarily treacherous shoals of Court fashion and favour.

'And what do you hear?' Gresham's tone betrayed no interest whatsoever in the answer.

'I hear the name of Henry Gresham,' said George, 'and rather too often – from people who hate you.'

'And why should they talk about me?' said Gresham. 'I haven't had an affair with a Court lady for … weeks. Unlike the Earl of Southampton. I hear he's got Lizzie Vernon pregnant. Or Kissie Vernon, as some of her female friends call her.'

'It's no joke!' said George sharply, taking a long pull at his goblet and motioning to Mannion to refill it. 'The vultures are gathering over the throne of England. It's a positive feeding frenzy. Old Burghley's been on his last legs for months. More important, the Queen can't be far off joining him. Forty years on the throne, for heaven's sake! Only a handful of people in England remember life without Elizabeth as Queen. There's no heir—'

'But there's lots of choices!' said Gresham, with mock enthusiasm. 'Our dear Queen has merely sought to make life interesting for her loyal subjects by leaving the issue of her succession so open! Imagine how boring it would be if she had children and we knew who our next ruler was to be! This way, there's a huge variety for us to choose from.'

George refused to be moved by humour.

'Good God, man!' he snapped. 'You can joke about this? When one heir is the King of our oldest enemy, and the other the heir of our bitterest one?'

King James of Scotland and the Infanta of Spain were two claimants to Elizabeth's crown.

'I can joke about those two. I admit my sense of humour is stretched by the Lady Arbella. No, you're right. I can't joke about her. That face of hers! And those dresses!' He raised his hands in mock horror.

It was a measure of the chaos that threatened an England with no heir that such a milksop was even talked about as a possible successor. Lady Arbella Stuart was a drab girl whose only claim to fame was a massive injection of royal blood in her thin veins.

'Look, I'm telling you,' said George, clearly angered by Gresham's flippancy, 'I've had people name you in plots to put all three on the throne. And the same for plots to put Derby and Essex there as well! Not to mention the Kings of Spain and of France! You're everyone's favourite conspirator.'

So Cecil had been doing his work.

Gresham had been recruited to the vast network of spies paid for personally by Walsingham when he had been a penniless undergraduate at Cambridge. His deep involvement in the underworld of Elizabeth's England had not ceased when he had inherited a fortune, and it had survived even the death of Walsingham.

All around them were the noises of a great household, cushioned by the thick oak doors and the sealed windows, but audible like a low, deep current of sound. The clattering of hooves out in the courtyard as the grooms exercised Gresham's fine stable of horses, the cheerful insults of the stable boys and occasional sound of water as they slopped out the vacated stables. Soft footfalls as maids went about their business; the creak of floorboards. A tide of humanity, each locked in their own world, each viewing themselves as the most important person within it. And all the time The House talked to them, its brick and timber frame expanding with the heat of the day, as if it was taking in a great breath of summer.

'And you're not doing yourself any good by being so friendly with the Earl of Essex!'

'I know you hate Essex,' said Gresham. 'Fine. It's your privilege. I find him amusing and good company. You don't seem to mind being entertained by him, do you? You've been to Essex House with me often enough. And when he's dined here.' And you're jealous of his wealth, his looks and above all his friendship with me, thought Gresham.

'I think the man's rotten to the core, corrupt even. The crowd he hangs around with—'

'Now there you do have a point,' said Gresham. 'I concede he chooses his other friends very badly. When we go out together I'm usually spared his friends.'

'Which makes them hate you for being his favourite,' said George, 'and gets you in even more bad odour. But the conspiracy theories – I'm telling you they're serious. And being seen with a playboy Earl who might well be a conspirator himself doesn't help.'

'They must think I've a lot of time on my hands.' Gresham stood up, and stalked moodily to the great window overlooking the river. There was even more traffic on it now, since George's arrival. The river was a quick and clean way to move round London, avoiding the dust of summer and the clinging, lethal mud of winter. Always provided one did not fall in, or look too closely at the lumps that swept by on the tide, bobbing half in and half out of the water. 'George, I've hardly been at Court these past six months.'

'That's part of what's inflamed the rumours. They talk about you behind their hands when you're there. They get even more nervous when you're not. And when has the truth ever mattered at Court? What matters is if the Queen gets to hear them: that you're involved in every plot against her? If she does, you're dead. She's ready to hang, draw and quarter any man or woman who even mentions death in front of her face, never mind anyone she thinks is plotting to put a successor on her throne.'

Gresham turned to face George, and looked him calmly in the eyes. Should he tell his oldest friend the truth? The truth that George was every bit as much under threat as himself? And all because of him?

'Black magic,' said Gresham, throwing himself down on a chair so hard that it squeaked on the floor. 'Worship of Lucifer. Ritual sacrifices. Of children. Have they mentioned that?'

'What?' said George, caught out for once.

'The latest story is that someone from the Very Top Circles is heavily into satanism.'

'Is it true?' said George. He was part irritated at a story he had not heard and part fascinated. Witchcraft was still an active and all-present evil to all bar the most educated of the populace and, as George's interest showed, to large numbers of those who were educated.

'God knows,' said Gresham. 'Or if he doesn't, presumably Satan does.' Clearly George knew nothing. Which could mean that the story had not spread widely. Or that it did not and had not ever existed except as a smokescreen to hide whatever Cecil's real message and intentions were. 'As for me, as I'm not at all sure that I believe in God it would be perverse of me to believe in Satan, wouldn't it? Northumberland's certainly been dabbling in all sorts of things, and Raleigh's been at some of the sessions more often than's good for him. I've seen nothing of it with Essex. But he compartmentalises his life, and I suspect I'm in my own compartment.'

The Earl of Northumberland was known as the Wizard Earl, gathering a group of people round him who conducted what they called scientific experiments but which others called witchcraft.

'Well,' said George, 'I haven't heard those stories.' His voice took on strength again. 'But I've heard stories connecting you to every plot in Christendom. You're in danger, my boy. You really are. This country is a powder keg poised to explode. You're in danger of being seen as a lit fuse, and of being snuffed out.'

Something in the plain simplicity of George's affection bit into Gresham's heart, though no man and only an exceptional woman would have seen it on his face.

'Thank you,' said Gresham in a flat tone. 'I mean it. I really do. But you see, I don't care very much, quite frankly, about God or Mammon. I suppose I have to admit I care just a little bit about the rather bumbling force of nature that I know of as you. And rather less – indeed, a mere tiny fraction – about that great fat lump who's just polished off a flagon of rather good wine that's wasted on him' – Mannion grinned – 'but otherwise I don't care for very much, except survival.' And perhaps I am starting to care even less about that, he thought. 'Look, I'm not a fool. I've heard the rumours. I'm trying to keep out of it, away from the whole bloody Court, spend as much time as I can in Cambridge.'

'Fair point,' rumbled George, recognising the concession Gresham had made in admitting so much, 'but the College want to tear you apart as well, don't they?'

Gresham was well on the way to refounding the decrepit Granville College where he had studied as a youth. Refounding a Cambridge College, even with all the money he had, had shown that Cambridge had just as many knives as London.

40

'When you've never been popular,' said Gresham with resignation, 'you learn to do without it. To be frank, I'm trying to get out of the world of spying. When I was younger and it was run by Walsingham it was more exciting. Now, most of the time it just seems dirty.'

'It always was dirty,' said George. 'It's just that you didn't want to see it like that and were quite excited by the dirt. Well, you'd better be warned of something else,' said George. 'All the rumours are that you're popular with the Earl of Essex for a different reason.'

'You mean for more than my charm, devilish good looks and cutting wit?'

'That's what it is, is it?' said George, witheringly. 'The Earl must have weak sight and hearing, as well as weak judgement.'

'He's got all three, and more,' said Gresham, 'but at least he's got a bit of life and colour to him. Essex lives life at full speed, beyond full speed. He's exhilarating. Fun. And lots of the time he doesn't give a shit, which attracts me to him.'

Essex and Gresham did not spend a great deal of time in each other's company, but various occasions spent together had gone down in the folklore of the Court.

'Essex knows how to enjoy himself,' said Gresham, thinking back to the last time he had spent an evening with the Earl. As far as he knew, or could remember, most of those involved had recovered from their injuries. But my, it had been fun. 'And even I need that sometimes.'

'You know he's locked in mortal combat with Cecil?' said George.

'Of course I do, idiot. You'd have to be blind and deaf not to know. But calm down. You loathe Essex – fine.'

Was George jealous of Gresham's burgeoning relationship with the Earl? Or was it a basic puritanical sense that rebelled against the Essex set, where one member had gambled away a fortune on the throw of one dice? Or was it simple envy of someone who seemed to have been given so much by nature?

'I'm free to like anyone I wish – even someone you hate. Essex is an occasional social companion – I'm simply a bit of rough he likes to amuse himself with every now and again. I keep out of his politics, and out of everything except his social life. Actually I don't like quite a lot of the people he surrounds himself with as servants and advisers.'

'But you must have an opinion on the battle between him and Cecil?'

'Oh, it's a fascinating contest between the pair of them, I'll grant you that,' said Gresham. 'The Queen's favourite versus her most regarded adviser, who happens to look like a rag doll that's been boiled in the wash. Noble versus commoner. Best out of twelve rounds, winner takes all and the chance to decide the next King of England. I'm best out of it. Let 'em fight it out between themselves.'

'But you say you like Essex, and you detest Cecil. And you're not taking sides?'

'I keep telling you: Essex is an amusing companion. He pulls the curtains back in a darkened room sometimes. Which is what you need, old friend – you're getting far too glum far too often.'

'Essex only believes in himself,' said George rather pompously. 'And he yearns to be seen as a soldier after Cadiz and the Azores.'

'Not much military glory there for him,' said Gresham. 'I'm amazed at how much credit he got.'

George jumped in. 'My guess is that he hangs out with you largely because you're a hero of the wars. A positive veteran! You were fighting in the Low Country long before it was fashionable. And because he's paranoid about people asking him for money, because he hasn't got any, the fact that you're a true old soldier and have more money than you need is another recommendation. Take those two supposed virtues alongside your reputation for womanising, and you're everything Essex wants in a man.'

'At least I'm not everything the Earl of Southampton wants in a man. Now that would be embarrassing.' Southampton was Essex's closest friend – the Court referred to them and their circle as the 'fantasty calls' partly because of the extravagant nature of their dress – and rumoured to prefer young boys to women.

'Talking of which,' said George, 'there's another reason why Essex is interested in you.' He grinned. 'Your favourite person. Your lovely ward.'

'My lovely ward!' spluttered Gresham, caught out for once in a show of emotion. 'You mean that bloody impossible girl who's driving me mad with her nagging and tantrums!' Gresham had spent a lifetime controlling his feelings, showing no emotion to the world. It was an art he lost at the mention of Jane. 'What's Essex done to deserve her?'

'You mean that bloody impossibly beautiful girl,' said George, laughing.

'I acknowledge her beauty merely as a detached observer,' Gresham said. 'I refuse to join those who pant after her like a dog in heat.' He had inherited Jane some years earlier when riding back from a long and debilitating campaign in the Low Countries. Inherited was perhaps the wrong word. Engaging in accidental conversation with a ragged, pre-pubescent girl in a village terrifying for its dirt and poverty, her guardian had rushed out and started to beat her. Gresham had broken his arm for him. For reasons hindsight could never quite properly explain he had found himself with the stick-thin little girl riding in triumph behind him, the young lady in question having screamed long and loud at any attempt to make her ride with anyone else. If Gresham had had any thoughts at all they were along the lines of bringing the girl to London and handing her over to some family who would give her a home as a servant, but instead she had wormed her way into the affections of his servants and by the time she was seventeen was virtually running The House and rescuing it from some of the neglect that Gresham had subjected it to. Why had he hung onto her? He told himself it was because only a madman would take her as a bride. More probably he saw in her someone whose background was similar to his own, someone who had dragged themselves up, someone for whom religion and morality were replaced by that simple virtue of survival. Jane was a survivor. Though whether Gresham would survive her was another matter.

43

'Essex apparently thought he did deserve her. Or that she deserved him. She's turned out to be a cracker, you know. A complete stunner, in fact.'

'I've got eyes,' said Gresham, 'and balls, for that matter. They tell me certain species of spider are made very attractive,' said Gresham, 'so they can lure the male to mate with them. And then eat them.'

'Well, Essex fell into her web. You remember you took her to that party Donne held?' The servants he most trusted, and the old nurse he had placed Jane with, had remonstrated that a young girl couldn't be kept locked up all day, and had to go out some time or other. Gresham had allowed her, suitably chaperoned, to attend a few dinners and one or two literary gatherings. She had taught herself to read in The House, and seemed to have her head in a book every time he passed her by. The Essex crowd, mostly drunk, had burst in on one such gathering held by one of Gresham's oldest friends, the poet John Donne.

'I remember Essex bursting in,' said Gresham. 'I was rather drunk, and I have a vague recollection that I had to threaten to fight that awful steward of his, that foul Welshman . . . funny name, hasn't he . . . Blancmange or something? And his dreadful mother's got another daft name, hasn't she? Lettuce.'

'Lettice, Lady Lettice Leicester, and Gelli Meyrick,' said George, trying to keep a straight face. 'Sir Gelli Meyrick, actually. In any event, Essex apparently took one look at Jane and started to fawn round her like a dog at a bitch in heat. You know how he does.'

If Essex's sexual organ was as large as his ego then intercourse with him must be very painful, Gresham thought. It was amazing how many people fell for it. The ego, that is. Essex was rumoured to have had a child recently by one Elizabeth Southwell, and was known to be panting after and probably between the sheets with Lady Mary Howard and a girl called Russell. There was a sort of a rivalry between the two of them, though Gresham did not approve of getting women with child. As a bastard himself, he had no desire to inflict that status on anyone else.

'Anyway, Essex apparently came straight out with it.'

44

'Did he, by God!' said Gresham, his mind stuck on one track. 'And in a public place! I know standards are slipping, but even for times such as these—'

'Not that, you fool!' said George, annoyed at the flow of his story being broken, but pleased that he knew something Gresham did not. 'Came out with how he loved her, how his love was of such an instant growth that it must have instant satisfaction, how he would die unless she would grant him her favours.'

'Sounds like a man who does too much reading,' said Gresham, 'and of the wrong type of book, too.' But he was intrigued, despite himself. He would no more mate with his ward than climb into bed with an open mole trap, but any match between two personalities as big as this had to be interesting. If he was honest, he was also annoyed that he had not found out this story himself. If Essex fancied his ward, he might have had the decency to tell him.

'So presumably his Lordship planned to give my ward a right noble seeing to, standing up against an outside wall when nobody was looking,' said Gresham enjoying the conscious use of barrack-room language, largely because he knew George found it offensive and unnecessary. Which it was, of course. That was why it was fun. 'Well, it stops them getting pregnant if you do it standing up. Or so my nurse said. Mind you, she had twelve children of her own, so perhaps she didn't speak with total authority. So what happened? Did my little fire-vixen spread her legs to a belted Earl, or rather an Earl about to take his belt and other things off?'

'She asked for a pen and paper,' said George, straight-faced.

'What?' said Gresham. 'Now I've never heard of anybody doing it with those before.'

'Pen and paper. And he was so surprised he asked someone to bring some. After all, you may not find food in Donne's house, or coal, but you'll always find a pen and ink. So eventually – and in the interim my Lordship's hot breath has put condensation on all the walls – she takes both pen and paper, writes a few lines, and hands it to him.'

'What did it say?' asked Gresham now intrigued.

'It isn't so much what *it* said,' replied George. 'It's what *she* said. Apparently she faced up to him – he's quite tall, you know, and so is she – and said, "My Lord, I may have no breeding but I am not a toy to be used by you and then discarded. I've written my polite rejection of your kind offer to copulate with me here in this letter. I've addressed it to your wife."'

'Did she do that, by God!' said Gresham, amazed and alarmed at the same time. He suspected women had been hung from the ramparts of Essex House for less. 'What did he do?'

'He went as red as his beard, my Lord,' said Jane, 'looked as if he was going to hit me, and then burst out laughing. He has been sending me notes and gifts ever since. I came to ask if you could intervene and ask him to stop. It's getting very boring. A girl must look to her honour, even an orphan such as myself. And you are my guardian, however much you might regret it. A good guardian would be incensed at this assault on his ward's virtue and seek to protect her with all his power.'

Dammit! How much of the earlier conversation had she heard? How had this woman got the knack of entering a room in total silence?

'You need protection as much as a grown lioness needs an escort from a sheep!' said Gresham. Jane was looking very cool, her dark hair worn down as befitted an unmarried woman, her dress a working smock that did little to hide the length of her limbs or the curve of her body. He decided not to look into her eyes. They were disturbing, as deep as the darkest pool and flecked with intelligence. And sulky. Very sulky. All sorts of things would have been much, much easier if she had been stupid. And ugly. 'Are you going to make my life hell over this, as well as everything else? What do you expect me to do? Challenge Essex to a duel? If I do, everyone will think it's because I'm sleeping with you. Or want to. If I kill him the Queen will kill me. Mind you, if he kills me your problems really would be over.'

Jane's perfectly composed features did not shift at all. 'Despite a life lived largely without luxuries, prior to your kind rescuing of me,

46

I have never felt the need to indulge in self-pity. It's demeaning for anyone, and, if I may say so, particularly for a man.'

'No, you may not say so!' said Gresham. Was it a shout? Of course not. He would never lose his dignity in such a manner. How this woman had acquired the capacity, not only of silent movement, but of breaking through his lifelong self-control was quite beyond him. Once, when she was younger and being equally outrageous, he had moved towards her fully intending to put her over his knee. For the first time in his life Henry Gresham had been halted by a look. He would not try that again. This was ridiculous. He had been shot at, pierced several times by sword and dagger blades, blown up by gunpowder, near-drowned and once actually stretched out on the rack in the Tower of London (most incidents, now he came too think of it, connected in some strange way with Sir Robert Cecil) – and managed to keep his self-control. Yet now he was losing his temper, yet again, with a chit of a girl. It was nonsense. With a massive effort he calmed himself down.

'Please knock before you enter a room,' Gresham said, in as mild a tone as he could muster.

'Yes, my Lord,' said Jane, dropping her eyes from his gaze, but looking up at him for a moment from under her dark, deep eyelashes. 'I was about to when your body servant opened the door and let me in.'

Gresham directed a look of pure hatred at Mannion, who gazed back imperturbably and simply shrugged his shoulders. In answer to the question Gresham had not asked he said, 'Only being polite, wasn't I?'

Damn the both of them! A more unlikely combination than Mannion and Jane could not be imagined in the wildest writings of the stage, yet Gresham had never seen the pair exchange a cross word. There was some deep, unspoken level of communication between them that he could dimly sense but not understand. It annoyed him, because he valued Mannion more than any other person alive, more even than George. He resented her relationship with Mannion, was jealous of it. Mannion thought most women

47

were like a meal, a necessary pleasure to be enjoyed at regular intervals. Yet never for a moment had Gresham sensed anything of that sort between the pair of them. Whatever their relationship was, it was beyond sex and, for that matter, beyond him.

If someone had suggested that what drew them together was a very full understanding of their joint master, Henry would have laughed in their face. No one understood Henry Gresham, not even himself. It was a matter of great pride to him.

'Well,' said Gresham trying not to be rude and managing to be so, 'I'll mention to my friend the next time we meet that you're off limits. Will that do?'

'Thank you for treating it so urgently,' said Jane, the sarcasm dripping like honey from a comb. Acid honey. 'Perhaps you might take care to mention it early on in the evening?'

'What's important about the timing?' asked Gresham before he had thought properly and saw the hole in the road opening up before him.

'Having seen you come home after an evening with the Earl of Essex, I'd have some reservations about your memory after the first hour.'

That was her going too far!

'You've no right to comment on what your master does either in his business or his social life. You are impudent and impertinent.'

She flushed at that, and bowed her head. It was a minor victory for Gresham. He decided to capitalise on it.

'I doubt you came here to discuss the Earl of Essex. Now that you're here what can I do for you?'

'I was hoping to request some money from you,' said Jane simply.

'More fripperies for yourself?' asked Gresham nastily, and regretted it the moment he spoke. Whatever her faults might be, and her continual nagging, she was scrupulous over money. She virtually ran The House and the accounts were superb. She never asked for money for clothes or jewellery. Indeed, it was the old nurse who came to Gresham every now and again and pointed out that even the poorest girl occasionally needed some money spending on her clothes. He had remembered the humiliation of his own childhood in the shadow of St Paul's, when the other boys at school had picked on the poor boy dressed in cast-offs, and had immediately handed Jane a purse that would have bought three gowns for the Queen. She had looked at him very oddly, and a week later had paraded herself in front of him with a sombre day dress in a cheap, dark-green material. At the same time she had given him the purse back, virtually all the coin still in it, together with an invoice for the paltry sum the dress and one other of similar economy had cost. After that he had gone to Raleigh's wife, got a figure out of her of what might be a suitable monthly allowance for a young girl to spend on clothes, and given it to her regularly. He suspected she spent most of it on books, but that was her choice. At least his ward looked presentable and did not disgrace him.

His jibe had gone home. Jane coloured up again, but she still had guts enough to respond.

'Not money for myself, my Lord. Money for the Library.'

'*More* money for the Library?' said Gresham. The realisation that he had been unfair to her was making him even more annoyed and vindictive. 'You have a small fortune to spend on this cursed house as it is. What need have you of more?'

Gresham hardly needed the money. He was one of the richest men in London, thanks to his father who had built The House. And he paid nothing to Jane for acting as housekeeper and saving him a steady fortune.

'I believe, my Lord, that I *save* a small fortune on this house.' Good God! She was reading his mind now. 'Unless you were happy with your servants feeding every vagabond in London and half the villages around it!' Jane was getting angry now.

Here we go again, thought Mannion. They're off. It was better than a play. Gresham could make another fortune by charging for tickets to watch.

'Well, you of all people should know about poor villages. And vagabonds.'

49

Her face registered the unfairness of the comment, but she clung to her point.

'My Lord! That is so unjust! This Library, the state of so many of the books in it, is . . . is a *disgrace*.'

'As you now claim to run The House, why have you allowed this to happen? If indeed it is true.'

'It is true, my Lord,' said Jane. 'Just look, here!' She turned to one of the dark, oak shelves and pulled out a book, one of those still with dust all over it. A small cloud shot forth in the beams of sunlight, as if angered to have its rest disturbed. 'See? The binding is going here . . . and here . . . and here . . . if I open this work fully the spine will crack and the pages will fall out. It will be ruined.'

'Here. Give it to me.' He took the book rather less gently than she had handled it. He opened the cover, suddenly remembering and slowing down so that he did not rip the binding from the pages. He had no intention of proving her point. *The Revenger's Tragedy*. There was no author. It was a cheap, hurriedly put together edition. Gresham knew. He had paid for it. The author, Thomas Kyd, now long since dead, had been one of nature's victims, subjected to torture and caught up with the truly dreadful Marlowe. Gresham had helped him out by paying for the book to be published, to give Kyd something to sell. He baulked at giving the man money, which would simply be converted straight to drink. Would the world suffer if this new pot-boiler was lost to posterity? Well, people were now producing new editions of Kyd's plays, claiming they had written them. But this book, with no author listed, would not solve that problem. And it would have fallen apart in five years, anyway.

'It's just a play,' said Gresham. 'Not even a very good one. All blood and thunder and not much poetry. What will it cost to repair and preserve this . . . light reading?'

'A few pence. The content of the book isn't the point. Books are . . . for posterity.' She was prim now, like a schoolboy reciting a passage he had learnt by heart. 'What we discard, later genera-

50

tions might revere or worship. We mustn't judge. We must preserve so others can judge.'

'Fine speech,' said Gresham cuttingly. 'Where did you read it? But if later generations worship rubbish like this you won't find me going to church.'

'You don't, actually,' said Mannion from the doorway. 'Go to church, that is. At least, not as when you can avoid it.'

'Did I ask for your comment?' Gresham whirled round and glared at him.

'You never do,' said Mannion.

'Though it never stops him giving it!' guffawed George, who was clearly failing to see how serious the situation was.

Jane was not backing off. 'Please, my Lord', she said, though it clearly cost her deep, 'the worms will have these unless we do something soon. It would be an act of blasphemy to let so much knowledge go to waste.'

Now was the time to play his trump card.

'You had Armytage, the old bookseller, in here last week? Yes?'

Jane was caught unawares. Was this a criticism? What had she done wrong? Did he think she was selling her favours to the old man in order to purchase more books?

'Yes, my Lord. I—'

'I need no explanation. I passed him as he was leaving, invited him up here. These continual requests for money for the Library have to stop. So I asked him to estimate how much it would cost. For the whole lot. To get them mended, de-wormed or whatever you have to do. I've agreed a figure with him. He will do the work. And now will you stop pestering me with these requests? You have what you wanted. You may leave us.'

'My Lord, *how much* did Armytage ask?'

Gresham had hoped she would ask. The size of the figure proved conclusively how generous Gresham was, the lengths to which he would go to meet his ward halfway. He named the figure, trying not to sound smug.

Her response caught him totally unawares. Jane turned scarlet,

51

and exploded, 'That's outrageous! A ludicrous sum! A third of that and Armytage will be able to repair all the volumes here and keep his wife and children in state for a year!'

'Are you complaining at my generosity?' Gresham yelled, pushed now beyond his limits.

'I'm complaining at your stupidity!' Jane shouted back. She thought about adding 'my Lord' but decided not to. 'It's criminal to waste money! It's amazing you have any to spend if you can be fooled by an old man!'

'How dare you talk to me like that!' roared Gresham. 'What's happened now to the "my Lord" this and the "my Lord" that? Well?'

'You told me not to call you "my Lord" because you were only a knight and not a proper Lord at all,' said Jane, She was still flushed, but back in demure mode now, hands joined in front of her, eyes downcast.

'Then why do you still carry on doing it?' asked Gresham boring in for the kill. 'Except, that is, when you're being grossly impertinent?' God, what must it be like to be a father like George, and have more than one of these wild young animals to cope with.

She looked up then.

'Because whether I choose it or not, you are my Lord,' she said simply. Then she burst into tears, and left rapidly.

Damn! That was her in her room for another two days at least! False tears? Genuine tears? How in heaven was a man meant to know the truth behind a woman's tears? Did she know the difference? And what did it matter? And what did this stupid girl matter to him anyway? He had actually been quite proud at getting the books sorted out. Despite the front he put up, the scholar in him hated to see a book being ruined by time. The trouble with these books was that they had belonged to his father. At one stage he had half decided to move the whole library to the new one he was funding at Granville College, Cambridge, the recipient of more and more of his time and money. Had it been the thought of the effect on the girl that had stopped him? No. Of course not. It had been the thought of his favourite room in The House lying bereft of the books that were its true furniture.

'She's right,' said Mannion, moving forward to pour the second flagon of wine he had brought. 'That old bugger Armytage must 'ave seen you coming. You could buy the Vatican Library, and get the Pope thrown in as a free gift, for that much.'

'Oh, shut up,' said Gresham unconvincingly. 'I'm paying enough in bribes to the Vatican as it is.' The Pope would be a crucial factor in validating any claim by a Catholic to the English throne. It was an area where Gresham needed the fullest possible knowledge.

The annoying thing was that Mannion was probably right. Gresham always knew when he was in the wrong, and then fought hardest to try and ignore what he knew. Usually, when the storm was over, he realised his mistake and owned up to it. Gresham never realised that for a man of power to be capable of admitting he is wrong is a truly endearing feature to those who work and live with him, even more so if they can see the struggle he has to face to meet the truth.

'Oh, shut up!' he said again to Mannion, and sighed. The fight had gone out of him once Jane left. 'And make sure to go tomorrow and negotiate a proper price.'

'Can I take the girl along with me? Old Armytage'll do anything for 'er, and she knows 'er business. 'E'll melt in 'er 'and when she flutters 'er eyelashes at 'im.'

And have her see him admit that he had been wrong? To hell with it!

'Oh, for heaven's sake! Take her if you really have to, on condition I don't have to see her. Just make sure her eyelashes are all she flutters.' He hated himself for making the concession. 'And make it clear that if she crows about this I'll wring her neck. Or, better, send her with a little red bow tied round a part of her that sticks out to Essex House, a gift courtesy of Henry Gresham. Except I'm not sure I dislike Essex enough for that.'

'Which takes us back to where we started,' said George. 'Essex. He's the key to all these rumours. Him and his battle with Cecil.

The Queen's failing, we all know that. Essex and Cecil are fighting it out for the Crown. Well, for control of it.'

The Earl of Essex moved in wild company. Gresham knew that. He was a major reason for it being wild.

'It may not be a prize worth having,' said Gresham. The row with Jane had left him tired and irritated, as meeting her always did. Why was he fighting on so many fronts? Was that all life held for him?

'What do you mean?' said George.

'You worry about the goings-on at Court. It's typical of the arrogance of Essex to think the only contenders for the throne are English. France, Spain and the Pope are actually more of a threat. And do you know the real problem? All these powerful men playing with countries and with crowns just as if they were chess pieces on a board! I worry about the country, and about London. You remember the three bad years in the 1590s when it seemed to rain for eleven and half months each year, and the crops just rotted in the ground?'

'Remember?' said George. 'I can hardly forget. We had people dying, children starving. I had to mortgage farms to feed some of the worst-off families. I'll be paying for those three bad years for twenty more years, and some families paid with their lives.'

'Your people were lucky. They had a master who was willing to pay to see them fed.' A master who mortgaged the estate more than it could bear, Gresham now knew to his and George's cost. 'Most didn't. Something snapped in England when it was clear the third year was going to be like the others. Remember all the preachers going around talking of the seven lean years? People really believed there'd be no good harvest for four, five more years.'

'So?' said George. 'Bad harvests and famine are as old as farming, as old as mankind itself.'

'Yes,' said Gresham, 'but it's always at its worst when things combine. It wasn't just three disastrous years. It was the fact the years came at the time when everyone had realised there'd be no heir,

54

realised Elizabeth'd never marry, there wouldn't even be a husband to call King when she died.'

'Most of my people working on my lands don't know or care who's Queen. Or King.' George was getting glum now, the wine depressing rather than lifting him. 'It's always been about survival for them.'

'They care in the Low Countries,' said Gresham. 'I've seen a dead family outside the gates of a big city, their eyes eaten out by the birds and their arms chewed off by wolves. They know what happens over there if there's no strong leadership, no one person in charge. And I think people are starting to turn on Gloriana, to hate her for her selfishness in having no heir, in naming no successor.'

'Evidence?'

'The talk in College is always a good guide. Every Cambridge College is full of men with shoulders looking for a chip to sit on them. But look round here in London: they no longer cheer when she drives through the city. The boatmen just about pull aside for her barge. They don't shout or cheer, or even put their oars up in salute. Sometimes they don't even look in her direction. They look away. And row on.'

'So?'

'They cheer when Essex rides past, cheer as if there was no tomorrow. And that's dangerous, don't you see? Essex has stood up to the Queen. He's handsome, he's dashing—'

'And 'e knows it!' said Mannion decisively. 'Don't 'e just love the attention! Not clever to love it so much, and to show it.'

'He's *new*!' said Gresham. 'The Court's like a musty old sheet that's been in the chest far too long. He's a breath of fresh air, not an old wrinkled lady with a Court that smells of lavender and cedar. A lady whose top servant is Robert Cecil. You know what someone painted on the walls of his home? Cecil's home?'

'Decorate me?' said George, who was dangerously close to getting drunk. 'Give me a new coat of paint?'

'No. Toad,' said Gresham. '*Toad*. Is that a country happy with its leadership?'

'Sure you didn't paint it yourself?' asked George, giggling.

'Wake up, George!' said Gresham. 'There's things going on out there that worry me too, unsettling things. Not just my survival. That's minor. Who'll care if I end up dead in the Tower? You and a servant. But if we unleash civil war in England? That has to be more important than you, or me. We may be coming to the end of an era. But we don't know what's going to replace it.'

'So?' said George. 'Do mere mortals ever know that sort of thing?'

'But what if we replace it by what's happening in the Low Countries? Twenty, thirty years of rival armies fighting over ordinary people's bodies for a power no one can ever truly win. What if the wolves become so bold as to come up to your door?'

Perhaps, thought Gresham, the wolves are here already, just dressed in sheep's clothing.

They had talked on, until George fell asleep by the fire. Gresham had left him, snoring gently, though it was only noon.

'You goin' to tell 'im the truth? About Cecil?' said Mannion. Gresham had told Mannion immediately.

'No,' said Gresham. 'At least, not yet.'

CHAPTER 3

Mid June, 1598
London

The extravagant and luxurious trappings of Essex House were a lie, of course, albeit a very pretty lie. A hundred tradesmen had been ruined by Robert Devereux's extravagance and his inability to pay for what he used.

'It must be Ireland, my Lord,' said Gelli Meyrick. 'It's been your destiny from birth. It's your chance for the future.'

Robert Devereux, Earl of Essex, did not glance in the direction of Sir Gelli Meyrick, his secretary. The Earl was stretched out on cushions, his long legs apparently carelessly cast in front of him, but not so carelessly as to fail to reveal either the fine silk of his hose, or the magnificent shape of the legs it hugged so closely. He was in his shirt, a goblet clutched in his hand. Dark sweat marks showed under his arms and across his back. He had come from the fencing master, whose session he had extended by nearly three quarters of an hour. Essex was good, and he knew it.

'Ireland,' he mused, the lilt of the Welsh accent he had never quite lost clashing with the more refined Court accent. 'You say is my destiny. Isn't it more accurate to describe it as my family's fatal attraction? Or perhaps you believe in kill or cure?' He tossed back what wine was left in his goblet.

The Earl's father, the father he had hardly known, had died horribly of dysentery in Dublin, his very innards seeming to turn to corruption. Power in Ireland was an enticing prize for the newly ennobled, those with no inherited land. Yet the lands and income Ireland offered had one weakness: much of the land had to be conquered before it could be raped for its income. Appointed by Elizabeth as Governor General of Ireland, the endless battles to suppress the wild Irish peasants and their treacherous feudal lords had worn out his father's body and what little wealth he had in equal measure.

'Your father tried and failed,' said Meyrick, unabashed, 'partly because he was never the soldier you are, partly because he went to Ireland for wealth.'

'God knows,' said Essex, 'I could do with the wealth! Is there no more money to be got from my lands?'

No, thought Meyrick, remembering the screams of the three men he had had whipped in front of their wives and children for hiding a few sacks of oats, there is not. However, the Earl should not be bothered with such trivia as the bleeding backs of his peasants. Indeed, he was soft enough to be moved by their sub-human wailing.

'We do all we can, my Lord. But Ireland is your Holy Grail. Take it. Drink from it. You'll be immortalised.'

'You flatter me,' said Essex, a faint smile crossing his lips. It was the smile that so helped him with women, suggesting as it did great sadness allied to great vulnerability. It was no lie. The Earl was a far more melancholic and vulnerable man in his own mind than he hoped his friends ever saw. 'And I know you flatter me. I'm like the child desperate for the nurse to tell him the same old story, the story that comforts not because of its content but because of its familiarity. So, carry on. Let me be the child I am. Tell me about immortality. My immortality.'

'Ireland is in turmoil. Tyrone is fighting to throw the English out of Ulster; has gone back on all his agreements. The Lord Deputy is dead and the Queen will appoint no new person. Our forces are weak and badly led, and one of our prime strongholds at Blackwater is under siege. Ireland awaits a true soldier. A man whose valour and leadership will finally wrest it from its warlords. And when Ireland finds its hero, so will England. It'll hail you as a saviour, as the man who finally marked out the greatest expansion to English rule since the loss of Calais.'

'Now tell me why all this will make me immortal?' whispered Essex, his voice dropping to almost inaudible levels.

'Because the Queen is dead!' hissed Meyrick. 'Not dead quite yet in her body, but nearly so. Dead in her mind. Dead in her leadership. Dead in her capacity to inspire the love and affection of her subjects. When you return victorious from Ireland, London and the whole country will be yours for the taking! This country has had Regents acting for the very young, when such a one has become King. It's a small jump for it to accept a Regent for the very old.'

'Or mount a rebellion,' said Essex. Some physical change had come over him, a hardening of the muscles in his face. His voice had changed as well, the rural Welsh lilt more pronounced now, yet the words more clipped. Essex did not like people to come close to him. Perhaps because he himself never quite knew what personality he would wear on any day, or even in the course of any one hour. He liked drink to act as a buffer between himself and those to whom he offered friendship.

'Crowns are taken by force of arms! Henry the Seventh felt no need to act as Regent for a failing King! To rebel against the Queen would be no rebellion at all. It would be a succession. A right and proper succession.' Essex's eyes were ablaze now and he swung himself off the couch, stood to his full height.

Was he as handsome as his admirers always claimed, Meyrick wondered? Probably not, but the combination of the clean body, the wide and handsome face and the money to dress it properly made for a powerful appeal, fired as it was by a mind that soared and crashed in an infuriatingly unpredictable manner.

Well, there had been no other career option for Meyrick when he had hooked his hungry claws into the handsome young noble-man, hoping against hope that this man would be the means of lifting him out of grinding, humiliating poverty. And it had worked, had it not? *Sir* Gelli Meyrick now ran the Earl of Essex's Welsh estates with a rule and a rod of iron that made him the most feared man in the Marches. Would this man, his master, become King of England? It was no more fanciful than the prospect of Meyrick gaining a knighthood had been ten years ago. Why not? How many of Bolingbroke's followers, when they had joined his service, had expected to end up wearing the King's livery?

'There is a tide in the affairs of men . . .'

Meyrick looked blankly at Essex.

'Shakespeare. *Julius Caesar*. It's spoken by one of the men who kill Caesar, and then try for his crown.'

It was typical of Essex that in the broad sweep of the idea he had forgotten that Caesar never had a crown, had been killed because he seemed about to claim one. He had also apparently forgotten the moment when old Lord Burghley had drawn a prayer book out of his pocket and pointed to the 55th psalm with trembling fingers, 'Bloody and deceitful men shall not live out half their days.'

Essex had been arguing passionately against peace with Spain at the time. But Essex was not finished.

'For each man there comes a moment, a moment of destiny, a moment of truth. It appears, it is there to be grasped . . . and then it goes, like a shooting star in the heavens. Grasp the right moment, and mere men become Kings and Kings become Emperors. Choose the wrong moment, and vaunting ambition turns into dust. Or kills the conspirators, as it did those who rose against Caesar. But who knows when that moment is?'

This was not Meyrick's strength. Intellectual debate bored him. Essex liked to patronise those around him, careful to keep his drink-ing companions to soldiers and bluff men of the world, or playactors who would sell their souls for another jug and one good line. If he had attracted a circle of true artists, perhaps they might have chal-lenged the sense of intellectual superiority he seemed to need so much. There was only that turncoat Francis Bacon perpetually whispering in his ear. Damn him! thought Meyrick. My life rests with this man, yet he can wear so many personalities in the space of one hour that he would tire out the very Devil himself. Which Robert Devereux, of the many available, am I talking to now?

'Am I Brutus?' asked Essex. 'Tumbling to my own destruction because I know my monarch is wrong, and simply clearing the way for Octavius Caesar to step in and take over the crown I should have won? Or am I Bolingbroke, making one strike because I know that all the fabric of government is rotten to the core, rotted from within, waiting merely for the one, savage blow to bring it all tumbling down in my favour?'

Or are you simply a vain, bloody and deceitful man who, for all that he seems to talk about others, can only talk about himself? thought Meyrick, and then dismissed the thought. It was not helpful to someone who had no other cause, and whose role was to stiffen in its determination the one cause he had.

Essex was standing by the window, victim of another sudden mood change. He spoke aloud, but Meyrick knew the words were private. He often did this, speaking out private thoughts apparently oblivious to the fact that others were hearing him. Essex was like a child, a fatherless child in desperate need of someone to tell him what to do.

'So little time!' he said. 'All that awaits the slow is the plague, or decrepit failing old age. So little time!'

'Make time your friend by grasping it,' said Meyrick, almost desperately, 'or lose it by delay!'

There was no answer. Meyrick waited, for seconds, for minutes. It was as if the Earl had frozen. Sensing something he did not understand, Meyrick bowed briefly, and left.

The image of a small boy swam before Essex's eyes. Eight or nine, perhaps, with unusually fine features, startling blue eyes and a mop of blond hair. Why? Why had he given in? Some were granted time. Others had it ripped away from them.

How could one decision so change a life? It was as if the vast, open plain that he had strode so confidently was narrowing down to a dark tunnel that led only to one destination.

Could the Devil speak true?

'I thought you was meant to be in charge of things?' asked an incredulous Mannion.

They were on the river, and eight men in the Gresham livery of purple and silver were rowing lustily, enjoying the sunlight and the exercise, and the fact that their boat was the smartest on the Thames, their master a dashing figure and their livery the best on the river that day. And not one of them was thinking that if their master was proved a traitor, they might well hang. The life of a servant was inextricably bound up with that of his or her master.

'I am. Meant to be, that is,' said Gresham.

'This ain't no joke, this really ain't. This is one o' your specials, this is, like the time you comes 'ome calm as a cucumber and tells me we're going off to join the Spanish Fuckin' Armada.'

'I understand in academic circles it's known as the Spanish Armada. Which it isn't, of course. Not *the* Spanish Armada. If you remember, they sent another one a year ago.' It had been blown away by gales in the Bay of Biscay.

'Well, I know it as the Spanish *Fuckin'* Armada. And I was fuckin' on it, which is more than your fuckin' academics ever were. And we were bloody lucky to get away wi' that little jaunt, and luck don't come twice – I bin thinkin'.'

'Don't,' said Gresham. 'Stick to what you know best – headaches from alcohol.'

Mannion swatted the sally aside. 'If we goes off to Scotland with a little love letter from Cecil to James, we might as well hang a bloody notice round our neck saying "TRAITOR! CUT ME BALLS OFF!" Secret mission or public, we're still on a hidin' to nothing'. There must be a way out of this.'

'You don't seem bothered I'm betraying Essex,' said Gresham.

'I'm as bothered as 'e would be about betraying us – and the answer is, 'e wouldn't give a sod. You 'as your fun with these toffs, but you never trust 'em.'

They were heading to a play commanded by the Queen, at Greenwich. It would be a comedy, Gresham knew. Her Royal Rotten Teeth would not contemplate a history or a tragedy, which would inevitably mention death. And probably a bad, anodyne and totally silly comedy, as that was the way the tastes of the old lady seemed now to be set.

The boat bit into a wave, and the oarsmen rocked back slightly in their seats.

'Cecil's set us up,' Gresham said bluntly. Better the truth. Better to let those who loved him see how stupid their love and loyalty were. 'You, me and Willoughby. We're over a barrel. I'm sorry. It's my fault for not seeing it coming.'

Gresham looked at Mannion who, to his surprise, grinned at him.

'Maybe. But I bet 'e ain't seen what you'll chuck back. You'll think o' something.'

Everything humanity didn't want went into the Thames, and it was unusual for Gresham to think of it as pure. Yet in comparison with the politics of Queen Elizabeth's Court, it seemed pure beyond belief.

'Still, I don't like it,' Mannion rumbled on. 'If ever you thinks you understands something Cecil's doing, it's the sign you've got it wrong. It's never simple, with that bastard. You missing a trick, are you?'

'Almost certainly,' said Gresham, 'but that's part of the game, isn't it?'

They were within sight of Greenwich now, its flags flapping in the brisk wind. It had always been one of the better Palaces. It held a special place in Gresham's memory. He had not lost his virginity there. That had gone a lot earlier, in a back alley near St Paul's. Instead he had lost something rather more important: his heart, making love to a girl who, for a brief moment, he had fooled himself into thinking he had fallen in love with. Now, in his dotage, he knew he had only ever been in love with one girl. And she had been a Spaniard who had chosen to reject him and marry a Frenchman. Still was happily married to the Frenchman, as it happened, with five children, three of them boys. He paid someone to report to him on her, though he knew he would never see her again. Did Anna ever think about him? He doubted it, yet she had chosen to give him her virginity when she had already decided to marry her Frenchman.

Gresham's mind was churning, and with more than the memory of puppy-fat romances. Mannion was right, of course. Cecil's plans were never simple. His only weakness was that the more complex his machinations, the more he believed that no others could penetrate their complexity. Cecil's Achilles heel was his deep-seated belief, sometimes hidden even from himself, that he was the cleverest man alive.

'Ever watched a fish in a net?' asked Mannion innocently. The river was passing them by at a satisfying speed. Mannion had once been a galley slave. He said it meant that watching other people row was one of his greatest pleasures.

'What?' said Gresham, his train of thought interrupted.

'Thrashes around, don't it?' said Mannion. 'Gets itself tangled more and more. Well, us, we're in that right bastard's net. We thrash around, we'll lose it. Clever thing is to stay calm. There ain't a net made that hasn't got a weak bit in it. We got to wait, that's all. Stay calm. Find the weak bit. And swim out through it.'

'Thank you,' said Gresham, his voice laced with irony. 'Exactly what I was thinking.'

As it had been, actually. As he so often did, Mannion had put into simple terms what Gresham worked out by a more tortuous and self-denigrating route. Gresham was in Cecil's net, and moaning about it would help him and his friends no more than it would help the fish. And, unlike the fish, they would need to think themselves out of this net.

There was always a way out! There always was!

The oarsmen were happy because they were well paid, well fed

64

and well clothed. There was no comparison between being a boatman for Sir Henry Gresham and the back-breaking tedium of a peasant's life. No labourer who bent over to pluck a weed received a cheer from passers-by, as Gresham's oarsmen had just received a cheer for their fine appearance from an Alderman and his whole family. But perhaps the eight lusty men who rowed Henry Gresham's boat and the Alderman with his fat wife and two fat children rowed by two sweating journeymen, shared one thing. They were going to the play. The sense of excitement was uncontrollable, one reason why the authorities frowned on the theatre so much. They claimed that the theatres were breeding grounds for the Plague, but it was the plague of ideas spawned by the players, their living pictures of Kings overthrown and rebellion unleashed, that they were most scared of.

As if marking it as a forbidden pleasure, the playhouses were largely outside the boundaries of the old city, one wall of which was the River Thames. Situated on the south bank, beyond the control of the City Fathers, they stood side by side with the string of brothels that everyone knew were owned by the Bishop of London. Visiting a play held at one of the royal Palaces was a different kind of excitement, though Gresham often thought that the only difference between sex from a whore and sex from a lady-in-waiting was that the whore told you how much it would cost beforehand.

'Funny thing, isn't it?' said Mannion, who liked nothing better than a good play, preferably with a horrible murder in the opening scene. He was reading Gresham's mind again. 'The bloody authorities'll close a theatre down at the drop of a sneeze, yet if 'er 'Ighness invites any one of 'em to a show they'll be there in their finery quicker than an 'are in March.'

He glanced back to where the Alderman's boat was bobbing in the swell, falling rapidly behind. His fat wife was starting to complain that she had known all along it was too rough to go by boat.

Judicious use of Gresham's money had secured them an empty slot on the jetty that fed the Palace, by the simple practice of parking a wherry there four or five hours earlier. As the wherrymen caught sight of the Gresham livery they backed neatly out, the larger of the two men grinning at Gresham and doffing his cap.

Gresham's men started to edge the boat into the vacant space; the jetty overflowing with boats and people, the boatmen concerned about their fine paint, the men and women far more concerned about their fine velvets, silk and satins. Amid the chaos, a ragged-arsed little boy stood gawping at all the fine folk, thumb in his mouth, one of the human flotsam and jetsam of the river. Half an hour either side of this particular rush hour and a guard would have moved him on, but now no one had time or energy.

There was a shout from behind them, and Gresham and Mannion turned instantly. A huge boat, eight oars a side and more like a royal barge than a private vessel, was charging full ahead into the space reserved for Gresham, seemingly oblivious to the smaller boat that was already halfway to the spot. At its stern and on its mast flew the proud pennant of the Earl of Essex, the rowers dressed in the tangerine-coloured livery that the family favoured. The Earl himself sat languidly on a throne at the stern, talking to a man whose appearance would have made a peacock feel underdressed, oblivious to the chaos his men were about to cause.

'CLEAR THE WAY THERE! CLEAR THE WAY FOR THE EARL OF ESSEX!' The man at the front of Essex's battleship was yelling at the top of his voice, and smaller boats were scurrying out of his way like ants, Essex's oarsmen not letting up as they raced to the jetty; if anything seeming to row even harder. It was a neat trick, if you could do it, to row for home as if chased by the Devil and then dig the oars in hard at the last moment and halt the boat before it splintered itself and the landing stage. Whether this lot were good enough to do it remained to be seen.

There was an outward civilisation in Elizabeth's England, but it ran only skin deep. The place at the jetty was clearly Gresham's. Essex was equally clearly trying to take it. Duals were fought for less. Honour was at stake, and reputation. Essex chose that moment to look up, casually, as if by accident, and his eyes locked on to Gresham's. He smiled, and waved a hand. It was a clear challenge.

He is enjoying this, thought Gresham. He has no need to fight for this poxy little mooring, except that it is a battle of wills and more exciting than the river on a normal day.

Gresham's men had not yet shipped their oars. There was time enough, just, for them to dip the blades into the muddy water and reverse out of the path of the Goliath heading at speed towards them. Most men would have done just that, if only to save their skins. Few who used the river, and even fewer sailors could swim. But Gresham's men were different. The river was a dangerous place, and they had to do more dangerous things on it following his orders than many liveried servants would have dreamt of.

Ramming. For all the social niceties of this situation, this was ramming. It was the best way of making a quick kill on the river. Head for the enemy, smash into their side, hole their boat, jump on board, grab whatever you wanted and back off to leave the evidence to sink behind you. Gresham's men were trained for this. He did not need to look at Mannion, or speak to him. It was at times like this that their intuitive understanding paid dividends.

'Fend off to stern.'

Gresham spoke in what seemed a quiet voice, but it carried to his men, to whom it was a familiar order, and somehow cut through the babble on the jetty, increased now by the excitement over what seemed to be a major collision.

The slight signs of uncertainty that had been visible among his men as they looked up in a moment of relaxation and saw a vast vessel bearing down on them at speed vanished, to be replaced by military order. The two men seated at the bow lowered their oars into the water, leaving them motionless for the moment, ready to give the vessel direction one way or the other as was needed. The next pair reached up the mast, where two vast boat hooks, stout timber with iron hooks at the business end, were strapped to the mast, almost equalling its height. Effortlessly they swung down the lengths of timber, so smoothly as to hide the difficulty of the act on a bobbing boat, and passed them forward for the stern pair of men. As if they were puppets, the men rose to their feet just as those behind them sat down to balance the boat, and the boat hooks were suddenly held like levelled pikes. This was the crucial moment. The two men at the stern had to direct the boat hooks, the two men behind them had to grab the end of the timber shafts as the impact threatened and give more strength to the lead man. Yet the seat of a pole has no point on which to fix, if it is to receive a big impact. The two men at the rear reached down into the lockers at their feet, and slipped a strange, leather contraption on their arms with a pouch slung beneath it. Into the pouch went the end of the boat hook.

'SECURED!' the two men yelled in unison. This was what had taken the time in training, endless hours when the boat hook seemed to have a life of its own, when in securing it the rear man had swung it so widely as to knock the front man off the boat. How many hours of men splashing and swearing in the water had they undergone to produce this situation, whereby in seconds a small tree had been unslung from a mast, placed securely in the hands of a strong man ready to guide it and secured from behind by another man waiting to absorb the shock on contact?

They had the time, just. Momentum, that was the key. For all the fearsome strength and weight of the Earl's boat, like all boats it was surprisingly easy to push aside. Essex's boat was bearing down on them from almost directly astern. To Gresham's left was a motley collection of craft, mostly professionals delivering their human cargo. To his right was a rather splendid, gilded royal boat, too small to be a barge but still very grand. It was no choice.

'Fend off right,' he ordered, as calmly as before, but his pulse racing as if this was a real battle rather than a stupid battle for honour.

If it worked, Essex's boat would skitter off down their right-hand side. The bow oarsmen on that side shipped their oars and checked that those of the two stern men, wielding the boat hook, were flush along the side. It was all they had time to do.

The man was still yelling at the bow of Essex's boat, rather more frantically now. He was used to people getting out of his way, and the significant obstacle in their path had not moved. His eyes opened wide in startlement as the two huge boat hooks swung out and pointed at him.

'CLEAR . . .' he shrieked, his voice in danger of going falsetto, before he felt the deck shift under him, lost his footing and, in rather stately fashion, fell into the Thames.

The boat hooks caught Essex's barge just to one side of the bow. The men took the strain, actually took the one step back that the boat allowed them, and then pushed with all their strength. A sudden snag, the sinews straining and then Essex's ship started to slew round. One more heave, and the job was done.

Then the men wielding the boat hooks did something they had not been trained for. In a real fight, they would have awaited the order to fend off again, or stowed the boat hooks and gone off after their attacker. In this case, they simply raised the boat hooks to head height, dipping them down again as the rigging swept by. The careering weight of Essex's boat was unstoppable. It drove it through. The heavy boat hooks crashed into the pates of one, two, three and four oarsmen, flattening them in the bottom of the boat, their oars flying, before those behind realised and ducked. As they did so they forgot their oars, which smacked in contact with Gresham's boat and whipped back, smashing the men on the chest or on their hurriedly lowered heads. At one moment a boat hook seemed to be headed straight for the Earl of Essex and the fine bonnet he wore; he glided aside at the last second and the hook passed through empty air. Was he still grinning, Gresham had to ask himself?

Then, with a massive, grinding and wonderfully expensive crash, Essex's boat drove into the Queen's gilded plaything, smashing its own bow fully halfway into the final quarter of the other boat. Shards of wood like daggers flew through the air. The boat heeled over with the shock, so much so that its mast nearly touched the floor of the jetty, and then half-righted itself, filling with water and still enmeshed with Essex's boat. The rest of Essex's men were flung forward, Essex the only one with the sense to wrap his arms

69

round a stanchion and stay more or less where he was. His popin-jay friend was hurled forward, caught himself a nasty blow in the crotch on the guard rail, and catapulted over it into the river.

What a pity, thought Gresham, grinning now it was all over. That fine velvet, satin and silk would not survive a ducking. Was it that awful man who acted as secretary to Essex? The unfortunately named Gelli? The vicious Welshman?

The mast of the Queen's boat had not snapped as it heeled over, but must have cracked on impact. Suddenly, and without warning, there was the sound of tearing timber, and the mast wobbled, then snapped its rigging, tumbling down onto the jetty.

The boy was still there, his thumb still in his mouth, bemused, even more wide-eyed as the great men and women crashed into each other. He must have seen or sensed the mast headed towards him, but was frozen to the spot. The chunk of timber landed two, maybe three feet to one side of him. One of the planks it hit flew upward under the boy's feet, like a see-saw, catapulting him into the water. He could have hit another boat, knocked his brains out. Instead he flew straight as an arrow into the only clear patch of water left in that area of the Thames, and started to drown.

Shit! Gresham's world narrowed down to the small figure in the water. Two stupid men doing man things and fighting over their honour and who won a parking place on the river, that was one thing. No real harm done, except some broken heads, some wounded pride and a lot of work for carpenters. Gresham never thought if this whole farrago was worth the life of a worthless child. People do not think in these situations. Either they do, or they step back. Gresham was incapable of stepping back.

The finery on his back, understated though it was, would have kept a peasant and his family in food for a year. Oh, to hell with it. Life was about more than possessions.

To the amusement of his men, guffawing now at the ease with which they had bested the Earl of Essex and oblivious to the boy in the water, Gresham mounted the stern and dived cleanly into the water, his hat flying off as he did so and bobbing gently behind him.

His breath left him as the cold of the water bit through his clothes and into his flesh. The boy was going down for the third time, and sank just before Gresham reached him. Mentally bisecting the angle, Gresham kicked his heels and dived under, hand out-stretched, knowing the murk of the Thames would hide the boy from him. His flailing hand grabbed hold of something – cloth? Gresham drove upwards. He drew in a huge gasp of air as he reached the surface, and saw with relief that it was indeed the boy he had grabbed. Flipping himself over on his back, he rested the child, spluttering and struggling feebly as he was, on his chest. He reached the jetty to a rousing cheer from a hundred or so bystanders, shouting partly because they were impressed, but also because they were ashamed that they, who had seen the drowning boy, had not felt inclined to risk themselves in the water. Reaching the scarred and tide-scorched rough wood of the jetty, Gresham heaved the boy onto dry land by sheer brute force. Overcome tem-porarily by exhaustion, he waited before heaving himself out, a ludicrous, drenched figure in Court dress, and hatless.

'Are you all right?' he asked the boy, who was wild-eyed with terror, and wetting himself. The boy's eyes connected with his res-cuer.

'Fuck off, mister!' he said with a squeak, and repeated it for good measure. 'You fuck off, you!' He picked himself up, and ran off with a shambling gait into the crowd, a master of urban disguise.

Gresham felt a hand grab the back of his sodden doublet and, with surprising strength, haul him out of the water. His own men had formed a protective cordon round him, once they had realised what was happening, but they had obviously let someone through. Was it Mannion? No. It was the Earl of Essex.

A hand plonked something on top of Gresham's head. It was his hat.

'Well, Sir Henry,' said the Earl of Essex, 'at least you're wearing something that's partly dry. I picked up your hat from the water just as you dived in.'

'Thank you, my Lord,' said Gresham, spluttering a little.

However hard one tried, water always seemed to get into the lungs in escapades like this. 'It wouldn't do to be seen hatless in company.'

'Quite,' said the Earl, as if the conversation they were having was the most normal thing on earth. 'Now you must tell me, how did you train those men of yours to be so superb? Outstanding. Quite outstanding. If Philip Sidney had had men like that around him he'd be alive now. You must tell me how you did it.'

As the realisation of the stupidity of it all hit him, Gresham could no longer restrain his laughter. It burst out of him.

And to his surprise, Gresham heard Essex join him in the laughter. After all, life was a farce, wasn't it? A bad joke played on humanity, their punishment for feeling pain? Was Essex the only other man in the world who saw how ludicrous it all was?

Gresham allowed himself to be helped to his feet. The laughter subsiding, he looked at Essex. 'Forgive me, my Lord,' he said, with a formal slight bow. 'You are most gracious, and I am very silly.'

Essex looked at him, something glancing behind his eyes, lighting them up. 'Fuck off, mister,' he said.

And both men collapsed into yet more uncontrollable laughter.

Gresham was leaving visible puddles behind him as he walked with Essex into the courtyard of the Palace. Mannion followed a dutiful few paces behind, clucking like an ancient hen over a lost chick. He made it clear, without saying a word, what he thought about people who dived in to rescue a child no one would miss. From behind came various gurgling and sloshing sounds, and a torrent of swearing. Gresham glanced over his shoulder. An incandescent Gelli Meyrick was being hauled out of the river, his extravagant dress reduced to a sodden sponge, ruined.

'Shouldn't we wait for your . . . secretary, my Lord?' asked Gresham.

'He will look after himself,' said Essex carelessly. 'Gelli is very good at that. It's actually what he does best. If he needs me for anything, you can be sure he'll ask.'

They walked on in silence for a few moments, past the guards at the water gate, who drew their pikes up to attention in a salute to Essex. He pretended not to notice. Gresham suspected that had they not shown him this sign of respect they would have had the roasting of their lives. That was the trouble with real aristocracy, thought Mannion: treat you like a brother one minute then have you up for being too familiar.

'I've a room here in the Palace, and some old rags,' said Essex airily. 'I'm taller than you, but they'll fit you passably, I imagine, and I'm sure we can rustle up a towel.'

They walked on for a few more yards. Only Gresham would have noticed the slightest of changes in Essex's step.

'An urchin,' said Essex casually. 'A vagabond of no worth, destined to grow up a thief or a villain, or worse. Why did you risk yourself for him?'

Gresham's tone was the only dry thing about him.

'He is of no worth to us. I suspect to himself he is worth quite a lot.'

Very few people other than the Queen's servants kept a room in the Palace, particularly a large, beamed room with a generous fireplace and splendid views out over the river. Even fewer kept a stock of clothing that would have doubled the wardrobe of many a gentleman.

'Just in case, Gresham, just in case,' said Essex, as a servant brought garment after garment out of chests. Another servant laid a fire and lit it. The cold was starting to get to Gresham now, and he was fighting his body's desire to shiver. He found himself welcoming the heat of the fire.

Just in case of what, thought Gresham? In case he found himself with an unexpected overnight stay at the Palace in the old Queen's bed? Essex's arrogance, his assumption of superiority, was supreme, yet at the same time Gresham felt himself strangely unaffected by it. He was . . . amused, that was it. Amused, rather than offended. Why? Perhaps it was because the arrogance was so much on the surface, so understood by its owner as to make it no threat. With Essex, what you saw was what you got. Except by all accounts what you saw and what you got could change several times in the space of one hour. However, he was all conciliation and concern now, though never mentioning once that the reason for Gresham's sodden state was the arrogance of his boat master in seeking to claim a berth that clearly was not his.

If life as a campaigning soldier had taught Gresham anything it was to disavow his culture's horror of nakedness. He stripped down to his shirt, and then pulled that long, dripping garment over his head, allowing Mannion for once to towel him rather more vigorously than was strictly necessary, still cross at his master for taking what he deemed unnecessary risk. Essex had not quibbled when Mannion had made to enter the room. He glanced at Gresham's naked body, not lasciviously, but rather in the manner of a Welsh farmer looking over a bull he was about to buy. Did he notice the slight discoloration down one side of Gresham's whole body, the slightly paler tinge of the skin where a stupid soldier's carelessness had ignited the powder store? Only Mannion knew why there were so few oil lamps in any room Henry Gresham had power over. Candles were likely to snuff out if they were knocked over; a knocked oil lamp spread its flame. If he did notice, Essex said nothing, and nor did he comment on the various scars that adorned almost every part of Gresham's body. Instead, he looked almost dreamily out over the Thames.

'You'll join me at the play? Sit with me? It's the least I can do . . . particularly if you tell me how you trained those men of yours. Superb! Quite superb! Put my lot totally in the shade.'

Something in Essex's voice told Gresham that the men on the Essex barge would be made to pay for what had happened out there on the river.

Gresham was dried off now, attending to the intricacies of unfamiliar buttons and fastenings. The doublet he had chosen was one of the most reserved in the Earl's spare wardrobe, but still had double-slashed sleeves and an immensely ornate neckline. The Earl wore his doublets cut high, probably to amplify the cut of his legs, and while Gresham thought it made Essex look faintly ridiculous, like a stork, it suited Gresham remarkably well. On the Earl there was the merest hint that the upper thighs were perhaps just a little too . . . fat? Perhaps he should ask Essex if he could keep the outfit . . .

'I'd take them out on the river and tell them that we would stay there until they got whatever manoeuvre it was we were practising right. We went out at high tide to some mud flats. If they kept on getting it wrong, we'd get stranded on the mud flats as the tide went out, and they'd have to wait till the next high tide to get home.'

'And did you ever have to wait?'

'Oh, yes. Twice, as it happened. The first time they didn't believe me. The second time they were so desperate to get it right they were all fingers and thumbs. Not a bad training for a real fight.'

Gresham had seen outwardly well trained men panic under the pressure of battle, and load two powder charges into a musket, or ram two balls down the barrel. The effect in each case was lethal, the barrel peeling back and the marksmen blinded by splinters and burning powder. Once he had seen a man fire his musket with the ramrod still in the barrel. For some reason the gun had held firm, and in crazy slow motion the wooden pole described a lazy arc through the air and caught an enemy horseman a smashing blow neatly on the chin, where it peeked out from under his helmet, and threw him to the ground. It was a shot the man could never have made if he had planned it. It had turned the skirmish their way, as it happened. They had been outnumbered and losing their will to fight, and the ludicrous sight of the flying ramrod had persuaded them that someone up there must be on their side.

'Did you arrange for yourself to be picked up? Surely you didn't stay marooned?' asked Essex, leaning forward now, his interest really engaged.

'I couldn't leave, even if I'd wanted to. There was no way off those mud flats – you'd sink seven, eight feet if you tried to step on them. No one could leave the boat, and no one could join it. Tides take a long time to turn, I can tell you.'

'Food and water?'

'No. None was allowed.'

'Not even for you? The commander?'

'Especially not for me. I was making a simple point. If a vessel gets boarded on the river, it's not because those boarding it want to say hello. They're not going to leave any witnesses alive, particularly the commander. If the men fail, the captain dies as well. It's a simple lesson.'

'Didn't discipline suffer? You can have no secrets crammed onto a small boat with eight men.'

'Sometimes four, sometimes eight, sometimes sixteen,' said Gresham. 'Did it suffer? I don't know. I certainly wasn't going to shout at them for seven or eight hours. The punishment was having to be stuck there. So I played dice half the time, and then kept sane writing sonnets for the rest of it. Bloody difficult, sonnets.'

Mannion, who had been helping him in silence, stepped back, and nodded approvingly. Mannion had little pride in his own appearance, but great pride in Gresham's. Gresham winked at him and gave a slight sideways nod. It was time for Mannion to leave, or rather for him to wait outside the door. Essex would talk more freely if the two men were alone. He was clearly in it up to his neck with James of Scotland, and God knew who else. For once it might be in Gresham's interests to sound out Essex's political thoughts.

Essex hardly seemed to notice Mannion's departure. As he often did, he spoke, but in the manner of someone talking to himself.

'You played dice with them . . .' Essex mused, his brow furrowed in thought for a moment. His eyes swung back to Gresham, a signal perhaps that his mind had returned to here and now. 'Didn't they lose respect for you?'

'They lost money,' said Gresham, with a grin. 'I learnt to play dice with Drake, and on the Spanish Armada. In fact one of those men on the boat this afternoon, Dick, he owes me five hundred crowns still. I keep reminding him, but I don't think I'll get my money.'

This new vision of a relationship between commander and men

was worrying Essex. He kept coming back to it, like a terrier after a rabbit that he was not convinced was quite dead.

'I couldn't do that,' he said with disarming honesty. 'I don't understand common men, not in the way I suspect you do. I've seen commanders in the field like you – on the very rare times I've been allowed to be a real solder!'

It was no secret that the Queen kept Essex on a leash, and that he wanted military glory more than anything else. The fury he descended into when the Queen refused him permission to go on one jaunt or another was legendary.

'Commanders like me? I'm hardly a great commander,' said Gresham.

'No?' said Essex. 'I can see the way your men look at you, the way they trust you, the ease of the relationship they have with you. I can lead such men, I think, but I can never feel part of them.'

'Perhaps, my Lord,' said Gresham, suddenly bored with the conversation. You did not talk about leadership or how to work a body of men. You just did it. Theorising killed the whole thing dead. It was all common sense, after all. 'But I've an advantage over you.'

'An advantage?' said Essex, sensing an insult but not sure what it was. 'What do you mean by that?'

'You were born a nobleman, born to lead, born to see yourself as a cut above other men. Brought up in the household of the most powerful man in England.'

Where apparently you learnt black magic and sodomy, thought Gresham, though this is probably not the best time to mention it. Except there was no sense of any great evil emanating from this man, unlike Cecil. Essex was surprisingly likeable. Spoilt, selfish and certainly arrogant, but no one brought up as the heir to an earldom could ever totally avoid that. He was a philanderer and probably a depressive, and his mood swings were renowned. Yet underneath was a genuine power, allied to that strange vulnerability.

'I was born a bastard,' Gresham continued, 'to a merchant who happened to make the greatest fortune in England but who had no

77

birth and no breeding. If I seem at ease with my men, and they with me, it's because we both recognise how similar we are. We're no different, really. I've just had more luck.'

Without realising he had done it, or why, Gresham's last words pushed Essex instantly into a different persona. Gresham saw at first hand one of those famous, meteoric mood changes in Robert Devereux, Earl of Essex.

'And if you can do what you have done without the power that breeding brings, how much should I do, who have had all that advantage, had the ear of the Queen ... I, who love the Queen more than any other of her subjects!'

Dark, black melancholia, a bottomless pit of sadness and hopelessness into which one could only dive, helpless. It was a mood Gresham recognised from himself.

The ear of the Queen? It was probably one of her more attractive bits, thought Gresham, but you're welcome to it and the rest of her body. Love the Queen? It was entirely possible that Essex did. Royalty had that effect on some people, robbed them of their senses, made proud men obsequious, filled them with a slavish devotion. Perhaps Jesus had had the same effect on his disciples.

Essex's mood had swung totally in the space of a second. He was angry now, hauled up out of the black dog pit, on his feet, his face reddening, almost shouting at Gresham. Did the man have a dose of the clap, as many said? The disease was endemic in Court, and Essex a known philanderer. These sudden mood changes, often followed by plunges into mad depression were a feature of syphilis. Yet Essex showed none of the outward physical symptoms.

'I was born to power!' he was shouting now, like a lunatic. 'God gave me the breeding, the body and the brain!'

But not, thought Gresham, the modesty to go with it. Nor, as it happened, the money.

'And what have I done with it? Done with my precious ration of time? The gift we are given only once?'

Was this an act? No. There was real insanity lurking behind the Earl's frothings. Yet at the same time there was something else, the strangest sense of a different, almost an alternative intelligence at work, observing and assessing while all the time the outer person gave a very convincing performance as someone who had lost not just the marbles but any sense of the rules of the game.

'You've become Earl Marshal of England,' said Gresham, deciding not to pander to the rage or the self-pity. The appointment had been announced in December of the previous year. This was new in their relationship. They had never talked like this before. 'You've certainly had your ups and downs in Court politics, but as things stand you're the favourite of the Court. You're also, gratifyingly but dangerously, the man the people cheer as he rides through the street. Oh, and you're Master of the Queen's Horse, and holder of her monopoly of sweet wines. Not bad, even for an Earl.'

'Pah!' The scorn in Essex's voice was tangible, a tearing, terrible thing. 'I am mocked for my failure in the Azores, my Lord of Effingham made Earl of Nottingham and so to walk ahead of me at the opening of Parliament!' Essex was conveniently forgetting that his appointment as Earl Marshal had restored his precedence over Effingham. 'To be sponsored by me for any post at Court is to have the kiss of death on one's prospects! The Queen ignores my nominations. *Laughs at me, even!*'

The expedition to the Azores in 1597 had been a disaster, the feud between Essex and Sir Walter Raleigh shaking and eventually breaking the whole mad-cap adventure.

'If naval engagements were subject to common sense and logic, or influenced by the effectiveness of their commanders, Spain would be King of England now and the leader of the Armada, Duke Medina de Sidonia, probably Earl of Essex, for all I know.'

It did not make sense under normal circumstances to remind a reigning monarch how many such had lost their thrones or their lives, nor to remind a proud Earl that his power was to all intents and purposes in the gift of the reigning King or Queen. Yet it seemed to have worked. Essex's head snapped round, his headlong descent into self-pity not stopped, but certainly slowed down.

'You were there, not just with the Armada, but on it? You've never talked of it. It was one of the great scandals of the time. They said you were a spy for Spain. They still do say so, some of them.'

'I was there,' said Gresham simply, this time looking into his own soul, rather than trying to fathom that of Essex. 'On board the flagship of the Armada, by the side of its commander. I was a young man then, and already a spy, that most despised of all things. On a fleet led by the person who I still think of as the greatest commander of all. By the side of that man a petty tyrant deliberately stranding his men on mud flats to teach them a lesson is nothing. Nothing at all.'

'And was Medina de Sidonia so good a commander?' whispered Essex, his mood changed yet again. 'They say he was a coward, that he failed in his leadership.'

'He's the best man I've ever served with or under.' Except Sir Walter Raleigh, but given the relationship between Essex and Raleigh it was probably not tactful to mention that now.

'why? Why was he so good?'

Essex was driven by what he knew in his heart he would never attain: military glory. It was one of the ways he would rescue his life, give it meaning. It was simple. You fought and won, or lost. If you were lucky you lost your life in the latter case, and gained sweet oblivion from the mess of life. Did Essex share with Gresham a wish for death, to end the struggle, the fighting for position, the endless pursuit of ill-defined goals?

'Medina de Sidonia had lands, estates, position. A happy marriage, children. When he was summoned, without warning, to take charge of the Armada, he knew it would fail. Too much damage had already been done, and his intelligence told him that this outwardly great fleet was like a child damaged beyond repair in the mother's womb. His King had given him binding orders that crippled his freedom of action.'

'So he served an ungrateful monarch,' breathed Essex, 'and yet he still took the duty on?'

'Of course he did!' said Gresham, scornfully and stung for once into an entirely open response. 'He was a grandee of Spain, wasn't he? In Spain, nobility justifies itself by sacrifice. He knew he would lose his honour by leading a fleet that was destined to fail. And his honour is the only thing a Spanish nobleman has that matters. Our poor noblemen . . .'

Careful! Essex was poor, his extravagance paid for by a monopoly on sweet wines.

' . . . our poor noblemen hang round like hungry dogs outside the doors of the Court, destroyed if they cannot don a new doublet. In Spain the poorest noble thinks himself rich if he has his honour. Yet his King had called for Sidonia to do something that he knew would lose him his honour if he accepted and lose if he refused. He knew he would lose. Yet still he sailed, because he had sworn his fealty to his King. He knew that when he lost he would lose his own honour and reputation, the things more important to him and his ancient family than life itself. Yet in losing his own honour he would ensure that the real villain, his King, preserved his. It was a conscious choice, don't you see?' Gresham was getting carried away. He decided to let it happen. 'Forgive me, my Lord Earl. Do you know how many times he led his own flagship into the heat of the battle, exposed himself to every sharpshooter in England? A cannon ball does not stop in mid-air and bow to noble blood. So I sink a little when I hear you bemoan your own lack of advancement. The noblest commander I've ever met sacrificed his own reputation for a higher end, the reputation of his monarch. In my mind, true nobility consists of sacrifice as much as self-advancement.'

'And do *I* have that quality of true nobility?' For a moment, Essex was like a child before his father, seeking approval.

Gresham ran through the facts in his mind. Essex's boat master had tried to ram his way into a berth to which he had no right by brute force. Yet in the aftermath of a battle he had clearly lost, the Earl had shown no rancour, and rather put himself out to be generous to his erstwhile opponent.

'You may have, my Lord,' said Gresham simply. 'Or you may not. The jury has yet to return a verdict.'

'And you, Henry Gresham? What is your verdict?'

Why was the greatest nobleman in the country asking a mere Sir Henry Gresham what he thought of him? 'I don't give verdicts,' he said. 'And I trust only two people on this earth, and view that as a major weakness.' A weakness Cecil had been able to exploit. 'My personal jury is likely to stay out for the rest of both our lives, give no judgement on your standing or on my own. But it's a little better than that. I can tell you one verdict it won't be uttering.'

'And that is?' Essex, for short periods, had phenomenal power of concentration, bringing such intensity to an issue that he threatened to burn it out.

'I won't be telling you to, "Fuck off, mister!"'

Essex rocked back, a great guffaw coming from him. 'I think the level of gratitude shown to you by that street urchin is an emblem for the Court, as it happens, a measure of the reward we who haunt this place get for our sycophancy.'

A servant had brought some wine and some sweetmeats in on a silver tray, emblazoned with the Devereux arms, and left as silently as he came.

'Have you been sent to spy on me?' asked Essex casually, as he reached for the wine. 'I understand Cecil summoned you last week.'

There are defining moments in our lives, usually ones we have not prepared for, often ones where we think afterwards what we should have said or done. Was this what it had all been leading up to? Had Essex planned the invasion of the berth simply to meet Gresham intimately, lure him into a false sense of companionship and then find out the truth about him? Gresham had less than a second to decide. If he hesitated, he was declaring his guilt. If he owned up to being Cecil's creature, a man with the vast resources of Essex could have Gresham dead within the hour. If he denied it and Essex believed him, all it would take was a disloyal and bribed servant in Cecil's household and Gresham would find a dagger in his back. Gresham had no illusions that Essex would put his own interests and survival on a far higher priority than that of a convenient and amusing drinking companion. And he had no time to think!

'Yes,' said Gresham simply. 'Of course I have. In a manner of speaking. Cecil uses me to clean up some of his rubbish, and I fear that's how he sees you at present. But we ought to be clear on one thing. Cecil thinks I work for him. I don't. I work for the Queen, and for peace and stability in England.'

'And for yourself?' asked Essex.

'If by that you mean will I put my own survival before yours, yes. As you will undoubtedly put your survival before mine.'

'True,' said Essex, as if this went without saying. 'And you are willing to tell me that you will put your personal feelings aside, and work for Cecil and the Queen even if by so doing you harm me?'

Essex was gazing directly into Gresham's eyes now, and Gresham returned his gaze. Essex had his sword belt by his side, while Gresham's had been rescued from the jetty and was now presumably in the hands of one of his men somewhere distant in the Palace. Gresham had stripped naked in front of Essex, who knew there was no dagger hidden on his person. Gresham was as defenceless as he would ever be, his servant outside the room, and he had just confessed to being in Cecil's employ.

'Of course I am, my Lord,' said Gresham, seeming immensely relaxed. 'If that situation were to arise. Better the spy you know. It gives us both so much more control over the quality of the information.'

'Is this . . . normal? In your line of business, I mean. To be so open?' asked Essex, the merest hint of a laugh in his voice.

'Well, no, actually,' said Gresham. 'Come to think on it, this is the first time I've told someone I quite like that if the need arises I'll shaft them with the government. But somehow it doesn't seem unreasonable, given the circumstances. Indeed, it seems rather a good idea. I'm surprised I haven't thought of it before. It takes so much of the tension out of things. And, of course, I hate Cecil, and in a strange, drunken sort of way I really am quite fond of you.'

'They said you were a very, very strange man,' said Essex. 'When

I asked my own spies about you. I've never known whether you shared my company because it interested you, or whether you were being paid to do it.'

'I did so because you interested me. And because life quickens when you are there. Was it deliberate on your part to force an encounter earlier?'

'No. There was no plan. But I could have stopped my boatman heading for your berth. I chose not to do so.'

'Why?'

'It was more fun that way. And the Queen has enough money left to build some more boats.'

'And why this sudden questioning about my motives? Our conversation today has taken rather a new turn.'

'I've become suspicious of everyone,' said Essex. 'Of necessity. The times are very … tense. My position with the Queen is not secure.' It was probably the truth. 'You're known to work for Cecil, and to hate him. And he you, so they tell me. Wasn't it you who gave the Queen his nickname? "My little pygmy" she calls him, to his evident distress.'

Cecil hated and despised references to his warped body. Gresham sighed.

'So the story goes, but alas it's untrue. Everyone believes it was me, but in fact the name was suggested to her by Cecil's father. It's more comfortable for Cecil to believe that it was me.'

'I can't understand how two people who loathe each other can work together as you and the pygmy appear to do. Or why a man as wealthy as you evidently are needs to do such work.'

'Yet you, my Lord, agreed a truce with Cecil when he was away on his ill-fated embassy for the Queen to the King of France. A truce which you honoured.'

'That was politics,' responded Essex airily. 'It suited him to be in France, and it suited me for that time not to be plotting. Simple mutual convenience.'

Gresham decided this particular conversation was going nowhere. 'Are we going to see the play, my Lord? Oh, and by the way, if you are going to kill me, would you mind starting now, while I'm wearing your clothes? It's so difficult to wash out the blood . . .'

Gresham had noted that Essex's hand was resting on the hilt of his sword. Essex's hand stayed where it was. There was no humour now in his voice. 'No, I am not going to kill you now. But, as we are making a very uncourtly honesty the flavour of the day, it is entirely possible that I may do so later. I do not like the little pygmy, or those who work for him. I do like you, but that fact won't stop me killing you. Or you me, I suspect, if the need arises. I'm really not so sure you are Cecil's man. Not in your heart. I take it he has some dirt on you? Some hold over you?'

Gresham smiled a slight smile, but said nothing.

'I'll take that as a yes,' said Essex. 'And, in the name of that same honesty, I shall try and wean you off that detestable little toad . . .'

So that was where the inscription on Cecil's wall had come from.

' . . . and make you my man, rather than his. You will find me a better master.'

And that, thought Gresham, as he and Essex rose to leave the room, is probably the truest thing said in this bizarre conversation.

But at least Essex's ploy was quite clear. He would try to seduce Gresham away from Cecil, thereby hurting and humiliating his greatest enemy. Robert Devereux wanted Henry Gresham as a trophy, a living and possibly even a notorious witness to the great Earl's capacity to attract men into his party. Well, it suited Gresham to play the game for the moment. He had no option.

Before they reached the door, it shook with two mighty thumps, and a noise like an iron sheet being dropped onto a door key. Gresham shuddered. He knew that noise. The Queen's guard always dropped their pikes to the ground with a resounding crash when they arrived at their destination. They were overweight, and so wore their breast- and backplates loosely tied. The result was that the two heavy pieces of metal were forever grinding against each other, and bouncing off belt buckles. The door was crashed open by a guard, whose helmet showed a serious dent on its left-hand side. Valiant action against an enemy, wondered Gresham? Or contact with a door post while drunk?

Elizabeth's dress might have been dark red, if much of the cloth had been visible beneath the pearls. She was fanning herself. Essex and Gresham both swept off their hats, and bowed low, forcing their eyes to the floor.

The Queen ignored Gresham.

'Robbie, Robbie,' she crooned as a lady might talk to her pet dog, 'how is it that yet again you cost me money?' She extended her hand, and bid him rise up. 'My poor boat is smashed, and my loyal boatman distraught.'

Essex, upright now, gave her a brilliant smile.

'Majesty, I shall build you a new boat with my own hands, finer than that which Cleopatra rode in to meet Mark Antony—' he began grandly.

'Which like you, will look beautiful, but sink at regular intervals!' the Queen cut in. They both collapsed into peals of laughter, more like boy and girl than Queen and noble. Gresham was still bent forward in his bow, his back starting to feel as if he had collected the harvest in single handed.

'You may rise, Sir Henry,' said the Queen, who until this moment appeared not to have noticed Gresham's presence. 'While you still can,' she added caustically. Gresham rose up, to his considerable relief. The Queen looked coldly at him. 'I hear that yet again it is you who have led this young man astray.'

Gresham had learnt to take risks – small risks only – with the Queen.

'Your Majesty,' he said, 'I have tried for some years past to lead my Lord of Essex astray, but for some reason he has always overtaken me and left me as a mere follower.'

What might have been a flicker of grim approval crossed the Queen's face, and she turned again to Essex. It was as if everyone else had vanished, Gresham, the guards and everyone, and the only people in the room were Elizabeth and Essex. Her old eyes were alight for a moment, sparkling with the excitement of flirtation and dalliance.

'And will you take me, an old woman, to the play, my Robbie?' she asked in an unusually soft voice. When she chose she could bark with the sensitivity of a fog horn. Her eyes softened for a moment, gave a hint of the girl she once had been. Was she in love with this man? And was he in love with her, or with her power and office?

'I will take you . . .' said Essex, pausing deliberately ' . . . even to the ends of the earth.' Somehow what should have been arch flattery was sincere. Adoration? Worship even? Essex needed the Queen's approval, not just for the money and the favours it brought, but almost more for the excitement, the sense of being at the heart of things. Yet at the same time there was a deep resentment, a burning anger at being in thrall, a fierce yearning to be free. God help Essex, God help England – and perhaps even God help Elizabeth – if ever she and Essex came to blows.

CHAPTER 4

Late June, 1598
Scotland

'I hate bloody Scotland!' said Mannion glumly.

'How can you hate it? You've never been there.'

'Don't have to 'ave bin somewhere to know you hate it.'

They were riding side by side, nearly at the moorings where the *Anna* lay ready to slip her anchor. The slaughterhouses at Deptford were pouring blood and offal into the river, turning the near shoreside sections of it a stinking brown. The ships jostled against each other in the moorings, the squeak and rattle of rigging vying with the thousand and one noises of a busy mooring. The slop of the waves on the stone steps was reassuring, but even they seemed tired. The day had turned heavy, hot and humid, with thick grey cloud lowering over London. There was nowhere for the air to go, and the stench of the slaughterhouses hung everywhere, sticking to clothes like an invisible devilish glue.

Gresham suspected that one reason for Mannion's reluctance to travel was that a relationship with one of the cooks in The House was starting to get interesting. The woman, recently widowed when her drunken husband fell into the Thames, was both good-looking and a good cook. The combination of sex and food was about as close to a vision of heaven as Mannion could go.

'Madge'll still be there when you get back, old man,' said Gresham with a singular lack of sympathy. 'Anyway, she's still in mourning for her husband, isn't she? Though why anyone would mourn for that drunken lout I'll never know. And how did he kill himself falling in? He came here looking for a job as a boatman and swore he could swim.'

'Tide was out when he fell in,' said Mannion. 'Twelve foot drop. Pity really.' Mannion's voice contained no shred of pity whatsoever. 'It's all silt down there, 'cept there's one rock within about a mile. He fell 'ead first onto it. The sharp bit of it. Stupid bugger.'

'Madge must have been heartbroken,' said Gresham drily.

Mannion did not see the joke, or chose not to see it. 'Bloody ecstatic, more like. She'd been tryin' to kill him for years. Anyway, that's not why I hate bloody Scotland.'

'Well,' sighed Gresham 'you're clearly going to tell me, so why not get it off your chest now and then we can all have some peace?'

'I hate it,' said Mannion, 'because it's cold, it's wet and it's a bloody long way away. And they eat oats boiled in water, cold with salt on top. And there's midges, and the beer's lousy. And,' he continued, warming to his point – it was clear he had been asking around in the taverns, 'they say as 'ow the people in the lowlands are all miserable bastards who don't like drink or dancing and wear black all the time, and those in the mountains are mad as hatters and so pissed by nine in the morning that they can't give you the time o' day.'

'Well, that last bit sounds attractive for someone like you.'

'I *enjoy* a drink,' said Mannion. 'When 'ave you ever seen me out for the count as a result of it? I likes to experience my pleasures.'

Never, now Gresham came to think of it. Which was quite extraordinary, as he had never seen anyone capable of drinking as much as Mannion. A surprising number of conversations with Mannion ended with him in charge. Gresham decided to give up. They were nearing the *Anna*, and it was time for business.

Gresham had not been joking when he said he kept a vessel in permanent wait for him. Or had done so, in recent months. His only sadness was that having confessed to it, he would now have to find a new boat and a new berth. Cecil would get his own men to identify the ship and where it lay, and a vessel that was known to his enemy was no use to Gresham, however beautiful it was. The *Anna* was small, a barque, yet with three masts, the first two square-rigged and the third lanteen-rigged, but for all her small size she was a thing of great intricacy and perfect in her form, well able to stand the storms of the Channel if the need arose. Her previous owner had died at sea; his widow wanted a quick sale.

Mannion may have hated Scotland, but he hated sea journeys even more. Yet even he had to admit that if one had to go to Scotland it was better to go by sail than to face endless weeks on a horse or, even worse, a bone-shattering carriage. They rounded a corner with a timber-framed house leaning crazily forward as if it wanted to kiss the earth, the horses slipping on the mire and filth that lay on the road, and before them was the *Anna*.

Gresham had been summoned to Cecil two days earlier, a measure of Cecil's concern being that he would only hand the letter to Gresham in person. An extra measure was the fact that the meeting was not in any Palace, but in Cecil's surprisingly modest London home. It was the place where he kept the servants most loyal to him. Gresham knew that much from having tried to bribe them all without success. The transaction had been brief and businesslike. The house and the servants were draped in black. Lord Burghley's death had just been announced. Had Cecil loved his father? If he had, he was not showing it.

If it became known that Gresham was going to Scotland with a message for its King, he might as well slit his own throat and save someone else the trouble of doing it. So how could he disguise his mission?

The answer had been Mannion's idea. It was highly audacious, so much so that Gresham did not bother to clear it with Cecil in advance. It was more fun that way.

'You've said it yerself often enough. Hide the truth by telling it. Tell 'em you're going to Scotland.'

'Brilliant!' said Gresham. 'And tell them I've a letter from Robert Cecil to the King of Scotland?'

'No,' said Mannion, 'tell 'em you've reason to believe that girl you took on board, and who's the biggest pain in your life, actually had a Scottish father. Tell 'em you're going to try and unite her with her blood relations – which is the best way you can see of getting 'er off your back, an' the sooner the better. You'll be very convincing on that score, I reckon.'

'Hang on,' said Gresham. 'Apart from the prospect of spending quite a long period of time with the bloody girl, and the fact that she'll almost certainly throw a fit and lock herself in her room for a year if I even mention it, I'm implicated in every plot that's going at present. So does it really make sense for me to announce I'm going to Scotland, when everyone knows James is one of the main contenders for the throne?'

'Makes sense if you gets a permit from the bloody Queen,' said Mannion. 'You know her well enough. Ain't many people going up to Scotland on a regular basis, things being what they are. Mebbe she wants a letter delivered as well.' Mannion obviously thought he'd made a joke.

The problem was that the old drunkard might be right. Going to Scotland with a passport from the Queen was the best cover of all. But the first problem was the girl, who was most likely to reject any suggestion that she might come simply because it came from him. The second problem was the Queen. Her body might be ageing rapidly, but there was no sign of the decay entering her brain. Could he fool her into granting him a passport? When she had knighted him ten years earlier in that terrible dungeon in the Tower of London, the sword she had used could just have easily gone through his neck as tapped him on the shoulder. The work he had done since had both harmed and helped his standing with her – if anyone ever knew what their standing was with the Queen.

He gained an audience surprisingly quickly considering everyone in England wanted a private audience with the Queen. Yet perhaps it was not so surprising. Increasingly the old lady seemed to act on a whim, living for the moment as if she realised that her own moments were more and more limited by time, the one thing over which she and no other human had control.

Delay. That was the problem. Elizabeth had always had an uncanny knack of letting time sort her problems out for her. Outsiders saw it as vacillation, but Gresham was not so sure. In this instance he needed a firm answer from a woman to whom firm answers were increasingly becoming an anathema.

The only thing shocking about her today was the extraordinary red wig she was wearing. The gimlet eyes were as hard as ever, her breath capable of knocking a fly out of the sky at fifty yards, and the jewels on her lavish dress enough to buy an army. It was early evening, when the majority of England whose lamp and candle was the sun were heading to their beds. Whitehall Palace proved its usual warren, but Gresham realised how serious things were when he was ushered through a string of rooms and suddenly found his male escort replaced by giggling ladies-in-waiting. His audience was being held in the chamber directly outside the Queen's bedroom. What was even more frightening was that, with a quick nod, she dismissed the female attendants. Gresham hoped for Mannion's sake they had been banished to whatever antechamber he had been forced to leave him in. Some of the ladies-in-waiting were known to be keen on a bit of rough.

If he had not known better he would have sworn the Queen had been crying. Her eyes were bloodshot and swollen, the make-up beneath them showing signs of rapid and rather ineffective repair. It was said that she had hand-fed Burghley the old man's last meals on earth, like a mother feeding her young child.

'So, Sir Henry!' the monarch exclaimed, 'the rare moment comes when you ask to see me! I seem to recollect that for much of my reign it has been my job to command you to attend my Court.' The tone was harsh, combative. It was as if she wished to banish any concept of softness.

He was alone with the Queen. She was in a black gown, with a high neck, its folds sparkling. It was what passed as casual wear for the Queen but still had enough whalebone in it to strip a decent-sized whale of its skeleton.

'Your Highness, I—' Gresham started to say.

'Your Highness,' carried on the Queen, in a fair copy of Gresham's tone, 'I recognise the threat you pose to my existence, and your absolute power over my fortunes. I am rich enough not to need your patronage, arrogant enough not to seek your approval in normal times and intelligent enough to be able to flatter you more amusingly than most.'

The Queen paused. Gresham doubted that the Italian who had just set up in London teaching people the manners of the Court would have an answer as to what one did when the Queen started to mimic you. She was seated in a high-backed chair that was not quite a small throne. A fine Venetian glass had been left by her ladies, and she leant over daintily to sip from it. It was as likely to be boiled water as wine, if Gresham's experience was anything to go by.

'Do tell me. Have I summed you up?' Her tone was deadly serious. And when the daughter of Henry VIII used anything deadly, wise men listened.

Ah well. Men – and women – only had one life. What was life without risk? And who wanted to die in their bed of old age?

'Your Majesty, the greatest flattery I can afford you is to acknowledge that my wealth can be confiscated by a wave of your hand, the seat of my arrogance severed from its neck by a wave of altogether different material, and intelligent enough to realise that I am at this moment desperately trying to think out stratagems that will avoid either eventuality. Or, to put it more simply, yes. You have summed me up. Rather too well, as it happens.'

The Queen looked at Gresham for a moment, her expression unfathomable. Then she spoke, 'I have tolerated you because even with your arrogance and shameless good looks you have done me good service, but also because of all the people I have known in my time your superb flattery has never been offered other than with a supreme awareness that it was simply flattery and not the truth.' She leant forward. There was real anger in her eyes. 'I know more than you think I know about your role in the fate of my sister, Mary Queen of Scots.'

Gresham had decided in his youth that to reveal one's fears and one's emotions was the ultimate weakness, and had imposed a rigid self-control on his body. It was only that which enabled him to stop going white.

'I know what you know about the first Armada. I think I could be said to have drawn it from you on the rack.'

The hint of a smile played across that small part of her lips liberated from make-up. Brave men had been known to burst into tears and confess their all when simply shown the rack. Gresham had been strapped into it and the torture about to start when he had held that particular conversation with the Queen. The strangest thing had not been her presence in the torture chamber, but that she had come to the Tower of London at all. She hated that place above all others, ever since she had entered in through Traitor's Gate, accused of treason by her sister Queen Mary.

'And then there are the other affairs, those I have known about, those I know about that were intended to be kept from me and those I do not know about.'

Damn her! Why could not the old body be matched in the mind? Was there anybody stupid in this mad, deranged Court, or did they all have the brains of the Queen, Cecil and Essex?

'So here you are,' said the Queen, taking a sip from her glass. 'Undoubtedly you want something from me. No one asks to see the Queen for love, only ever because they want something in her power.' She held up her hand, as Gresham opened his mouth. 'Enough! Cease before you start. I have had enough of oiled words. Tell me what it is you want. Spit it out, man.'

There was no pause in Gresham's answer.

'I wish your passport for me to visit Scotland with my ward and a servant.'

94

The words hung in the air.

'You always were clever, Henry Gresham. Cleverer than anyone, except perhaps for my little pygmy, and certainly clever in a different way from him. Others would have spun me a cock and bull story about why they wished to visit the country of the impudent young man so hungry for my throne.' There was real venom in her voice. Gresham had a strong impression that Queen Elizabeth of England did not much like King James of Scotland. Perhaps the fact that she had ordered the execution of his mother did not help. 'You choose to say nothing.'

Gresham continued to choose to say nothing. The strain was actually harder than filling the air with noise would have been. Babbling is easy.

In earlier years the Queen would have got up at a moment like this, and started to pace the room restlessly. It used to annoy Gresham because it was exactly what he did. Instead, she stayed seated. Gresham noted the cushions piled high beneath and around her. They were new. The Queen had been renowned for sitting on hard wooden seats for hours on end. How times were changing.

'Well, now,' said the Queen, actually settling back into her cushions, but with a wicked gleam in her eye. 'As Sir Henry is apparently struck dumb for a moment, let us see if an old woman . . .' She paused momentarily and cocked what remained of an eyebrow at him, as if daring Gresham to challenge as any courtier would do the assertion that she was old. Gresham continued to say nothing, his face impassive. ' . . . can come to some conclusions. It is a long, painful journey to Scotland, and an inhospitable country with few charms for a man of wealth and taste. Therefore Sir Henry has strong reason to go there. His ward, who they tell me he has not bedded yet, is unlikely to be the real reason. Given the importance of Scotland to those who are already playing dice for my throne and who believe me dead already, the real reason is therefore likely to be a plot. But whose plot? And is Sir Henry for or against the plotters?'

Gresham was challenging his own body not to sweat, his own face not to redden. This was getting dangerously close.

'My little pygmy hates Henry Gresham, but uses him.' She was looking intently at Gresham now, daring him to show by a flicker of his face that she had hit the mark. 'As he, for some reason, seems willing to be used. But there are others, of course. Sir Henry is a lifelong friend of the greatest rogue in my Court, Sir Walter Raleigh, who as so many of my Court would like nothing more than to have a line of communication open with the ... King of Scotland. And my Great Lord the Earl of Essex has been heard expressing admiration for Henry Gresham the soldier, just as so many others have been whispering that this same Henry Gresham is in this plot, or that plot or the other plot. And my Great Lord of Essex is not above suspicion in seeming willing to bend the knee in obeisance to the north.'

There was a long silence.

'Which one is it, I wonder? Which of those professing undying love and loyalty towards me as their Queen wishes to send a covert message to my rival in Scotland? Or perhaps it is all of them? Or is it the King himself who has asked to see you? Is the whole pattern in reverse, with His Royal Highness of the frozen north making the running, seeking to use this same Sir Henry Gresham as his intermediary with one of those named earlier? Or, God forbid, with all of them?'

There was another, even longer silence.

'I command you to make answer,' said the Queen simply, and Gresham knew that his time of silence had ended. 'Why do you wish to go to Scotland?'

'Majesty,' he said, 'I have a lust for porridge and it will not be denied.'

For a moment he thought he had gone too far, as a flicker of yellow flashed across the Queen's eyes, and then she burst into a peal of laughter, so intense it rocked her fragile body. When she had stopped laughing, and had wiped the traces of spittle off her lips with a delicate handkerchief, she looked at him again.

'And was I stupid enough to expect a straight answer from you? Tell me one thing. Just one thing.'

'Your Majesty?'

'I have lost my father.' The mood change was sudden. God knows how anyone could keep track when she and Essex were in the same room together. Lose her father? Henry VIII had been dead these many, many years. Gresham could see the tears rising up in her eyes. Real tears. Good God! 'My Lord Burghley is the nearest thing I had to a father, and now he is gone. I have already lost my executioner, Walsingham, who bankrupted himself for me. I have lost . . . so many of those who were my friends. And you, with your good looks, your money and your wit, you who were trained by Walsingham, you could have stepped into his shoes had you so wished. But you never showed any interest, fled to the Low Countries to fight in stupid wars and no doubt prove your manhood in the lunatic way men seem to have to do . . . you are the only person I know, Henry Gresham, who gave up a position of power in my Court when it beckoned him, when to acquire it would have been so easy. Why did you spurn advancement?'

'Your Majesty,' said Gresham, who felt it was time he strung more than two consecutive words together, 'I am one who believes that most of life is a pretence, and who struggles more and more to see or to find meaning in it. Life at Court, even in your service, would for me simply have been another pretence. I am sorry.'

'Yet you miss out the most important thing of all,' said the Queen, 'if you wish to keep your life and your liberty.'

'I do?' said Gresham, nonplussed for once.

'If you were simply seeking to flatter me, you would have pointed out the mere truth. You have done several things for which you should have been hung, if not drawn and quartered. Yet never to my knowledge have you once undertaken an action that would threaten my life or my throne.'

Well, that was true, thought Gresham, though all too often that had not been the motive in his actions. He nodded, acknowledging the truth.

'So tell me this. If I give you my passport to Scotland, will anything that takes place there threaten my life or my throne?'

For a brief moment he saw the real fear that haunted this woman in the small hours when she was alone. Her powers were waning as she lost the battle with time. The men who had put her on the throne and kept her there – Burghley, Walsingham and the rest of the pack – were dead or dying. How easy now to speed up nature: a subtle poison in her food; the assassin's knife; even a carefully mounted rebellion. Ring out the dead wood, ring in the new. The Queen is dead. Long live . . . a new Queen? A new King?

Gresham did actually take time to think this one through. Slightly to his surprise he found he was not willing to lie to Elizabeth. She was foul-breathed, not infrequently foul-mouthed, infuriating in her procrastination, had probably denied the country an heir simply to preserve her own power for as long as she lived and was the most devious person he had ever known, as well as the most selfish apart from himself. Yet she had brought peace to a ravaged England for forty years, and given her people in exchange for all that it gave her the one thing a monarch could give their country: stability. The Spanish had not invaded, for all that they had tried. Ireland may have been falling apart for most of her reign, Tyrone threatening to wrest the whole country back into Irish hands, but it was of more use to royal vanity and land-starved nobles than to any normal Englishman. The harvest might be bad, the bottom fall out of the wool trade, and a thousand natural calamities befall Jack and Jill. But at least in the reign of Elizabeth their problems were from natural calamities. No wild horsemen trampled their crops at harvest time or ran with their babies on the end of a pike, and no marauding armies took their wives and daughters even as they burnt their house down. Unlike Essex, military glory had never ranked as an ambition in Elizabeth's mind. Like Burghley and Cecil, she saw war primarily as a waste of money. So Gresham ran through at break-neck speed all that might result from his rescuing the reputation of Cecil with James. Try as he might, he could find no scenario that would threaten the Queen. It would probably be better in the name of stability if Cecil was cleared in the eyes of James. It might stop the both of them plotting even more.

It was the time he took thinking that saved his life, he realised afterwards. A dishonest man would simply have denied any threat to the Queen. The sight of him almost visibly testing each scenario against her question, his reserve forgotten for once and his brow furrowed in concentration, was the greatest testimony to the honesty of his answer.

'No, Your Majesty, there is nothing associated with my journey that could threaten your throne or your life. Or rather,' and he allowed himself a dry little smile, 'I give you my word that there is nothing I know of or can predict that would be counter to your interests. No man can ever predict with exactitude what a journey will produce.'

He thought again. Clearing Cecil's name might even allow for a smoother transition of power when the moment came for the Queen to die. And Cecil would never hasten that death. James of Scotland had spent most of his life fighting for survival amid the rabid politics of his homeland. He knew better than most that those who killed or deposed a monarch acquired a taste for it. If Cecil did anything to hasten Elizabeth's death he would not only never gain James's trust; he would hasten his own death at James's hand.

'My journey will help preserve the life and fortune of those few I call friends. And, if anything, it will help rather than hinder your own assured long reign and good health.'

The Queen sat back, suddenly looking very tired.

'Take this ring.' She scrabbled in a box by her side, and produced a fabulous but crude emerald set ostentatiously in gold. 'Show it to the men outside this room, and they will let you pass. Had you not had this, my token, you would have left here under their escort for the Tower. And this time you would not have emerged.'

Something approaching despair filled Gresham's heart. He prided himself on being one jump ahead of his pursuers and those who threatened his life. Yet he had been trapped by Cecil, didn't know whether Essex was his ally or his rival and now had damn nearly been executed by the Queen, all in a state of blissful ignorance as to what was happening. To be in control was central to Henry Gresham's life. What was he playing at, letting these people out-manoeuvre him? Had the depression that had beset him these past six months finally corroded its way into his very soul, draining his will to live and dulling his judgement?

'You may present the ring to King James in secret. It is an agreed token between us.'

An agreed token? Why was there an agreed token between the Queen and the man to whom she had just written a foul and abusive letter, warning him off her kingdom and accusing him of gross presumption? 'And you will give him this as well.' It was a thin, sealed package. A letter, obviously. How interesting. It appeared that everyone in England wanted secret packages delivered to King James of Scotland. There was a tidy little business here for the right person.

'Yet you will cling to your initial stratagem, and take the girl along with you. She will be your given reason for making the journey. Your meeting with the Scottish King will be in secret, as will the exchange of the ring and the package. As no doubt will be the exchange of whatever other information you wish to give. Show the ring to the right people and it will gain you a secret audience with the obnoxious little sodomite.'

It was strange how sodomy and black magic kept cropping up together in Gresham's life.

'You will not under any circumstances let others know you are carrying my message. Those who have commissioned you must continue to think they are the sole reason for your visit, and that you cajoled me in my dotage by your charm and good looks into granting you a passport. And you had better bring the girl to me tomorrow, so I can be seen to question her in private. Yet from now on, you are not undertaking this journey on behalf of those who first asked you to make it, whoever they are. A higher authority now commands you. You are doing it as my messenger. A messenger of your Queen.'

Wheels within wheels. Deviousness within deviousness. What better way to cloak a mission from her enemies than by letting them think it was their mission? And now Gresham knew that beneath the public bickering and exchange of letters there was a different relationship between Elizabeth and James. Whatever it was, it was clearly both separate from the public domain and not based on a true meeting of minds. 'Obnoxious little sodomite' she had called him, with no lack of sincerity.

'And understand one thing, Henry Gresham.' He had never known King Henry VIII, but something in his daughter's tone made him understand the fear that man could provoke in others. 'If it becomes known that you have exchanged my ring and that package with the King of Scotland, if word ever leaks out, you will return to England not as one of its richest men, but as a pauper. Every piece of land, every house, every hovel and every asset you own will be stripped from you and fall to my Crown. You will become the penniless bastard you were before your father decided to rescue you.'

There was a third, long silence.

'I have no Bible here,' said the Queen of England. 'No witness, even. Yet I ask you to swear a simple oath, and to stand by that oath as if every Bible in the world was here for you to lay your hand on, and every witness including God. Will you swear to do everything – everything – in your power to preserve my reign for as long as I live? And will you swear to do everything in your power to ensure that when the moment of my death comes, it is through nature and God's will and not the actions of men?'

Gresham thought about this for a few moments.

'I wish you had not, Your Majesty, preceded your request by your threat. As for the threat, I take it as one of the most powerful I've received in my undoubtedly misspent life. I shall deal with it as I've dealt with all such other threats.'

A spark of imminent death flickered in Elizabeth's eyes. Not her death, which her soul could not contemplate. His death. He hurried on.

'As for the swearing . . . yes. I swear to what you ask. You've brought internal peace to England for forty years. You've fought off our enemies and kept them from invading our shores. I swear to preserve your reign and your life, for so long as you do naturally live.'

He dropped to one knee, and bowed his head. It seemed the right thing to do. The silence which followed was one of the longest in Henry Gresham's memory.

'You may leave my presence,' the Queen said finally, in a tone of impenetrable neutrality.

It seemed somehow inappropriate to thank her. He left her presence.

He was silent as they rode home, having given Mannion the briefest summary of what had taken place. Mannion had sucked on the hollow tooth he claimed had been there all his life but which he had never had seen to, and said nothing.

Scotland was renowned for killing its monarchs, and about as welcoming to its own kind as a steel-quilled porcupine, never mind a spy from the English Court. Things could get very unpleasant in Scotland, thought Gresham. As if the trip did not present problems enough, there was the added complication of the girl. Or two added complications, as it happened – coping with her on the trip, and not least getting her to go in the first place. She was his agreed cover, even more essential now the Queen had validated her as the reason for his going, but short of tying her up and stuffing a gag in her mouth he was damned if he knew how to get her up north, and the last thing he wanted was to have to try to do so with her kicking and screaming. Still, it was not in his nature to postpone a problem. As soon as they rode into the yard of The House and handed the reins of the grey over to a groom, he asked to see her. Asked. It was not as if he had rescued her, paid for the clothes on her back and the food in her belly, was it? No, he had to ask to see her, not command it.

She came in to the Library demurely enough, her eyes downcast, her hands folded neatly in front of her. He could see why she drove men mad. Yet his deliberately casual questioning of others had suggested she still had her virginity. Why had he chosen to meet her in the Library? Of all the rooms in The House, it was the one he most identified her with, except for the uncharted territory of the kitchens and servants' quarters. Yet it was, ironically, the room in which he felt most at home. So be it.

She was late, of course. She always was. She did it to show him who was in charge and to infuriate him. He stood by one of the huge windows overlooking the Thames, determined to remain ice-cold and not let her lateness affect him.

A more astute man would have realised that his summons had put her in a panic. Desperate to appear her best before him, she had thrown out every one of the pathetically few dresses she owned onto her bed, the clucking maid who was with her if anything more nervous and thrown than she was. At least her hair was washed, and the last of the infuriating spots had vanished from her face. What dress? *What dress?* The dark-green offering was her newest and, verging on the formal, hardly suitable for a young woman whose day would be spent helping to run one of the largest households in London outside of the Palace or Essex House. It would have to do. And she would only anger him more if she was later than she had already made herself!

He prided himself that none of his true feelings showed as she arrived a full ten minutes after what was reasonable. He turned, and nodded formally to her.

She prided herself that none of her true feelings showed as she arrived, desperately wishing she had had time to put at least the tiniest smidgeon of powder to her face and neck.

Well, the stick insect he had picked up as a child from the side of a muddy pond was no stick insect now, thought Gresham. No wonder she turned heads wherever she went. She was a fine crop to be harvested by some suitable young man, and the sooner he arranged it the better: for her and for him. Though God knew how you organised such things. Bess Raleigh would know, must know. In the meantime, he needed her. Please, God, if you are there, just this once, make her do what I want . . .

He had written a fine speech in his head, but he looked at her and gave up. His conversations with Cecil and with the Queen had contained very real threats of death and ruin, and he sensed danger in his relationship with Essex. And these were threats he had failed to see coming! A sudden wave of tiredness swept over him, like the water closing over the head of a drowning man. He looked at her.

'I need your help.'

It was as simple as that. For a fleeting moment he appeared vulnerable, rather like a brave little boy who had lost his parents and was standing in the market place determined not to show his fright.

'I need you to do something for me which will undoubtedly be uncomfortable and . . . and which might even be dangerous, perhaps.'

If he failed in his mission for Cecil or for the Queen he would be ruined and Jane cast back onto the streets at best, and at worst hacked to pieces for the edification of the mob. And he had a growing sense of dissolution, of impending terror. Was England about to be plunged into civil war? Would the four horsemen be unleashed on England? Whatever the answer, it lay in the Queen, in King James, in Cecil and in Essex, all of them interwoven into the fabric of this bizarre journey he was required to make.

And then one of the most surprising moments of Henry Gresham's life happened.

'I will do as you ask,' she said, looking him in the eye. Not sulky. Not reluctant. Matter of fact, no argument.

What had gone wrong?

He started to gabble, 'We must travel to Scotland by sea. In my barque, the *Anna*. Though it's summer, such a voyage always has risks. And . . . I need you to pretend.'

He was struck by her extraordinary eyes, wholly dark but with tiny flecks of light in them.

'What is it you wish me to pretend, my Lord?' Again, matter of fact. As if this conversation was the most normal thing in her life.

Gresham sighed. 'The real reason for my journey is difficult to explain. No. I'll be more honest with you: it's better that you don't know. If things go wrong, which of course I'm almost sure they won't, it's vital that people think you know nothing. If they think that, they'll leave you alone. If you know nothing about the real reason, it's far easier to give that impression.' He looked at her, and saw her intelligence. 'I'm not trying to patronise you,' he said simply. 'It really is that ignorance is your best defence. But I need an excuse, and the one I have arrived at is to invent some Scottish ancestry for you, make the reason for the trip a search for your real parents. The Queen's agreed to grant us a passport on that basis.' Unconsciously, he let his humour show. 'It's usually a good thing to agree with the Queen.'

He realised as he said it how insulting his suggestion was. Jane must have cared about who her parents were. And now he was proposing to use what was central to her concept of self as a mere cover for other, more important things which at the same time she was not allowed to know. He waited for the explosion.

'I'll find it difficult to summon a Scottish accent.'

He started to formulate an answer, and then realised just in time that she was making a joke. And in making it, saying yes to the whole thing. He allowed himself to grin.

'You and me both,' he said. 'There are certain sacrifices I wouldn't ask anyone to make.' He paused for a moment. 'Oh . . . there is one other thing. Before granting the passport, the Queen wants to meet you, tomorrow. If she's seen—' At his words Jane's control vanished. She squeaked, and put a hand to her mouth in shock. Well, it was almost like a squeak. It was a noise that clearly she wished she had not started to make, and which she tried to stifle from somewhere around stomach level, where it appeared to begin. It lost a little momentum as it progressed from stomach to breast, from breast to neck, from neck to throat and from throat to mouth, but there was still enough left of it to burst out in what could only be described as . . . a squeak.

'My Lord!' she said in desperation. 'I have nothing to wear!'

105

Oh God! How could he have forgotten? Even a man such as he could not fail to recognise that honour, reputation and life itself for a woman depended on the dress she wore to meet the Queen. It was entirely reciprocal. How could he have forgotten that to present a young girl to the Queen in the wrong dress was as if to present her naked?

A sudden calm descended on him. This was a life or death crisis. He was good at those. It was only young girls for whom he was responsible who threw him. This was different. He looked Jane up and down, and a separate part of his brain noted the startled and even rather fearful effect this produced on her. He was undressing her in his mind, right enough, but not for that reason. Not yet, anyway. This was business.

Lady Downing. Sarah. Married at around Jane's age to a semi-senile suitor, she had enjoyed her husband's wealth and compensated for what he could not provide by starting an affair with Gresham, one of his very first acquaintances with a lady-in-waiting. Except that Sarah had been very bad at waiting. Their physical relationship had lapsed when she had married her second husband, but they had stayed good friends. Sarah had married a mere stripling of forty-six after her first husband died, and been plunged into mourning when he too had died of a canker some three years later. They were about the same height, Sarah and Jane, and seemed to push out against their dresses in more or less the same places. Sarah would help. Thank God they had remained the best of friends when the business between the sheets had ended. As for seamstress, alterations, ribbons and . . . and things girls cared about, it was still daylight, and money talked.

'MANNION!' Gresham bellowed. In time of need . . . Mannion was never far away from Gresham, but this time the old fool must have been hovering outside the door.

Gresham turned to Jane. 'I'm sorry . . . I should've thought. There's an answer. Lady Sarah Downing. She's an old friend of mine.' To his credit, Mannion kept a straight face. 'She's got a stock of Court dresses a mile high.' Did Jane's face lift a little at

106

this? 'She's about your size. We'll go there now in the coach. You –'
he turned to Mannion – 'find me three seamstresses and two jewellers. Get them here, the first with their kit and the second with
their wares. Tell the seamstresses they'll be working through the
night and most of the morning. Tell 'em why – it'll make them
more committed – and offer them three times the going rate. This
is a crisis.'

He turned to Jane. 'I hope . . .' What he saw with his intuitive
instinct for reading faces was the most extraordinary kaleidoscope
of emotions he had ever witnessed. In business mode now, he was
detached, needing to cut to the quick and to identify what the
quick actually was. 'Please tell me what it is you want to say?'

Jane appeared almost in despair. 'My Lord,' she said, 'I have
never appeared before a Queen. Never dreamed that I would be
presented at Court. I have nothing to prepare me for this. But . . .'

'But what?' said Gresham, impatient.

'But Lady Sarah Downing? Two jewellers?'

She waited. Gresham said nothing.

'I am a person of no breeding!' she said at last. 'I can't appear
before the Queen in rags. But at the same time I can't appear as
mutton dressed as lamb! Overdress me and I'm as humiliated as if I
was under-dressed.'

A number of memories of Sarah floated before Gresham's eyes.
Some were unprintable. All were happy.

'Sarah's a great Court lady,' he said, 'but she's human, and surprisingly normal. Try to trust her, if you can. Tell her just what
you've told me.'

Mannion had left, and the yard was full of the noise of a great
house being woken up.

'Thank you,' said Gresham, still in business mode, 'for making
something I was dreading surprisingly easy.'

'Thank you,' said Jane, 'for letting a girl of no breeding meet the
Queen of England.'

Why had it all gone so easily?

*

107

Gresham had not heard the brief conversation that had preceded her meeting with him. By some strange coincidence, Mannion had bumped into the hastily dressed Jane on her way to the Library.

'He needs yer to say yes to goin' with the both of us to Scotland.'

'And?' said Jane, cocking an eye to one of the very few men she had come to trust. If she had learned anything from Henry Gresham it was to mask her feelings, although her heart seemed to have speeded up to three times its normal rate.

'It's bloody dangerous,' Mannion said factually. 'But fer Christ's sake, say yes, and give 'im an easy time of it.'

Jane looked him in the eyes for a brief moment, then nodded carefully, before going to meet Gresham.

Gresham was relieved at the outcome of his request. He was staggered when, the next morning, he saw its product. The dress Jane and Sarah had chosen was of the finest dark-green velvet. It seemed to hug Jane's upper body, and then glance splendidly off her waist, cascading like a waterfall. Yet she had reserved the greatest stroke of genius for herself. Such a dress would be slashed to reveal perhaps an irridescent blue or even a pure black silk. Against the dressmaker's entreaty, Jane had insisted that the rich slashings show underneath not an oasis of blue or black, but simply more of the dark-green velvet. The only concession she had made was to ask for the openings to be lined with a modest number of small pearls. We are here, the pearls seemed to say, and if we thought we were more than we are we could be used to reveal a glow of colour that would rival a mallard's neck. But we are not so. We are simply a young girl in a borrowed dress, and we know who we are. As ever, the lack of pretension made a more powerful point than a week's artifice would have achieved.

Gresham's jaw dropped when Jane was presented to him. He had not seen this girl – this woman – before. She was extraordinarily, stunningly beautiful. It was not the dress with its cunning line, or the make-up so sparingly and skilfully applied, nor the wonders they had done with her lustrous hair. She was not made beautiful by what she wore. She made what she wore look beautiful. He looked at her for a moment, his face expressionless, sensing her yearning for his approval.

'Wait here a moment, please,' he said, and left the room. Five, ten, tense minutes passed before he returned, bearing a box.

'Something so beautiful deserves something equally beautiful,' he said quietly, as he drew forth the necklace. On a simple gold chain, the ruby was like an open heart pulsing with extraordinary colour. He moved behind Jane, slipping the necklace over her neck, feeling the warmth of her skin at his fingers' ends.

'It was my father's,' he said. 'It seems a shame for such a thing to lie in the dark. It'll be your only jewel. They'll know whence it came. And they will not call you mutton dressed as lamb.'

Well, at least he had struck her speechless for once.

He had thanked Sarah from the bottom of his heart. There had been no malice in their meeting, and when their time was done there had been no malice in their parting.

'I enjoyed it,' she had said simply. 'It made me feel young again.' She did not mention that she had no children of her own. 'Tell me, have you slept with her?'

'No I have not!' said Gresham with a vehemence partly fuelled by the thoughts he had had at the sight of Jane in her finery. Because of these thoughts, he could guess other men's reactions. As a result he felt himself aggressively protective towards Jane.

'Do you really know what you've got there in that girl?' Sarah asked.

'A target for every man at Court?' asked Gresham glumly. 'I hadn't realised she would make me act gamekeeper as well as poacher.'

'However beautiful, the body will always decay over the course of life,' answered Sarah. 'The mind,' she added gnomically, 'stays with us all our lives, God willing.'

It was difficult to say whether the radiance that lit Jane came from the superb job Sarah – and Jane – had made of an instant

Court dress, or from within her own sense of well-being. Gresham never doubted that the meeting with the Queen would go well. Whatever her failings, Elizabeth had a soft spot for young girls, provided they did not marry against her will or bed one of her favourites.

'What did she ask you about?' asked Gresham, as they went back to The House in the Strand.

'Oh . . .' said Jane vaguely, 'woman's stuff.'

He decided to leave it at that. The real business was about to start.

Gresham and Mannion dismounted at the quayside, handing the horses over with a pat to the grooms who would ride them home. The cobbled wharf was littered with the debris of the sea, and stank of tar and foul water, thick in the heavy air that barely flapped a sail. The tiny waves were slapping angrily yet ineffectively at the hulls, as if warning the ships of their bigger brethren waiting out at sea. Jane was due to come in the huge coach that Gresham's father had adopted in his later years. Already the arrival of the fine gentleman and his baggage was causing a stir, with men turning from the mending of sails or the lugging of stores to watch the new entertainment and relieve the boredom of their working lives.

How did you train your men? Essex had asked Gresham. With great difficulty and at great length, was the answer. Only two of those same men were with Gresham now, Jack and Dick, to act as porters for the luggage. Other men would have taken servants to care for their clothes or shave them on such a trip. Gresham chose to take two people who knew how to handle themselves in a fight.

The same was not true of the crew of the *Anna*. The master was a competent seaman, in part-retirement now. His crew were no better and no worse than many of their type – jobbing mariners who moved from one boat to another as work came up – and who would stay only a few months or even weeks when it became clear that the *Anna* would only leave her berth for short trips to shake out her sails and stretch her hull. Some three or four, the more permanent ones, were members of the master's own family. Gresham's instinct had been to use the *Anna* for the trip to Scotland rather than take passage on a boat of which he had no previous knowledge. At least he knew that good money had been spent on her rigging, that her timbers were sound and the vessel in exceptional repair. He would sell her afterwards, he reasoned, and buy another escape route in another mooring.

But he had not trained the *Anna*'s men. Her crew did not know him, had no particular loyalty towards him. The elements were only one of the dangers for a sailing ship.

What if his enemies were watching him, even now? How much would Cecil's letter, or that from the Queen, be worth to someone angling for the Crown? How much was the Queen's ring worth? Anyone bringing it to James would be granted private access. On a secret mission, how would James know whether or not the bearer was the man to whom the Queen had handed her token, or the man who had murdered the initial bearer? Worst of all, was Essex skilled enough to hear of Cecil's rebuttal and try to intercept it?

Nagging at the back of his mind was the way he had been tricked by Cecil. Was he losing his touch? Was using his own boat another sign of the decaying mental powers of someone who had lived on the edge for so long that he was now taking the easy route? And all the time the sense was growing in him of the importance of what he carried. A letter from Cecil to James was bad enough, possible proof of treachery. Yet even that was insignificant by the side of a secret letter from Queen Elizabeth of England to King James of Scotland. How many of those fighting over the flesh of the English crown would give a fortune to know the contents of that letter?

He cast his eyes over the roadstead, from the bits of rough timber, fish scales and assorted unidentifiable lumps of matter washing up against the strand, to the boats with the precious berths by the shore out to the less fortunate moored in the tideway. Would one of these nondescript, assorted vessels, the lifeblood of England's coastal and near-continental trade, drop its sails as the *Anna* set out, and follow it silently out to sea? How many of the seamen and rabble on the quayside were in the pay of Gresham's and the Queen's enemies? Was the spy being spied upon at this very moment?

Mannion was oblivious to Gresham's fears, casting a professional eye over the *Anna* and grunting in satisfaction at what he saw. Mannion had been a ship's boy, groomed to be a captain, until the owner of the vessel had fallen into the hands of the Inquisition and been burned alive as a heretic in front of his wife and crew. Just as Gresham hated oil lamps, so Mannion would never stay in a room where pork had been overcooked. The similarity to the smell of human flesh burning was too close.

The master of the *Anna* was standing on her tiny quarterdeck, and hurried over to greet Gresham. Old now, every storm he had weathered had left a wrinkle on his face, but he had a toughness that Gresham found reassuring. What was less reassuring, and what Gresham had not seen when he had interviewed the man, was his tendency to move sideways all the time like a restless crab, and to rub his gnarled hands together like a moneylender striking a deal. Nor would he look Gresham in the eye. Interesting. Alarm bells began to ring in Gresham's head. The man was sweating, nervous. What had scared him so much?

'You seem to have a full crew,' said Gresham noting more men than he remembered scurrying round the deck. They ranged from another wizened old man who the captain assured Gresham was the best ship's carpenter sailing from London, to a boy for whom a razor seemed an impossible dream.

'I hope I haven't acted out of turn, sir,' the man was now saying. As well as not looking at Gresham his rheumy eyes flickered left and right, as if expecting someone to rescue him. 'The voyage to Scotland is long and sometimes treacherous, even in summer. It would be greatly in our interest for us to have two watches, but that means doubling the crew. Trade's not good at present, and there's plenty of good men around, so I took the liberty of hiring another watch. I know it's more expensive, but it will be safer, and with the lady on board . . .' He nodded obsequiously towards Jane, who had just arrived and whose trunks were being lugged on board by a cheerful Jack and Dick, and kept his eyes on her for longer than was strictly necessary. 'I've also taken on board a sailing master. He can navigate and con the ship, let me have a little sleep every now and then.'

Damn! Damn! Any one of the original crew might have been paid by one of Gresham's enemies, though as a safeguard Gresham had instructed the master wherever possible to recruit from his extended family. But the new men? Recruited in a hurry from the taverns that served as employment exchanges along the river, they could be anyone's man. Damn! Why had he not thought of this beforehand? For someone who liked above all to be in control, too much of his life was out of his hands at present.

'Master,' said Gresham, 'I do mind.' The man's face fell, and Gresham worked outwardly to reassure him. 'No, the responsibility is mine. I didn't explain to you the reality of what it is we do. The voyage we are embarking on is . . . sensitive. It's possible my enemies may have tried to place someone on board.' Had he hit a spot? Or was the old man simply angry at the implicit accusation. God! What a way to start off with someone who might at some stage in the voyage have their lives in his hands. In any event, the man showed anger, started to bluster. Genuine? Difficult to tell. Patches of his face were dead, unmoving, the nerves perhaps atrophied by too many stormy days and nights gazing head on into the wind and the spray.

'Sir Henry! I'm an honest man and I ply an honest trade!' Why, when a man felt the need to tell you that he was honest, did it always mean the opposite? 'The idea that I would allow – a *spy* – on board my ship – your ship,' he hastily corrected himself, 'is a deep insult.' Did he realise what Gresham was? If he did, he was about to allow the deepest insult he had ever met board his ship. For money of course. Which would be why he would have let others on board of the same type, if that was what he had done. Gresham let him rant for a while longer, then cut in.

'What's the minimum number of men you need?'

The man's brow furrowed in concentration. It was clearly with only the greatest reluctance that he spoke. He was caught in a dilemma: when Gresham had hired him it had been plain as a pikestaff that the man was not only rich, but knew about boats. There were some as said that he had sailed not against the Armada but actually on it. 'Well, two more might let me stand down most of the rest, I suppose, so that we run with a full crew in the day and have only two on watch at night, if the wind is steady and the boat's working well. It's not ideal, but it'll do. There must be a good man at the helm, of course, and one as a look-out. It's dangerous out there, and I don't mean just the chance of running into another vessel.' He thought for a moment. 'But I would implore you, sir, to let me keep my new sailing master. The only other man I could have trusted to take charge on a watch left me last week to take up his own command.'

Gresham would probably have to compromise on that. Experienced sailor that he was, he was no navigator, nor qualified as a captain. He spoke as if granting a great favour.

'By all means keep your sailing master,' said Gresham. And I will ensure that either Mannion or myself are awake whenever he is on duty. 'And you'll have four extra men. My men. These two here and two more I'll send for. They've all been at sea. The two you see here are quite experienced.'

Was fate playing against him? There were ten, perhaps twelve men in The House he would trust in a fight. Apart from Jack and Dick, he knew of only two remaining whom he could call on as reinforcements. The rest he had allowed to go home to their villages, knowing he would be gone perhaps for months, knowing also what a difference the men would make to their families and their villages for the harvest. Many of the great London houses ran on a skeleton staff in the summer, the owners fleeing the heat and increased plague risk in London for the country, the servants desperate to get back to their homes to help in the crucial time that could decide whether a family starved over the winter.

Yet at least he had two men at The House, men with no family to return to. Gresham's boatmen were all originally sailors. They were tough, adaptable and very happy to swap the sea for the Thames. There was little glamour in life at sea. Take the *Anna*. Drake had taken ships as small with him around the world. It was standard policy to take twice the men one needed on any long cruise, on the assumption that half would die of disease or injury.

Even though Gresham sweetened the signing off of the new sailors who had been recruited with a week's wages, two of them took it very badly, looking poisonously at Gresham and rubbing their foreheads. Gresham's sense of danger grew, was screaming at him now. He knew that when a man touched his chin in talking he was uncertain, when someone played with their earlobe they were considering a lie. His life had depended at times on knowing these things, reading the language spoken by the body as well as hearing the words spoken by the mouth. And he knew that the man who rubbed his forehead in that manner was not only angry and disturbed, but scared and rebellious as well. Why so? The men had received a week's wages for no work, and sudden appointment and dismissal were as much a part of a sailor's life as fighting the sea or eating badly salted beef. Had these men been paid to act as spies on the spy? To steal the packages he carried from Cecil and from the Queen, and her ring? If so, he was well rid of them. But it meant that the secret of his trip was out, to someone at least.

He motioned to Mannion.

'Sure you're not just getting into a panic?' asked Mannion gruffly. 'You've been in a right old mood for months past now.' It was the nearest Mannion would ever come to criticism.

'The master talked about our voyage to Scotland,' said Gresham flatly.

'Well, that is where we're bloody well goin', ain't it?' said Mannion.

'But he doesn't know that!' said Gresham. 'When I ordered him to get ready, I mentioned a long trip. Supplies for two months. I didn't say where we were going!'

'But there's others who knows, ain't there?' said a perplexed Mannion.

'Think about it,' said Gresham. 'I know. You know. The girl knows. Cecil has every interest in keeping my going a secret until I've at least embarked and am well on my way. The Queen likewise – which is why I never mentioned the reason for my request to see her to anyone before the audience, and why she agreed to issue the passport in secret and make no announcement. Of course people will find out where I've gone. There are no secrets in England – or, probably, in Scotland. But I bent over backwards to keep the knowledge secret until we were halfway up the coast and out of harm's way, too late for anyone to stop us. We did everything to make sure our destination was a secret. And an old sea captain doesn't exactly hob-nob with a lady-in-waiting who might just conceivably have been listening outside the door, or spend time with one of Cecil's servants. Someone else told the master we were going to Scotland.'

'And?' said Mannion.

'And the only reason, the *only* reason, must be to suborn him, buy him. The quick blow on the head, the search of us and our baggage? Or the arrangement to meet with another vessel off a certain point at a certain time?'

'So what do we do now?' said Mannion, looking around the quayside. 'Call it off and go 'ome?'

'What for?' said Gresham. 'Cecil'll pull the plug on us if I don't get going. The Queen'll have my balls, likewise. And if we do turn round and get another crew in time, what's to stop it happening all again? We've got the two of us, two good men we've trained ourselves and two more we can get in time. And we can lay on a few surprises. We've faced lots worse odds. And we know what might be coming. Better out than in, I say. If someone's after us, let's bring them on, find out who it is.' He paused for a moment. 'I'm tired of all this shadow-dancing. Let's get this out in the daylight. I'm tired of running away. Let's run into it, head first.'

Gresham felt a cloud lifting from his soul. It was madness to walk into a trap with himself, five men and little more. But it was doing the unexpected, taking a perverse control. If his instinct was right, he would soon have an enemy to fight. A real, physical enemy, tangible and visible.

'Right you are,' said Mannion, simply. He rarely agonised over decisions. 'We got some more work to do, then, ain't we?'

There was time enough to get some extra supplies from The House and the two men – Gresham hoped they were still there and had not already gone off to some tavern – and still catch the tide. He had planned for everything to be ready two hours earlier than was strictly necessary, assuming Jane would be late by at least that much.

Jane appeared on deck.

'Lucky bugger!' an onlooker shouted, as Jane bowed politely to Gresham.

Lucky? The particular bugger who had cried out did not know half of it – the tears, the tantrums, the moral blackmail . . . well, at least she had agreed to come and not made his life difficult. He owed her something for that. If she kept to it, of course. Storms at sea could take on a new meaning over the next few days.

The age of chivalry could not be allowed to die entirely, and so the master's cabin had been given over to Jane, tiny as it was. She shared it with her maid, Mary, who was thankfully ugly enough to put off even Mannion's roving eye. Gresham had never doubted that Jane's maid had to come with her. It was not only that the girl would need help dressing, particularly if as part of their cover, she was to be paraded before a King as she had just been paraded before a Queen. Sarah had been persuaded to part with two more Court dresses, so there were now three packed carefully in a chest all their own, carefully sealed against damp and salt spray. It was also the more mundane matters. It would be wholly unseemly, for example, for a man to enter the cabin in the morning and ditch the contents of the chamber pot over the side. That was definitely another of the maid's jobs. Gresham took over the one other, even tinier cabin, knowing without asking that Mannion would sleep at the foot of his truckle bed. The master, pushed out by the need to house Jane, would make do with a hammock slung at the rear of the hold, an old sail slung across to mark out his space even though the hold was empty apart from Gresham's baggage.

Jane was excited by the prospect of the voyage. It was quite pathetic really, and if Gresham had had any spare emotional capacity he would have found it rather touching. He knew they could be in for weeks of damp boredom, a tiny deck their only exercise. Yet for Jane, who suddenly at the prospect of the voyage had turned from a sulky young woman into an excited young girl, this was clearly an adventure. She saw little outside the confines of The House, her visits to St Paul's to buy books and her occasional visits to Cambridge. She had invented a role for herself in The House, becoming in effect its steward; the old man who occupied that role had been only too willing to allow her to take over.

Jane had been little more than a foundling when she had first been entrusted to the care of The House. Unlike Gresham she worshipped it; its architecture and its grandeur staggered her. Its comfort seemed to her as if heaven had indeed arrived on earth. Its Library was proof that paradise did indeed exist. So much to find out! As a little girl rescued from the cruelty of being a bastard in a mud-soaked village, she was simply another whim of Henry Gresham, the man who had scorned one of the biggest fortunes in England to go and fight in the Low Country, risking death by bullet or pestilence with every step he took. To those he paid to work in The House, the man who had rescued her was little more than an absentee adventurer and rather too many of them remembered their master as a ragged-arsed urchin who, like Jane, had wandered the endless corridors and passages of The House, owned and loved by no one. She too had been free to wander The House from its finest rooms to its lowest cellars. And she had listened. Oh, how she had listened, a mere child, wide-eyed and posing no threat to anyone. What she had heard had horrified her. The

Gresham fortune was feeding half of London. Even worse, basic repairs were being neglected. She had never had any position of power; she had always been cast as the victim: 'Ah, there she is – the poor little bastard girl rescued by that strange man who does the dirty work for the Cecils!' Jane could remember the moment, the single defining moment, when she had declared war on life as a victim. It was when she saw three sides of beef being delivered to The House, and two of them just as quickly being whisked off to destinations unknown; a nod and a wink the only currency that changed hands. It was then that she had given herself a purpose in life. Henry Gresham – Sir Henry Gresham – was a book she could not even lift off the shelf, never mind open and read the pages. His House was a different matter altogether: that she could read and understand. From that moment it became her aim to run The House as it should be run.

How to do it? Very difficult, as she had no status and was nothing more than a discardable whim of her master. Yet she had one thing, one thing only, on her side. None of those in the employ of The House and her master knew the exact nature of the relationship between them. The fact that there was no such relationship was as true as it was not widely known. She had traded shamelessly on that ignorance. She had waited until she had turned sixteen, the age at which many a girl was married and nominally at least became responsible for running a household. She had positioned herself in the right place when the sides of beef arrived, and at the crucial moment when a grinning labourer was about to cart the majority of the delivery off elsewhere she had asked, in a loud voice, 'Does my master know where his beef goes?'

There had been a stunned silence, and the grin had frozen on the face of the man with one of the sides of beef hung over his back. The cook had fought back, inevitably. Jane had planned for this.

'Stop your nonsense, girl!' she had said. 'What do you know about such matters? Get about your business – and while you're at it, out of my kitchen!'

'I know you're cheating Sir Henry!' Jane had said with an air of absolute finality; inwardly she was quaking. 'And if you carry on doing so, I shall tell him.'

They had reached an agreement, the elderly cook and the young girl. These sides of beef would go their way, as they had done for so long, but would cease to do so after that. As of now. And if the lucrative business ended, her conversation with Henry Gresham – the one he would never in reality have allowed her to have – would never take place.

She had then gone immediately to the steward, and demanded that *she* scrutinise the meat orders in future. Reduced to panic by the thought of what could be revealed about his mismanagement, he had agreed.

Slowly, Jane had thought. One piece at a time. It had taken her two whole years to gain control, to do the steward's job while he continued to receive the rewards. Yet it gave her a strange satisfaction to know that The House was now well managed, albeit at one remove.

And Mannion had proved her greatest ally. The stables in The House were as corrupt as the rest of it. Certainly Gresham's fine horses – one of the few things he really did seem to care about – were well fed and well looked after, but so were many other horses in London from money siphoned off from The House. The Head Groom was a vicious bully, renowned for the violence he inflicted on prostitutes in the stews of Southwark. Jane had left him until last, partly through fear, partly through realisation that he would be her greatest enemy. He was no cleverer than the others, the sum of money he was taking from his master no greater than others, but he hated women. He, of all the power figures in The House, would not bow down under a threat from a woman, and he also had the strongest position. Gresham cared more about his horses than he ever did about his ward, and the Head Groom was good with horses, one of the best in his profession. Would Gresham care how much money was wasted if his horses were well cared for? In her heart of hearts, Jane thought not. And she had no doubt that if it came to a choice between the welfare of his horses and her welfare, there would be no competition. She actually went to her show-down with the Head Groom convinced that he would win, for the moment at least, and that she would be lucky to emerge from their conversation with anything less than a black eye or a bloodied lip.

It had certainly been heading that way. He had actually stood up and started to walk towards Jane, his right hand clenching into a furious fist, when suddenly he stopped. The stable door had opened. Someone was standing there, blocking out the light.

'If you lay a finger on 'er,' said Mannion, 'you're dead. Tragic episode. Man killed by 'orse. Except it won't be an 'orse that kicks your pathetic little life out of you. It'll be me.'

The man looked at Mannion, stunned. There was an air of absolute finality in what he had said. When he chose to exercise it, Mannion carried massive authority.

'And while you're at it,' Mannion said, in the same flat tone, 'pack your bags. You just resigned. You got an hour. Otherwise, I'm telling you, one of these 'orses is going to behave out of character tonight.'

The man left the stables, his white face suggesting that The House would have a vacancy for a new Head Groom within the hour.

Jane was stunned. She had not even realised that her master and Mannion had returned to The House. She had not seen Mannion at work before. The sheer, blunt force of the man in part overwhelmed her, made her feel fragile and will o' the wisp. And no one had ever helped her before, not like this, except for the one moment when the fine gentleman had rescued her from poverty and humiliation. Jane was used to being alone, and acting on her own.

'Why did you . . . how did you know . . .?'

'Pleased I 'appened to be around.'

She felt she ought to say something, started scrabbling for words.

Mannion put his finger to his lips.

'Look, girl,' he said, and somehow the 'girl' was not patronising. Rather, and very strangely, it made her feel an equal. 'People like 'im upstairs' – it was clear he was referring to Henry Gresham – 'they need 'elp from the people who really know how it works. You give it your way. I give it mine. Truth is, we're both on the same side. 'Im upstairs, 'e'd use a sonnet to say it, and then not get it right. Us, we don't need fancy words. We just need to know as 'ow we're on the same side.'

He grinned at her, gave an ironic touch to his forehead, and left, leaving the stable door open. A few of the horses had become restive at the tension and the voices, and before she left, almost without thinking, she walked down the length of the stables, reaching out a hand here and a hand there, talking nonsense softly. The smell of horses was all around, not offensive like the stench of human sewage, but somehow rich and warm, tempered by the delicate scent of straw and fodder.

It was a strangely assorted trio that watched as the *Anna's* scratch crew dropped her dun sails and eased gently out of Deptford, enough hours of daylight left to get her safely out to sea: the young man of fashion in his prime, the waif-become-spy and the great bulk of the serving man.

For two of them at least, it was not the blustery wind nor the rapid, chopping motions of the boat that held their attention. It was the other vessel that also slipped its moorings at exactly the same time as they did, let them build up a lead and then started to follow a suitable distance behind.

'Coincidence?' asked Gresham.

'You must be jokin',' said Mannion. 'But, you know, you get feelings, don't you? Even before your business with the captain. I got a feeling about this one.'

'I've got a feeling about the whole bloody trip,' said Gresham, under his breath. No point in alarming Jane. The wind streamed her hair behind her as she gazed excitedly at civilisation slipping past them. Her maid was puking over the side. She had told everyone she was going to be seasick, and was determined not to let them down.

122

'We can still turn round,' said Gresham.

'Yeah,' said Mannion, 'we could.'

They watched as they made more open sea. The sails behind them, even darker than their own, stayed steady, neither coming nearer nor turning for France.

CHAPTER 5

1 July, 1598
At Sea

They rigged and lit the running lights as night came on, one at the stern and one at the bow. Then, unusually, two bright lights at the mast head, one to port, one to stern, hung from the widest yard of the mainmast. A landsman would have thought it routine. For someone like Gresham, who had sailed with Drake, it was extraordinary. Was it his imagination, or were the shadowing sails catching up on them?

Mannion thought so. 'What's it look like to you?' Gresham asked him. There was complete trust between them at moments like these.

'Well,' said Mannion, 'I ain't seen this many lights outside of a Palace. Must want someone to see us. As for that ship, they're smaller than us, but faster.' Mannion paused to collect his thoughts. 'Smuggler's sails, probably not heavily armed.' Smugglers tended to favour the darkest possible sails to avoid recognition at night, even darker than the traditional dun sails that a number of the London vessels favoured. What was following them was a smuggler's boat – large enough to take a decent cargo, but small and nippy enough to make the Channel crossing at speed, probably with a few popguns to discourage boarders. 'Room for lots o' men on board, mind.'

'If you were them and you wanted to do us damage . . .' asked Gresham.

'I doubt they want to do us damage, at least not right off. It's what you're carrying they wants, and that means keepin' you alive, at least until they've found it. After that . . .' Mannion needed to say no more on that count. When Gresham had been milked of his information, he and the rest of them would tell no one of the assault, pursue no vengeance, provided of course they were at the bottom of the Channel. 'I'd wait till it's real dark, pull up on us, grapple and board. They could have ten, fifteen men, easy, spare for a boarding party. Mebbe more, God help us. There's two of us, and fer all they know we've only got a couple o' piss-pant servants with us, 'stead of four trained men. The crew 'ere, most of them'll be asleep. And any road, they ain't goin' to shed too much blood for us, are they? Even if they haven't got their own men among 'em, which they probably have. Like 'im up there.'

A thick-set sailor with a villainous low forehead was crouched in the tiny crow's nest. The vessel behind them could simply crack on sail and overtake them within the hour if it so chose, but that would give Gresham an hour to prepare if a suspicious look-out called the alarm. If it could be managed, it would be far better to creep up on the *Anna,* the look-out and whoever was in command bribed to silence. As if to echo their thoughts, the master came up to them, touching his forelock in the traditional salute.

'I'll be taking myself off for a while now. The ship's in good hands.' He motioned to the sailing master, a surprisingly young man with a shock of fair hair under a woollen cap and a ready grin.

'Could be coincidence,' said Gresham.

'Yeah?' said Mannion.

They gathered their four men in the tiny space of Gresham's cabin, bent almost double, and gave them instructions. If anything, the four of them looked more excited than frightened. Jack and Dick were both dark-haired, well-built men, the difference being that Jack had twenty years on Dick, most of that spent at sea. Tom

125

was the man with the broken nose Mannion had brought along to knock some respect into Cecil's messenger: no great brain, but brilliant fists. Edward was thin, lugubrious, and the best oarsman on the Thames.

The *Anna* carried four small brass cannon on either side, but the one addition Gresham had made to her when he had bought the ship were four swivel cannons on the stern, two on either side of the upper deck. The for'ard pair could cover the tiny main deck as well. Such a gun was usually designed to sweep grapeshot across an enemy's deck, but its size was limited by the fact of it being more often than not simply secured to a strengthened guard rail. Too powerful a load, and the recoil would smash the wood and unseat the gun, making it useless. On the *Anna*, each gun was secured on a metal rod that passed down through the deck and was secured deep within one of the main frames of the ship. As a result, the guns could take and fire quite a sizeable ball, as well as grapeshot.

'Do we tell the girl?' asked Mannion.

They knocked on her cabin door. She had not undressed, but was clearly about to. Gresham felt stupid, bent low under the deck timbers, the girl sitting on the crude bed that jutted out from the side of the hull.

'We think we might be being followed, by another boat. There's a chance it might try to board us. Things could get violent, I'm afraid.'

'Why should they want to board us?' asked Jane, outwardly reasonably calm. Gresham had been terrified she would get the vapours, or whatever women did.

'I . . . I'm carrying . . . material that could be of advantage to any number of people.' He found this very difficult, but anyone successfully taking the *Anna* would be likely to take her and her maid, before dumping them over the side. It seemed unfair not to tell her as much as possible, given what would happen to her if they lost. 'But the truth is, we don't really know who they are. It's what I do. I live in a world where . . . where for a lot of the time we know very little, particularly where the threat comes from, or even why it comes.'

He was impatient to get back on deck. There were things to do.

'Here, take these.' He handed her two pistols, expensive flint-locks primed and half cocked. They were part of the extra supplies he had ordered at the last minute from The House. 'Bar the door when we leave. Do you know how to use these?'

'I've watched others do so,' she said, looking distastefully at the gleaming, oiled weapons.

'Check the flint is here.' He motioned to the firing mechanism. 'And that there's powder there. See? The metal cover lifts back if you do . . . this.' He tossed a small, oiled, canvas bag onto the bed. 'There are spare flints and four separate charges of powder. The guns are on safety now, the hammer pulled back, so it won't fire unless you pull back a little further, until you hear the second click and it locks. Then it'll fire when you pull the trigger. Hold it with both hands. The recoil is vicious. Aim at the middle of the body, then you'll have more chance of hitting something.'

Her face turned white, and for a moment he thought she was going to be sick.

'I'm sorry about this,' he said lamely. 'I'd no idea it would happen, or that it would happen this early.'

She was pale, but in control. 'Perhaps the other boat isn't following for a reason,' she said gamely. 'Perhaps it's just a coincidence.'

'I'd hoped so, for a while. But the other boat is faster than us, designed for speed in fact. No one spends longer at sea than they have to, even in high summer. She's holding back, using only half her sail. If she'd other business, she'd be about it by now and long out of our sight. Sorry.'

It was nearly dark now, and if the other vessel was an enemy it would be loosening out the remainder of its sails, surging through the heavy swell to catch up, the sound of her bow pushing through the water lost in the wider noise of the sea. The enemy vessel reminded Gresham of a hawk, gliding silently through the air, the fat thrush in its sights. The *Anna* ploughed contentedly on, dipping into the waves and then rising in an easy steady motion. She was no greyhound, but she was still a sturdy, long-legged creature, gobbling up the miles.

Timing. It was all about timing. He placed himself casually on the quarterdeck, as any grand noble might do on board what was in effect his private yacht. He noted a thin sheen of sweat over the sailing master's face, despite the rapidly increasing chill of the evening, and felt the change that came over his body when he knew he faced action. He fixed the enemy sails – they had become the enemy now, guilty until proved innocent – with his eye, and measured the distance. How long for her to catch up?

So many variables! There was her speed, which he could only estimate: in open sea, there was a tidal drag for or against each boat which affected speed. An hour. That was his guess. An hour between the moment when he lost sight of the shadowing sails in the dark and the moment when the other vessel could be expected to be alongside.

The sailing master was looking at him now, worriedly. Owners did not pace the deck when light had gone, and there was nothing to see except for the occasional flash of white as a wave broke.

It was time.

Mannion appeared on the main deck, a flagon in his hand. He was swaying slightly, and not with the buck and heave of the deck. He looked up at the main mast, where Lowbrow was still crouched in the crow's nest. Mannion hailed him, clearly to offer him a drink, and made for the stays, starting to climb the mast.

'Stupid bugger!' said the sailing master, at the wheel. He looked at Gresham. 'If that man o' yours falls in, he's a dead 'un. We'll never find him in this dark.' Rather ominous thick cloud covered the moon and stars. This on its own had interested Gresham. Without the stars there was no aid to navigation except an ancient compass. A ship within sight of the shore should have hove-to, put out a sea anchor, strove to remain where it was until dawn showed it its path again. Yet the sailing master had made no effort to halt

the *Anna*. Perhaps he knew by intuition where they were. Or perhaps a moving vessel would cloak the sound of another vessel
coming alongside, homing in on their stern light. And why was the
sailing master handling the helm? Traditionally on a reduced night
watch, he would give the orders, and a seaman would take charge
of the wheel.

Gresham decided to play the aristocrat.

'Serve him right!' he said grandly, and with a laugh. 'Drowning'll
teach him not to get drunk at sea!' It was a comment that could
have come very easily from numerous of the chinless wonders who
spent their time pomping around Court.

Gresham retreated to the stern rail, directly behind the wheel.
The sailing master's attention was distracted by the sight of
Mannion, apparently clumsily climbing into the crow's nest, despite
the protestations of Lowbrow which were whipped away by the
wind before they could properly reach the deck. Mannion was half
in and half out of the vantage point when he raised the flagon he
still clutched in his hand in what appeared to be a salute. Except
the salute turned into something else as he brought the flagon
crashing down on the skull of the look-out. The man collapsed
forward, hanging half in and half out of the wooden structure, arms
dangling faintly ludicrously.

If they had known for certain that the look-out had been bought
by an unidentified enemy, Mannion would simply have hurled him
overboard and left the sea to do its job. But what if this was a false
alarm? Were their suspicions worth the life of a possibly innocent
man? Gresham had reckoned not, so Mannion tied the fiercest of
gags round the unconscious man's mouth, and produced twine
firstly to bind his hands, then his arms to his side and finally his
feet. Finally he bound him to the mast, so it looked as if he were
still on duty. One thing was certain. If the *Anna* sank tonight, she
would be taking its erstwhile look-out along with her.

The sailing master looked aghast as the blow struck, and started
as if to move from the wheel when his sailor's instinct told him
what happened to sailing vessels whose helmsman suddenly left

their station; the wheel and the helm as a result swinging wildly in the wind. Still grappling the wheel, he turned with open mouth to remonstrate with Gresham when suddenly more stars than there were in the sky exploded in his head, and he fell unconscious. Gresham pocketed the short wooden club and grabbed the helm, the *Anna* already having started to swing head to wind. Jack appeared as from nowhere, and dragged the sailing master to one side, binding him as effectively as Mannion had done the look-out. Then he came to the wheel, taking it over with a nod from Gresham.

There were flittering shadows on the deck now, moving quietly with shoes removed so as not to wake the rest of the crew sleeping in the forecastle. The extra chests that had been brought from The House were opened, some of their contents removed. This was the tricky part. The *Anna's* guns were not on her lower decks, firing through ports cut into the hull. They were rather on the upper deck, firing through the guardrail. The result was that their snouts barely projected over the side, but under any normal circumstances they would still have been rolled back to muzzle load. Yet even these light brass guns would send noise and shuddering pounding through the hull if they were rolled back on their wheeled mountings, and if that did not wake the crew and the master nothing would.

Could they load the guns without rolling them back? The men had assured Gresham they could. It was devilishly difficult, though. They were under half sail, and a ship moving through the sea under sail is never a steady platform. One man had to lean out over the bulwark and push the powder charge down to the end of the barrel using a shortened rammer. A second man held onto his legs for all he was worth. The charges, brought from The House, were in the finest of linen bags. The loader had to ram a metal spike down the touch hole of the gun, piercing the linen and exposing the powder. He would then pour a charge of powder down the touch hole. He could then light the powder directly with a slow fuse, or use the new-fangled flint-and-wheel mechanism on the gun to fire it. In the meantime, the loader had taken the ball, and rammed that down the barrel as well, while leaning out over the side. Except in this case, it was not a ball the loader was ramming down the barrel, but another, more coarsely bound package – grapeshot: loose, sharp pieces of metal, lethal at short range to any crowded deck. While Mannion and three of the men sweated to load the cannon, Gresham and Dick loaded the swivel guns. Here again convention was being denied. Just as the main deck cannon were for ball, so the swivel guns were for grape. Yet Gresham was opening packages from The House that contained not one but two small cannon balls, linked by chain. Chain shot. Designed to wrap itself round masts, bringing them crashing down. There was some satisfaction for Gresham in the recognition that these had been part of the original stores he had brought to the *Anna* for this journey. The first thing he had done when he had bought the ship was to have ball and grape cast for her cannon. Many did not bother. You could fire almost anything out of the mouth of cannon, including balls far too small for its bore. If you did, you simply increased to ludicrous proportions windage, the effect the air had on a cannon ball that was not perfectly round, or the ball ricocheted round the inside of the barrel as it was fired to the vast detriment of any capacity to aim it.

They were hampered by the need to load on both sides. If the enemy came, which side of the *Anna* would they come alongside? There was no way of knowing. In three quarters of an hour it was finished.

Gresham remembered to ask Mannion to go down and brief Jane on what was happening. He then had a sudden feeling of panic. Would she fire through the door and kill him?

They had shifted the allocation of men in the light of what they were expecting. Jack had taken the helm, even putting on the sailing master's stupid little woollen cap that had covered his blond hair, and trying to shrink himself in size. Gresham and Dick crouched behind the bulwark, two pistols each in their belts, both clutching boat axes with a cutting blade on one end and a sharp spike on the other. Gresham had his sword, despite the extraordinary ability of the sword and scabbard to get between the legs and trip up the owner. Mannion and the others huddled under the lee of the quarterdeck. A slow match in a tub of sand was burning between each of their cannon.

The *Anna* ploughed on, gently plunging her bow into the slight swell, the whoosh and swish of the waves strangely regular and settling. The dim light of the stern lantern showed nothing clearly, but cast a faint luminosity over the quarterdeck, the angle changing and rolling with the motion of the sea.

Who was master and who was servant now, thought Gresham? They were simply six men, with the same skin to feel pain, the same skull to be broken and the same heart to be pierced, six men united by the intensity of risk and fear. The fear that none of them would admit, but which ate away at their guts like a worm eating its way through flesh.

They strained to hear a change in the noise of the waves, a change that would signal another vessel pounding alongside. The minutes dragged on. Had it all been imagination? It was over an hour now since darkness had closed down on Gresham's last sight of the sails. He was about to convince himself that a look-out and a sailing master had been given seriously unnecessary headaches when he heard the noise. A different sound of water being pushed aside, one that did not match the motion of the *Anna*.

Without conscious thought on Gresham's part the other person who shared his soul took over. This person is calm, icy calm, and does not feel fear. This other person has heightened senses and awareness, can smell every tang of salt in the air, actually hear the wind as it passes through the rigging. This person views the world as if everything has slowed down. This person, back pressed against the upright of the guard rail, seated low on the deck so no head was visible, felt able to twist round and look out into the noisy gloom of the sea. Yes! He had guessed right: put himself on the port side, assuming the enemy vessel would come at them from the land side.

They were carrying stern and bow lights, and two lights hung at the masthead. They cast a ghostly, flickering light onto the deck, and for a surprising distance on either side of them. It was a shock when the enemy vessel suddenly appeared as if it had surfaced from under the very waves, sweeping up from astern, low, lean and menacing, like a sharp-beaked sea monster. Dark as it was, the dim light meant that Gresham could see the men packed onto its deck. Damn! There must be nearer to twenty of them, and a bundle of seamen. Twenty against six. Well, it was time to lessen the odds.

Scrabbling along the deck like comical tortoises, still invisible to their attackers, Mannion, Dick, Tom and Edward moved to each of the four cannon. On the other vessel, two men were swinging grappling hooks, preparing to throw them over the rapidly diminishing gap between the two ships. Half the remainder were already climbing onto the rail, holding with one or both hands to the rigging, waiting to jump across to the other ship. They were good, give them their due, no noise, no excited chatter. All very businesslike.

Hell can be replicated here on earth. Just as the grappling hooks were about to be thrown, Mannion put his fuse to the touch hole of his cannon. Dick, Tom and Edward were a second behind him, if that. The sharp, eye-burning, red and orange tongues of flame that leapt out across the void were more startling than the crashing noise of the explosion. Gresham, his eyes firmly closed, desperate to preserve his night vision, hoped the others had heeded his instruction to do likewise. The glare of the light cut through his eyelids, determined to sear and scar his memory.

The impact of the grapeshot was appalling. It was as if a massive scythe, Death himself, had cut through the men standing on the rail, the nails and metal shards tearing into flesh, gouging and spoiling. There were shouts and screams, but as always they were from those left relatively unscathed. Those scoured and stripped red by the cannons were either dead in an instant, or their bodies forced into instant shock. One man looked in silent horror at where his right leg had been a moment before, and toppled over the side in silence. Yet the irony of war was still in charge, the terrifying random nature of death. One man stood still on the guard rail, unmarked, while those around him were blasted to butcher's meat. He looked to left and to right, uncomprehending, too stunned to realise the nature of his luck. Bodies, still or trembling and in spasm, littered the deck, covered now in sticky blood and human debris.

The men on the *Anna* were not finished yet. As soon as they had fired the cannon, before the attackers could react from their shock, all four men and Gresham on the quarterdeck bent down and picked up fragile jars, pilfered to great complaint from the stores of the cook at The House. Filled now with lamp oil, oily rags stuffed in their necks, Gresham and all except Jack, glued to the wheel, touched the fuses to them and lobbed them over the gap and onto the deck of their attacker. One, infuriatingly, bounced on the deck but did not break, and a seaman kicked it through the scuppers and over the side. The other four burst into flames, which licked satisfyingly at the deck timbers of the attacking vessel. Two spread their oil over bodies, one dead and one wounded. Gresham swore that the flame of one of them was soused out by the blood pumping from a wounded man. As the fire bit into his clothing and over his hand, the man started to scream. Suddenly it was easy to spot the sailors who were the normal crew of the attacking vessel. For sailors in a wooden vessel held together by tar, fire is second only to water as an enemy. Three or four men broke away and started to stamp out the flames, one of the four clearly in charge, giving orders. He was a small man with a goatee beard.

A surprising number of men had survived the withering blast of grapeshot. How many? Difficult to say in the dark, despite the flickering light of the lamp oil still eagerly seeking to turn the deck to ashes. Certainly ten men, not less, perhaps a few more. Shock. Then anger. And a fierce desire for vengeance. Gresham had seen it so many times. Men either broke when faced with a sudden shock, or became consumed by blood lust. These men would have been hired because they were fighting men. As such, they were responding the only way fighting men knew how. Blood for blood.

A life for a life. Heartbreak for heartbreak. It was the oldest plaint in the world.

Gresham had always known they would be outnumbered, could not rely on the four cannon doing the job for them. The oil was a diversion, dangerous but within the compass of any competent crew to stamp out, literally, before it became a real threat.

He moved to the swivel gun and, as if on an order, Jack slung a loop of rope over the wheel and secured it. It would steer the ship for a minute or more, but if luck turned their way a minute was all they would need.

The wheel of the attacking vessel was manned by one man. The deck of the *Anna* was still rising and falling, the sea refusing to change its habits simply because men were killing each other.

> Earth and Water, Fire and Air,
> Which nothing know of human fears.
> Earth and Water, Fire and Air,
> Which bore hemlock for Socrates.
> Earth and Water, Fire and Air,
> Which held a cup for Christ's blood tears.
> Earth and Water, Fire and Air,
> Will hold your cup of death and years.

For some reason the doggerel he had written years earlier came to Gresham's mind. The sea would not mourn the men who had died, or the men who were going to die. In the great scheme of things, no man or woman could be said to matter.

Waiting until the upthrust of the waves, Gresham aimed the swivel gun as carefully as he could at the enemy's wheel, Jack firing at almost the same moment. There was a double-tongued explosion of flame, and caught in it was the helmsman, open-mouthed. One ball ploughed into the deck two foot away from the wheel, cutting a furrow and sending lethal splinters flying through the night air. The other caught the wheel housing at its base, shattering it to pieces and filling the helmsman with so many splinters that he looked like a human porcupine. The ropes in the wheel housing disintegrated, and the rudder of the attacking vessel was no longer under control.

What should have happened then was that the attacker, its steering blasted to hell along with half its complement of crew, should have sheered away uncontrollably, unable to follow the *Anna* even if the spirit of its men had not been broken.

But war is not an exact science, as Gresham knew to his cost. Seconds before the wheel housing was shattered, a grappling iron arched through the air and hooked into the *Anna's* guard rail. One man had kept his head amid the panic and bloodshed, and bound the two ships together. It was the same man who had ordered the sailors to stamp out the flames, the small man with the strange beard. For a moment those hauling on the grappling iron were distracted by the carnage unleashed on the wheel housing, but then they renewed their efforts.

Damn! If that one throw had missed, the other ship would be careering away, by now, its steering ropes broken, the *Anna* free to make her escape. One throw. One stupid throw. The difference between life and death. He must cut that rope.

The two hulls came together with a grinding crash.

Sails full set, the attacking ship tried to veer away, helmless, but met the resistance of the *Anna's* hull, its wheel still set for the wind. For the moment the greater mass of the *Anna* took charge, and the two intertwined hulls charged on through the dark.

The remaining men on the attacker raised an exultant cheer. There were no prisoners taken at sea. And this had become personal. There were eleven of them left, a couple of them wounded but not seriously so, and only four men on the main deck of the *Anna*, two on the quarterdeck. What was there left to lose?

Gresham knew that in an instant the remaining enemy would launch themselves onto the deck of the *Anna*. They would do so to the accompaniment of the awful, shrieking and grinding sound of two hulls bound unwillingly together, and the frantic banging on the hatches that secured the forecastle and the hold. Mannion and the others had thoughtfully battened both of them down, as one would when securing for a storm. The result was that the normal crew of the *Anna* and her captain were locked in below, just in case they might decide to take the side of the attackers.

The defenders had one surprise left. Those attacking had to step up onto the deck of the *Anna*, exposed. Men expecting to board a ship, where those on the receiving end had no warning, armed themselves with axes and sabres, cutting weapons for close work. Pistols were heavy, cumbersome, and tended to lose their priming powder if joggled. There was less hindrance for those who stood waiting for an assault.

As eleven men launched themselves onto the deck of the *Anna*, six pistol shots rang out. One missed completely. Dick had been shown how to load and fire such a weapon, but at the last nerves had overcome him. One other ball caught a glancing blow to the shoulder of an attacker, tearing his jacket but only nicking his flesh. He swore vociferously but swept on. One, obscenely, caught an attacker full in the mouth, and blew his head into a foul red jelly.

Unlike a rifle bullet, a pistol ball leaves the barrel at a relatively low velocity. This has many consequences that reduce its lethalness as a weapon. The recoil is more blunt and savage, reducing aim. The short barrel means that the ball receives less sense of direction from its carrier, and is freer to decide where it goes. The ball travels less far. Its accuracy is in part a function of the speed with which it leaves the barrel.

But the pistol ball has one, great advantage. The far faster rifle bullet hits the body at high speed and passes through it, there being little difference in size between the entry and the exit wounds. The lead pistol ball does not have the speed to pass through the body. It flattens as it meets its first impact with flesh, and even more so if the first impact is with bone. So much of the human body is fluid, and the slow pistol ball sets up a shock wave as it first hits and then settles into living flesh. Fire a pistol with a lead ball into a lump of clay, modelled to have the same constituency as human flesh and the exit wound will be six times larger than that on entry.

Thus a pistol bullet does not have to kill a man to incapacitate him. It can, quite literally, knock him out, deliver such a shock to his body that it shuts down and goes into total shock.

Of the six pistol shots fired by Gresham and his men, one killed a man instantly, three condemned men to lingering, gangrenous deaths, blowing flesh out of their bodies for which nature could not compensate. More importantly for the defenders, the odds were reduced: eleven functioning men reduced to seven. Seven against six. Except for the four upright seamen on board the attacker, still stamping out flames but capable of joining the attack at any minute. One of them, the small man with the goatee beard, seemed in control.

Seven men leapt on board the *Anna*. Seven men who a short while earlier had been in a company of twenty. Seven men who had seen two thirds of their companions diced into bleeding red meat. Seven men crazed by combat, by the loss of their fellow men, by sheer blood lust. Seven men who had nothing to lose.

Gresham and Jack vaulted the front rail of the quarterdeck, landing hard on the deck. Two of the attackers veered towards Gresham, seeing in his finer clothes his status as captain. There was a shout, a command. It was the small man with the beard. His first words were strange. Then he shouted again, more clearly, 'Not him! Not him! Keep him alive!' Was it accented? The faintest hint of something unusual in the inflexion?

The two men backed off, sabres pointing warningly towards Gresham. On either side of him, fierce, hand-to-hand fighting was skidding across a deck slippery now with blood. Mannion was locked in a gut-wrenching exchange of blows with a man as big as he was, the clang of their blades something primeval. Jack seemed to have the better of his man, probing at him thoughtfully, deflecting his enemy's wilder and wilder blows with almost intellectual precision, forcing the man back further and further, with occasional feints with his boat axe confusing his enemy even more. Edward, as thin and lugubrious as ever, was dancing across the deck, showing the agility of a dancer, drawing the tall, thin man on, attacking him, tiring him out. He had noticed the thin stream of blood flowing from the man's leg, where the grape must have brushed against him. Young Dick, dark hair matted against his forehead, was losing ground, out of breath, on the edge of panic, flailing out widely and wildly. He was being played with, as a cat plays with a mouse, as Jack was playing with his opponent. Dick's opponent, the one whose shoulder had been nicked by the pistol ball, was showing no sign of any serious injury, and was eyeing Dick with the same predatory caution with which Jack was eyeing his man. It was only a matter of time. Tom ... where was Tom? He was nowhere to be seen. The seventh attacker, his cap ripped off his head to reveal a startlingly bald pate with a diagonal scar across it, had seen Dick as the weakest of the opposition, was turning to attack him. At the same time, the two men who had been called off Gresham had retreated enough to leave a gap through which Gresham could see the grappling iron, cutting deep into the wooden side of the ship. Cut them free? Or help Dick?

Gresham's sword was out, the boat axe in the other hand. He turned as if to head for the grappling iron, and his two guards instinctively turned with him. With extraordinary agility Gresham swung round the other way, and in the brief moment that one of the men exposed his chest Gresham plunged his sword directly under his ribcage, twisting and turning the blade as he did so and ripping it back out with a savage downward heave. The man screamed, more in anger and fear than in pain – and dropped his sabre to clutch at the gaping wound through which blood was now pouring. The other man backed off, fear in his eyes. Gresham had turned in a moment, impossibly, the blade a mere flicker. There was no time for finesse. Dick had seen bald pate coming towards him, and was almost crying now. His first attacker chose not to wait for bald pate, and suddenly leapt forward, smashing Dick's blade aside and raising both hands to bring his heavy edge down on Dick's skull. An expression of surprise came over his eyes, and he looked down to see a sword blade protruding from his chest. Gresham had pirouetted round in one seamless movement and lunged forward again. As the man gaped and blood began to dribble from round his mouth, Gresham put his foot firmly in the man's back and pushed with all his strength. With a sad, sucking, sighing noise the blade pulled out of the man's body, as he was hurled forward onto Dick, who screamed and half scrabbled out of the way of the descending body. Dick's face was a mass of blood now. Not his blood. The blood of the man who had so nearly killed him. Gresham faced up to bald pate, who suddenly halted his onward rush. Gresham saw something in the man's eyes, and started to turn.

The man behind him, one of the two who had been told not to kill him, was about to make a last brave effort and disobey orders. Scarface. He had a scar down one side of his face, a scar which had closed off his left eye. Whether the eye was still there or not, God only knew. Scarface had seen Gresham's skill, knew there would be no prisoners from this fight, knew it was kill or be killed. He was experienced enough, whoever he was, to see that this was his one chance, even if he had only one eye left to see it.

Gresham had lunged at one man, then turned and skewered the other man, but it had taken time to kick the body off his blade. He had then turned a third time to face the bald-headed man. Reacting to three opponents was miraculous. Reacting to four was simply impossible. For a brief moment Gresham was unbalanced, exposed. Scarface wielded his crude blade like a scythe aimed at Gresham's neck. Gresham turned his head to see it heading inexorably for him. Even as he brought his own aching sword arm up he knew he would be a fraction too late, even as he tried to spring back away from the gleaming steel. He had killed two men, and parried a third. The fourth would kill him. He greeted the prospect with something approaching relief.

There was a clang that could have come from Titan's armoury, and the swinging blade hung in mid-air, stopped. Mannion and his opponent had been exchanging blows of vast force with monotonous regularity, almost taking turns, when for no apparent reason one of Mannion's massive strikes did not stop at his enemy's sword, but seemed to carve down straight through it, snapping the defending blade as if it was glass and carrying on to split the man's skull, grey brain matter and blood spurting out like a newly constructed fountain in a noble's garden. Mannion had not waited to see the man's body drop to the ground, but had turned just in time to cover the four paces to Gresham and stop his attacker's blow. Gresham, half on his knees, looked for a brief moment into Mannion's eyes, a moment in which both men said all they needed to say to each other, and thrust up at his exposed attacker. The shock of Mannion's block had sent a stinging blow up the blade and hilt. The cheaper the weapon, the more likely it was to let its user feel every hit in nerve-tingling detail. Slightly off balance, Gresham would have compensated for his awkward position, half kneeling and half falling, had his foot not slipped on a patch of blood and skidded out from under him. The sword thrust he had intended to go up and under the ribcage of his assailant instead went low, the superb steel slicing straight into the man's genitals. The scream was as if someone had rubbed razors across the man's eyes, a screech of pure agony. Almost pityingly, Mannion brought his heavy blade down on the man's head, mercifully cutting short the inhuman noise.

'Bet that hurt,' he said, turning to face the bald-headed man, who was looking nervously from Gresham to Mannion and back again, unsure as to who was his opponent. Gresham leapt to his feet, a throbbing, burning pain in his head, and the man's eyes swivelled to him. Mannion leapt forward and enacted an exact replica of the blow that had just been intended to kill Gresham, a scything, sweeping cut of sheer brute force. There was no one to help bald pate, and the blow half severed the man's neck. Perhaps he wanted to scream but all that emerged from his mouth was a frothy, red, bubbling gurgle.

Jack had been aiming blows at his opponent, swinging them at head height, forcing the man to raise his arms, tiring him even faster. Suddenly and without warning he swung low, breaking the man's knee with the force of his blow. His enemy sank to the deck, gargling, face up, pleading. Jack centred his blade, and pushed it

141

hard into the man's neck. Dick had scrambled out from under the body of the man Gresham had killed, and was standing wild-eyed on the deck, looking for someone to kill. Edward was still dancing around his man, who suddenly looked up and saw that he was alone on the deck, five blood-stained men facing him. He stepped back, dropped his blade, put up his hands palms outwards to his attackers. There was no mercy in their eyes. Before any of them could move, he jumped onto the guard rail, dropping his hands. The *Anna* gave a sudden lurch, and the two hulls started to pull apart, opening a three-foot gap between the two vessels. The man began to slip, paddling his arms ludicrously to try and keep his balance. He fell between the two hulls just as the wind and the waves forced them together with a grinding crash, mellowed by the sound of something soft being crushed, like eggshells being trodden on.

There was screaming from the other boat. The small bearded man was shouting at the three seamen left on board his vessel, pointing with a sword to one of the two small cannon on his deck. He was yelling at the men to fire the guns, but they were huddled under the forecastle, clearly scared out of their wits and mutinous.

The man stopped yelling, realising it was a lost cause. He turned, and looked at Gresham. Then, remarkably, he gave a brief bow.

It was simply business. A gesture of recognition from one professional to another. He laid his sword blade across the rope of the grappling hook that still tied the two ships together. The blade must have had the sharpness of a razor. With only two or three strokes, the rope was cut, and the enemy vessel veered away, vanishing in seconds into the gloom.

Damn! thought Gresham, not for the first time in the past few hours. There went his last real chance of finding out who had decided to try and take the *Anna*. Then an awful recollection dawned on him.

'Where's Tom?' asked Gresham. 'Did anyone see what happened to him?'

'Yeah,' said Mannion. 'I saw. That bald-headed bastard came straight at 'im, and 'e forgot where the rail was, backed into it 'e did, and fell straight over. No point in looking. He caught his 'ead a right crack as he went over. Must 'ave been unconscious as 'e 'it the water. Stupid bugger.'

'God help him,' said Gresham, a part of him starting to die alongside the man he had lost. 'He was my responsibility. He was only here because of me.'

'It's bad,' said Mannion, 'but don't fret yourself too much. We all of us know the odds. Loved a fight, did Tom. Knew what 'e'd signed up to. Best way for man like 'im to go. 'E'd never have made old bones.'

There was the crash of a pistol from below deck. Gresham looked up, the burning pain in his head getting worse by the second, and a shockwave went through his body as he saw that the sailing master was no longer tied up by the wheel, strands of rope suggesting he had somehow found a knife and cut himself free.

Gresham started to run for the door that led into the cabins, but fell back as it was kicked open.

The master was dragging the sailing master on deck. The sailing master's left shoulder was a mass of blood and pulp where the master had clearly fired one of Gresham's pistols at him.

'You bastard! *You bastard!* Betray me would you? Betray me and my crew? I'll kill you! I'll fuckin' kill you!'

The master kicked the sailing master hard in the groin, his muted groan a measure of the pain overload he was already in. There was a seaman's knife in the sailing master's belt, the one that had cut him free, and the master reached for it, and was about to plunge it into the sailing master's neck when something cold touched his temple.

Jane was holding the second pistol at his head. Her hair was streaming in the wind and she was barefoot. She looked insane, the intensity in her eyes the hallmark of the truly mad. As if to emphasise her insanity and the insanity of life, the bodies of those killed by Gresham and his men littered the deck, surrounded by dark brown pools. The deck of the *Anna* would never be the same again.

'I heard him talking to the sailing master,' she hissed, the pistol rock steady. 'There's a hatch from the hold through to the cabin space. You can only unlock it from the cabin side. That man there let the master out, and they started to argue. When there was that terrible noise of fighting.' Some hint of the agony she had undergone from the moment the cannons crashed out came into her voice.

'They were accusing each other. Then the sailing master said they should take me hostage, use me to bargain with you, force you to put them ashore and take the rowing boat. Then they broke into my cabin, and the master here shot his friend. Without warning.'

'Now why would he do that?' asked Gresham softly, starting to edge towards his ward.

'Because he must have thought that if he could blame this man he could pretend to be innocent. Keep himself on a big boat. Not have to trust himself to a rowing boat.'

It was the girl's icy calm that was more frightening than any display of emotion would have been.

'Good thinking,' said Gresham conversationally. 'What do you intend to do now?'

'I think I very much want to pull this trigger,' said Jane, with an intensity that would have cut through ice-hardened rigging. 'I want this man to know that I am no one's property, that I am not owned by anyone, that I am not something to be used.'

'And you think shooting him will let him know that?' asked Gresham. He was nearly by her side now, but if she knew of his approach she was showing nothing of it.

'Perhaps,' she said, 'and perhaps not. But it will help me know that I am a person. It will help me to have fought back. Not to have been passive. Not to have been a . . . victim. I am so tired' – and there was the faintest crack in her voice now – 'of being . . . nothing.'

'Please give me my gun,' he said gently.

'Why?' she said calmly, and he saw her finger start to tighten on the trigger.

Because it cannot be good for a young girl to blow a man's head off. Because if you did kill this man it might leave more scars than it healed. Because there is something awful, something terrifying about the cold dedication of your voice. Because girls cried or got the vapours, or came over all feeble. Or spread their legs to the invaders. Girls were defenceless.

'Because I would like you to.'

He put out his hand, very, very slowly, and laid it gently over the barrel. It was cold under his fingers. She had not looked at him at all, and did not do so now. There was the briefest of flickering moments when he felt sure she would pull the trigger. Then, as slowly as he had put his hand out, she started to lower the pistol, looking fixedly all the time into the eyes of the master.

'Know I could have done it,' she said to him, as if they were the only two people left in the world. 'Know that I would have done it.'

No one who heard her doubted her words.

Gresham closed his hand over the barrel, and very carefully removed the pistol from her grasp. The butt was warm where she had held it. It was at full cock.

Gresham swung round, making all the watchers except Jane jump. Suddenly the pistol was jammed against the master's breast.

'I rate loyalty above all other virtues,' he said simply, and pulled the trigger.

The lock came forward, the pyrite sparks fell down into the now open priming chamber. There was a dull click.

He ignored the expression on the master's face, and spoke conversationally to Jane.

'The powder's fallen out of the priming pan. Happens a lot. Next time, check it before you mean to fire. You're probably right to carry out a threat like that, if you can.'

The girl's face was white in the darkness. Was there the faintest hint of a passing smile on her lips? Not in her eyes, certainly.

'Take her below,' said Gresham to Mannion, still speaking softly. 'She's cold. Jack, get back on the helm. And you . . .' he turned to the master. 'Drop that rubbish.'

Mannion took Jane under his wing, and with an arm round her

shoulders led her below, muttering something that no one else could hear. She went uncomplainingly, suddenly docile.

She has courage, Gresham thought. Real courage. He was not used to it in a woman, other than the Queen of course, and he had never thought of her as a woman. But where did Court ladies have a chance to grow or show courage? Perhaps only in fighting the mysteries and pain of childbirth.

The master let go of his grip on the sailing master, who was in a swoon, and crumpled to the floor. With a quick nod to Edward and Dick, Gresham stepped back. Dick was potentially as unhinged as Jane. Some action would help him.

'Take him,' he said.

'Over the side?' asked Jack, mildly.

'Over the side,' confirmed Gresham. The master watched in horror as his sailing master was dragged to the rail and rather unceremoniously hurled into the sea.

'He can't swim!' said the master stupidly.

'Well, there's never been a better time to learn,' said Gresham casually. There was a faint splash, hardly audible amid the noise of the sails and the sea. 'Now, tell me. Where are we?'

'We're bein' driven up the Channel. Shore's about two maybe three mile off. We're safe enough, unless the wind veers. Which it hardly ever does here.' Desperate to please. Now, at least. A short while ago he had been willing to sell Gresham to the highest bidder.

'Final question. How many others of your crew were suborned?'

'None of them, I swear!' The man was shouting now, pleading. 'It was jus' the sailing master and that look-out there.' Lowbrow was still strung to the mast, showing no signs of returning to consciousness. The flagon Mannion had crowned him with had not broken, despite the force of the blow, and could be heard rolling around the bottom of the crow's nest. 'It warn't my fault!' The toughness Gresham had noted on their first meeting had gone, replaced by a wheedling sycophancy. 'They threatened my family! They made me do it.'

146

'Who is "they"?' asked Gresham, quietly.

'Dunno. I really dunno. Small man, with a beard like . . . didn't talk at all, got his 'enchman to do it, man was a sailor . . . just wanted to know when we were goin' to sail. We had to let 'em board. Said they'd be no harm to anyone. All they wanted was the package they reckoned you were carrying. That's all.'

Gresham looked pityingly at the master. He nodded to Jack and Dick. Without warning, they stepped forward and grabbed him.

'*No!*' he screamed.

There was a second splash, and silence.

Mannion had come back up on the deck.

'Pity if 'e can swim,' said Mannion.

'He can't,' said Gresham. 'I asked him when we hired him. He said it was a good thing if the master couldn't swim, meant he took more care not to sink the ship.'

They released the crew, but not before they had reloaded the two forward swivel guns with grapeshot, and pointed them down at the well of the ship where the crew gathered. They seemed more confused than mutinous.

'Your master and your newly acquired sailing master betrayed me,' said Gresham factually, trying to pretend that white-hot iron bars were not beating against the inside of his skull. 'The noise you heard' – and which had clearly terrified them – 'was a vessel manned by those who had bribed him to allow it to intercept us, to rob me and then to dispose of my men and my ward over the side.'

Had they known? Gresham doubted it. The master had seemed to Gresham not only a man who liked to keep things close to his chest, but to keep as much money as possible as well. Sharing the truth meant sharing the spoils, and he only needed the sailing master and the look-out to be in the know.

'They were both killed in the action.' Let them work out the detail. 'An action that fought off around twenty armed men, as it happens and cost the life of one of my own men.' The odds shocked them. Somehow they knew this man was not boasting, that he was telling the simple truth.

147

'I need to know who was family among you. You have my word that I will not harm you, but put you ashore in the morning. But I must know who you are, because I cannot trust any blood relation of your master. I must and will place them under guard until they are landed. If you do not tell me,' he said calmly, 'I may have to torture you to find out.'

Would he have done so? With his head hurting as it was . . . He need not have feared. At the mention of torture there was a collective gasp of horror, and the three crew members who were family to the late master owned up seconds before the rest of the crew pointed them out. One of them was the little ship's boy. Family they may have been, but they were not showing any remarkable sadness for the loss of their relative.

Did Gresham realise the impact he made? Probably not. A dark, menacing figure, he stood casually on the quarterdeck, one hand holding a superb sword, the other on the firing mechanism of the swivel gun. In the dim light, he could have been the Devil, and several of the crew were persuaded that he was.

The three family members were taken to the hatch that led to the hold. Suddenly, without warning, the older of them kinked left, right, and ran for the side. Vaulting the side rail, he put his arms out before him and made a perfect dive into the blackness of the night.

'Bugger!' said Mannion under his breath.

'I think we can assume that one can swim,' said Gresham. It was a good distance to the shore. The other two were put back in the hold and the hatch battened down again, the door from the hold to the cabins securely locked and a spare piece of timber nailed over it for good measure.

'Who among you is the best sailor?' A middle-aged man stepped forward. 'Is there someone who can sound the depth?' The man nodded. 'Then get him to do it now.'

The chosen sailor stood at the bow, and swung a lead weight easily in his hand. The bottom of the lead was stuffed with tallow, so that when it touched the bottom it would come up with sand or gravel or whatever lined the sea at that point, telling the experienced mariner where they might be. The rope onto which the lead was tied had cloth or small metal items attached to it at regular intervals. Even in the dark the leadsman could sense when the lead had touched bottom, draw up the line and by feeling the item woven into the rope know how far down it had stretched.

Three times he flung the lead forward, three times found no bottom.

Gresham turned to the sailor who had nominated himself as the most experienced. 'Can you and the remaining men rig a sea anchor? Take in the sails?'

'Best thing to do,' said the sailor, knuckle to his brow. 'We're in deep water, and the sea anchor'll keep us there. Can't be more'n four or five hours to dawn . . .'

At dawn they would put in to the nearest port, find or send for someone to pilot the ship to Scotland.

'How's the girl?' asked Gresham. They were sitting on the stern rail each clutching a pewter tankard full of wine. Mannion always packed the essentials. The wind, which had threatened to get up at one point, had settled to something not quite strong enough to whip up the white horses on top of the waves, and seemed to be easing even more. Action always left Gresham exhausted, and with the same burning headache. Sleep was impossible, and he was haunted by the image of the broken-nosed Tom, and the girl, standing on deck with the pistol in her hand like some awful goddess who had been spirited up from the deep.

'The girl?' said Mannion. 'Asleep. I thought she'd pop 'im, you know,' he said in a tone of wonderment, and no small admiration, 'I really did.'

'I think she did too,' said Gresham. 'And I'm damn sure he did.'

'Well, watch out next time you and 'er have a row,' said Mannion, 'and make sure she ain't near a gun.' He thought for a moment. 'I 'ate fuckin' people who try to kill us,' he said finally, taking a pull on his tankard and smacking his lips. There was something special about

149

food, drink and, for that matter, sex, after a man had looked death in the eye and beaten it. For this time, at least.

'More than you hate fucking Scots?' said Gresham. The drink would not help his head the next morning, but it was helping to dull things now, which was what mattered.

'Depends if the fuckin' Scots try to kill us. What a right bloody mess!' Mannion said. 'Everyone thinks you're plotting against everyone else. Cecil would kill you at the drop of a hat – if you don't deliver that bloody letter. The Queen'll reduce you to rags – and me as well, come to think of it – and probably have you knocked off in the Tower while she's at it, if you don't deliver her bloody package. Essex – God knows what 'e'll do, 'cept I wouldn't trust him as far as I can spit and he ain't goin' to like it if 'e 'ears you've carried messages gettin' Cecil off the 'ook. And now we've got someone else – or mebbe one 'o them trying to kill us.'

'Not trying to kill us exactly,' said Gresham wearily, 'though they would've done, I'm sure. All this business tonight was about getting what we carried. But which one? Cecil's message? Or the Queen's? Did Essex get wind of a message that would stop his campaign with James? Or have we walked into plots from the Pope, from Spain or from France, without realising it? And how did who- ever it is know about either package? Has someone infiltrated Cecil's household? Or the Queen's? The Court leaks like a sieve, but when it really matters, both Cecil and the Queen are past mas- ters at keeping secrets.'

'I'll tell you somethin',' said Mannion. ' 'Ooever organised that boat that attacked us . . . it's not someone used to dealing with you.'

'How so?' said Gresham. Mannion's mind was clearly working on a different track to his own.

'Tailing us like that. How often does another ship weigh anchor and leave a mooring at exactly the same time as another? Why would a faster ship like that one stay just so far behind us? A *courtier* wouldn't notice it. We would. That boat, and the man who ran it, it's someone who don't really know you, someone who's got you down as just another stupid messenger.'

The miscalculation had cost twenty men their lives. Gresham tried to get his aching brain around the problem. Who was trying to kill him? Was it just for the messages he carried? And if it was, why were they so important? Whoever it was had access to real money. Hiring a decent boat and the men to sail it did not come cheap.

'What about 'im up there?' asked Mannion. The look-out had regained consciousness now, could be seen straining at his bonds.

'We'll decide about him in the morning,' said Gresham tiring suddenly of the killing. 'Your watch or mine?' he asked, aching from the core of his soul for Mannion to take over.

'I reckon I'll manage the first two hours,' said Mannion. 'You get your head down for a bit. But there's summat we 'ave to do before that.'

They could have just heaved the dead bodies over the side, would have done so without a moment's thought in the heat of the battle. But now it seemed different. After the red mist of battle something like sanity returned. Or was it simply a different form of madness? They would give each man a cannon ball tied round his ankles, and Gresham, who they had been trying to kill a short while earlier, would say a few words he did not believe over them as they slid off the plank into the sea. We cling to these rituals, thought Gresham, and where there is clearly no meaning in life we try to give it some significance in death. It was a necessary farce. He moved wearily, needing to check that the stiffening bodies had indeed been laid out with their legs and their arms straight. It did not do to have the sickening crack of an outstretched elbow in the middle of a funeral service as the body slid down the smoothed wood.

The Council Chamber seemed empty, but much of the power of England was there – the Queen, Essex, Lord Admiral Howard of Effingham, now Earl of Nottingham, Robert Cecil and the Clerk of the Signet, Thomas Windebank.

151

They were standing, the great men, as they often did. Essex was red in the face, almost shouting. The other men were pale-faced, nervous, sensing something wild and uncontrollable in Essex. The Queen was impassive, her head bent low. No smiles now between her and Essex, no sparkling eyes or fine compliments.

It was Ireland, of course. The need for a new Lord Deputy in Ireland was beyond pressing, was now a dire necessity. Elizabeth had decided on Essex's uncle, Sir William Knollys. Essex had started to argue passionately against his uncle, one of his greatest allies in Court, and was forcibly putting the case for Sir George Carew. It was transparent. Carew was one of Cecil's men, and his absence from Court would aid Essex greatly and inconvenience Cecil to the same extent. In addition, Ireland had a wonderful habit of either killing its Lord Deputy or ruining their political future.

Elizabeth raised her head, interrupting Essex's tirade.

'I thank you, my Lord Essex,' she said imperiously, 'for your wise counsel. But I am Queen.'

Essex did not have the sense to shut up. He tried to interrupt her. Mercifully, she chose to ignore him, and carried on. 'Sir William Knollys will go as my Lord Deputy to Ireland. It is decided.'

Essex's fists were clenching and unclenching, the colour rising higher and higher in his face. With an expression of sheer contempt and a gesture that would have been more suitable for a man rejecting the advances of a whore, he turned his back on her.

He turned his back on her.

It was an inconceivable insult to turn one's back on the monarch, unthinkable, unspeakable.

Elizabeth's head jerked upright, and what little control she had left she lost. With one swift move she leant forward and delivered a stinging box on his ears. The sharp smack of her slap echoed in the appalled silence of the stone-vaulted chamber. One might deliver such a blow to a silly lady-in-waiting, or to an idiot servant. To do so in public to an Earl, at a Council meeting, in the full panoply of state business, was unprecedented, unbelievable.

Essex turned and shrieked at Elizabeth. And worse, inconceivably worse, he clapped his hand to his sword hilt, and pulled perhaps two or three inches of the steel out of its scabbard.

There was a gasp from the other men. To make to draw one's sword on the monarch was high treason. It was not an insult that would have the perpetrator banished from the Court. It was a gesture that would have the culprit kneeling on the block at Tower Hill.

'*This is an outrage!*' screamed Essex, apparently oblivious to the dual outrage he had just committed. '*I will not bear this!*' He took his hand off his sword hilt, more in the manner of someone making a great concession than of a man recognising a great error. 'I would not have borne this from your father, and I shall not bear it from you, a woman.'

The men were transfixed, gazing in horror at the sword hilt. It was Nottingham who stepped forward, put himself between the Queen and the errant Lord, pushed him back. Nottingham said nothing.

There was silence in the Chamber.

Essex was flushed, standing at his full height. He looked round the room, saw no help from the other men there, looked in the eyes of the Queen and saw what Anne Boleyn must have seen in Henry VIII's eyes at the very last.

He rushed from the room. Had the first two or three steps been an attempt to retire gracefully, facing the Queen? Or had it taken him that long simply to turn?

All eyes were on Elizabeth. She gazed in silence for a moment at the door through which Essex had left. Then, without another word, she swept past the other men, and left.

Essex stormed down the corridors of the Palace, oblivious to where he was. Suddenly he came to a dead end, a dark, brick-built avenue ending starkly where what had once been a door had been filled in. He paused, as if waking from a dream. It was the dark, narrow tunnel that had been the stuff of his dreams. Here. Now. Real.

What had he done? What had he done!

He had always been obsessive, prone to swings of mood. Yet always before he had been able to pull back, a deep instinct warning him in time to allow his charm to work its wonders. Always, until . . . What was the figure forming in his imagination in the pattern of the brickwork? Was it the pensive face of a small boy?

Alone, with no servants and certainly no Queen to see and hear him, Robert Devereux, second Earl of Essex, sank to his knees, and sobbed. Sobbed almost like a little boy.

CHAPTER 6

Late July, 1598
Scotland

Their arrival in Scotland was an anti-climax. Blustery, sharp winds chased them up the coast, threatening a storm that never quite happened. They saw numerous other sail, but none seemed to want to follow their exact course, none seemed threatening. Gresham eyed with grim memories the towers of Dunbar Castle, perched on its twin rocks, and the vast three-towered bulk of Tantallon Castle, but no boats scuttled out to chase the *Anna*, and Tantallon seemed deserted. There was no quayside berth for them at Leith, but the anchorage seemed half empty by the side of the bustle of London. A cloud of smoke, coal and wood seemed to hover permanently over Edinburgh, even though it was the middle of summer.

The first disappointment was horses. All they could seem to hire were small nags, underfed and as grumpy as their owner. Still, Gresham had dressed in the most sober and sombre manner to avoid attention, and the horses were at least in keeping with his clothes. The second disappointment was what was rumoured to be one of the best hostelries in the city. It was dark, cramped and stank of stale piss, where previous inhabitants had clearly not bothered with chamber pots. He set Mary, the maid, and his three men working to scrub the rooms, even cajoling some hot water out of the kitchen and some half-decent soap. He left the job to Jane's ministrations. She seemed settled now, quiet but calm, and had made no mention of her brush with the master since it had happened. Before Gresham left, he noted that she had donned a simple smock, and was on her hands and knees, scrubbing away like a washerwoman. How extraordinary to move so quickly and easily from being the most beautiful woman at Court to this. Dick had returned to the world of the sane alongside her after the battle, yet Gresham could detect no familiarity between the young man and the beautiful girl of the same age. Whatever else Jane had mastered, she had the ability to send out the strongest possible signal to any interested male that she was not available. If rumour was to be believed she was the first woman in England to turn Essex down.

Gresham and Mannion set off to get the sense of the city. James held Court at Holyrood Palace; it was a poor thing from the outside compared to the Palaces Elizabeth owned. The forbidding bulk of the castle and Arthur's seat dominated the city, overlooking the stinking pond that they call Nor' Loch. It was not a place to bring cheer to the soul, Gresham thought.

Cameron Johnstone was the name Gresham had been given when he had asked for a contact in Scotland. A thin, straggly lawyer dressed from head to toe in black. Part of his garb would have been fashionable in London five years earlier, but part showed a strong French influence. The impression of legal respectability was spoilt by a thin scar that ran from his chin to just under his right ear. His accent was as thick as Scottish rain, but understandable. His office was also clean, and Gresham and Mannion had learnt enough about life in Scotland to relish what seemed to be the absence of fleas on both their host and his furnishings.

'Ye'll be wanting refreshment?' asked the man, and a fat servant girl with freckles and great plump cheeks brought in wine. It was good. French, by the look and the taste, and had kept well.

Something nagged at the back of Gresham's mind. He knew he had never talked with this man before, never met him face to face. But had he seen him before? There was something vaguely familiar about the slightly shambling figure, the way the head was held slightly to one side . . .

'Now,' said the man, 'I'll be of the mind that you'll no want to be wasting your time or mine. Any friend of the Earl of Northumberland is a friend of mine – though not of all my countrymen, I might add.' He allowed a brief grin to flit across his features. The Percy family, Earls of Northumberland, had been fighting the Scots, when they had not been fighting their own King, for time immemorial. It was a relationship based not so much on love and hate as familiarity and hate. Percy had business interests in Scotland, had recommended this man and had provided him with a letter of introduction.

The lawyer glanced at Percy's letter. He listened as Gresham gave his invented story of being told of a Scots couple who had briefly lived in the village from where he had rescued Jane, who had paid a local man to look after the girl while they were away 'for a few months' and who had never come back. East Linton, that was the name of the village they claimed to have come from. Jeffrey was the name that had been given, said Gresham. Angus Jeffrey and, perhaps, a Belinda Jeffrey. He knew it was not much, but it was all he had to go on. Johnstone looked at Gresham, having taken brief notes, and Gresham felt he was being looked into and through.

'Well,' the lawyer said, 'East Linton's maybe twenty, twenty-five mile out of town. No a long ride for a gentleman such as yousel'. You have good horses, do you?'

Gresham said where they had hired their nags.

'Aye,' said the lawyer, 'well, it's always a guid thing to help old animals in their distress, but I think we can do a wee bit better than that for ye.' He rang a small bell by his side, and a man his own age came in. 'My client here will be needing some decent horses. And some others taken back to where they belong. Sir,' he turned to Gresham, 'will you trust my man to find you mounts?' Gresham nodded. 'In which case, might I suggest you wait here for the hour or so it will take my man to acquire them? Will you remind me how many men there are in your party? And the lady, of course.'

'There are . . .' Gresham wanted to say six men and the lady, but stopped himself in time. Poor old Tom was drifting onto the Essex or Norfolk coast now, if he was lucky, and if he was luckier might even get a pauper's burial. Or he was full fathom five, down among the dead men until his bones – and his broken nose – were returned to sand. 'There are five men. Myself, my . . . secretary here . . .' Gresham motioned to Mannion, who he had promoted to a secretary in case the Scotsman was conscious of rank and wanted to boot out the servant, 'the girl and three male servants. Oh, and we'd better add in the maid, if she ever recovers from her sea-sickness.'

Mary could have been shot, skewered, ravished and drowned when the *Anna* was attacked and, had they lost the battle, would almost certainly have had three of the four administered to her. Despite being locked in a cabin while the battle raged above, hearing men die and scream and so on, she had hardly mentioned those passing inconveniences, preferring instead to keep up a continual and very taxing diatribe against the sea and all surfaces which did not stay still. Gresham had only shut her up by threatening for the journey home to put her in the rowing boat and tow it however many hundred yards behind the *Anna* that it took for them not to hear her whining voice.

'Will the lady and her maid require a small carriage, then?' asked the lawyer.

Gresham thought about it. 'Does the weather look set fair?' he asked. Something of a rather good summer's day appeared to be emerging from under the smog. Jane could ride well, and so could the maid after a fashion. It would do both of them good to be out in the open, and they would probably be more comfortable on horses than in a hired, bone-rattling carriage.

'It will be fine,' said the lawyer firmly, as if God communicated these things direct to him, 'for at least two more days. Ten mile a day will be enough for you with ladies, I believe? There is a good inn at East Linton. It is on the main route, of course.'

Gresham made a decision. 'They can ride, in the first instance. Can you get us a carriage and horses, for it to ride with us should the weather change, or for the return journey?'

Had he made a mistake? The lawyer did not blink, nor did anything in his expression change. Gresham had been introduced by Northumberland not as a nobleman or a courtier, but simply as 'someone who holds my trust', which in the diplomatic language of the day put Gresham as little more than a senior employee. The cost of the small coach would be the same as that for all the horses put together. By ordering it as a reserve Gresham had revealed that money was no object to him. *Ergo*, either Gresham was not what he appeared, or someone very wealthy was paying for the trip.

'Will you grant me the pleasure of entertaining yourself and your . . . secretary to dine with me over noon?' This lawyer was no fool. Then again, few lawyers Gresham had met had been fools. Total and utter bastards, yes, but fools, no.

Under normal circumstances Mannion would have perked up at the offer of food, slugged back whatever was left in his drinking vessel and started to loosen his belt a notch. Instead he looked up at Gresham with unusual respect, and said in a passable middle-class accent, 'We do have business elsewhere in the city, sir, as I am sure you are aware.' Mannion was dressed like a secretary, and appeared as comfortable as a wolf suddenly asked to don a woolly fleece. Despite this, his combination of servility and disapproval was superb.

'I can tell the time,' said Gresham dismissively. 'I would be delighted to accept your offer. You are most kind.'

'I apologise for the humbleness of the fare,' said Cameron Johnstone. 'You are very welcome, but nevertheless unexpected guests.'

The food was actually surprisingly good. There was excellent beef, a venison pie, a pigeon baked whole and several varieties of fish. There was also hot soup, crammed with vegetables, and rough bread that belied its appearance with a wonderful, nutty flavour. There was local ale, and more of the good French wine.

'I must be open with you,' said Cameron, eyeing with the slightest hint of amusement the inroads Mannion had made into the food. 'I know of you by reputation. The work I do for the Earl of Northumberland is not only . . . related to his business matters. I also deal for him in . . . political issues.'

'Political issues?' asked Gresham.

'The border between Scotland and England is the most troubled in the world, perhaps,' mused Cameron. 'You will have heard tell of the reivers, and their like?' Gresham had indeed heard of the legendary border raiders. 'The Earl of Northumberland stands as the gate to England, but it is a gate that opens two ways. It is also the gate to Scotland, of course. Over hundreds of years certain . . . understandings have built up. Certain ways of doing things. Were it not for these understandings, the border lands would have drowned in their own blood years ago. These understandings do not stop warfare, of course. They limit it, and restrict some of the consequences when it does take place.'

'And you . . . broker these "understandings"?' asked Gresham genuinely interested.

'I think the phrase is "go-between",' answered Cameron. 'I quite literally go between my Lord of Northumberland and his party, and certain Scottish nobles on the other side, and sometimes talk to the wilder elements who inhabit the borders, for one set of nobles or for both.'

'Isn't it dangerous?' asked Gresham. 'The wilder elements are unlikely to respect the nobility on either side. I can see that the nobility – on both sides – might be inclined to blame you for everyone else's faults.'

Cameron gave a dry laugh. 'You have a rare understanding of these things. As I would expect from Sir Henry Gresham.'

Gresham looked at him levelly. 'Did you suggest to the Earl of Northumberland that he might place your name before me? And if so, how is it that you knew I would be coming to Scotland?'

Cameron's smile, thought Gresham, was like that of a snake before it killed its prey.

'I knew the Earl would recommend me, and that you have been part of his circle,' said Cameron. Which neatly avoided answering the question while seeming to do so, thought Gresham. 'And someone who is actually no more and no less than a spy would be mortified not to meet a man who in England is one of the best-known of that breed. Whatever the reason for your visit to Scotland, I hoped you would do business through me.'

Or arrange to have me robbed and killed at sea, thought Gresham.

'My business can at times be dangerous. As I'm sure is yours,' said Gresham calmly.

'Aye', said Cameron, 'but I care little for that. You see, no member of my family has lived beyond the age of forty. We all die, the male members at least, of what seems to be a canker, a growth, usually in the stomach, sometimes in the lungs or groin. So when I met my girl, my wife, and we had two fine bairns, I did everything in my power to make a living for them before I reached the age of forty. Including selling my loyalty and probably my soul to men such as your Northumberland, our equivalent here in Scotland and the worst parcel of border-raising rogues on God's earth into the bargain.' Cameron paused for a moment.

'And?' Gresham prompted him.

'And so it was a great surprise when my dear wife and our two bairns died within a week of each other, of what you would call the plague, though I who had held them and kissed them survived without a scratch or a single stinking pustule. So here I am, with a fine estate and, to be honest with you, Sir Henry, no one to leave it to. So your arrival here lightens up what is to be frank quite a dreary existence, and the prospect of death holds no fears for me. Quite the opposite, as it happens.'

161

In Gresham's experience men only used a phrase such as 'to be honest with you' as a preface to dishonesty, and a phrase such as 'to be frank' as a preface to dissembling.

'So why reveal all this to me?' said Gresham. He had heard Cameron Johnstone speak and for a moment heard himself speak. The prospect of death holds no fears for me. Quite the opposite, in fact. It could have been Gresham speaking of himself. Perhaps that was why Cameron had said it.

'Because I do not for a minute believe that you are here to chase the antecedents of your ward. And because my native curiosity makes me interested to know why you are here. Not out of mere idle curiosity, but in the vain and rather conceited hope that I might be able to help.'

'I'm sorry to hear about your family. Truly sorry. It's difficult to imagine your pain and suffering,' said Gresham.

'Do you have wife and children?' asked Cameron.

'No, I do not,' answered Gresham.

'Then it *will* be difficult for you to imagine what it means to lose them.'

Cameron Johnstone was hiding infinitely more than he was revealing.

'I need to meet your King,' said Gresham. 'As a matter of urgency, and in strictest secrecy.'

'For reasons you will not tell me, of course?' asked Cameron.

'For reasons I will not tell you,' confirmed Gresham. 'Of course. Can you do this for me?'

'Oh, yes,' said Cameron almost casually. 'But understand one thing. I can set you up such a meeting, but our King James has more than a mind of his own. He will decide. Yet there are many in the capital city,' he waved to encompass Edinburgh, 'who can not only promise but deliver you as much. You see, we are less formal here in Scotland than you are used to in your great Court of London. All sorts of men, and women too, have their secret assignations with the King, as well as their public ones.'

All sorts of men? And women too? Secret assignations? Was this

162

sodomy and black magic? Were Cameron's comments premeditated, or simply a lucky hit?

'Arrange this meeting for me,' said Gresham, 'and I will be for ever in your debt spiritually, though I'm happy to make sure any debt is not financial.' He tossed a bag of coin over the table.

Cameron eyed the purse with an expression of amusement, and flicked it back to Gresham's side of the table.

'I fear you were no listening, Sir Henry. I've no need of money. A little pride, or even a reason for living, now that would be helpful.'

'And you think I can supply either?'

'If I'm being honest, no,' said Cameron. 'But you offer more hope than most. So I can return to you within two hours and tell you whether or not the King will see you, when he will see you and where.'

'And what if a party of troops returns in two hours to arrest me? Or a group of border bandits to kill me and leave no questions?'

'Most risks are shared, are they not?' asked Cameron cheerfully enough.

'I think it would be best if in accepting your offer,' said Gresham, 'I did so with one caveat. Please row out to me on board the *Anna* with your answer. With one boatman only.'

Cameron did not blink. 'That will be fine,' he said, 'though please acknowledge it will take me longer to reach you there than it would had we a rendez-vous here in the city. Please describe your vessel, and roughly where she is in the anchorage.'

They loaded the cannons and the swivel guns just in case, but need not have worried. Cameron rowed out to them alone, with much splashing and missing of the water.

'I thought you said you were wealthy?' said Gresham.

'Aye,' said Cameron, 'and I did not get so by wasting money on men to row me when I have a body that can do the thing myself.' Not only had Cameron arranged a meeting with the King, but had done so for that evening. Things were indeed different in Scotland. Cameron was quite apologetic.

'I'm sorry you had to wait until this evening,' he said. 'The King has been hunting all day.'

'Is my meeting secret?' asked Gresham.

'It is so arranged,' answered Cameron.

And so it was that they entered the Palace by a back door, a whispered conversation between Cameron and two guards opening the crude wooden door criss-crossed with iron bars. They walked through an open courtyard, then entered a labyrinth of stone passages. A thin drizzle was coating the dirty stonework now, which glistened in the light of the few torches that were burning in sconces on the walls.

'Are you an agent for the King?' asked Gresham. He and Mannion were walking behind Cameron, Gresham with his hand on the hilt of his sword.

'It is as I explained it to you,' said Cameron, not turning his head, concentrating on the turnings, 'I work for the King on occasion, and for Northumberland on occasion. And, on occasion, for others. And, on this occasion, for you.'

'And on occasion for yourself?' asked Gresham.

'Always for myself,' answered Cameron succinctly, but said no more.

They came to a door with a huge lintel, so low they had to bend to enter. Before they did so, Cameron turned to both Gresham and Mannion. 'Leave your swords by the door. And any daggers or other blades you may have. When the King was in his mother's womb she saw a group of armoured noblemen knife her music teacher, Rizzio, the man many thought was her lover, to death in front of her. It's left him with a horror of bare steel. He'll sense if you have a blade. Remove them all. Even the hidden ones.' Cameron looked meaningfully at Mannion, who stared back impassively.

'Do it,' said Gresham. 'But if there are armed men in that room, or armed men enter,' he said to Cameron, 'I'll break your neck as my last act on earth.' He realised what a small threat it was to a man who had professed to welcome death.

'Please do,' said Cameron. 'But do look inside the room first.'

He swung the door open. It was small, sparsely furnished with a crude table and four stools. Two torches flared in the ubiquitous cast-iron sconces, guttering and sending out dirty smoke that stained the walls even more and made the eyes sting. An unarmed man in Stuart livery, dirty and grease stained, was in the room, his back to an unlit fire. He greeted Cameron briefly and with no evident affection, and left through another low door on the opposite end of the room. It measured perhaps twelve foot by twelve, and cheap tapestries adorned two walls.

'Don't sit down,' hissed Cameron, after Mannion had unloaded a small armoury and Gresham his sword and dagger, leaving them by the door. They were still horrendously vulnerable, Gresham realised. A rush of men to either door and they were effectively defenceless. They waited.

The door opened suddenly, and a man entered the room. He was of medium height, though slightly hunched in his back, his head seeming almost too thin for his body. His tunic and hose were dotted with jewels and pearls, but like his retainer the fine material was greasy and marked with stains. Cameron bowed low, and Gresham and Mannion followed. This presumably was James VI of Scotland; perhaps shortly to be James I of England.

'Your Highness,' said Cameron, 'Sir Henry Gresham, from the Court of England, asks your gracious permission for an audience.'

James did not return the bow, but plonked himself down on a stool. He did not ask the others to sit.

'Has the man no tongue in his own head?' he asked. The tone was perfectly polite, the content distinctly aggressive. The accent was thicker than Cameron's, on the edge of intelligible.

'Your Majesty,' said Gresham, 'my tongue is constrained by my being in a foreign country and at a foreign Court, and in the presence of a King. I intended no disrespect in allowing your countryman to speak for me.'

'That was well said, enough,' conceded James. 'So now you've started, what else is it you have to say to me, now that you've dragged me down here.' Gresham was getting the feeling that the King had not had a good day.

'Your Majesty,' Gresham said, 'I would be grateful if it were possible for us to speak alone.'

'Alone, then,' answered the King, 'except for my servant here. You may trust his capacity to bide his tongue. Or, to put it the other way, with him present to guard me if need be you may hold a conversation with me. Without him, your conversation will be with yourself.' The King seemed very bored, listless even.

Gresham bowed low, accepting the deal. Cameron and Mannion backed out of the room. Mannion banged his head on the stone lintel, and Gresham gritted his teeth, waiting for him to swear. The only noise was the door shutting.

Gresham pulled the Queen's ring out of the sealed pocket he had been carrying it in, and placed it on the table. It gleamed dully in the torchlight.

The King leant forward, suddenly interested.

He looked up at Gresham, and Gresham saw the flash of intelligence in his small, dark eyes.

'There is something to go with this token? Something from the Queen your mistress?' There was an eagerness in his voice now, an almost childish excitement.

Gresham bowed again, reached inside his tunic and brought out the sealed package that Elizabeth had given him. He placed it on the table. The King looked at it for a moment, and then nodded to his servant. The servant leant forward, picked up the sealed document, put it in his pocket.

Why was the King not reading it? It was almost as if it he already knew its content, was patting himself on the back without having to read it.

'Your Majesty,' Gresham said, hoping to capitalise on the King's evident good mood. 'I have another letter for Your Highness, if you will care to receive it.'

'Another letter?' said the King. There was even a hint of humour in his voice now. The man was dirty, Gresham realised, ingrained

166

muck in his fingernails and in the creases on his forehead. There was a strange smell around him, a musky, musty smell, not the sharp and acrid tang of sweat but something older, rather like a maturing cheese. 'You've been a very busy man, Sir Henry Gresham.'

'Others have wished me to be busy on their behalf, Your Majesty,' said Gresham.

'You've been kind enough to call me Your Majesty four times now,' said James. Gresham checked through his memory: James was right. '"Sir" will do right enough from now on. Tell me about this other letter.'

Then a crashing realisation dawned in Gresham's head. James was drunk. He was in the first stage of drunkenness, when the drunkard knows the state he is in and almost over-compensates in the exactness of his language. Gresham had known a host of men, and women, who were far better at conducting their business drunk than sober. The realisation of King James's state did not shock so much as intrigue him. It was only early evening.

'Sir,' said Gresham, 'it comes from Sir Robert Cecil. As with the Queen, he has asked for it to be treated as most secret. I should add that he does not know of the letter from Her Majesty, any more than Her Majesty knows of his letter.'

'You would be wise not to make too many assumptions about what Her Majesty may or may not know. But you will tell him, as his man?' said James.

'Sir, I will not tell him.' Gresham had almost said 'I will no tell him', his brain already picking up the Scottish idiom. 'I am not his man. I have merely agreed to deliver this letter for him.'

'And what does it say?' Was James toying with him now, implying that he had opened the letter? And therefore perhaps implying that he had opened the letter from the Queen? Oh God! Gresham was on trial again for his life. Was it thus with *all* monarchs, or only those bounded by the North Sea? Well, if in doubt, try the truth. It was such a rare commodity in Courts that it had rare healing powers as well as shock value.

'Sir,' said Gresham, 'it is true that once before I opened a letter from Robert Cecil that I was carrying while sailing with the expedition by Sir Francis Drake to Cadiz. I found that it ordered my death. Since then I have tried to avoid reading anything penned by him and placed in my trust.'

'Well, you clearly survived,' said James, 'unless it's a ghost I see before me now. But I guess you may have an inkling of what this second letter contains.'

'I believe it reassures Your . . . you, sir, that Robert Cecil is neither a sodomite nor a servant of the Devil.'

James's hand had started to rise to his chest, as if to make the sign of the cross, at the word 'Devil', before he corrected it.

'And am I right to accept that reassurance?'

Robert Cecil had tried to have Gresham killed on several occasions and was holding him to ransom even now. He loathed Gresham, had done so for years. Just as his father had been the strength behind Elizabeth's throne, so the son hoped to be the strength behind James's throne when he came to be King of England. A word now from Gresham that Cecil was either a sodomite or a Devil-worshipper could remove Cecil from the power he lusted after, do him irreparable damage.

But would it? Or would it damage Gresham more? Well, the truth had worked so far. Try it again.

'Sadly, sir,' Gresham said and watched James lean forward, as if desperate to hear the bad news, 'you are right to accept that reassurance. At least as far as I am in a position to judge.'

James rocked back, but the alert interest was clearly still there.

'Sadly? Why sadly? What is sad about clearing a man of two grievous accusations?'

'What is sad, sir, is that we are sworn enemies who yet work together. And I count myself as a friend to one who is a bitter enemy of Cecil, the Earl of Essex. It grieves me not to be able to confirm Robert Cecil in any accusation made against him, as it grieves me not to support my friend. Yet to convict him of sodomy or Devil-worship would be wrong, I believe.'

168

'And is this a man I should trust, this Cecil who is your enemy?' asked James. 'Or should I trust this man who is your friend, this Essex?'

In a few months this rather unprepossessing man might be Henry Gresham's King. It would not do, for purely practical reasons, to lie to him.

'If, sir, you become King of England with the support of Robert Cecil, he will do more than anyone else to preserve you in that state. If you become King of England with the support of the Earl of Essex, you will reign far more dramatically. It would be two very different reigns.'

'But what of their different loyalty to me before I achieve that happy state?' In the bitter turmoil of Scottish politics, James had proved himself a survivor. He had good reason to know and to fear changing loyalties, shifting allegiances and fickle friendships.

'That, sir, is a matter between yourself and them. I can only state that I do not consider Cecil a sodomite or a Devil-worshipper, but that if I were to choose my company I would choose Essex over Cecil.'

James thought this over for a few seconds. He motioned to his servant, ordered him to bring drink.

'Tell me about the English Court,' said the King of Scotland. He had still not asked Gresham to be seated. 'Tell me about Essex,' prompted James. The servant returned with a decanter and two fine, cut-glass goblets, Venetian by the look of them. The King looked up at Gresham, motioned him to sit. He did not ask Gresham if he wished to drink, but ordered the servant to hand him a glass. Sweet white wine, by the look of it. Ironically, it was the monopoly on all sweet wines imported into England, granted from the Queen, that allowed Essex to lead the life that he did. Gresham preferred the drier, Alsace wines.

'Essex I know only as a social companion, a drinking partner if you will,' said Gresham, waiting for the King to take the first sip. Or rather, the first glass, Gresham saw, as the King knocked back the opening salvo and motioned for a refill. Was Gresham meant to do the same? He compromised by taking a large swig of the stuff. Was this to be trial by drink? 'He is a charismatic figure, glamorous and brave, foolhardy and moody, ambitious for military glory, highly intelligent but at times stubborn beyond belief, spoilt yet vulnerable. He is loyal, though taxed by the demands of loyalty. He is a leader, though a flawed one and in some strange sense a broken personality. He has a zest for life, and something of a desire to lose it.'

'You sum up a man well, Sir Henry,' said the King, taking his second glass slightly more slowly. 'But tell me, who does England want as its next King?'

'If you mean England as the country, sir, the truth is that it cares little who is King or Queen if there is peace and a chance for prosperity to flourish. If you mean England as the Court, there are as many factions as there are nobles. I believe that at present the majority would favour you. Spain has given too many painful memories to England, and as for Arbella Stuart, our country no longer wants to anoint a silly woman in order to make the throne the prize of the first man who wins her favours. We did that with Mary and King Philip of Spain.'

'Drink your drink, man,' said the King. 'There's truth in wine, as well as folly.' Gresham obediently knocked back what was left in his glass. Without a word, the servant filled it up to the brim. Gresham felt an obligation to take a significant sip from the refilled vessel. 'And will you tell me about the Queen?'

Gresham thought about that one for a split second.

'I would prefer not to, sir, if such were to be granted me. A man who gossips about one monarch to another is likely to gossip to everyone.'

James sat silent for a moment.

'Well, you've passed your first test. You've managed not to poison me against anyone, despite one of them being an enemy of yours. You'll wait in Leith for me to pen a reply to both these letters. They'll be delivered by Cameron Johnstone.' There was an ever so slight slurring of the King's words. 'Within twenty-four hours. You will know they are my letters by this seal.'

James snapped a finger, and the servant produced a candle and some sealing wax. The candle was lit from the sconce, and James melted wax onto the table, stamping his fist down on it. The ring on his finger left a clear seal imprinted in the wax. James made sure Gresham had seen the mark, and then the servant picked the still warm wax from off the table, broke it into pieces like communion wafers and threw the remnants into the cold fireplace.

James stood up. Giving a brief nod to Gresham, he left through the same door he had entered by. The servant followed, not repeating the acknowledgement to Gresham by even a nod.

And where did that little exchange leave him, thought Gresham? None the wiser was the truth. James had clearly been expecting a message from Elizabeth, looking forward to it even. He had not been expecting a message from Cecil, but had accepted it with relative equanimity. He wanted to know about the English Court; no surprise there. And having been handed a messenger, he wanted to make use of him to reply by return. All very reasonable. And he had been rather drunk at the same time as being very reasonable. What message was there in that for England's future prospects?

Jack and Dick had been ordered to go back to the *Anna*, once cleaning duties were complete, if only to keep an eye on the crew. The lugubrious Edward had been allocated as Jane and Mary's escort for a tour round Edinburgh. Jane had come back excited by her first sight of a new city. They were in Gresham's room now, the largest of those they had taken. It smelt of scrubbed stone and hay, copious quantities of which had been strewn across the floor once it had dried.

'Do you know,' Jane said to Mannion, finding it easier to confide her excitement to him rather than Gresham, 'they don't live like we do in London with separate areas for the rich and for the poor. Oh, the rich have town houses, but a lot of them here, they all live

171

on top of one another, quite literally – the higher up the building you go, the better class you are.'

She turned to Gresham. 'And do you know what a lot of the lawyers are called?'

'Tell me,' said Gresham, who knew he was going to be told whatever he answered.

'Bonnet-lairds!' Jane exclaimed, who for today had decided to be a young seventeen-year-old, rather than any of the other things Gresham had seen her be. A shrieking fish-wife; a cool matron, seventeen rising fifty; a sulky seductress; a chief librarian . . . that was only the start. 'A laird is a noble around here, what we might call a gentleman. Apparently a lot of the lawyers buy small estates just outside Edinburgh, and call themselves landowners. The people call them bonnet-lairds. "Bonnet" means . . . not quite real. Something you put on and off too easily. When do we ride out to find the parents I'm meant to have had?'

Her capacity to change the subject was not the least infuriating of her mannerisms.

'We have to wait the arrival of a package from Cameron Johnstone,' said Gresham. 'We can't make any plans until then.'

Early next morning there was a rattling at the door of Gresham's room, and the Scots lawyer fell rather than walked through it. His left sleeve was torn and there were blood streaks all the way down his arm. He had a livid bruise on the side of his head. He was gritting his teeth with pain.

'What happened?' asked Gresham, rising to his feet, sword out, peering through the door to see if Cameron's attackers had followed him.

'In the street!' muttered Cameron. 'In full view! That's what caught me out. I was expecting something in a back alley, not in the full glare of public approval.'

'Did they try to kill you?'

'I think it was this they wanted.' He grimaced as he brought out two sealed packages. It was James's seal, the one he had stamped into the table. 'Three of them, great lumps of offal that they were.'

'How did you escape?'

Mannion had come in and, without a word pushed Cameron into a seat. He was expertly stripping the man's jacket off. A bowl and the cleanest cloth they could find were soon sending red streaks into the clear water. Mannion had initially scorned Gresham when on campaign he had always insisted on the water being boiled before it was used to treat wounds. It was advice given to Gresham by Dr Stephen Perse at Cambridge, and Mannion's view of academics was equivalent to his view of Spaniards and Scotsmen. Yet even he had come round when the infection rate in Gresham's men had been insignificant in comparison to the other troops on campaign.

'They came up from behind,' said Cameron, feeling gently with his tongue at a loosened tooth. 'Tried to rush me into an alley, but I heard their noise, sensed what was happening. So I stopped and ducked down, and they bounced off me rather. Then one of them clubbed me on the head. He'd have got me, I think, but we were in the public street and he had to try and half hide the blow. So I saw most of the stars but kept conscious and tried to run between the legs of the nearest one. He used the knife, caught me here on the shoulder.'

'What then?'

'I stuck my knife into his guts and cut the other one's face. The last man backed off and I was able to run.'

'When did you last appear in a law court?' asked Gresham, bringing a mug of ale to him. 'It doesn't strike me that your legal skills are your greatest strength at the moment, or the ones you use most often.'

'Ouch!' said Cameron, as Mannion touched the entry point of the wound. Cameron felt round the wound gingerly, grimaced, and then yanked something out. It was a tiny splinter of steel. 'Thought so,' he said. 'Point of his dagger. Cheap stuff. Like the men. Och, me and the law? I was in court only last week, actually. I do like to keep my hand in. Unfortunately the woman in question's supposed

173

marriage to the man who walked out on her wasn't supported by any documentary evidence, unlike his actual marriage to the other woman he'd lied about to the first. If you follow me.'

'But the law isn't your primary concern?' continued Gresham, who was beginning to realise that the Scottish advocate was a more interesting figure than he had first thought.

Cameron sighed. 'You could say that. I fear my . . . other activities have tended to dominate in recent years. Not least of all because they were more profitable. That was at the time, of course, when I had a reason to want more money.'

'Forgive me,' said Gresham, 'but did your wife and children actually exist?'

'Oh yes,' said Cameron. 'I take the point, and in the spirit it was intended. Wonderful sob story, isn't it? But, as it happens, it is true. With one final twist. I became a spy, as distinct from a respectable if rather dowdy lawyer, because it gave me more money. And, if I'm being honest, because it was more exciting. I thought the only danger in it was to me, that I was running the risk. Imagine my surprise, therefore, when my wife and children caught their illness from an agent who asked us to shelter him for two nights in our home. We gave him the children's bedroom. Space is at a premium here in Edinburgh, even for reasonably wealthy families.'

He took a drink from the mug, ran his hand up the side of his face, examined his fingers. There was only a little blood on them.

'You have to admit that life has a sense of humour. We'd just sacked a maid, but let her stay on for two days out of kindness to find somewhere else to go to. Her last job was to change the sheets on the bed. My wife was scrupulous about these things. Except the maid never changed them, and for the first time in her life my wife did not check. She was going to, had actually set off, when there was a knock on the door and her dear mother made one of her unannounced visits. I suspect my friend the agent left some of his fleas as a parting present. He was dead a week later anyway, my wife and children a few days after that. So that's the story. I seem to

174

be left with the job I did for them. And I do seem unable to get myself killed.'

'We're leaving, now,' said Gresham, the alarm bell tolling in his head. The intrigues in the Court of London were like walking through a deep marsh in a thick fog. In Scotland it was like doing the same walk not only in fog but in the pitch black of night.

'I need a fast passage to England,' said Cameron. 'May I take passage on your boat?'

So as to knife me in the back all the more easily, thought Gresham. Out loud he said, 'Why so urgent?'

Cameron grinned. 'For some reason James trusts you to deliver this package to Elizabeth.'

'We sail within the hour. If you can be there by then, you may take passage. If not, we leave regardless.'

Gresham and Mannion both noted the man who scurried away as soon as they left the lodgings, but if he was going to call out help to stop them he failed to do it in time. They made it to the *Anna* unmolested.

'Why the hell are you lettin' that freak come along with us?' asked an incredulous Mannion. ''E's about as trustworthy as a spoon with an 'ole in the middle of it!'

They were on the quarterdeck, watching the smoke of Edinburgh recede. Cameron was somewhere down below. ('Probably knocking holes in the bottom of the boat' muttered Mannion.) Jane was standing nearby.

'Trustworthy?' said Gresham. 'Women are witches when it comes to judging character. Here, Mistress Jane, what do you think of our new acquaintance Cameron?'

Jane thought for a moment.

'I think he is evil,' she said, 'and you are mad to bring him with us. Why have you?'

Gresham tried not to show his shock at the certainty of her judgement and its intensity.

'Like you,' he said, 'I don't trust him. Yet I'm like a tennis ball being hit between the factions at Court, and being hit from one Court to another. Already someone's tried to murder us. Cameron is the only enemy I can see! If I can keep him in sight, he might lead me to the others.'

Cameron chose that moment to join them. Before he could offer the time of day, and without dismissing Mannion or Jane, Gresham spoke, 'You're clearly up to your neck in the intrigue of both Courts. You're clearly trusted by King James. It was quite clear he only saw me because of your intervention and that he didn't actually want to come, so you must have serious credibility with him.'

Cameron waved a hand, neither confirming nor denying.

'And I remember where I saw you before. In winter. In the English Court. You were hanging round at the back. I only remember you because you looked so odd in your drab clothes. I only caught a glimpse of you. But you walk in a peculiar manner, slightly sideways, like a crab. You did it as you got off the horse on the quayside. *What were you doing in Elizabeth's Court?*'

'Saving her life, as it happens,' said Cameron.

'How so?'

Cameron sighed. 'In front of these?' he asked disparagingly, motioning to Mannion and Jane.

'It's the price of your passage,' said Gresham. 'Unless you want to swim home.'

'I suppose you have to know,' Cameron eventually replied, after a good few seconds when he looked to be seriously considering the swim. 'James received a tip-off that there was going to be an assassination attempt on the Queen's life. All we knew was that the assassin was Scottish, an exile who no one had seen for three or four years. It was his father who tipped us off, though God knows how he knew. Scottish families work like no other. James sent me down to the Court. Under cover of doing work for the Earl of Northumberland. The Earl agreed without knowing why. The Earls of Northumberland and the Kings of Scotland have been trading like this since time began.'

'To stop the assassination? Those were your instructions?'

Cameron looked uncomfortable. The motion of the boat was rising and falling in the easy swell, now they had cleared Leith, but Cameron's discomfort had nothing to do with the sea.

'Well, no, as it happened. My instructions were simply to identify the boy, find out who he was working for, if the plot was real.'

'And did you?'

'Identify him? Yes, though he was surprisingly well buried. Find out if the plot was real? There was reason to believe so. The boy was living above his means, had purchased two very fine pistols and so on. As for finding out who he was working for, no. That was our failure.'

'And your master would have let him do his work?' Gresham asked.

'Aye, well . . . that was left rather open.'

'It would be, wouldn't it? James must be desperate for the throne of England. Elizabeth's death might be seen as simply speeding up an event that is going to happen anyway.'

'If you mean that the relative poverty of our country and the perceived wealth and splendour of England has given many of our noble families a gleam in their eye that outshines the star at the nativity, yes. And James himself would deeply love to leave the intrigue – and, aye, the threat to his own life – behind him.' Cameron paused for a moment. 'That was why I had to think long and hard before I stopped the man. In the act, as it happens.'

'You stopped him?' said Gresham, fascinated.

'We'd actually been given a date for the attempt. Except it was a week later than when the fool actually tried it. At Court. Simple, really. He planned to move forward at the start of the procession, when Elizabeth first marched from her bed chamber through the antechamber, fire a pistol at her head from the closest range and presumably back that up with a dagger. I'd been watching him for a week, and sensed something was different in him.'

'Why was there no scandal?' asked Gresham incredulously. 'Why didn't we hear about this?'

'Luck, mainly,' said Cameron. 'I grabbed him at the back of the crowd, as he was making to break through, tumbled him through an arras and an open door. I hadn't realised how much all eyes are on the Queen at moments like that. Anyway, we got away with it. Only a few guards saw the disturbance, and they were easily settled.'

'And the assassin?'

'Dead, unfortunately. He fought like the Devil, and it was him or me. Which meant we never did find out who he was working for.'

'So why did you decide to stop him?'

Cameron sighed. 'It was damned difficult. For all I knew James wanted her dead. But the truth was, the boy was Scottish. I can't help but believe that if he'd been paid by the Scots I'd have heard somehow. The father didn't know who the boy was working for, just knew he was planning to do something dreadful in England and had said goodbye to them all in a letter. He only wanted the boy's life saved. Which we failed in as well.'

Gresham said, 'But even if the boy wasn't working for the Scots no one would believe it. James would have been seen as setting up the murder, and the effect might have been to rule him out of the succession. So you decided that your King's chances of becoming King of England would actually be lessened if the murder succeeded, and so stopped it.'

'Summed up like a professional!' said Cameron. 'And then I decided that we might as well get as much advantage from the situation as possible, and told Cecil, having disposed of the body. I told him the boy was Scottish, told him how we'd heard, and was very forcible in my denial that James had any part of it. He believed me, I think. After all, the assassination would have turned people against James. Cecil told your Queen. I suspect that letter was her thanks. And possibly even a promise.'

'The promise of a throne?'

'It seems likely. You see, I'm a cynic. Most Scots are, and if you look at our history you'll see why. I think Elizabeth hates James. I think she wants him as the next King to throw her reign into glory. I think she's starting to hate her country for letting her die, and making James her heir she sees, in a perverted way, as her revenge.'

'My, my,' said Gresham. 'You are cynical, aren't you?'

'All too likely to be bloody true, though,' said Mannion. 'She's always been too much of a bloody woman. Can't make her mind up, changes it all the time when she does. It'd been all right if she'd had babies. Babies makes women stop being selfish.'

Mannion's summary of half of humanity was at least clear and simple.

'So that's why you like giving women babies so much?' asked Gresham. 'You see it as your social duty to help out womenkind?'

'Well,' said Mannion, 'you upper-class bastards – beggin' your pardon – spend enough time ensuring the line doesn't die out. You can't deny the same privilege to the working classes.'

There was a slight expression of confusion on Cameron's face. He had not heard too many interchanges between Mannion and his master before, and clearly had much to learn.

'All of which leaves the interesting question of who it was tried to kill the Queen,' said Gresham. 'The Pope? Spaniards?'

'They've tried before,' said Mannion glumly. It was common knowledge in the Court that King Philip of Spain had tried up to ten times to have the Queen killed.

'Or one of the English factions wanting to put a puppet Queen on the throne?' Gresham continued.

'Unfortunately for my credibility, you miss one other candidate out,' said Cameron. 'The Scots.'

'But you said it would be political suicide for the Scots to try and assassinate Elizabeth now,' said Gresham.

'Political suicide is what my kindred have been best at these past five hundred years,' said Cameron. 'We have nobles who can't think beyond the end of their bonnets, are even stupid enough not to see the consequences if a Scotsman murders the Queen. And some with memories of the last time one Queen murdered another. A Scottish Queen.'

'You were at Court,' said Gresham. 'Someone must have authorised that. Someone like the Queen.'

'I believe she knew of my presence. Unofficially,' said Cameron, sniffing.

'So you were the intermediary between Elizabeth and James? Placed in her Court with her consent to take that role? And when you had to go back to report to James because guards had seen you and your cover had gone, she was left with no messenger . . . which is presumably why the role descended on me.

'You'll be pleased to stay as my guest in The House,' said Gresham. Cameron started to demur, but Gresham held up his hand to silence him. 'The price of your passage is having you where I can keep an eye on you. And knowing an instant messenger is there should I need to write to King James myself. And,' Gresham continued, 'think how convenient it will be for you to keep an eye on me. And be so near to Essex.'

Cameron stayed silent. He realised this was an order, not a request.

PART 2

The Road to Ireland

CHAPTER 7

January to March, 1599
London and Ireland

Jane had bought books in her brief foray into Edinburgh. She seemed to have an instinct better than any homing pigeon for them. The journey back to England had been as idyllic as any such journey could be. The sun had shone, the wind had blown just enough to give them good speed but no scares and Gresham had found Cameron to be knowledgeable in both Italian and French poetry, as well as the works of Machiavelli. Gresham and he were careful to keep off issues relating to their mutual existence as spies, talking poetry and politics instead. Jane was buried in a book, and Mannion listened to the exchanges between Gresham and Cameron pretending not to understand. Every now and again, he would stagger the remaining crew of the *Anna* with his nautical knowledge.

The journey proved to be the calm in the middle of the storm.

They came back to an England in uproar. The Earl of Essex had been banished to the country after the Queen had boxed his ears and he, in high dudgeon, had drawn his sword on her! The fiendish rebel Tyrone was sweeping through Ireland and English bodies littered every river and every ford in Ireland! Essex was ill! Essex was dead! Essex was not dead, but seriously ill – really ill this time, not the pretend illnesses he usually contracted when the Queen was piqued with him. Essex was better! Essex had been murdered on the orders of Cecil! Essex had been called to raise and command a new army in Ireland, the army that would sweep the rebels into the sea!

'You are in total neglect of your duty!' said Jane to Gresham, standing defiantly in front of him. Things had rapidly got back to normal. 'You will not replace your steward, who is in his dotage, and you will not order repairs to The House! The result is that the roof of the west wing will collapse unless something is done soon.'

'It is my house, and I will do with it – or not do with it – as I wish!' said Gresham stingingly.

'It is something you hold in trust, as does any man who owns a great house, and you are betraying that trust!' said Jane equally vehemently.

He had been too nice to her when she was young. It never did. Treat them rough and they grew up respecting you, Gresham thought, denying the fact that every shred of his actual experience proved the contrary.

'And how about the people who will die when the roof collapses? Do you own them and their souls, as you own this House?'

'You are impertinent!' said Gresham. 'Leave my presence immediately.'

Jane gave the most skimpy of little bows, turned on her heels and left.

Gresham realised he had quite enjoyed the row. Jane's cheeks coloured and her eyes flashed when she was angry, and he liked the way her chest rose up and down.

'Me, I never went to college,' said Mannion.

'That's because they only let intelligent people in!' retorted Gresham.

'Good thing, probably,' said Mannion, undisturbed, 'cos uneducated men like me are dead stupid with words.'

'Stupid with words?' said Gresham caught off guard for the moment. 'What words?'

'Words like "impertinent", for starters,' said Mannion. 'I allus thought it meant cheeky, impudent. Never realised it meant bein' right.'

'It doesn't,' said Gresham.

'Must do,' said Mannion. 'You told 'er she were impertinent.'

'So?'

'Well, she told you as 'ow the west wing's about to fall down, and it surely is. So if she tells you, and you tells her she's being impertinent, it must mean she's right.'

Gresham felt himself deflating.

'Oh, Christ. Is the sodding building about to fall down?'

'Building ain't,' said Mannion. 'Roof is. Much the same thing when you comes to it.'

'Why do you always side with her?' asked Gresham. 'Have the pair of you got a thing going?'

'No, we haven't, as it happens,' said Mannion calmly, 'as you knows full well. She's family, ain't she, in a sort of way. I don't bed family.'

'It's about all you don't bed,' muttered Gresham.

'Jealousy'll get you nowhere,' said Mannion. 'And me, I just goes with those who're impertinent.'

'What?' said Gresham.

'Those who're impertinent.' He looked at Gresham pityingly. 'Those who're impertinent. Like what you've told me the word means. Those who're right. I mean ter say, you're a Fellow of a grand college and all that. Me, I'm just a working man. If you tells me as 'ow the meaning of impertinent is being right, who am I to argue?'

'Can we end this conversation?' asked Gresham.

'Course,' said Mannion easily. 'You're the master. You can end any conversation when you likes. In fact, you can do that a lot easier than rebuild the west wing. Which is what you'll have to do before long if you don't recognise that 'er who annoys you so much

185

is actually very impertinent when it comes to the state of that roof.'

'For God's sake! All right! Go and get someone to mend the bloody roof! And hire a new steward while you're at it! The old one's been loyal, hasn't he, even if he is ga-ga. Give him a room in the bloody attic – the west wing of course – and a pension and free food. Let's have all London feeding off me.'

'Better if she does all that,' said Mannion. 'You know, 'er that's impertinent.'

'Can't I even keep my dignity?' said Gresham.

'No,' said Mannion, 'you can't. Leastways, you can't order a new roof when you're buggering off to Ireland. And taking me with you. She can. And she'll look out to make sure they does a good job.'

Life went into hibernation over winter, the celebrations for the twelve days of Christmas a brief glittering interlude. Despite that, the Court had been a frenzy of activity following Gresham's return in September. The incredible row between Elizabeth and Essex had been patched up; Essex was widely seen as the man who would lead an early spring offensive in Ireland. Recruitment had started by October, and showed no signs of lessening off. The army for Ireland was shaping up to be the biggest land force Elizabeth had ever sent out in her name. She was not prepared to be the monarch who lost Ireland for England. For once, she even seemed willing to put her money where her thin mouth was.

Gresham had gone immediately on his return to deliver his packages to the Queen and to Robert Cecil. The Queen had been cursory, verging on dismissive, her thanks perfunctory and her whole manner that of someone whose mind was elsewhere. Cecil had been cold.

'Thank you,' he had said, fingering King James's letter but managing to hide what must have been an intense urge to open and read it. 'The Earl of Essex will in all probability lead the expedition to Ireland. You will accompany him.'

186

'And tell you if the man commanding the largest army Elizabeth has ever mustered is likely to turn it round and bring it back over the sea to conquer England and not Ireland?' asked Gresham. The incident with Elizabeth had not lessened Essex's popularity with the masses, if anything had increased it. Many at Court felt there was a very real risk in letting Essex take command of one of the largest land armies England had ever seen. In Gresham's opinion they were right.

'Precisely so,' said Cecil.

'And I do this for love, my Lord?' asked Gresham. 'Love of my greatest friends, I mean, rather than for love of the Earl of Essex?'

Cecil sniffed.

'There are consequences for you and for your closest friends if you fail me, yes,' he said. 'Those consequences have not changed. As I have said, I believe your friendship with Essex to be born out of a flagon, not out of any true meeting of minds.'

'I think the consequences have changed, my Lord,' said Gresham trying not to sound too smug, 'not least of all because there are now consequences for you as well.' Gresham had been looking forward to this for some while. He liked to be in the driving seat, and anyone not in that position with Cecil was likely to find that the alternative was to find himself under the wheels.

'How so?' said Cecil, trying not to appear interested.

'You were kind enough to give me a letter, with your own personal seal on it, to give to King James of Scotland.'

Cecil said nothing.

'As you know, it's extraordinarily difficult to make an exact forgery of a seal, particularly one produced by an expert. They can be made to look similar, but the finer lines are almost impossible to replicate exactly because they're cut by hand and each hand is slightly different. An expert will spot the difference in minutes.'

Cecil remained silent, his eyes boring into Gresham's.

'Here,' said Gresham, tossing a sealed paper in the direction of Cecil. 'I've tried to forge your seal on a number of occasions. I've used the best people, the very best people. This is the finest example I've managed.'

To all intents and purposes the seal on Gresham's letter matched that used by Cecil. Cecil strove to appear disinterested, but the colour had left his face.

'You can relax, my Lord,' said Gresham. 'It's good, I grant you, as good as money can buy, but it wouldn't fool an expert, not for long. But there's a technique for lifting an original seal off one letter and fixing it to another.'

And a devilish complex business it was, as Gresham could confirm, having witnessed its use on Cecil's letter to James.

'It works,' said Gresham confidently, 'most of the time at least. And it worked, thank God, with the letter you gave me for James. After rather a lot of effort, I was left with your seal complete and unbroken, and an opened letter.'

Cecil stayed silent.

'Congratulations, by the way. Your letter to James was excellent. Respectful, dignified, precise. An excellent refutation of two most serious accusations. But back to business. While duplicating a seal is very difficult, forging handwriting is far less so. You wrote to James in your own hand, of course. You couldn't trust it to any secretary. Your hand is a fine one, but it's College-taught, a standard script. Please open that letter. The one I passed you with the false seal on it.'

Reluctantly, slowly, Cecil reached for the letter, glanced briefly at the seal and cracked it open. The letter thus revealed was a letter in the hand of Robert Cecil. Every detail, every swirl was exact and precise. It was his own handwriting. Except that at the bottom of the page was a vast ink blot. It happened. The pot was tipped over. The quill took on board too much ink, and decided to drop it randomly on the page. How the person forging that letter must have cursed his own carelessness!

The letter, blot and all, was an effusive paean of praise for King James of Scotland, regretting bitterly the time it would take for him to inherit his rightful throne, pledging undying loyalty to him and making some terse and deeply wounding criticisms of the 'old lady' running England from a red wig.

Cecil had the grace to go really white this time.

'Did you—' he started to ask.

'Did I place your proper seal, after taking it off your actual letter, put it on a clean version of this forgery and hand it to James? No. That would have been too easy.'

'So what did you do?' asked Cecil, his voice that of the snake.

'I took your original letter, the one I'd lifted your seal off, and re-sealed it with the best forgery I had of your seal. King James of Scotland got your original letter, right enough, albeit with a false seal. As I said, the forged seal isn't perfect. But it was probably good enough to fool the King of Scotland. After all, the letter you wrote does a good job of exonerating you from blame, actually makes a strong case for your not being either a sodomite or a Devil-worshipper. Why would anyone bother to forge a letter that in all probability puts you back in King James's good books? You can relax about that at least. The King of Scotland received the letter you wrote him, as you had written it to him. The only difference was that the seal was a forgery. A forgery he is unlikely to notice.'

'And my original seal? The one you tell me you lifted off my letter? To what use did you put that?'

'Well, I had to find a *good* use for it, didn't I? It's not every day I get the chance to make a letter look as if it came from you. That went onto a fair copy of this splodged letter. Same text, more or less. Except no blot this time. The one that protests undying love for King James, deep resentment at Queen Elizabeth and sufficient treasonous comments to have you hung. If not drawn and quar-tered.'

'And its whereabouts?' asked Cecil.

'In safe keeping. A treasonous letter with an apparently unbro-ken seal. A seal that matches in *every* line and whorl your seal, because it *is* actually your seal. A treasonous letter, written in your hand. A letter which the loyal Henry Gresham was tasked to deliver, but through loyalty to the Crown refused to do so.'

Gresham paused for a moment.

'The scene is positively tear-jerking. I really don't know why someone hasn't put it in a play. This loyal servant of the Crown, the humble Sir Henry Gresham, is blackmailed by the evil Robert Cecil into taking a message to the King of Scotland. Knowing that the letter will inevitably be traitorous and disloyal, he is far too terrified to open it. Instead he uses his vast wealth to substitute it for a letter that merely protests my Lord Cecil's innocence of accusations of sodomy and Devil-worship, sealed with a hastily forged copy of my Lord's seal that only the King of Scotland would be fool or drunk enough to accept. He achieves his mission. My Lord Cecil seems happy with the delivery of the letter, and his threat to Gresham is placed at the least on hold. King James seems happy enough with what he has read. Everyone is happy. Including Henry Gresham, who of course has retained the original letter in the certainty that it is treasonous, who can produce it unopened, who now knows that the altered content is quite explosive. So Henry Gresham can now blow Robert Cecil out of the water on demand, at least while the Queen lives.'

The silence was long enough for a competent spider to have built a significant web.

'And where does this leave us?' asked Cecil. His composure never left him for long.

'Equal, I think,' said Gresham. 'You hold the mortgages on my friend's land and forged letters that will send me to the block. I now hold the equivalent on you. *Touché*.'

'And the Earl of Essex?'

Cecil was nothing if not consistent.

'I've been asked by him to go on his Irish expedition. As a captain, with my own troop. At my own expense, of course. I said yes.'

Did Cecil's expression change?

'It's quite ironic, really. You see, the dashing Earl knows I work for you, and it would flatter his ego hugely if he could seduce me into his service. You have very few secure sources of information on Essex – for all his faults, those who serve him do tend to be very loyal – and you're equally desperate for me to go with him as your spy. Well, I am going, but not in answer to your threats or to his entreaties. I'm going because I have chosen to go.'

'Why did you do so?' asked Cecil.

'Ever since I met Essex I've had this sense about him. A sense that he is a mover and shaker, a sense that he is someone who will make and change history. There are two types of people in the world: those who simply live, and those who make a difference. Essex has the power to make a difference – for better or worse. And my sense is that his time is now. And because I'm beginning to realise that what's driven me to dirty my hands in the filthy game of power is the desire to make a difference, I'm drawn to him. Have you ever watched a good swordsman at work?'

The question threw Cecil.

'Violence is the last resort of the intellectually incompetent,' he rasped as if his saliva was acid. 'I despise it as a waste of resources. Why on earth should I watch a swordsman?'

'Because if you had,' said Gresham, 'you'd see that a huge part of his skill is to go with the flow, let the weight and mass and momentum of the blade do most of his work for him. So it is with me. I'm fascinated by Essex. I'm also frightened by his power to influence people – frightened because he himself does not realise how much he can use that power for good or evil. If you wanted me to spy on Essex, all you had to do was to use my natural inclination, my fear of Essex, and for once I'd have been a willing partner, matching your very different fear. As it is, and because you chose to enlist me by a crude threat, you've lost me as an ally. I go to Ireland as a free agent who might choose to report back to you, but who is under no compunction to do so.'

'I think you lie to yourself,' said Cecil. 'I think the Earl of Essex has cast his spell over you as he has cast it over so many others. I think you are his creature.'

'Your lack of imagination catches you out. One can observe a spell without falling under it. I go to Ireland, knowingly, because Essex intrigues me. He's Icarus. He'll fly too near the sun, and it'll destroy

191

him. And I go because I care for peace in England, and his raving ambition's a threat to England. And because as I quite like him I might be able to stop him doing the stupid thing. But most of all I will go to Ireland because I can sense things happening, great, momentous things. Things that might change history. Oh, I know you see yourself as the spider, sitting at the centre of the web, controlling everything and everyone. But I tell you, there's more afoot than even you can imagine. The Earl of Essex is somehow at the heart of it all so if I am to find out what's going on, I need to be with Essex.'

Gresham left Cecil's presence a great deal happier than he had left it the last time. He had not destroyed the threat posed by Cecil, but he had offered a counter balance, and the two were now in the state of an immovable object up against an irresistible force. It was good enough. It would have to do.

'This,' said Mannion, 'is a right bugger's mix.'

One end of the Library faced out onto the Thames. The other overlooked the courtyard, where what appeared to be a minor battle was raging.

Gresham had put word about that he wished to recruit a company of men. As a result the house had been besieged since dawn. There were 'captains' in their hundreds out there, big, swaggering burly men with huge moustaches and extravagant hats whose brims nearly bridged the Thames, some of them with weather-lined faces marked by smallpox, others with battle scars, one with a huge black eye patch that seemed to make his other eye glare even more. There was a man with a wooden leg, seeming to move faster than his two-legged companions, and one with a hook instead of a left hand. Rather than the sharp end pointing back to the user, it pointed upwards in a grotesque U-shape, the better to rest the shaft of a musket on.

It was late January, and bitterly cold. Braziers had been set up in the yard and, on Gresham's orders, on the street as well, the red-hot coals roasting the fronts of those who huddled near them while the raw wind froze their backs.

Many of the men knew each other, veterans of endless campaigning in the Low Countries. They accosted each other with hollow fellowship or rich insults, their wary eyes glancing round all the time. The cold of winter held no threat for them; they were the survivors. They had overcome bad food, sweating fevers that had swept through the camps in winter, dysentery, heat and cold. They were the ones who the musket balls and the cannon balls had missed, the ones who had scrambled ashore when their transport sank off the Scheldt, the ones who had brought their mounts under control when they bolted and looked set to run straight at the enemy. It was luck, of course, more so than skill or judgement. Warfare took no account of morality, cared nothing for character, for wife or for family. The good died, the bad lived on, or the other way round. Attendance at communion before the battle was a primitive, primeval act, designed to placate an angry God just in case he did exist, to grab the luck to oneself even if it meant taking it away from someone else.

Among their number were the young ones, some dressed in the height of fashion, some in rags, second, third or fourth sons whose only inheritance would be a small annuity. Men who had been conceived as insurance in case the eldest born died young. Shuddering at the thought of a career in the Church or life as a hanger-on, they placed their faith in becoming a hanger-on to the gods of war. War offered excitement and the prospect of reward. And because they were young, they thought they were immortal, and it would be someone else who would die or be maimed. Ignoring the evidence of the older men around them, men for whom war had run its iron fingernails across the soft matter of their brains as well as their bodies, men whom war had corrupted and robbed of half their sensitivities, these young men hung around the edges of the group, the veterans deigning to notice them only if their clothing or equipment suggested they might be good for a free drink.

Gresham and Mannion chose their men finally, fifteen officers and 150 foot soldiers; it took them most of the day. A major factor was the men's kit: a rusty sword, a pistol not gleaming with oil, a leather sword belt that was torn and likely to fall off in battle, and the man was dismissed instantly. So too was anyone with a clearly new, gleaming and unused pistol which had probably been hired for the day. What Gresham and Mannion were looking for were pistols showing signs of usage, carefully oiled and cleaned. The *braggadocios* wore their pistols openly. The soldiers would even cover the wheel, flint or matchlock mechanism with a carefully cut piece of oiled canvas, to protect it from the weather. If in doubt, Gresham asked to look at the ammunition bag carried by each man. A number had no pistol balls or powder. An equal number had a few balls of different calibre, none of which fitted the gun they were carrying. The real soldiers had at least ten or twenty balls, all as perfectly round as the foundry allowed, and the true veterans would have cast the balls themselves. A misshapen ball could stick in the barrel, blowing up the gun, or simply roll out of it. The less round the ball, the less accurate its flight. As for the sword, it must show signs of use, be oiled and sharpened on one side only, and show no signs of a sudden application of the sharpening stone that morning. A blade that was lovingly tended every day revealed itself to an expert as quickly as some men can sense a virgin. Another key was the length of the blade and weight of the sword. The worst of the soldiers carried swords far too long and heavy for their size and build; carried it for show rather than for use. The true veterans matched their sword to their body mass, height and reach.

So much for the trappings. Then there was the man himself. There would be illness enough on the campaign – Ireland was riddled with a particularly virulent form of dysentry which seemed to eat up men's insides – so to take someone already ill or brewing a sickness was madness. Was the face pale from drink or a wasting sickness? How about the cough? Was the limp an honourable wound or a suppurating sore? Then there was the final and simplest check of all: did the man look you in the eye?

Gresham and Mannion made their way the short route down the Strand to Essex House where there was a level of apparent chaos that made The House look positively calm. Yet it was ordered chaos, Gresham noticed. For someone so mercurial, Essex could be a surprisingly good organiser. While he was a strange mixture, he had some good officers round him, and while his command decisions had been suspect in his few real experiences of warfare, his administration had always been surprisingly good.

They heard the Earl long before they saw him. Most of London must have heard him. He was sitting by a map-covered table and he was screaming. Not just shouting, but screaming, so carried away that spit was flying across the room from his mouth. 'God's blood!' he yelled, 'Am I to endure this? Can a man not breathe? Must I be thwarted at every move?'

None of his entourage were willing to deny him. That had always been part of Essex's problem. The loyalty he inspired was that of the Messiah to his disciples, and only Judas had disagreed with Jesus. Gelli Meyrick, over-dressed in a turquoise doublet and a hat that could have shaded most of Cheapside, was standing by the table, looking vaguely menacing with a dark scowl on his face. The Earl of Southampton was standing by Essex's side – a sensible place to be in the face of the flying spittle – and he and Gresham exchanged guarded nods. Southampton was a fey creature, with a rather languorous manner and an ivory complexion that always looked pale and damp. Gresham thought him a vicious little pimp and, on the few occasions they had met, Southampton had shown every sign of returning the feeling. It was noticeable that on his drinking and wenching bouts with Essex, Southampton had not been present. Also in the room was Sir Christopher Blount, Essex's stepfather. He was more of a mystery than Southampton. Anyone who could survive Essex's mother had to be saintly, and Blount had always struck Gresham as more straightforward than his reputation for deviousness merited.

'Good day, my Lord,' said Gresham.

Essex swung sideways to face Gresham standing in the door.

'I am tried beyond my patience!' he shouted, but this time it was a shout, not a scream.

'Why so?' said Gresham.

'The Queen has denied me, not once, but twice over! The Earl of Southampton here, who I wish to be my Master of Horse ...' Good choice, thought Gresham ironically. Southampton, the devious little prick, was about on the same level of intelligence as a horse, though not nearly so beautiful. ' . . . I am told cannot have that position, and nor will My Royal Pestilence allow Sir Christopher here a place on the Council for Ireland.'

The problem, thought Gresham, is that there is no reason whatsoever why Blount *should* have a place on the Council for Ireland, save that he was Essex's stepfather and his duties might keep him for a little longer out of the company of Essex's mother. Anyone in their right mind would want that. Essex's mother was the most dreadful person Gresham had ever met.

Essex stood up suddenly, and his stool flew back, skittering, across the room, to land with a bang against the wall.

'I am tied to my own reputation!' he shrieked again.

No one jumped up from their seats. No one had any. Essex had adopted the royal prerogative of having no one sit in his presence. It was a dangerous sign. This is not a man in control of himself, thought Gresham. This is a man driven by a demon, or perhaps by the pox. But why no other symptoms? The Earl's face was as unmarked and handsome as ever, the hair flowing without need of a wig and there was no sign of the high, prancing step forced on pox victims, who lost all sensitivity in their extremities and so could not sense where their feet were landing.

'They call on me,' the Earl ranted, 'because there is no other, yet when I go, it is to leave my enemies behind me to triumph.'

A tremendous sense of loneliness, that was something else Gresham had noticed about Essex. That and the melancholia drew them together.

'My Lord,' said Gresham, taking a deep breath, 'isn't it about time you stopped shouting? It fails to impress the men. It is not what a top commander does.' A top commander, thought Gresham, strikes poses and makes calculated speeches to win over the hearts

196

and minds of simple men, before leading them to their death.

A look of stunned disbelief swept across the faces of those in the room, not to mention that of Essex himself. People did not talk to Essex in this way, particularly when his river was in full flood. His face suddenly fell, his body slumped as if it was a corpse full of corrupt air, bloated in the sun, which had suddenly collapsed at the prick of a spear. He still had energy enough to scowl at Gresham.

'Come!' he said, imperiously. The others glared at Gresham as he went with the Earl into an inner sanctum. This fool of a man was the Earl's drinking companion! They were his officers! Gresham felt their hatred almost as a physical force beating at his body.

The back room had a bed in it. A retreat for seduction? Gresham thought not. It was a hastily erected thing, on three trestles. Interesting. Gresham wondered if it went wherever the Earl went. Why did the Earl of Essex need a bed? Was it the pox? Or was it some other illness?

Something Gresham did not wish to remember crept into his mind. There had been a Fellow at Granville College. A loud, overbearing and frequently drunk man, he let it be known that he dabbled in the black arts. Few believed him. Gresham had been forced to undertake servant duties for lack of money. It was either that or starve. He had gone into the man's room one morning thinking him gone, and only five minutes into his rudimentary cleaning had realised that the bundle of rags in the far corner was a man. It had stirred, groaned. Thinking him ill, Gresham had helped him to the bed, sat him on it.

'It takes its toll,' the Fellow had muttered, acting as if drunk but in some way that Gresham sensed not drunk at all. Confused would have been a better word, but this was a man of outstanding intelligence, one of the most fluent debaters in the College.

'What takes its toll, sir?' Gresham had asked innocently.

The Fellow had looked at him, and Gresham remembered the livid, red rings round the man's eyes. Eyes of fire. Then the man had said, 'When the cycle . . . has finished and the . . . the blood is . . . used – gone – then the . . . tiredness comes.' The man could hardly speak. He was looking not at Gresham but through him to something so endlessly dark that Gresham could not see or even conceive of it.

'What blood?' asked Gresham.

It was as if the man had suddenly woken up. He blinked once, twice, three times, even shook his head.

'Why,' he said, 'the Blood of the Lamb. The Devil has no sheep in his field. Only the young ones. Only the lambs. Now leave me.'

He had rolled over on the bed, seemed to drop into an instant sleep. The Blood of the Lamb? It was the reference to the blood of Christ in the communion service. The Devil has no sheep in his field? Troubled, for no reason he could understand, Gresham had gone to one of his few friends in College. The friend had blinked.

'Sacrifice,' he had said. 'The Devil-worshippers make live sacrifice and drink the blood after they have performed a ritual over it, a reversion of the Mass, in Greek, not in Latin.'

'They sacrifice a lamb and drink its blood?' asked Gresham. 'What wonders! I do little more when I eat rare meat. If I'm ever lucky enough to taste a lamb at all.'

'No,' said his friend, looking very discomfited. 'Not a lamb. A child.' He had refused to say more, pleading a lecture to attend despite Gresham knowing there were none scheduled for that afternoon.

Was there a circle of red round Essex's eyes? Why was there a worrying reminder of the same extraordinary tiredness the Fellow had shown all those years earlier?

The Earl's voice was on the edge of slurred. Seemingly oblivious to Gresham, he flung himself on the bed, laid full out and put his hand to his brow.

'I need you to advise me,' the Earl said suddenly, just as Gresham had persuaded himself that Essex had fallen asleep.

'As I explained, my Lord,' said Gresham, 'I've agreed to equip a company at my own expense. Should you wish to consult me, I'll come, as I've come today.'

'Why does she thwart me at every turn?' asked Essex, his voice almost a whisper. 'Why? Does the past mean so little?'

Gresham shuddered to think what the past held between Essex and Elizabeth.

'My Lord,' said Gresham, 'there's reason enough, if you but calm down.'

'Reason?'

'Of course,' said Gresham. 'The Earl of Southampton made one of the Queen's ladies-in-waiting pregnant. You know better than I Her Majesty's whims. She hates her ladies having affairs with younger men, God knows why. She hates them even more when they have babies. Perhaps it's too cruel a reminder for her of her own past, her own failure to complete a woman's duty. Yet she can no more stop the flow of sex in the Court and its inevitable result, than stem the Thames. To add insult to her injury, your friend then went and married the girl, again without her consent. He's lucky enough not to be still in the Tower. The Queen's certainly not going to give permission for him to mount anything else for a while, never mind give him command of her horse.'

And the man's a silly little idiot with no more military training than a rag doll and even less brain, whose sole idea of military service is riding around on a horse looking glorious. God knows why Essex favoured him. It was one of the endless complexities of the man.

'And as for Sir Christopher, he's a good enough soldier, but he has no links with Ireland except through your family, and he's an unashamed Catholic. I've no reason to doubt his loyalty . . .' said Gresham, thinking he had no reason to confirm it either – he suspected Blount's loyalty was to the Essex family alone – 'but Ireland is a Catholic nation ruled by Protestants. To those who don't know him, Sir Christopher is potentially one of the enemy, not one of their rulers.'

Would Essex start to froth at the mouth again?

'I am not well,' was all he said. 'Those who tax me do not realise what they take out of my poor body. I sense it within me, the illness that killed my father, the rotten inner core that can break out at any minute. My curse is to have been born fair, so that people look no further and see my real state of health.'

What a wonderful actor the Earl would have made. The problem was, he dramatised everything, turning life into a script for a play.

'I know a good doctor,' said Gresham, thinking of Stephen Perse and feeling immensely stupid once he had said it. Even Perse had limited remedies for a gross attack of self-pity.

'It is not a doctor I need,' said Essex, managing to combine a huge sigh with an equally huge sense of melodrama. Oh God, he was speaking as if reading from one of the player's scripts now. 'It is our country that needs a doctor.' He looked straight at Gresham, an unfathomable bleakness in his gaze. 'There is no doctor for my illness, and no cure.'

'In the meantime,' said Gresham, 'we can't offer the whole country a drink but we can certainly have one ourselves.' There was sweet wine on the table. Without waiting for permission, Gresham poured two glasses and offered one to the Earl.

Essex started to sit up, looking angry for a moment and then allowing his face to relax.

'You aren't like the others who serve me,' he said, rather plaintively.

'That's because I don't serve you.' said Gresham. 'I'm here by my choice. It leaves me free to say what I want to say, as distinct from what you want to hear.'

'Before you think yourself too much in charge,' said Essex, 'do you wish to know who tried to leave you at the bottom of the sea, on your recent northern trip?'

Gresham hid his annoyance. Essex had an excellent spy network. Gresham's was better, and London was a city of tongues. If Gresham had not been stuck on a boat, or had dared put Mannion ashore to start an investigation while he flogged up to Scotland, he too would have found the small man with the beard. It must have been the sailor who owned up to being 'family', the one who had leapt overboard. He must have run back to London, told his story in the taverns and walked into or been reported to someone paid by Essex. Essex had had a flying start to find the man. It would explain why Gresham's efforts had been so fruitless. The attacker must have been a prisoner of Essex's all the time. What a waste of time and money on the agents Gresham had sent out to scour London for the man.

'What even you mightn't know is that they were after you, not the messages you carried.'

Damn! How did Essex know about the messages? Or *did* he know about them? Was he just shooting in the dark, hoping to land a hit?

'I envy you your certainty,' said Gresham.

All of a sudden, this was a different Essex. He was the efficient mastermind of a complex spy network.

'Then you envy me something I don't have. The man in charge was betrayed to me by a fluke. One of the men he had trusted to sail with him, or at least hired to sail with him, owed a debt to my father. My long-dead father. Telling me that the man had sailed to attack you was his way of saying thanks and repaying the debt. That and the fact that you appeared to massacre very nearly everyone else he had hired. He was rather shocked. My informant sees you as a cross between Satan and Ghengis Khan. As for the man who hired *him*, I had him taken immediately I was given the story. Smallish, with a goatee beard and a strange hint of an accent. You wouldn't envy him. It took him ... some time to tell what he knew. What little he knew.'

'How long did you torture him, my Lord?'

'Long enough,' replied Essex, 'or so I'm told. I wasn't present in person. I find that sort of thing rather distasteful.'

Gresham saw in his mind the flickering torches on dripping stone walls, the metal heated in the furnace, the stench of red-hot iron on human flesh, the pincers, the bloody mass at the end of a man's hands, the mouth agape with blood where the teeth had been slowly, ever so slowly pulled.

Essex could never quite wait long enough. Huge impatience was the price he paid for his occasional bouts of vast energy. If he had waited, knowing Gresham was bound to be interested in what he said next, and forced Gresham to ask the next question, it would have given him a moral ascendancy. As it was, he lost patience first and spoke.

'He was most insistent that his aim was to kill you. Not to gain access to whatever packages you carried. Those interviewing him were of the opinion that it was true. They're experienced in such matters.' The narrow, watery eyes of Southampton came to Gresham's mind, and the cruel malignancy in the eyes of Gelli Meyrick.

'Men under torture say what their torturers want to hear, to stop the pain, regardless of whether or not it's the truth,' said Gresham. 'Even the Queen knows that, which is why she so rarely has men tortured.'

'That's certainly true,' said Essex conversationally. There was strength back in his voice again, though he still sounded exhausted. 'But as I said, those doing the business were convinced that in this instance it was the truth. Perhaps because they had only started on him that day. Unfortunately, they could find out no more, including who paid him and why. He killed himself.'

'That was casual of your secretary,' said Gresham.

'They were moving him from being chained to a wall, to chaining him on a table, so I understand.' Gresham noted that Essex had not denied the presence of Gelli Meyrick. 'They thought he was unconscious, let him drop to the floor and turned round for a moment to prepare the table. It gave him enough time to grab a blade that was nearby – one of the one's they had been heating up for him, in fact – and stick it under his own ribcage. He died immediately. Warmly, but immediately.'

'Well, he would, wouldn't he?' agreed Gresham.

'Now tell me about Cameron Johnstone,' said Essex, who was proving full of surprises that day.

'What do you already know?' asked Gresham.

'That he has been at Court claiming to have the ear of King James. That he has recently come from Scotland courtesy of a trip

202

on your ship. And that he has been commanded by the Queen to accompany me to Ireland, for reasons Her Divine Majesty has not seen fit to tell me.'

'He's a Scottish spy who was of use to me in Scotland, and came recommended from Northumberland,' said Gresham, 'and he masquerades as an advocate. He's spying on me and on the Court and will undoubtedly send reports back to King James on both you and on Elizabeth. Except I'm not so sure it can be called spying if you own up to it. He's attractively transparent about the whole business, and very good on Italian poetry.'

'Well,' said Essex, putting the goblet down, 'it'll make a difference to have someone spying on me for King James, bearing in mind that half my army is spying for Cecil, for Raleigh, for the Pope, for the King of Spain, for the King of France, for the Queen, or for all of them. I take it you've been able to find out no more than I about who is loyal in this army of knaves?'

'I don't think I'd tell you, my Lord, even if I had. I'd view it as my business. Unless, of course, it transpired that the plot was against you. You see, I've always valued our relationship as personal, rather than one soured by politics or anything other than a shameless interest in pleasure.'

'There's a plot against me,' said Essex. 'At the same time as you were despatched to Scotland, the Queen sent a messenger to Hardwick Hall.'

Hardwick Hall was the present residence of the Lady Arbella Stuart, resting prior to what many saw as her inevitable call to the throne.

'From which you assume what?' asked Gresham.

'That the Queen is selling her Crown,' said Essex bluntly, and the redness of rage began to rise again in his face. 'She will take the blood line of that damned woman and sell it to a foreign power. England will have a Queen in name but a King in reality. What will happen to this country if another Queen ascends the throne, tied by marriage to one of the crowned heads of Europe? What if terrible history repeats itself, and Arbella Stuart is used to legitimise the new King of Spain as King of England? What if the King of France is her choice? England conquered by a turncoat Protestant whose allegiance to his faith is based simply on the Crown of France being worth a Mass?'

'A little knowledge is a dangerous thing, my Lord,' said Gresham quietly.

'A little knowledge? What do you mean, *a little knowledge*? How can you claim to know more than I?'

The arrogance was there again. You could see this man as Icarus, full of vaulting ambition and in his heart of hearts believing that he was greater than the sun. You could also see him craving the sun's blessing, and as an arrested child desperate to do the right thing.

Gresham gazed levelly at Essex. 'Spain's plan isn't for the new King to marry Arbella. Or at least it wasn't when I last heard. Even they recognise how the memory of Mary's marriage to Philip of Spain has ruined the prospect of repeating such a thing for many years to come.'

The two men Gresham paid in the Escorial Palace reported a new outbreak of realism among those who advised the Spanish monarchy.

'The plan rather is for the Duke of Parma to ascend the throne. He has a blood claim. He's a powerful figure. He'll make a treaty that allows Protestantism to continue in England. The Spanish believe that Parma will be an ally of Spain, but be sufficiently divorced from it to justify to the English a strong, male ruler. More importantly, the plan for Parma to be next King of England has the support of the Pope.'

Essex was looking horror-struck at Gresham. There was also an element of petulance in his face. Gresham had stolen his fire.

'And how can you claim to know this? You, a mere . . . *gentleman* at Court?'

'I may be just a gentleman who is an occasional attender at Court,' said Gresham, 'but I did once offer the Duke of Parma – the present one's father – the throne of England on Elizabeth's behalf. I have . . . contacts . . . in France, in Spain, and in Rome.'

'You did what?' said Essex, aghast, disbelieving yet drawn to the sheer cheek of the idea like a moth to a flame. 'You offered the English throne to the Duke of Parma?'

'Yes,' said Gresham, 'it's long story.'

'And Elizabeth agreed to this?' asked Essex.

'No,' said Gresham. 'There was a slight problem over that, now you mention it. A slight problem that involved the Queen, Cecil, the Tower of London and being put on the rack. As I said, it's a long story.'

'What have you done in your life?' asked Essex. 'What else do you know?'

'I know the rack's bloody uncomfortable, even before they start to yank the handles!' said Gresham.

'You're the greatest fool I've ever known!' said Essex, exasperated. 'What else do you know about the present situation?'

'The King of France is actually the main contender for the hand of Arbella. He's been led a merry dance by the Queen. She's spent her whole life giving suitors for her hand a merry dance.' Careful. Essex had probably been proposing to the Queen once a month on principle for the past ten years. 'Now she's doing the same thing with the suitors for a stupid girl who has royal blood. France has high hopes for chaos on the Queen's death, chaos into which it can step. I know letters have gone to Hardwick Hall from the King of France, and that so far there's been no response. I know Elizabeth is determined to have no woman succeed her. I know the Duke of Northumberland has swung behind the candidacy of King James, on the understanding that James will allow him "to hold a Mass in a corner" and not persecute Catholics. Cecil thinks he has it all under control, playing with Spain, with France and with James, worming his way into the favours of all three of them until he makes up his mind. Elizabeth also thinks she has everything under control: believes she has Arbella under her power, and is playing her usual game of encouraging both France and Spain to think they might be granted Arbella's hand, endlessly spinning out the secret negotiations. Most of the time, I couldn't judge who the

205

Queen will anoint as her successor, if she can ever bring herself to do it. Sometimes, I think it could be the Earl of Essex she anoints, and that her anger at him is a measure of the gift she knows she might give him.'

Essex's head shot up. There it was. A distinct, red ring round both his eyes. There was a long, a very long silence.

Gresham drew a deep inward breath.

'And just as Elizabeth wants no woman to succeed her, so I believe your gorge, my Lord, rises at the prospect of any man other than yourself becoming King of England.'

'On what grounds do you say that?' asked Essex, eventually. 'And who are you saying it to?'

'I say it on the same grounds that lead me to believe Elizabeth will allow no woman to succeed her. Instinct. It rarely lets me down. You're tied to the Queen by your oath of loyalty, and tied down by your dependence on her for the majority of your income. As for who I say it to – no one else, as yet.'

There was another very long silence.

'And by the way,' added Gresham, 'I believe there is a plot against you, though not one with Arbella Stuart at its heart.'

'You tie me in tangles!' said Essex, the colour even more marked in his face. 'You are worse than the Queen! Whose is this plot? What is this plot?'

'Cecil's,' said Gresham bluntly. 'Cecil doesn't care who gets the throne, as long as he can control whoever it is. He'll never control you. Therefore what he's trying to do is very simple: he's provoking you to rebellion. He's feeding your anger, your resentment of the Queen, in the hope that you'll rebel. When you do, you'll destroy yourself, and do his job for him. Cecil wants your body in two pieces on a scaffold on Tower Hill.'

'But if I return from Ireland the victor, the people will call for me!' said Essex. 'I will be their champion. I will be ... unstoppable!'

'And Cecil knows that. But it was Cecil who was so forceful in suggesting to the Queen that you take command of the army for Ireland. What does that suggest to you?'

'That Cecil is a fool?'

'Cecil is never a fool,' said Gresham. 'He's someone who hates war. Not because of the killing and the maiming, or the suffering, but because of the cost and because war is random. Yet in this instance, he's done his research.'

Cecil had talked to several soldiers who had served in Ireland. Gresham had been intrigued when he had heard, knowing how much Cecil despised soldiers, his scorning of war and its waste. It had caused Gresham to interview those same soldiers, to get reports of the conversations they had had with Cecil.

'He believes that Ireland will defeat you. It's the biggest gamble in his political life. It's also the first time he's gambled anything on a war. He thinks the war in Ireland can't be won, and that by sending you to inevitable defeat you'll be shamed, and stake your all on a final blow, an act of rebellion.'

It was as if someone had put a dart straight into Essex's heart. He collapsed back on the bed, the redness gone from his face and replaced by a pallid sweat.

That's it, thought Gresham. You've been through this in your mind, faced up to the fact that Ireland destroyed your father, and decided that if you lose the war to make your final play for the throne! Cecil is right! You *can* be provoked to futile rebellion!

'And how can you know this?' asked Essex, his voice a whisper.

'Know it? I can't *know* it. But I know Cecil, and I know a little of you. You're passionate, impetuous, full of an outdated chivalric energy that ignores the real dirt of war. Cecil's cold-blooded, cautious, always planning in advance. If I were Cecil, I'd gamble on your losing in Ireland. It has, after all, been a bottomless pit for English military commanders, a stinking black hole that's swallowed up bodies and reputations. And the joy of it all is that he can't really lose. If you sink into the mud and the bogs of Ireland as so many others have, either you'll die as your father died or you'll come back discredited and in all probability be forced into a rash act of rebellion by your own overweening ambition.' Selective hearing. Gresham had just accused Essex of overweening ambition,

207

but it was as if he had not heard. 'But what if you win? You'll be the hero of the day and perhaps even the month, but such fame rarely lasts. Cecil will have gained all the credit with the Queen for suggesting you so strongly, and proved what a selfless adviser he is. And in your absence he can secure his power base and attack yours, packing his allies more and more into the Court.' Gresham paused for a moment. 'I tell you this, my Lord. You're in danger of becoming another victim. Not of your own vanity and ambition, with which you're well supplied. But rather of the vanity and ambition of Robert Cecil.' As many of us, including myself, stand in danger of becoming a victim of Robert Cecil, thought Gresham. 'Cecil wants you to rebel. For the first time in his life, he wishes a rebellion. Is trying to engineer it, to provoke it. He needs to do something big if he is to take over in power and influence from his father. You're being manipulated.'

'Why does no one else tell me these things?' asked Essex.

'Because they've got more sense. Because they depend on you for their livelihood. Because all great men surround themselves with people who say what they want to hear. And because though I sometimes think you're one of the biggest fools I know, and I wouldn't trust you most of the time for more than the price of a drink, you make me laugh and at least you've got a personality.'

'I'd hoped to tell you things you didn't know,' said Essex. 'Instead, you've told me things I should've thought of. If Cecil is plotting Ireland as my doom, I'd better make sure I understand the country. Hadn't I?'

There was shock on the faces of the others when Essex emerged. Quite clearly, when their master had one of his fits of passion they were used to him retiring to bed for days. Rather than welcoming his return, they seemed almost resentful of it. If one gets accustomed to dealing with a madman, the return of sanity can be as taxing as the madness itself. Systems, thought Gresham, systems. We all live by systems, learn how to cope with the idiocy of life by systems. Disrupt the system and you disrupt the person.

'You're an experienced soldier with a high reputation' said Essex to Gresham. 'Few of those close to me have such experience.' Well, that would do Gresham a lot of good with Meyrick, Blount and Southampton. 'Give us your opinion of Ireland.'

Campaigning had nearly killed Gresham, yet being a soldier was like an illness that once in one's veins could never quite be got rid of.

'I've never served in Ireland,' said Gresham, with no trace of pomp or circumstance, 'but I've talked with those who have. I'm sure you've talked to them as well. I doubt you need my pearls of wisdom.'

'Try us, *Sir* Henry.' It was the weasel Southampton. 'I am sure we are all desperate to learn from your knowledge.'

Gresham eyed Southampton with a contempt he did not seek to hide.

'I can believe you're desperate for all sorts of things you can't get,' said Gresham. 'My knowledge isn't one of them.'

Southampton could have, should have challenged him to a duel for such an insult. Instead, he snickered, a simpering, sickening little giggle.

'So . . . forthright!' said Southampton. He meant rude, of course. Then his face narrowed. 'So full of breeding! As one might expect from a man whoring his services as an informer and a spy to the highest bidder!'

The challenge hung in the air. The others in the room froze.

Gresham took off a glove, carefully tugging at each finger.

'There you have me, my Lord,' he said, in a regretful tone. He looked calmly at Southampton, and the man suddenly took a pace back. Something in Gresham's eyes chilled him, cut through even his spoilt arrogance. 'I've no breeding, whereas you have more than you can handle, I'm sure. As for the whoring bit, I'm truly a bad man of business; I give my services for free, alas. But I do have manners. And manners tell me that a gentleman responds to a challenge.'

Gresham tossed the glove towards the table. Before it could land, a hand plucked it out of mid-air. Essex's hand. Well, if he was ill it had not yet affected his reflexes.

'No,' he said. 'I will not permit this. I will have no squabbling among my allies or my friends.'

That was a little rich, coming from Essex, who had nearly torn apart the expedition to the Azores by his permanent and unreasoning feud with Sir Walter Raleigh.

'As you will, my Lord,' said Gresham easily. He and Southampton would have their day. 'But please do tell this brat of a Lord to keep inside his kennel for fear that it's he who gets bitten by something bigger, better and more dangerous.'

Southampton made as if to respond, but again caught Gresham's eye and halted with his mouth half open. It made him look even more vacuous than usual, and Gresham caught the slightest hint of a smile from Gelli Meyrick. It was not a smile of friendship, more a sharp-toothed recognition from a predator of a fellow animal that had been wounded.

'The campaign in Ireland,' said Essex. 'I wish to hear your views.'

Gresham looked round the room. Playboys. Adventurers. Blount had seen some service and was a bluff enough soldier. Outside there were some good men who would serve in Essex's army. But in here? Essex's previous military ventures had been distinguished by the tangerine livery of his men, many trumpets and the excellent playing of drums, rather than by any military success or sign of strategic planning from the commander. Brave, yes: no one could take that away from him. But a great general pays others to be brave. He is paid to command and to think. Could Essex think for long enough to get the job done? As for the rest of his crew, they were hangers-on, men like Meyrick who were excellent at terrifying tenant farmers and peasants, bullies to the core, or young, spoilt idiots like Southampton who thought war was about pretty uniforms. Oh, well . . .

'I'm sure you've heard all this before.' Essex was about to say something, but Gresham held up his hand. As he fingered the maps, Gresham seemed to grow in stature, become less of the shadowy figure of vague menace, more the commander. 'The land itself appears to be your greatest enemy. It's uneven, marshy, treacherous to foot and horse, subject to wild swings in weather, with bogs even on top of mountains. All this seems to breed a strange marsh fever. The Irish seem to be able to melt into their landscape. They've skills our soldiers haven't even begun to learn. They can shadow an army for days and give no hint of their presence, rising up out of the swamp, the bog or the grassland as if they were wraiths. So many of the ways are treacherous, fords over rivers so few, that it is folly to stray from the beaten path. Yet the Irish can find their way over bog and marsh and will adopt a favourite tactic of dropping one or two trees across a path, blocking a route, then punching in from the sides and rear, melting away if they meet fierce resistance, wiping out the party if they don't.'

'So can a campaign in Ireland ever be won?' asked Sir Christopher Blount.

'Any campaign can be won,' said Gresham. 'The Irish weakness is their lack of unity, which Tyrone is addressing; their lack of artillery, which means that forts and strongholds can be held far longer than would be the case in the rest of Europe; and their fear of our cavalry, which has always been our strongest hand in Ireland.'

'And *our* weaknesses?' It was Essex.

'The English Pale, our sphere of influence, is based in relatively few counties and is supported by English settlers. There's a host of Irish chieftains who will support whoever pays them most. Vast tracts of Ireland have never been actually conquered by us. There's a fierce patriotism in Ireland, and we've profited as we have only because so many of the Irish hate each other more than they hate us. Now they are starting to unite. England and its troops can command Dublin and some of the counties, working from castles and strongholds, while the Irish can command the countryside with their wild kerns. They can overwhelm our troops if they gather in sufficient number as they did at Yellow Ford. If they

211

receive troops and artillery from Spain in large numbers, they will be able to match us in the fixed battle and take our strongholds by siege.'

Gresham was saying nothing that was new, but a part of his heart fell as he realised from the glum expressions round the table that some of it at least was new to his listeners.

'So what would your plan be?' It must have cost Essex much, with his dreams of military glory and vision of himself as a commander, to ask that question. What did he think Ireland was? A gentle version of the Forest of Arden?

'Go for the heart of the matter. Head straight for Tyrone's base in Ulster, kill him or drive him into the countryside for ever. Tyrone is the key, England can divide and rule well enough in Ireland. It is when Ireland unites that we face defeat. Tyrone is the key to Irish unity.'

'How goes your recruiting?' asked Essex, changing the subject in his infuriating mercurial manner.

'I'll bring one hundred foot, fifty horse and fifteen officers to your command. If we have until March to train them, they'll be passable.'

'And will you join my command team?' asked Essex.

'I will not, my Lord,' said Gresham. There was the hiss of indrawn breath from someone in the room. 'I will be too busy whoring my services. But I will fight for you, and for the Queen, and fight long and hard.'

'So we're off again,' said Mannion, as they walked away from Essex House, the mud frozen on the paving that made the Strand one of London's better-favoured streets.

'Does it make you unhappy?' asked Gresham.

'No,' said Mannion. 'Seems to me life's just one fight after another, always has been, always will. If yer not fightin' people, you're fighting life. I know war's bloody horrible, and from the sound of it Ireland's worse than most. But at least out there you know who the enemy is, you know who you're fightin'. Way we lead our lives, we're spending most of the time fightin' without knowin' who it is we're fighting.'

'I suspect,' said Gresham, 'that there'll be the enemy we can't see and the enemy we can see in Ireland as well as in London.'

'Well,' said Mannion with a grin, 'we'd best get down to trainin' those buggers we've just recruited to make sure when we does get shot it's at least by an Irishman!'

'Why can't I accompany you?' asked Jane.

'Don't be monstrous!' said Gresham. 'You're a woman!'

'I'm glad you've noticed,' she said tartly. 'Mannion tells me there are literally hundreds of women who follow the army. I've shown I can be useful. In medieval times Kings used to take their wives away with them on campaign. Queen Eleanor had two of her sixteen children on campaign.'

'Good God! You're not pregnant, are you?'

'No, I am not!' said Jane, going a deep red. 'I was using it as an illustration!'

'The women who follow the army are not normal. They – they are . . .' How could Gresham explain to a young girl what the women who followed the army were?

'They are common-law wives,' said Jane, 'that's what Mannion told me.'

'They're whores!' said Gresham, desperately. 'Give them any fancy name you like, but they're whores for the comfort of the men. Many of them are . . . shared between men. I'm sorry. I can't put it any more plainly.'

Jane stood silent. It was impossible to know what she was thinking.

'Don't they cook? And wash? As well as . . . do the other thing?'

'What?'

'Well? Don't they?'

'Yes, I suppose some of them . . . look after their men, I suppose—'

'Well!' said Jane triumphantly, 'I can come as your housekeeper! I can make sure you get decent meals and clean clothes and—'

213

'Why on earth do you want to come?' asked Gresham. 'This is war, for God's sake. People will die, half of them from marsh fever! It is no place for a proper woman. It just isn't.'

'I want to come because . . . because . . .' her face went red again. 'I want to come because it gives me a role! If you leave me here . . . I'm not your wife! I'm not your mistress!' She had the grace to blush. 'I'm not even a servant! I'm a nothing! An expensive mistake who spends your money, wears the clothes you pay for, lives only through you. At least on the boat I was serving a purpose, was doing something. Here, with you and Mannion in Ireland . . . I'm nothing, doing nothing, being nothing.'

For almost the first time he felt a tinge of sympathy for her. But he had no option.

'Look, I'm sorry,' he said, and perhaps he was. 'I'll have enough to worry about with my own survival in Ireland and that of my men. If you were there I'd have to worry about you. And I'm not prepared to be the person who's responsible for your death.'

'But you don't think twice about being responsible for your own death? Or the men you take with you.'

'I know what I'm doing. So do they.'

'What if I know what I'm doing? What if it's what I want?'

'I'm sorry. Campaigning is no place for a young girl.'

There was a rebellious, angry expression on her face which carried through to the whole way she stood.

'Do you want me to be really blunt with you?'

'Aren't you always?' she retorted.

'There's no way I could guarantee to keep you a virgin on such a campaign as this is likely to be. And before you say anything' – he had seen her about to speak, to remonstrate – 'what I mean is rape. Pure, simple rape. There are men there, possibly many men, who would simply bide their time, take their chance, wait till I was out of camp. They would come to your tent – and no one I know has ever been able to lock a tent – and put a bag over your head so you couldn't identify them. Then in silence, their silence at least so you couldn't recognise their voices,

214

they'd rape you. With a rag stuffed in your mouth to drown your cries.'

That got through to her, he could see. She gave a bow, lower than her normal cursory bob, and retreated.

The odd thing was, a part of him was sorry to leave her behind.

There was a great banging and crashing down in the yard, the boom of a voice and the sound of a door being assaulted. George almost fell into the room.

'I'm coming with you!' he announced. 'Now shut up and understand one thing. I'm bored out of my mind at home, this is a great adventure and I am not, I repeat not, going to let you go to Ireland without me to keep an eye on you. Fetch the wine.'

Dear George, thought Gresham. You won't be raped, but I've just moved heaven and earth to stop Cecil from ruining you, and now you insist on coming to Ireland where a great clumsy oaf like you will be the first to get an Irish dart in his breast or catch dysentery, and so you will kill yourself after I have been to all this trouble to stop you getting killed or worse.

But in his heart of hearts he was glad.

The horses were restless, pawing at the ground and snorting, impatient to be off on the journey they sensed was imminent. There must have been fifty at least gathered in front of Essex House, and a straggling line of men and baggage carts, together with 200 men dressed in the tangerine finery of the Essex livery. They were blocking the Strand and attracting a vast crowd, all of whom had fallen silent for the prayer.

They had hoped for the Bishop of London, but he had declared himself ill. Essex's chaplain, who had the advantage over the Bishop in that he actually believed in God, read the specially written prayer. Heads bowed. Even the horses seemed to sense the occasion, and calmed down. It was so silent that the brisk wind could be heard flapping the pennants tied to the spears.

'Almighty God and most merciful Father . . .'

The chaplain's voice was thin, half blown away on the breeze.

215

The vengeful words, asking for destruction to be hurled on the heads of England's enemies, seemed more futile than threatening. The final 'Amen' rolled round the street and its close-packed houses like a subtle roll of thunder.

There was a shouted order and, led by the Earl, the mounted men wheeled round and rode for the embarkation at Chester. Old women, men and boys started to shout and cheer, a gathering crowd crying out their good wishes and blessings, an old woman with tears in her eyes at the sight of the fine Lord on his magnificent charger.

The weather seemed set fine until the party, swelled by even more hangers-on, reached the fields of Islington. There, out of nowhere, black clouds boiled up. Within seconds the fine plumes on the hats of the officers lay slicked down onto wet cloth, horses and men were drenched by the sudden downpour and large lumps of hail bounced off the track, turned instantly into mud.

The old woman who had cried at the sight of Essex had followed the slow-moving train of baggage carts, despite the evident pain in her legs. She stopped now, tears of rain dripping down her lined cheeks.

'It's an omen,' she whispered, 'an omen.'

There was no one to hear her, the driving noise of wet rain on cloth, flesh and ground drowning out all other noises except for the jingle of harness and the squelch of hooves and feet on the roadway.

CHAPTER 8

April to July, 1599
Ireland

''E can award knighthoods – and is doin' it by the sackload, as it 'appens,' said Mannion. He was referring to the Earl of Essex. ''E can proclaim someone a traitor, 'ang 'im or pardon 'im, as and when 'e wants. 'E can raise taxes – in fact, the only bloody thing 'e can't do is mint money with 'is 'ead on it.' Mannion took another bite at the chicken leg he held in his massive paw, leaving a shred of meat hanging out of his mouth as he carried on. 'And the only other bloody thing 'e can't do is decide what to do!'

The Council of Ireland had been meeting endlessly, while the army kicked its heels.

'I suppose 'e'll ask to see you again,' said Mannion. ' 'E usually does. Though God knows why, seein' as 'ow he don't show any sign of listening.'

Gresham shrugged his shoulders, and dropped off the low stone wall on which he and Mannion had been sitting. George had gone off earlier for a meal.

'He knows what I think . . .' As if on cue, a man in tangerine livery stepped out from round a corner of the castle and asked

217

Gresham if he would accompany him. At least Essex's servants were more polite than Cecil's.

Essex had moved from the Council Room to a side chamber. He was without Southampton, Blount or Meyrick, the only other person present a young page with a bruised face. Gresham had heard about that. Apparently the boy had dropped a jug of ale at supper the night before, and splashed the Earl's doublet. Essex had stood up and punched the boy, hard enough to fell him to the ground, then dragged him up by his hair, bent him over the table and thrashed him with a horsewhip. It had shocked many of the Irish there, not least because of the sudden violence of the action. The boy stood, eyes red, trying not to tremble with a jug and two simple pewter mugs on a tray. He had blond hair and pale-blue eyes.

'Pour,' said Essex, and the page did so without being able to conceal the trembling of his hands. Gresham winked at the boy, feeling sorry for him. No one ever had much time for a page. He would let the dust settle for a day and then get Mannion to take him hawking for an afternoon, give him a decent meal. It usually didn't take much to cheer up a boy like him, and his stripes would heal soon enough.

'They tell me, my Council, very different things from your advice. They say Tyrone is reinforcing rebels in the south, in Leinster and Munster. They say we need to march there and destroy these reinforcements and only then move north and attack Tyrone.'

'There's no evidence of these reinforcements, other than hearsay that could easily have come from men paid to say it. Settlers in the southern counties always stress the danger they're in, to persuade you to give them support. The sight of our army in those provinces is as important to the settlers as any battles we fight. And if Tyrone's unwise enough to reinforce those in the south, it's all the less people to fight if we meet him in his stronghold.'

Gresham was getting tired of saying the same thing over and over again.

'They say there is no transport to resupply us if we take off to the north,' said Essex, undeterred.

'They mean,' replied Gresham, 'that it's far more dangerous to resupply you in the north. They forget how an army can forage for itself, or go on hard rations for a while.'

'What think you of my new Master of Horse?' asked Essex. Had he heard Gresham's earlier replies? For all the attention he paid them Gresham might as well have spent the time mouthing silently. This was getting very boring.

'My Lord, you know what I think of the Earl of Southampton. And he, no doubt, likewise of me. I think he's a piece of shit, with the same ability to rise to the top whatever water he's in. You also know what I think about your appointing him your Master of Horse, despite a direct prohibition from the Queen. You've enough enemies, without making a further one of the person you most need as your friend. And why, oh why do you have to make so many people knights? It infuriates the Queen – and some of the people you've knighted are just plain apologies for humankind!'

Essex had awarded knighthoods in profusion, as was his habit. Gresham knew why he did it. Underneath his bravado the Earl craved popularity; this was a cheap route to it.

Essex's brow furrowed. As usual, he ignored the question he did not want to answer.

'The Queen is ill-advised, has always been ill-advised.' He looked up at Gresham. 'You know my problem? I have no *feel* for Ireland. I can't sense it, as I can sense England – its fields, its seasons, its pulse.' At times Essex looked like a little schoolboy, lost and rather forlorn. Yet this was the man who had savagely beaten a page.

'You've decided to take a large party to the southern counties,' Gresham said flatly.

'How did you know?' asked Essex.

'I guessed it a week ago. It'll let you "sense" Ireland, as you wish and need to do. It will reassure the settlers. It might allow you some easy combat to bed in the army and test the opposition. It'll

219

mean there will be rich pasture in the more barren north when you do move there after Tyrone.'

It will also let you prance ahead of your army on your fine horse and receive the cheers of the settlers as you come into their towns, thought Gresham.

'You've summed up what was said at the Council meeting admirably,' said Essex. 'And still you think I'm wrong?'

'Yes,' said Gresham. 'But when people tell you you're wrong you dig your noble heels in and become even more stubborn, and determined.'

'Your plan? What would it be?' asked Essex.

'Head for Tyrone, force him to fight or to flee. Our intelligence is that he can call on up to twenty thousand men, but they're scattered over the country. If he's sent his men to the south then he's weakened his northern force even more. Yellow River proved how good his men are. But they aren't used to formal battle. Ours are. Now is our time to strike.'

'I dare not.' There was a tone of finality in Essex's voice. 'There you have it. England's noble commander dare not head straight for his enemy. I daren't because I come here to our Irish friends as a man given command firstly only by his link with the Queen and his position as her favourite, and secondly as a man with a reputation for rash and imprudent action. Someone has done their work well,' he added darkly. 'If I'm to retain the support of my Council I have to show that I listen to them.'

It would be Cecil, Gresham knew. Ireland was divided by the English who came over when there was war to be fought or new land to be grabbed, and the resident Anglo-Irish, some of them from the Norman stock that had originally invaded the country. No power from England could be sustained in Ireland without the support of the Anglo-Irish, those who lived in Ireland, farmed its lands and had based their whole future on their continued occupancy. Someone had done a good job in advance of poisoning many of the Anglo-Irish leaders against Essex; the rumours had been spread that he was a philandering popinjay. It had all the hallmarks of

Cecil's work. Essex had worked hard to show he was a steady hand, had done well. There had been no rages, no illnesses, no retiring to his bed. The only extravagance had been the strange business with the page.

'I'd like you and your company to come with me on my expedition; to be the vanguard.'

Gresham bowed. It was an order, not a request.

George emerged from one door, wiping his mouth, as Gresham emerged from another. Mannion soon made a third and together they enjoyed the warmth of the sun in the courtyard.

'Did you mention Wallop?' asked Mannion, after Gresham briefly told them the gist of his conversation. 'Or Kildare? Or Ormonde, for that matter?'

'No,' said Gresham, 'and I'm not sure I will.'

'What about Wallop and Kildare?' asked George, confused. 'Have you been keeping secrets from me?'

'Not deliberately,' said Gresham. 'I've been doing some research. Now I have found out as much as I can, I can bring you in on it.'

'What research?' asked George.

'Sir Henry Wallop was Treasurer to the Irish Council and one of its most experienced people,' said Gresham.

'He's the one who died, didn't he, the evening we got here?' said George. 'Everyone said it was a bad omen.'

'Yes,' said Gresham, 'he did die, in agony, spewing his guts up. Mannion found out that two of his servants left the next morning, haven't been seen since.'

'What's odd about that?' asked George. 'Servants know their job goes when their master goes. They often clear off, after seeing what they can steal, of course.'

'Servants who are closely connected with preparing their master's food?' asked Gresham.

'Ah,' said George. 'I see what you mean. And Kildare? I take it you mean the Earl of Kildare?'

'Yes. Drowned in a storm in the Irish Channel. There's a strange amount of confusion surrounding the Earl's death. He was another stalwart supporter of us English, the good Earl. No one quite seems to know why he was out in the Irish Channel at the time, or understand a drowning in what one sailor described as "just a little bit of a blow". And no one seems to know for certain if he fell overboard, or even if his ship sank, or what. There's a rumour on the quayside that he was pushed.'

'Rumours on the quayside!' scoffed George.

'Perhaps,' said Gresham, 'but isn't it odd that two of the steadiest and wisest people in Ireland are suddenly out of the way — permanently — when the new Lord Lieutenant arrives? And then the wisest of the lot, the Earl of Ormonde, gets called away just when the Council is deciding whether to hit Tyrone in his lair, or go gallivanting off to the counties we already control for a beauty parade?'

'Well,' said George, 'these things happen. Trouble at home, trouble with the estate . . .'

'It'll be interesting to see when Ormonde returns whether or not the summons was genuine, won't it?' asked Gresham.

'Look, dear boy,' said George in his most annoying avuncular manner, 'are you sure you're not seeing conspiracy under every bed? I know I was the one trying to warn you in London about plots and plotting, but here in Ireland — surely it's simpler here?'

'Could it be as simple as Cecil trying to guarantee the failure of this expedition?' asked Gresham bluntly. 'Thereby helping to destroy Essex and his reputation? And since this army will undoubtedly fight at some time or other, and Essex will undoubtedly be unable to keep out of the fighting, and commanders in Ireland have an unfortunate habit of being killed in action or dying in agony in their beds, what might you do if you were Cecil, and wanted to destroy your chief rival for good?'

There was a long silence. George, subdued at last, spoke to his booted feet. 'I'd have Essex killed,' he said, in what was almost a whisper.

'Precisely!' said Gresham. 'Best way? Bribe one of our men to "accidentally" fire a ball into his back in the heat of action. Friendly fire. Happens all the time. The great hero killed in action, falling as he would have wished in action facing the enemies of his Queen! It would probably never even come out that he had been shot by one of his own men. Get rid of Essex while he's safely out of the country, give him a magnificent state funeral to make the mob feel better. Back-up plan? Have him poisoned. Less glamorous for Essex, same result for Cecil. Oh, and take all the right people out or away to ensure the campaign's a failure.'

George was refusing to look at Gresham.

'Come on, George. Spit it out!'

'Henry . . .' he started clumsily. He hardly ever used Gresham's first name. 'Is . . . is this your way of telling me that Cecil has ordered you to kill Essex?'

Gresham looked aghast. 'Me? Kill Essex? Of course not, you great booby! Exactly the opposite in fact. I came to *protect* Essex!'

George smiled thinly, wanting to be convinced.

'Summat else you must 'ave worked out,' broke in Mannion. 'If Cecil wants 'im dead, he'll most likely 'ave to kill you too, gamble on finding that letter you forged before it did any 'arm. And if he wants this campaign to fail, 'e's gonna go for you on that score as well, seein' as 'ow you're the only person talkin' military sense to 'im.'

George looked at them both.

'So we assume that even now someone paid by Cecil is out there looking to kill you *and* Essex?'

'Seems reasonable,' said Gresham casually.

'And you knew that before you agreed to come out here?' asked George disbelievingly.

'Why else do you think I came?'

There was a long silence.

'I've been doing some research on Tyrone as well,' Gresham broke the silence. 'Do you know the one word that comes out time and time again when people talk about him? Dissembler.'

'Educated in England wasn't he?' asked George, trying to gather his thoughts. His knowledge of Irish history was sketchy. George had spent most of his time in Dublin writing letters home. Whatever the problem was with his estates, it was taking up more and more of his time.

'Not only educated there, but seen as an Irish lord friendly to England. Even had some of his troops trained by us, knows our military tactics inside out. Fell out with Elizabeth when he was made one of Ireland's top chiefs and had to choose between supporting one of his family arrested by us or sticking with us. He chose family – not that he had much choice. His own lot would have skewered him if he hadn't. But everyone who knows him speaks of his charm, his intelligence – and his total and utter unreliability. This man lies like you and I have a piss – it's the most natural thing we do, and something would go wrong with our day if we don't do it regularly and frequently.'

'So?' said George.

'So we're being outmanoeuvred,' said Gresham, 'by someone who's as much English as Irish. Tyrone's sending us exactly where he wants us to go.'

'Will Tyrone kill Essex? If Cecil can do it, surely Tyrone can,' asked George.

'He won't 'ave to, at this rate,' muttered Mannion. 'If Essex goes off gallivanting all over Ireland in the opposite direction to this bastard Tyrone, 'e'll either kill 'imself or make the fuckin' Queen do it for 'im. I reckon if she don't get Tyrone's head, she'll want the Earl's.'

In early May Essex marched out with 300 horse and 3,000 foot. It was all he had left after reinforcing garrisons and positions in the rest of Ireland. The rather tawdry little castle at Athy had surrendered after firing a few token musket shots, and the old Earl of Ormonde had arrived at last bringing 700 foot and 200 Irish cavalry along with him, as well as the Lords Cahir and Mountgarret, both of whom had dabbled with the rebels, and now, in the most theatrical manner possible, begged forgiveness of Essex, who loved every minute of it.

Gervase Markham, one of Essex's young bloods, rode up to the head of the column, where Gresham was riding with Mannion and George at the head of seventy of his men and twenty-five of his horse.

'Sir Henry!' Markham called out. 'My Lord of Essex seeks your company!'

'Does he want me to write a victory sonnet?' asked Gresham.

Essex was sitting on a glorious grey, looking for all the world like a young god. Southampton rode by his side, instead of with the horse he was meant to be master of, looking like a sour lemon with mould on its skin.

'I see you copy my horse,' said Essex. Gresham was riding a fine grey.

In London, Gresham would have replied that Essex copied *his* horse. Here, in Ireland, on campaign, he said nothing to his Commander in Chief.

'I need to draw the enemy out, give them a challenge they can't back away from,' Essex said. 'How many men do you have with you?'

'Seventy foot, my Lord, and twenty-five horse.'

'I am heading to the Pass of Cashel. You know of it?'

'I know it on a map,' said Gresham.

'It's ready made for ambush, I'm told. There are rough woods and bogs on either side of the roadway, excellent cover for the enemy yet providing a barrier on either side that we'd be ill-advised to try and cross.'

Essex reined in and looked at Gresham.

'I propose to invite the Irish to ambush us at the Pass of Cashel. I'll swing the army round with much noise and sounding of trumpets, take the road that leads only to Cashel. We'll delay subtly in our advance, so that those who're undoubtedly spying on us even now can ride or run ahead and gather a suitable force, if such a one exists.'

Gresham said nothing.

'Do you understand?' asked Essex. His horse was restless, as if sensing his rider's mood. 'I must see how great a force the enemy can muster, see how they fight, draw them into conflict.'

'And if they muster a large force, as at Yellow Ford? If they fight as well as the Irish appear to have fought there, beating over three thousand English troops?'

'That's where I need you.'

'Sir?'

'You've some of the best-trained and equipped troops in the army. I wish you to act as an advance party. Go to the pass ahead of the main army. Draw the enemy fire, allow me to gauge their strength, so that I know whether to attack with all my force or, if the enemy are too strong, retire before any proper ambush can be enacted.'

'What if the Irish read your mind,' asked Gresham, 'and hold their fire?'

'You're the experienced soldier,' said Essex. 'You must ensure they don't do so. Your force is large and threatening enough, I believe, to draw them out to reveal their full strength. Of course, if you're afraid I shall ask someone else. Or do it myself.'

It was the crowning insult, the one no gentleman could forgive. It had come out of the blue, shocking, unexpected and above all, unfair. The only saving grace was that none of Essex's other commanders were near enough to hear. Essex and Gresham had drawn away from the column and the slow-moving army moved on ponderously by their side.

'Of course I'm afraid,' said Gresham witheringly. 'Only fools feel no fear, and brave men are those who carry on despite it. But, my Lord, if you call me coward again, I'll kill you.'

He said it so simply that for a moment a listener might have let it pass by, before he realised not only that Gresham meant every word, but that Essex believed him.

'So be it,' said Essex. 'But if I call you it again, it'll be because you've failed me at Cashel, and if you've failed me there the Irish will have killed you long before you can kill me.'

*

Mannion was less than enthusiastic at the news Gresham brought.

'"Act as an advance party"?' exclaimed Mannion. 'Fuck me! This ain't no advance party! This is a fuckin' suicide party!'

'Is he testing you?' asked George, worried more for his friend than for himself. 'Is this him seeing whether, when the crunch comes, you'll fight for him, or whether your priority here is to stay alive and spy on him for Cecil?'

'It could be,' said Gresham, 'or it could be that he wants me dead.'

'What?' said George.

'I didn't just come here to protect Essex. I came here because I sensed, have sensed for months that terrible things are brewing, plots within plots, wheels within wheels, twistings and turnings. And that in some way I still don't understand, Essex is at the heart of it all. It's entirely possible I've misread the whole situation. Suppose Essex just wants a few easy victories to boost his image. Then he'll return to England and either blackmail Elizabeth into giving him Chief Secretary on the back of his popularity, or go for broke, lead a rebellion and either make himself King or marry one of his sycophants off to Arbella Stuart. In either case he either rules himself or rules by proxy, and he knows I'll stop him. This is a brilliant way to kill me with no blame attaching to him at all, and no suspicion.'

'I read the Bible once,' said Mannion. The interjection was so unexpected that George gaped at him. 'Bloody difficult it was, too. King David fancied this woman, didn't he, and sent out 'er husband – Uriah the Hittite, warn't it? Daft name – to the front line so 'e'd get killed and King David could 'ave the wife.'

'The difference,' said Gresham patiently, 'is that I'm not married.'

'No, but 'e don't half fancy Jane, don't 'e?' said Mannion. 'With you out of the way, she might be best off 'opping into bed wi' 'im. Better than bein' out on the streets.'

'I've left her money,' said Gresham, 'if I die. Leave the thinking to me, will you? If Essex wants me dead, it's not because he wants to bed Jane. It's because I might stop him doing what he wants to do.'

227

'Or it might be that we've got the best bloody company in the army to do it,' said Mannion.

'Well,' said Gresham, 'let's get them together and see if that's true.'

'We've got a little job to do,' said Gresham with the men gathered round him.

Gresham had asked to keep his men hidden in the centre of the column until their dash out. He had no desire for the Irish to guess his intentions, or see what some of his horsemen carried on their saddles, nor did he want his men picked off by Irish marksmen before the battle itself. He, Mannion, George and the three sergeants rode to the front of the column, still quite a long way from the start of the pass, but with much of its length visible.

'Round that bend, there,' said Gresham, pointing, 'that's where they'll drop the barricade. Trees, I guess, probably lashed together lengthwise so the whole thing can only move as one. Right. We know what we've got to do.'

It was uncanny, the way the same feeling always came over him before battle. It started with him seeming to go cold, yet not with a cold that would ever provoke a shiver. His sight became sharper, his senses peaked so he could smell every nuance on the wind, hear every twig crack. Doubts, fears, uncertainties – all started to erode, until all that was left was a single-minded, ruthless vision.

There was a shouted order, and trumpets blared. The column staggered to a halt, just as it would if a commander had suddenly sensed the chance of an ambush ahead of him and needed to take time to assess the situation. The road itself was firm enough, but Essex's Irish horseboys had told him the truth. On either side of the pass was a boggy, rough terrain, bordered by thick woodland that could conceal a whole army. The woodland was in musket range, just, or the range of a man throwing the short spears or 'darts' favoured by the Irish.

Suddenly Gresham's seventy foot soldiers emerged from the middle of the column. They had taken off their heavy coats, were in their shirts, to the amusement and laughter of the rest of the army. Forty of them had muskets in their hands, the other thirty swords and bucklers, with muskets slung securely over their shoulders. They were jogging, moving surprisingly fast over the stony ground of the road, faces set in fierce determination, breath starting to come hard. The men looked lean, wiry. Gresham had trained them well.

'There!' said Gresham, at the head of the column. Shadowy figures had risen up from the very edge of the woodland, sunk down again quickly as if to a warning order. But it had been enough. Gresham looked at Mannion.

'Good fifty or so on each side. Mebbe more.'

Gresham nodded. The timing was crucial. The rebels would have their musketeers close by the trees. The heavy weapons would slow them down, make it harder for them to melt back into the trees unless they were close. The advance party would turn the corner, meet the barricade, stop in some confusion, probably detach some men to try and shift it. The Irish would choose their moment to fire on them, perhaps only a third of them, to give the impression they were a smaller force. They would hope to knock out five or six men, no more at that range. The English would falter, then form up to return fire. A few Irish would show themselves, at extreme range, invite fire. The Irish would wait until the first volley, then their sword and spear men would rise up from the ditches in which they had been hiding, closer than the musketeers, hurl their darts and rush in while the men were fumbling with the clumsy muskets, reloading.

Fire. Ground the musket. Ram a charge of powder down the muzzle, hoping there was no smouldering powder left in the barrel, in which case the new charge would ignite and blow your face off. Ram a piece of wadding down on top of the powder. Take out the ball, ram that down hard. Raise the musket. Pour the priming charge, check the firing mechanism. Fire. It took an agonising time, with wild, mud-coated and half naked savages leaping down the hillside towards you.

With any luck, it would seem to the Irish as if they were about to overwhelm the advance guard. The rest of the English column would be drawn in, ordered on. The Pass was the only way forward. To encourage the English to advance into the Pass, men would suddenly appear from the rear of the column, and on either side, opening fire or hurling their darts before vanishing into the turf. There would be some panic and confusion, no room to spread out on the treacherous ground, the army being pushed forward into the defile, still blocked by the trees lain over it and cunningly tied together. It was a technique the Irish were very fond of using.

Well, thought Gresham grimly, let's see if we can rewrite the script.

His men were about to round the corner, where he had gambled they would meet the barricade of trees. There! Two pistol shots in quick succession, followed by two more. Blanks, double-loaded with powder but with no ball in the barrel. A louder noise than a simple pistol shot. Unmistakable. It was the pre-arranged signal. The barrier was there, as predicted.

A trumpet blared, and Gresham and his twenty-five horse rode out at the gallop, scattering stones and earth as they went. It was a warm, muggy day, a thin layer of cloud or mist over the sun, no wind to move anything. The clattering of the hooves seemed to hang in the air, motionless. Ahead of them rode six Irish horseboys, local recruits whose loyalty had been shown in previous encounters. Great, unwieldy bundles were strapped to their horses' sides; bundles of faggots. Like those used to burn heretics. Gresham, George, Mannion and his three sergeants held smaller bundles tied by a single rope to their saddles. And on the other side, smouldering slow fuses.

As if on cue, a number of Irish emerged from the edge of the wood, advanced a few paces and either knelt to rest their muskets on top of a convenient mound, or drove sticks into the soft earth with a Y-fork at the top on which to rest the heavy barrel. The trumpet blast caught them unawares, the sight of the horsemen giving most of them cause for pause. By the time the Irish realised that the ground was too rough for the cavalry to attack them, Gresham's foot soldiers had jumped into the ditches, largely dry now, that ran along each side of the road. Resting their muskets on the front edge of the ditch, twenty men lined each ditch.

The Irish muskets were confused. They had expected to see the advance party milling around in the middle of the roadway, firing off at a virtually unseen enemy almost at random. Forty men dropping in disciplined style into the ditch, half hidden with not a shot yet fired, was not part of the plan, any more than thirty swordsmen dropping in behind them. There were a few, desultory shots from the edge of the woodland, no more. The English were hardly visible. Puffs of smoke hung motionless for a moment on the edge of the woods.

Gresham and his horsemen had only their speed as their protection. They rode pell-mell at the barricade. Every shock as his horse's hooves hit the ground was transmitted into Gresham's body. A wild, heady excitement took him over, the cold of combat being replaced by a fierce fire that seemed to rise from his stomach. He had seen men hit who were in this state, men who had ridden on unaware of the blood streaming from them. He was yelling now, screaming, as were his other horsemen, the dust and the noise incredible. Some of the Irish chose them as the better target. Every time a plume of smoke showed the whereabouts of an Irish marksman, at least two of the English muskets would crack out, aiming at the source of the shot. One of the horses faltered, but picked up and rode on. It had been nicked, no more. At that range a serious hit, particularly when the ball was losing momentum, would be more luck than judgement. Gresham felt his own horse stagger, tensed himself for the fall, but it too picked up and drove on, every sinew and muscle straining. There were one, two shots from the English side.

The horseboys stuck their slow fuses into the heart of the pile of faggots roped to each horse, and with a wild cry stood up in their stirrups, cut through the rope with a wild slash of the knife and hurled the faggots over the heads of the men in the ditch into the woods. For a few seconds, the piles hung in the air, and then with a whoosh of flame they ignited. Oil-soaked in the middle, the outer layers were damp and thick smoke started to pour from them. One horseboy suddenly crumpled like a shot bird, caught by a lucky musket ball. His horse panicked, reared up, dragging the dead body of its rider along the ground, the man's head bouncing obscenely up and down on the stones, a mass of blood and torn skin. The horse crashed into the barrier of trees, swung round and galloped back up the pass, leaving its rider draped across the dead branches like an offering at a sylvan altar. A thick pall of smoke hung now over the barricade, robbing Irish and English alike of their targets. There was just enough visibility to see the English horsemen arrive at the barricade, two or three tree trunks lashed together and laid right across the road. It was too high to leap, the great branches sticking up like the masts of a ship; the greenery of the leaves telling how recently the trees had been felled.

Gresham and five others reached the barricade, took their packages and jammed them hard under one of the tree trunks. As they did so, the other horsemen flung the heavy canvas coverings off the grappling hooks they had been carrying, threw them over the bulk of the same tree, yanked them tight and then rode back paying out long lengths of rope as they did so. The twelve charges of powder Gresham and the others had laid under the great trunk went off almost together; the fuses had been kept deliberately short. The force of the explosion lifted the great lump of wood several feet into the air. When the smoke and dust settled, it had been split in two. The horses had reared and bucked savagely at the explosions, but the hours spent training them to cope with noise paid off and none bolted. Their riders took the strain on the ropes, and dug in their spurs. With a great, grinding roar the two pieces of the once-great tree separated even further, leaving a clear gap in the road. There was a two-foot crater where the powder had bitten most hard.

Forty or fifty Irish on either side of the road, confused by the roar of twelve almost simultaneous explosions, rose from the rough ground in front of the woodland where they had lain hidden armed with swords or short spears, one or two with bows. The wisdom of where the English had gone to ground now became clear. Far enough away from the explosions to be unharmed by them, they had also for the most part held their fire. A rattling volley crashed out from the men on either side. Five, six of the Irish were flung back by the impact of a musket ball on their bodies, human flesh punched into rag doll. Seemingly uncertain, the Irish began to edge forward to muster a charge when, in what seemed an incredibly short space of time, a second, ragged volley came from the English, equally accurate.

A trumpet blared from back up the road, and the English column started to advance on the now cleared road. The remaining Irish hesitated for a moment, then with more and more flitting round the edge of the woodland they began to fall back. It was clear that, though they knew the terrain, they were finding the boggy ground on either side of the road difficult. More and more left it to join the hard surface of the road fifty or so yards beyond the broken barricade. The advancing English army were round the corner now. The cheer that went up at the sight of the opened pass was replaced by a more bloody roar, as the men saw the Irish scuttling back along the road in retreat. Uncontrollably, a mass of horses leapt forward from the column, swept down the road in pursuit of the Irish. Many of them were the young bloods Essex had recruited, wearing outrageously plumed hats that were no match for a full gallop, and which caught the wind like sails. Gresham and his troops had reined in, were standing by the side of the road. They let the horsemen thunder by in their vain pursuit – the Irish would melt back into the surrounding terrain and leave the road the minute they realised they were being pursued, and the ground was too treacherous for the horses to follow. As the dust of their passage settled, and before the main body of foot drew up, Gresham looked down and saw three or four fine hats lying in the dust, their high plumes sadly bent and broken.

'The Pass of Plumes,' he muttered and felt the stinging pain behind his eyes that always came after action. Essex rode up to him, hard. Clearly he had wanted to ride off with his young men, chase and cut the Irish down. A lone musket shot from down the road and the agonised whinny of a horse showed the folly of what the young men had done. They would turn about soon enough, when the initial excitement wore off and they realised they could be picked off one by one by hidden marksmen.

'A victory!' said Essex. 'Revenge for the Yellow Ford!'

Two and a half thousand men had died on the English side at the massacre of Yellow Ford. Here there were fifteen, perhaps sixteen Irish corpses. The body of Essex's horseboy lay draped over what was left of the barricade. One of Gresham's men had caught a musket ball in the mouth but had had the decency to fall unconscious and would be dead within the half hour, his face smashed to a pulp. A victory.

'Is it a victory from which we can claim to have learnt a great deal, my Lord?' asked Gresham, trying to keep the irony out of his voice. The pain was tightening now, sending hot needles into his eyes and down the whole side of his face. He yearned for darkness and a cold compress on his head.

'We've learnt that the Irish will run if they meet a foe of sufficient determination. Your men did well.' Essex looked carefully at Gresham, perhaps disappointed by his flat response. 'I'm grateful. Truly grateful. More perhaps than you might realise. I'll go and tell your men what I've just told you.' With that, he hauled his horse round, and galloped off to where Gresham's men were climbing out of the ditches. Essex sat beautifully on a horse. The men gathered round him, and after a few words Gresham heard cheers and huzzahs thinly on the air. The fools. Yet it was no more than he would have done, and his time to say well done to his men would come.

Mannion tapped him on the shoulder. Gresham turned and looked round. He was wearing a padded coat for riding, deliberately loose fitting, its tail flapping behind him on the saddle. A neat hole had cut through the cloth where the coat had ridden out behind him at full gallop. An inch further forward and it would have smashed into the small of Gresham's back, pulverising his spine. Mannion had not finished. He leant forward, started to yank the strap off the saddlebag on Gresham's horse. It sat just behind his kneecap. A ragged hole had been torn in the leather. Mannion withdrew something from the bag. A flattened lead ball lay snugly cut into the cover of a book, where it had come to rest. *The Revenger's Tragedy*. With both shots the marksmen had allowed just a little too much for Gresham's speed, placed the ball a few inches behind where it should have gone.

'I think what we might 'ave learnt,' said Mannion, tossing the book to Gresham, 'is that the Irish have some fuckin' good shots. It ain't bad to hit a horseman at full gallop from that range, not bad by 'alf. Can't 'ave bin more than a dozen shots fired at us. That's bloody good shootin'. And they knew enough to pick out the officer, too.'

Something in Mannion's tone cut through Gresham's tiredness.

'You telling me this isn't an Irish ball?'

'I'm telling you. And I saw who it was fired it at you. Two of 'em, I reckon. One fired at the Irish, took everyone's attention. Other bugger swung round at you. Bloody good shot, too.'

As the excitement drained from Gresham the double reaction – to action and to a separate attempt on his own life – set in. He pulled gently on the reins, and his horse, which had been vaguely poking at some grass, ambled off under his lethargic control to where his men stood, Essex just having ridden off to lead the main column through the broken barricade. They cheered as Gresham reached them, grinned at him, and he leant forward out of the saddle, slapping hands and occasionally grasping and shaking one. They had reloaded their muskets, he noted, before mounting their celebration, so if more Irish had risen up from the woods behind them they would have at least received one full volley before their charge. That was good. That was training.

He noticed a bare leg sticking up over the side of a mound, some ten or twenty yards beyond the ditch. Leaping lightly from his horse, he handed the reins to a soldier, and picked his way to where the Irish body lay. The ground was littered with huge tussocks, soft marsh between each one; he felt the earth sucking at his boots.

''Ere,' said Mannion, catching him up. 'You sure about this? It only needs one man in those woods . . .'

Gresham said nothing. He needed to see the enemy. He reached the figure, pathetic now in death. He was a young man, perhaps not even sixteen. He wore a ragged shirt and some sort of pantaloons that looked as if they could have been made of canvas, with something that looked like a woollen plaid over one shoulder. Knitted and spun by a mother? By a lover? Even by a wife? The musket ball had caught him full over the heart, smashed into his chest. Death must have been instant. He had long, straight legs, at his age more like a woman's than a man's. They were muddy, scarred with scratches from brambles or thorns. He had no shoes, but the sole of the foot that was sticking up had hard, brown skin on it that Gresham suspected was tougher than any leather. The boy's face had a strange innocence, and though his lips were drawn back in a grimace of pain – or was it hate? – one could see how good-looking he had once been. The body was filthy, the boy's hair sticking out in spikes and also covered in mud – a smear of mud across his face. Foul living? Or disguise? A disguise that broke up the whiteness and the symmetry of his face, a disguise that covered him not just with the earth but the smells of the earth, so that the human smell a horse or dog might sense was battened over and covered?

Something glittered. Gresham knelt down, and saw that round the boy's neck, mostly covered by the plaid that had been thrown up round it by his fall, was a silver decoration. He moved the material gently to one side. It was thin, fragile, a thing of rare beauty, with tiny, intricate interwoven designs. Was he a chieftain's son, this young man? Sent out on his first foray to test his manhood. He had no musket by his side, merely a quiver of the darts the Irish favoured and a sword, workmanlike but with no decoration to it. Youth. He had moved forward too close to the enemy, and paid the

236

price for his courage. Perhaps he had wanted to show the other men that he was not afraid, not knowing that all men knew fear.

'Don't move! Stay down!' Mannion hissed at him urgently. Gresham looked up.

A man was standing at the very edge of the woods. Tall, middle-aged, he had the wild beard and hair of the Irish, the same mud-stained appearance. He held a musket, pointing it straight at Gresham. It rested on nothing, no stick or mound, and the barrel was rock steady. Whoever this man was he had muscles of steel.

A wave of tiredness came over Gresham. It was his own folly that had taken him off the road within musket range of this wild man; his own folly that had made him stay by the body. He looked up at the man. Who cared? Would the world cease because this boy had been torn uselessly out of life? Would the world change when the musket ball tore into his own heart? Would death be like the longest sleep possible, pure oblivion and an end to terror and trial? But then there were the dreams. Who could know what the dreams might be?

Very carefully, aware all the time of the musket pointed at him, Gresham straightened the boy's legs before they froze in death at their grotesque angle. It was always a kindness; it saved someone the unpleasant task of breaking the corpse's legs to straighten them out. He laid the plaid carefully over the broad shoulders and exposed the silver ornament to the thin sunlight only now starting to creep out from behind the clouds. He cleared the clotted hair from the boy's face, folded his arms across his chest, closed his staring eyes. And stood up.

He looked across the void into the eyes of the man pointing the gun at him. For once, he did not feel fear. It was always going to happen like this, wasn't it? On some God-forsaken field in the Low Countries, in a back alley in London or in a palace in France. It could have happened so many times before, when the galleys had chased him at Cadiz, when Drake had shot at him, when the Armada had so nearly ground itself, at Tantallon Castle, in the Tower of London. So many times, so many escapes, each one chipping a tiny part off his soul, each one shrieking the question why. Why bother? Why go through this dance to the nonsense of time? To what end? To what purpose? So it happened by a pass that no one had heard of, after the most feeble of little victories. So be it.

He smiled a thin smile at the man, and turned to face him full on, dropping his hands to his side.

'Jesus!' he heard Mannion mutter beside him.

There was a rustle from behind him. His men had seen what was happening, were scrambling to join him. Though he could not see them, he could imagine numbers of them gauging the distance, deciding whether a shot at extreme range might be worth it. Slowly he held out his hand, never taking his gaze from the man with the musket, palm up, in the unmistakable gesture that says no. Do nothing.

The man waited an eternity, the barrel rock steady. Then, quite clearly, Gresham saw him nod. He let the musket drop, butt first, turned on his heels. And vanished into the woods.

'Fuckin' 'ell!' said Mannion. 'He came out o' nowhere, just as you started to finger that necklace thing. 'Ad 'is musket up before I could move.'

'He thought I was going to steal the necklace,' said Gresham. 'Thought I was a grave robber, a battlefield scavenger.'

'Why didn't he fuckin' shoot you anyway?'

'He was sending me a message.' Two of his men had reached him now, puffing and perspiring; four or five others were just behind him.

'If you're going to climb through these tussocks and this bog with your musket at full cock we'll lose more men from friendly fire than we ever do from Irish,' said Gresham with total calm.

The first man looked open-mouthed at Gresham, then almost comically down at his musket. With a shame-faced grin, he hooked his thumb over the hammer, let it click forward so that it was on safe. The story would go down in the books of course, though that was not why Gresham had said what he said.

238

There was Gresham, doin' the funeral rights over some Irish bastard, and up pops this savage, few feet away he was, and points 'is musket at him. Old Gresham e' don't even flicker. He carries on laying out the Irish bastard's limbs, like 'e were 'is mother, and then stands up. Stands up, I tell you! Not only stands, but turns and faces the bastard. Then 'e 'olds his 'and up, clear as daylight, tellin' us who're rushin' in to 'elp not to fire. An' they stand an' look at each other for Gawd knows 'ow long. And they nod at each other. I'm not kidding you – 'ere, pass the jug – they nods at each other. And the Irish bastard, 'e shoulders arms and fuckin' vanishes into nowhere, like these Irish bastards do, and Gresham, he turns round cool as a cucumber and tells me orf for 'avin' me musket at full cock! Would you believe it?

They would believe it, and embellish it, and men would look at him and think of it every time they saw him.

'It really doesn't matter, you know,' said Gresham to Mannion, when they were back on the road and out of earshot. 'None of it matters at all.' Yet by recognising it, he suddenly felt more free than he had for years. The pain in his head was lifting, and he had enough strength left to grin to himself. Something had changed within him when the wild man with the musket had nodded briefly at him.

A number of Essex's officers, mostly the younger ones and some of those who by now had returned from their vain chase, came up to clap him on the shoulder and shake his hand. Cameron Johnstone, increasingly seen alongside Essex's cronies, was hanging round at the back of the crowd. He was wearing what he called his campaigning garb, a coat even longer than Gresham's and fiercely clean white linen. When asked, he said simply that one had to keep up civilised standards.

'Thank you,' said Gresham.

'What for?' said Cameron. 'I very clearly didn't involve myself in your heroic charge. Unlike yourself, if I'm going to die, I'd like it to be on a matter of some significance.'

'You think this campaign is of no significance?' asked Gresham.

'I think its outcome will be of no significance. As a campaign, that is. Your leader has taken us off on a wild-goose chase, your recent so-called victory was in fact nothing more than a minor skirmish in which the Irish proved that they have refined running away to a proper military virtue. And I'm afraid the effect of this rather petty little victory on Essex won't be good. It's the idea of fighting that he's in love with. He's out of touch with the reality.'

'I still owe you thanks,' said Gresham, 'for the explosives.'

'Why?' said Cameron. 'You knew before I told you that gunpowder is far more effective if the force of the explosion is channelled. After all, that's only what a gun or cannon barrel does.'

'Yes,' said Gresham. 'But I hadn't thought of how to channel it. You gave me the idea of using a helmet, so all the force went upwards into the trunk.'

'Using a troop of horsemen to pull aside the trunk would probably have done it,' said Cameron generously. 'For some reason no one seems to have thought of that in Ireland before.'

Cameron touched his hand to his hat, and rode off. Gresham realised how much the gallop had bruised him, and gingerly started to rub his arms and legs. He took the copy of the play and, using his thumb, eased the musket ball out of the cover, stuffing the damaged book back into his saddlebag. His horse whinnied, jerked its head up and down three times, impatient to be off.

'Hold there, hold,' said Gresham, reaching out to stroke its head.

The rain. It had started to rain, a damp, all-pervasive drizzle that threatened to become a warm downpour. Soon the road would be turned to mud, the men and the carts slipping and sliding, the tents and the woollen clothing damp, nowhere for a man to get dry. Then the illness would come, the coughing, the stomach cramps, the retching sickness, the boils and the carbuncles that seemed to produce two more for each one that agonisingly burst.

'We're far from home,' said Gresham almost to himself, 'in a wild country that doesn't want us. It could be weeks before we're dry again, and soon the men'll start to fall sick, and die. What's the point?'

'The point,' said Mannion, 'is that you decided to bring us on this bleedin' expedition, and as we are on it we might as well make the best of it. So stop moaning and let's get back with the rest of this rabble before the Irish come back and pick us off.'

The walls of Dublin were just visible through the drizzle and low-lying mist.

'Thank Christ 'fer that!' said Mannion with real passion. 'Well, that were fun, weren't it?'

There was no answer from George or Cameron. The latter had attached himself to Gresham an hour ago. They rode with their chins dug into their chests, hats pulled down over their eyes, the rain defeating their eyelashes and driving into their eyes.

'The fun's about to start,' said Gresham.

'What fun?' asked George, suddenly alerted.

'Do you think the Queen's going to be delighted that after over two months campaigning we've got nothing to show for it – no major rebel army defeated and no major rebel stronghold taken? Nearly half our horses are sick or dead, the men are depressed and we've lost over four thousand of them. If Essex has any sense he won't be opening his letters in a hurry.'

But sense never was the commodity in greatest supply for Robert Devereux, Earl of Essex. The Queen's letters were vicious. He showed them to his followers, increasingly favouring the younger ones, the hotheads. At times Essex seemed to despise the Queen. At other times he showed a total dependency on her goodwill.

'We are misunderstood and grievously wronged!' the young man shouted. The Dublin tavern was full, the low ceiling smoky from the guttering candles and lamps. There was a roar of approval from round the table. The others – fifteen or twenty or so – were well on their way to becoming seriously drunk. Spoiling for a fight, in fact, except that the enemy lay outside the walls of Dublin, unreachable, vanishing as quickly into the mists of Ireland as the mist itself could vanish at the first brush of sunlight.

The young man himself – thin, wispy-bearded with delicate

hands and almost ludicrously long fingers – was the third son of a none too rich country squire from Shropshire. He had sold his annuity to buy his equipment for the campaign, hoping in some ill-thought-out way to gain fame and fortune in Ireland. Now his fine leather belt had rotted through in the damp, his horse had died shivering and he was relegated to little more than the status of foot soldier, too impoverished to buy another horse. He seemed to have found enough money for drink, judging by the state of him.

'We risk our lives for England,' he was saying, 'and those at home mock us for our efforts!' That went down well. There was another roar of agreement and approval. 'How can they understand this God-forsaken country, how even the bravest of men cannot fight with honour here?'

That got the biggest roar of the lot. The bogs, the perpetual rain, an enemy who would never come out to meet you but always melted away, an enemy who would simply burn a castle to the ground rather than stand and fight for it, an enemy who could not be drawn out to fight for any reason . . .

''We're criticised and condemned by those who stay at home and grow fat! And the Queen's advisers tell lies about us!'

Mannion watched silently from his corner, his tankard for once forgotten.

'They was stokin' themselves up right good and proper,' he reported. 'It's not good. 'E warn't alone, that young fool. There's 'undreds of 'em out there.'

'Well, Essex's answer won't help him with the Queen, or his own people,' said Gresham morosely. 'Decimation, it's called. It's a Roman idea.'

Sir Henry Harrington had been heavily defeated while out on a supposed punitive raid. Essex had court-martialled him, confined him to prison and executed his lieutenant for the crime of wrapping the English colours round his body and fighting until he dropped from exhaustion. Essex had also executed one man in ten of Harrington's force.

242

'So that's what you gets from a bloody education!' said Mannion morosely. 'Better off without it, in my opinion. We're losing enough men as it is from illness, without needing to help the Irish along and kill 'em ourselves.'

What need was there of a plot by Cecil, thought Gresham? Essex was his own plot against himself. The only time he had appeared to show any real energy or drive recently had been in pursuing revenge on Harrington's miserable troops.

Since his success at the Pass of Cashel, Gresham had been dropped from Essex's Council. Was it from envy of Gresham's heroic action? More likely it was the perilous loneliness of his relationship with Essex, all his other advisers seeming to see Gresham as the anti-Christ. There had been one attempt on Gresham's life already. If he was right, one was prepared for Essex. But when? And was another attempt on Gresham's life overdue? The animosity shown towards him by Essex's inner circle was palpable, almost a physical presence.

He and Mannion had found a decent room in the castle, high enough to be above the stench of the place on all but the hottest days, days which came rarely in Ireland. They were sharing a flagon early one evening, with Gresham worrying that he was falling into George's trap. Letters had come from home and plunged George into melancholia. He had refused all offers of consolation, refused even to divulge their contents, and had retreated off on his own. Again. If George had meant to come on this campaign as a friend something had clearly changed his mind. Now he spent most of the time on his own, consumed by his own devils. Nothing Gresham could say or do seemed to snap him out of it. It was unlike George, and Gresham felt intense worry for the man whose unfailing good cheer had been one of the mainstays of his life.

Even though it was not yet dark and only August, they had lit a fire, paying a King's ransom for coal rather than the smoky, heat-free lumps of peat that the Irish favoured. At least the peat smoke did not sting the eyes, which was more than could be said for the rough coal they had acquired.

'I think I made a mistake coming over here,' Gresham said finally. It was dark enough now for the flames of the fire to dance lightly on the walls and reflect in his eyes: in their centre, not like the crimson ring he had seen twice in Essex's eyes.

'Pity you didn't realise that months ago,' said Mannion.

'I came to protect Essex. Or maybe just to stand in Cecil's way. And to draw out my enemies. But I'm not helping Essex, and no clearer about who wants me dead.'

The two men identified by Mannion as Gresham's would-be assassins had deserted that same evening.

Gresham was impatient to get home. At the back of his mind was the fear that Cecil had engineered his presence on this trip to get him out of the country, so the next assassination plot against the Queen could succeed. Was Gresham overestimating his own power? Yet he knew he was the only force Cecil really feared, and the only agency in the Court that might, conceivably, pick up wind of such a plot before it happened.

England was like a vast pot, simmering with its rivalries and its tensions hidden under a calm surface. Now the occasional bubble was breaking that surface, the fire stoked up. Any moment now that pot would boil over.

Robert Cecil was in audience with the Queen. At his request, in an almost unheard-of concession, he had asked for Sir Walter Raleigh to be present, as well as Lord Mountjoy, Thomas Howard and the Earl of Nottingham. It was a rare combination. It was a Council of War, that much was clear, Elizabeth thought as her eyes flicked round the chamber. She was dressed outrageously again, the off-white material so hung with pearls and jewels as to distort its shape, its length too short, its sleeves somehow too cramped.

'The information is valid, Your Majesty,' Cecil was saying. 'Indeed, the Spanish force may already have set off. We must mobilise our troops and our ships now.'

It was always dangerous to tell the Queen what she must and

must not do. Equally, if he had not done so, it would have belied the apparent urgency of the situation.

'Is this force heading for England or for Ireland?' asked the Queen testily, as if its sending had been on the orders of Cecil and not the new Spanish King.

It was Nottingham who answered. He and Cecil had rehearsed this carefully.

'We cannot know,' said the Earl. 'We believe in all likelihood the Spanish force is for England. We have sent many, many troops over to Ireland, and our most acclaimed general. It is possible that the Spanish are convinced that with our eyes set to the west we are vulnerable, as well as stripped of men.'

'And I have been persuaded to send two thousand more into this bog!' The Queen looked accusingly at her advisers, who dropped their eyes. In response to her angry and accusing letters, Essex had replied with a mixture of self-pity, self-justification and high drama. He had also included a few facts, such as that he had fewer than six thousand fit men left to him for the attack on Tyrone in the north that the Queen was pressing on him so urgently. The two thousand reinforcements she had finally agreed to send had had to be virtually dragged out of her with red-hot tongs. 'I am paying my Lord of Essex a thousand pound a day to go on progress!'

Queens went on progress. Elizabeth did not need to add 'royal' to the word 'progress' for her meaning to be clear. It was the opportunity Cecil had waited for.

'Your Majesty, I am sure the Earl of Essex will use the men you have sent wisely, and will launch the offensive we are all anticipating. Yet . . .'

'Yet what?' snapped the Queen. 'Out with it, man.'

'Yet in your next message to him, it might be wise to insert an instruction that he should not return to England before Tyrone is subdued.'

Cecil did not add 'not return to England with the army with which you have equipped him', but all present heard the words even if they were not spoken. News of the dissent and anger in

Essex's force had reached home from the thousand and one spies in its midst. Like two contrary tides meeting in the middle of a great open channel, the anger and disillusion in Ireland met the anger and disillusion of those in England.

'So be it,' said the Queen, her eyes fixed unmoving on Cecil. He did not lower his gaze.

Excellent, he thought. Let the Earl of Essex mull over that message. Let him add it to the news that Cecil had been awarded the Mastership of Wards, the highly profitable post that his father Lord Burghley had held and which had built half Burghley house, the post which Essex coveted above all others. Let him realise who was master now in England.

'You're in favour again,' said Mannion. 'Summoned to a Council of War. 'Cept it's been goin' on for two hours already, so you probably missed the best bits. Messenger grabbed me outside. Get a move on.'

Gresham hurried off to the Council Room. Why this sudden summons?

Essex had been ill for weeks since his return from the fruitless but mercifully brief expedition to the west. It was an old and familiar pattern in the face of adversity: long, sudden bouts of supposed illness typified by deep melancholy and soul-searching, the need to be alone, the self-pitying wallowing that so annoyed Elizabeth. Perhaps as a child and a much-needed heir, illness had been a bartering tool, a way of reminding people of his true importance. Perhaps it had simply been a way of getting attention. All it achieved now was impatience on the part of those who followed him, and derision from those who did not. Yet in a strange way it seemed to add to his lustre with the common people, those who did not know him. A string of well-wishers, many of them of humble origins, had flocked to his door, some with pathetic gifts of fruit and food. Gresham had gained permission from the Master-at-Arms to have one of his own men guard all such gifts, and had even found

246

a team of peasant labourers to act as tasters. How easy it would have been for Tyrone to slip poison into such gifts.

Essex was thinner than when Gresham had last seen him, slightly bent in his gait, and for the first time Gresham saw the hint of wrinkles beneath a man's eyes that predict the coming of age. How would Essex fare without his beauty if it ever left him? wondered Gresham. Very badly, he suspected. The knowledge of his physical attractiveness was a central building block, almost a cornerstone, of the man's whole personality.

It took only three or four seconds after he entered the room for every alarm bell in Gresham's head to start ringing. The expression in Essex's eyes, flashed a warning to him. Whatever had just been going on in this room, Essex had been opposed to it. His face had the mule-like expression Gresham had come to realise Essex wore when he was thwarted in his wishes or denied.

This was not a Council of War. It was a trial. And Gresham was the accused. It was there in the glares of those in the room, virtually all Essex's top commanders and allies, and in the smirk of Southampton, the gleam in the eyes of Gelli Meyrick. It was there in the fact that the conclave was being held in the main hall of the castle, a room big enough to dwarf the twenty or thirty people in it. Why hold the meeting here unless it was intended to summon many more to receive one of Essex's grandiose pronouncements? The outcome of a trial, perhaps?

'Sir Henry!' Essex jumped straight in. 'We receive news from London almost daily that our efforts here are derided and dismissed, that we are held in scorn, that our honour and our reputation are besmirched.'

Of course they were. Essex's young entourage in particular would be receiving letters from their friends back at Court all the time, would hear of the Queen's displeasure, of the promotion of Cecil. Gresham stayed silent.

'Many here among my Council believe you are a spy for the Queen, or for Robert Cecil or for Sir Walter Raleigh. Many here believe that it is your words that poison the Queen against me in my absence. They wish to call you to account. Is it your letters that tell the Court I and this army, its officers and its men are incompetent and cowardly?'

So that was it! Essex had managed to make it clear that the simmering frustration in the camp had finally boiled over. Essex's officers wanted a human sacrifice. What better than a man rumoured to be a spy, someone who seemed to have taken over, in small part at least, some of the favour of Essex?

'Because if it is so,' said Sir Christopher Blount, Essex's stepfather, 'then you are the traitor, not my Lord of Essex, and it is you who should suffer a traitor's death.' Blount could well have had the 'o' missed out of his surname when he was born. If Blount was gunning for Gresham, he really was in trouble. Scapegoat. That was what he was being set up as: a scapegoat for the disapproval the expedition was getting in London. Not just a scapegoat: a sacrificial lamb. The credit that would accrue to Essex if he executed one of Cecil's spies could be vast, particularly among his own army and its collection of hotheaded young officers. Yet Essex looked as if he was doing his best for Gresham. Given Essex's capacity to go for lost causes, perhaps he should worry about that more than anything else.

They had executed a brave Irish officer who had wrapped the English colours around his body and fled the battlefield only when all seemed lost, inviting any Irish who caught him to rip his guts out before killing him, so he could watch his own blood stain those same colours. Gresham's money was no use to him here in Ireland. Essex had the powers of a King. Essex's wild young men wanted a sacrifice. The more he thought about it in the split second he was allowed thought, the more Gresham realised what a perfect sacrifice he would make. It would assuage the army's need for blood, and it would also send a clear message back to England that Cecil's men were as vulnerable as any other. It was known that Gresham had some form of special relationship with the Queen, dating from the days of the Armada when she had knighted him, and never properly explained why. His death would show that Essex was powerful enough to execute even one of the Queen's creatures. And no one loved a spy.

I'm dead, thought Gresham, unless I can think of something very fast indeed.

He placed his hand on his sword hilt and drew its glittering length in one, easy movement. Thirty men recoiled, thirty hands went to their own swords, and with a strange rasping noise like a crocodile taking its last breath, thirty swords came out of their scabbards.

'I had this sword by my side,' said Gresham conversationally, 'when you, my Lord Essex, asked my men and myself to go on a suicide mission into the Pass of Cashel. I did not need to use it, but I did ride at the vanguard of my men, and I showed what man I am by my actions in that skirmish. I picked this musket ball out of my saddlebag, after the action. The one that caused this darn in my coat I could not keep, as it passed an inch behind my spine.'

Thank God he was wearing that same coat. He reached into a pocket with his other hand, found the musket ball he had kept with him since that day and tossed it onto the rush-strewn floor in front of Essex. It bounced once, and lay still.

He had their attention now. But how often and how quickly had he seen the audience turn against the actor holding the centre of the stage?

'At the Pass of Plumes' – some of the audience could not resist the slightest of titters – 'I hope I showed my loyalty, as I hope I have shown it at other times in this campaign.'

He did not need to mention the capture of Cahir Castle, after Cashel the only significant victory in the whole campaign. Most of those here knew that it was his plan of action that had led to its capture, and that Gresham had led the charge across the island where the castle lay.

'As for letters, I issue a simple challenge. I have not put pen to paper since my arrival in Ireland, nor instructed others to do so on my behalf. Not a single word of mine has gone back to England, to Robert Cecil or to Her Majesty. You may put that assertion to any test you wish. Ask them, or ask any man who can write in this our army, and if you find any proof that I have written to England these past months, I will deliver you my head on a platter, and save you the trouble of removing it from my body.'

He felt strangely calm now. All he had to lose was his life. As it so often did, that calmness was working on these men who moments earlier had been baying for his blood.

'And I issue a second challenge. Let any man who has proof against me, either of my cowardice or my disloyalty, let him come forward now, and face me as a man. Let God and trial by combat decide the issue.'

And with that, he plucked off his glove and dropped it neatly over the musket ball. It was his only hope. Essex was in love with chivalry, loved the idea of personal combat, of man-to-man challenge. It spoke to his belief in a chivalric code that had only ever existed in the minds of those who wrote romances.

Well, that had been very theatrical. Never mind that Gresham was far from sure he believed in God, and was certain that trial by combat always resulted in the victory of the bigger brute over the smaller one. Or perhaps God simply favoured the bigger brute? Part of Gresham's brain realised that this was actually a very interesting moment.

One of Essex's lickspittle supporters might be just stupid enough to pick up Gresham's glove, in the hope of gaining Essex's favour. Well, it was done now. He looked round the chamber, with a rather vague and philosophical interest. He really, really did not feel like killing anyone today.

No one moved.

Gresham leant forward and offered his sword, hilt-first to Essex in the ancient gesture and, with a reluctance he hoped he was not showing, dropped down on one knee before him.

'My Lord, the decision is yours.'

Well of course it was bloody well his. This idiot who happened to have been born in the right bed at the right time to the right woman had the power of life or death over countless humans, not least of all one Sir Henry Gresham. The fact that it was cruelly unfair had nothing to do with it, and never had. Was God like the Earl of Essex? Very beautiful, and quite terrifyingly random? It might explain a lot.

It was not until many years later that Henry Gresham realised one reason why, against all the odds, he had liked the Earl of Essex so much: it was his capacity to do the unpredictable. It was a talent that Gresham had used to save his life on a number of occasions, but which at times seemed very lacking in other members of his species.

Essex stood up from the mini-throne on which he had been seated, and drew his own sword. He advanced the short distance to Gresham, his sword extended before him.

Oh well, thought Gresham, win some, lose ... He had always imagined he would not be able to complete the last word when the moment finally came. Or did the brain continue to work for a brief while after death?

'In England,' said Essex, clearly speaking now for all to know, but with his sword still held dangerously close to Gresham's neck, 'there is a Court based on rumour, falsehood and envy. In that Court, brave men can have their reputations and their honour tarnished by false report.'

Gresham could still hear him, so presumably he was still alive.

There was a ripple of approval from the members of Essex's Court.

'Here in Ireland, deserted and misunderstood by our country-men, we have no Court as such. Yet in this, our temporary Court of Ireland, we recognise courage and bravery more than intrigue and politics!'

He had struck a chord there, no doubt.

'Test your word? Prove your word? Henry Gresham,' Essex paused for effect, 'you proved your courage at Cashel and at Cahir.'

Then the stupid man flung his own sword on top of Gresham's. Gresham could not but help notice that both blades now pointed towards the Earl of Essex. He hoped no seers were watching.

'I will throw in my sword with that of a brave man, and believe the word of a fighting man before that of a flatterer, a sycophant or a courtier.'

Oh God! thought Gresham. Now I have to rise to my feet, clasp him in my arms and hail him as a brother. As I would willingly clasp a nettle, or a snake. And the others will roar, clap their hands, respond to this wonderful piece of theatre, without realising that I, Henry Gresham, rewrote the script while on the hoof, and changed its ending, so that I lived instead of hanging from a scaffold. And the only other person who knew what a farce, what a vast joke it all was, Gresham was holding in his arms now!

The onlookers were roaring, clapping their hands. It was better than a play. Southampton, Blount and Meyrick were looking like spoilt children denied a treat.

As Essex clasped him like a long lost brother, he whispered two words into Gresham's ear. Finally he released Gresham and went back to his chair that looked suspiciously like a throne.

'Sound the trumpet!' Essex announced grandly. It was the signal for a full meeting of the garrison, and Essex had used it once or twice before. The blasts on the trumpet were squeaky and out of tune – the trumpeter was clearly not expecting to be called and had to wipe beer and cheese off his mouth before he put his instrument to it – but effective enough. In ten minutes the hall was crammed with every officer in the garrison, and many of the men. The remainder gathered outside to wait for whatever news was to be passed out to them. Where were George and Mannion, Gresham wondered, with a slight twinge of worry? Cameron was one of the first to arrive, looking both studious and eager.

Essex stood up, and struck a pose, one leg out in front of the other, one hand on the hilt of his sword, the other on his hip.

'I have reached a decision,' he said as loudly as he could without shouting. The acoustics in the hall were good, something a born actor such as the Earl knew full well; they gave his voice a slight echo and resonance, deepening it. If Essex heard the *sotto voce* mutter of, 'About fuckin' time!' from a man at the back of the hall,

252

he did not show it. 'We march on the foul traitor Tyrone, march to bring the infamous rebel to his knees!'

There was a faint cheer at this, enough of a flame for Essex to fan. Gresham had heard so many of this type of speech that he more or less ceased listening, having learnt over the years when to cheer, stamp his feet or clap his hands. Essex's decision meant, presumably, that in a relatively short space of time men would be hacking each other to pieces. It was going to happen, and nothing could stop it. Why bother if a few words from the man who ordered it made the men feel a little better, even if only for little while?

He left the meeting feeling strangely light-headed. Perhaps only he fully realised what a lucky escape he had had.

'The strangest thing just happened to me on the way to the gallows – Oh, and Essex is off after Tyrone at last, now he's lost two thirds of the army and—'

Then he saw who was sitting at the back of his room, flanked by George and Mannion – Jane.

'What the hell are you doing here?' he exploded, disbelieving, shocked almost out of his mind. 'I gave you express orders to stay behind!'

'My Lord, I—' she began.

'How dare you defy me! Is this my reward for having taken you in to find my wishes flouted in this shameless manner? I explained to you the appalling difficulties if you joined me on this campaign. I actually took the time and trouble to explain to you, tried to treat you as an adult—'

'My Lord—' Jane was desperately trying to speak.

'I want none of your words!' ranted Gresham. 'You will turn straight round and—'

'You better listen to 'er,' said Mannion flatly. 'You really 'ad.'

Gresham looked at him.

'What?'

'You better listen to 'er,' said Mannion.

Angry beyond belief, Gresham heard something in Mannion's

253

tone. Gritting his teeth, he glared at Jane. 'For his sake, and for his sake only, I'll let you speak. But make it short. Very short. And then turn round and head straight for England.'

Jane was thinner than when he had last seen her, with bags under her eyes, eyes which had dark rings round them. She wore a mud-spattered riding dress – was clarted in the stuff. There was also a wild look in her eyes, a look he had not seen before, a look of total desperation. She seemed suddenly very vulnerable. He moderated his tone. Was he going soft in his dotage? 'Sit down. Now, tell me your story.'

Was there a flicker of gratitude in her wild eyes?

'It's so . . . stupid,' she said.

Why had he not noticed that her voice was a slight register lower than most women's?

'I was in the stables. I go there sometimes. I like the horses, and they know me now, at least the ones you left behind do.' She sensed herself rambling, visibly took a grip on herself, and carried on. 'There was a commotion outside in the yard. Your breeder had sent you three new horses, they were just being taken in. One of them was rearing up, he must have been spooked by something, I don't know, and there was a man almost pinned up against the wall, a man I'd not seen before. He looked terrified. Two grooms calmed the horse down, and the man, instead of walking, sort of ran. The horse had his back towards him by then, must have caught the movement out of the corner of his eye, lashed out with his back legs. One hoof caught the man on the side of the head . . .' She was living the horrific sight in her head now, almost talking to herself. 'His head was like – like an eggshell. It just . . . cracked open.' There were tears running down her face. 'I went to try and help, but it was too late. Everyone was shouting and screaming. All I wanted to know was who he was, if he had a wife or someone we had to tell about the accident.'

She stopped to compose herself.

'I asked everyone. One of the grooms said he'd seen the man before; he'd been to The House once, maybe twice before. He'd come in by the stable door and asked the groom to take him to Cameron Johnstone's servant. The one who keeps going over to Ireland. I didn't know what to do. You weren't there, Mannion wasn't there and Mary just screams all the time when anything happens. The steward's drunk by late afternoon, and because you were away we'd let half the servants go home for the harvest.'

'So what did you do?' asked Gresham, gently.

'All I could think of was how we could make the man look presentable for his widow or his family, with his head . . . so horribly smashed in. I ordered people to take the body inside, thinking perhaps at least we could wash it. They took it into the kitchen, dumped it on one of the slabs we use to carve up meat . . . I told the men to leave, and sent orders for two or three women to come and help me wash and dress the body. And this . . . this letter fell out of his clothing. Onto the floor. The kitchen floor.' She stopped for a moment, eyes wide now, full of the horror of the moment. 'The horse must have caught him twice, once in the head and once on the chest. His ribs were all broken as well, and the letter must have caught the full force of the hoof. The seal on the letter was broken. As I picked it up the top fold bent outwards and . . . and . . .' She looked up at Gresham. 'And I saw your name. So without thinking I started to read. I thought perhaps it was a letter for you, a letter that needed to be sent urgently to you in Ireland – I don't know!'

'And?' said Gresham as if talking to a child.

'And I read the letter. Decided you had to see it. But I couldn't trust anyone else, not after I'd read it. So I made Jack, Dick and Edward agree to ride with me to Ireland, the ones who'd been with us on the *Anna*. I felt I knew them, and they knew and sort of trusted me, and Dick is in love with me, sort of, and will do anything I ask . . . and I asked Jack, because he's the oldest and the wisest, to pick three other men they could trust. I remembered what you said about – rape, and other things. And I knew it was terribly important that you see this letter, and I thought six of your men would fight off anything other than an army and if we met an army it would all be lost anyway . . .'

She sensed she was starting to ramble again, and made a massive effort to control herself.

'I'm so sorry. I didn't mean to disobey your orders, and I took six of your men and lots of your horses without asking you, and it cost a fortune for Jack to get us on board a ship, though I'm sure he got the best deal he could, but we rode as fast as we could and hardly slept.' All the tension, the emotion and the horror was rushing out of her now, uncontrollable. 'And all the time I was convinced that if we got here you would be dead.'

'Can I see the letter? Please?'

She leant forward, the paper clutched tightly in her hand so tightly that the paper was screwed up and wrinkled where her thumb and forefinger had held onto it. She had to make herself let it go. Gresham thought she would have died rather than release it to anyone else. Mannion had clearly been told of its existence, but equally clearly, from the eagerness with which he crowded forward to lean over Gresham's shoulder, had not seen the thing itself. In some way the girl had driven herself to cross an ocean by the belief that this letter could only be handed over to him.

He gently prised it from her grasp, opened the folds and read.

It was a curt, peremptory letter. It blasted Cameron, to whom it was addressed, for staying out of contact for too long. It reminded him that he who pays the piper calls the tune. And it ordered him, quite clearly and unequivocally, to kill Henry Gresham. It was even more specific than that. It ordered Cameron to kill Henry Gresham 'Before my Lord of Essex can return to England from his Irish folly.'

Gresham looked up at Jane, who was poised on the edge of her seat, tear stains visible on her cheeks where they had cut through the grime.

'Have you shared its content with anyone else?'

She shook her head. 'No. I did tell Jack that if anything were to happen to me on the journey, he should take the letter if it were at all possible from my – body – and make sure that he handed it to you in person.'

Gresham looked at Jane; it was as if he had seen her for the first time.

'Even here in Ireland they have hot water and rooms that can be made warm. Please go and refresh yourself after your – journey.'

From the state of her, the ride from hell might have been a better description.

'Then, if you wish, please join myself, George here and Mannion for supper.'

'Thank you, my Lord,' said Jane, for whom exhaustion had become normal. 'Please ...'

'Yes?' said Gresham.

'Please don't punish Jack and Dick and Edward! Or the other three who came with us! It wasn't their fault. I *made* them do it.'

Gresham looked at her, and for all his control a smile started to play around his mouth. Dammit, he was becoming more attracted to this girl by the minute.

'I bet you did,' he said. 'My plan, actually, is not to hang, draw and quarter them – in front of their families, of course, just for good measure. Rather, I propose to thank, and reward them. They did well. Yet they had the lesser role. As for you, whose role was the greatest, all I have is ... my thanks. Just a few moments ago, I thought I was fighting for my life with the Earl of Essex and his cronies. Now I realise the real fight may well have been behind my back. You may well have saved my life.'

He looked at her, and grinned. The way he grinned at Mannion, the way he grinned at George. He only half realised what he was doing.

'Thank you,' he said, simply and cheerfully.

She left, giving him a hesitant, almost fearful smile. As if she could not quite believe her luck. She managed to look stunningly beautiful despite – or was it because of? – her disarray.

There was a long silence after she had left the room.

257

'Bastard!' said Mannion.

'The one who's in this room?' asked Gresham mildly.

'No,' said Mannion emphatically. 'Not that bastard. Cameron Fuckin' Bloody Buggerin' Johnstone. *That* bastard.'

Gresham had registered the occasional visits of Cameron's servant. Registered them. Thought nothing of them.

There was always hope for Mannion. It was usually not a spiritual or a metaphysical hope, but a physical hope and expectation: of the next meal, the next drink or the next woman. He had decided long ago that thinking was probably a bad thing. Yet he was thinking long and hard over this one, and suffering.

'You believe the letter? Believe it's genuine?' Gresham was the calmest of all of them.

Mannion and George looked at each other. George was pale as a harvest moon, no colour in his craggy face at all. Something was wrong with him, something Gresham could not define.

'Yes,' said George. 'The girl wasn't lying.' He looked as if he was about to say something, but it never came.

'But you're all missing the interesting point,' said Gresham. 'Actually, three interesting points.'

'That a Scots bastard wants to kill you?' said Mannion.

'That's not the point at all,' said Gresham. There was a faraway look in his eyes. 'The first point is a lesson for us all.'

'A lesson?' said Mannion, only half managing to restrain his look of concern to George. Was his master losing it? 'You ain't in College now.'

'We're none of us ever out of College,' responded Gresham. 'The first lesson is that we can't plan for everything. Least of all a maddened horse. We think we're in control, we think we have it all planned. Then something happens. Something out of our control. Something that doesn't obey our orders. Something we didn't think of – like Jane finding this letter.'

'So where does that wonderful bit of philosophy leave us?' asked George.

'With the second point,' said Gresham. 'From the start of this business, I've been running to catch up. I'd ignored Essex and seen him as the Queen's plaything. I'd become complacent about Cecil, hadn't realised he was building a plot against me, let him steal the advantage. Right from the word go I've been reacting to events, instead of dictating them. I've been following, not leading. And I hate to be a follower.'

'Is there a point to all this?' George suddenly seemed very tired, and rather old. It was the first time that Gresham had considered his friend might be getting old.

'The most important point of all,' said Gresham, suppressing his pang of worry over George. 'Who signed this letter? Who ordered Cameron to kill me?'

George shook himself.

'The signature's indecipherable. It could be anyone.'

'But don't you see?' said Gresham, exasperated and showing it. 'I've made the basic mistake!'

'Being born?' asked George glumly.

'No! Not finding out who it is wants to kill me. If I find out who wants me dead, then there's a strong chance I find out why. And if I find out why I start to see some sort of path through this forest that's threatening to make me lose my way.'

'That's Cameron then, isn't it?' said George, more animated now there was something to be done. 'He's the only definite link you have. He's bound to know who gives him his orders. I suppose you'll just have to torture it out of him.' George's lips pursed in a grimace. He disliked even the idea of torture, and Gresham knew that when its possible need arose there were moments when George began to regret his friendship with Gresham, and the avenues it sometimes dragged him down. 'But I don't think you should,' said George. 'I think if you do, you become just like your enemies, and no better than them.'

'Torture?' asked Gresham. 'I'll use it if I have to, but apart from the fact that Cameron's very tough, you can never guarantee that a man in physical pain tells the truth, only that he tells what he thinks will make the pain stop.'

'Physical pain?' said Mannion, picking him up. 'What other pain is there?'

'Mental pain,' said Gresham.

'What's that when it's at 'ome?' asked Mannion scornfully.

'Physical pain is when someone denies you your next meal, drink and woman. Mental pain is when you think that's what they're going to do. Can you get Cameron here, without showing what you think of him?'

'Course I can,' said Mannion. 'I'll be politeness itself.'

'Do that and he will spot there's something up. Just be normal. Tell him Essex has given me a job to do.'

Cameron came in ten minutes later, outwardly cheerful and fumbling in his bag.

'Here, I've a book for you if you . . .'

He looked up and into the barrel of the pistol Gresham had levelled at him. Instantly he turned and made as if to duck under both the pistol and Mannion, using the speed of his reflexes to get out of the room and gambling that Gresham needed a live man to talk to rather than a dead one to gloat over. His speed of thought was extraordinary.

He turned and the full force of Mannion's fist crashed into him. The impact knocked him two or three feet backwards, and he was unconscious by the time he hit the floor.

'I can't tell you how much I enjoyed that,' said Mannion, rubbing his sore knuckles.

When Cameron came to he was tied to a high-backed, ornate wooden chair, a separate strand of rope round his neck, pulling it back against the wood. He must have been in agony, but he only blinked once. There was a livid bruise down the side of his face already, and a tooth gone on the right-hand side, with a dribble of red blood coming out of his mouth.

Gresham held the letter in front of him so he could read it. Nothing changed in Cameron's face.

'How did you get hold of that?' he asked, slurring his words because his mouth was so swollen.

'In circumstances that were as accidental as they were fortunate. The man who delivered it is dead. We'd noted his earlier visits, and were watching him.' It would do no harm for Cameron to know that Gresham had in some way been responsible for the death, or that he had outguessed him. Jane had not known, of course, that Gresham had ordered Cameron and his servant watched like a hawk, or that all Cameron's outgoing letters had been intercepted. The irony was that Gresham had perhaps been too clever by half. He had not ordered incoming people to be searched, fearing it would tip Cameron off, preferring to have him believe he was unwatched in the hope that he might thus reveal more about who and what he was. The other irony was that despite all the money Gresham had spent on surveillance it was an angry horse that had revealed the real threat. And a watchful girl who happened to be able to read. 'In any event, the circumstances leave me in no doubt that it's genuine. Are you going to deny it?'

'The fact that the letter is genuine? No. The writer certainly intended to give me an order that he intended me to obey. What I do deny is that I would necessarily have carried out that order. Of that you have no proof.'

'Rather difficult to prove,' said Gresham, 'if the evidence one way or the other is likely to be my corpse.' His voice would have turned boiling water to ice. 'Except for one thing. Essex's officers just tried to have me hung, on the grounds of my being a spy for Cecil and passing back bad news to Court. I managed to get out of that one, just, with Essex's help, and as he clasped me like a long-lost friend he whispered two words in my ear. *Cameron Johnstone.* He was telling me that it was you who set up his Council. That it was you who were behind the idea of making me a sacrificial lamb. Perfect: you get someone else to do the dirty work for you. And you stand by the scaffold, wringing your hands over how unfair it is and trying to offer consolation to George and Mannion.'

Cameron said nothing.

'I believe you're taking money and orders from someone who wishes me dead. I need to know who it is, and why.'

'And I won't tell you,' said Cameron simply. 'If you're vulgar and brutal enough to torture me, I'll hold out as long as I can, but then give you one of a hundred names any of which might be true. You're not a man short of people who want him dead, and your history goes back a long way. You'll never know if the information is the truth or not.'

Cameron was not denying that he had set out to have Gresham killed.

'I wasn't planning to torture you. Not in that way,' said Gresham.

'Am I meant to say thank you?' asked Cameron caustically. He was showing remarkable bounce for a man in his position.

'You told us a very interesting story when we first met. A very moving story about your wife and children.'

There! Something had changed in Cameron's impassive face, something behind the one eye that was still open.

'And it was the truth. You see, I rarely take things at their face value. I had people check up on you. More difficult than it would have been in London, but money always talks and Mannion is very good at going to taverns and inns where people do things for money and not for morality. Your wife and children did die, and there's every possibility they caught the plague from a spy sent to you from my Lord of Northumberland.'

'So?' asked Cameron, eyes steady now.

'The best stories are always the ones that are true. Or at least, true in part. I enquired a little further. It appears that your marriage was foisted on you by your advocate father as a condition of your inheritance, that it was functional at best and that it is possible that one of your children was actually the child of you and your mistress. Your childhood sweetheart, as it happens, the girl you always wanted to marry, and who you brought to Edinburgh and set up at no small expense with her other child who was certainly yours and lived with its mother.

'Apparently you were quite a good lawyer, but the need to keep two households and the sheer excitement of it all started you doing dirty work for the King, for Northumberland, even for Scotland's ally France and, so it's rumoured, even for Spain. There are those in the taverns who believe you also have a route to Rome.'

Cameron said nothing. Gresham could almost see and hear his mind working, putting up idea after idea to meet this new and unexpected situation, testing each one and discarding it, all at lightning speed.

'It took me three months. The easier task was to find out where your mistress lives, far harder was to find where you keep your money. But I did find out both. Or those I paid so handsomely did. So let me be plain. I won't torture you, even if you tell me nothing. I will keep you prisoner: we'll knock you out again, and bundle you back to England with a good half dozen of my men. What I will also do if we finish this little talk without my having found out the truth is to arrange for the place your mistress and child live to be burned down, and for the same favour to be afforded the place where your money is. Neither will survive. It's as simple as that.'

Did he mean it? Gresham knew he did. A life for a life: those he loved had been threatened, could die; it was the way of the world. And the final irony was that he, Gresham, was using exactly the same threat on this man as Cecil had sought to use on him. Had Gresham so cheapened himself as to become his enemy?

Cameron knew Gresham's threat was genuine. He was a man whose continued life was testimony to his success in measuring risk.

'Cecil,' he said. 'It's Robert Cecil who ordered your death, at least as far as I know.'

Gresham raised an eyebrow.

'It is truly as far as I know. I have never met Cecil, never spoken to him. All my orders – and my money – came through the little weasel of a man you tell me now is dead.'

'Your evidence for thinking your master is Cecil?'

'My actual evidence? Laughingly little. I was approached shortly after I landed with you, by this man. Asked if I would be willing to spy on you. And then to kill you. Naturally, I was interested to find out who wanted you dead. There was one obvious candidate. Cecil.

So I casually dropped his name into a sentence, in a way that made it seem clear I assumed I was now going to work for Cecil.'

'And?'

'And the man went ballistic, turned a bright shade of pink, and spent so much time persuading me that Cecil was the last person he was working for as to convince me the opposite was true.'

'And why should Cecil want me dead?'

'I assume you can work that one out yourself. Firstly, he hates you, for personal reasons that have no basis in logic, but are simply a fact. More importantly, he's desperate to have the same position with the next King or Queen of England as his late father had with the present one. For that reason he is trying to manipulate the succession with every means at his disposal. I know at first hand that he's wooing my master, King James. I've recently come to believe that he's also wooing Spain with equal fervour. I think you call it riding two horses at the same time.'

'So how do I feature in all this?'

'The recent death of King Philip changed things for ever in the Court of Spain. The most trusted allies and secretaries to the King are now no longer certain of their place, new men of influence are coming on the scene all the time, making exactly the same sort of play for power that Cecil is hoping to do on the death of Elizabeth. Cecil's terrified that his dealings with Spain will be revealed. He's never trusted your relationship with Spain since you survived sailing on the Armada. He believes you may have links there, even be a secret Catholic and admirer of Spain. He believes you're the person most likely to ferret out his illicit correspondence with Spain, and that if you did you'd delight in using it to destroy him.'

'Why employ you as my assassin?'

If a bound and tied man could look pityingly on his interrogator, then that was what Cameron did.

'If a man known to be in the service of King James kills a leading English courtier, and one who seems to have a special relationship with the Queen, he could use that as a form of blackmail on James. Plus the fact that Cecil will then kill me.'

'Well,' said Gresham, 'I didn't think it would be simple. Now, do please tell me why Cecil will have you killed as well as have you kill me?'

'Because he knows that I'm close on his heels with regard to his dealings with Spain. I made the mistake of asking too many questions of too many members of the Spanish community in London, before I knew who I could trust. One of them talked to Cecil. The answer's obvious. Get me to kill you, his prime threat, then get someone else to kill me, his secondary threat. Why do you think I was so keen to come with you to this God-forsaken country on this God-forsaken expedition? I'm actually safer here than I would be in England. Or even Scotland. But I guarantee you some person in this army has been paid a tidy sum to knock me off once it becomes clear that I or someone else has performed the same favour for you.'

Gresham looked for a long moment at Cameron. His eyes gave nothing away. Cameron met his gaze with equal fortitude, neither wavering nor blinking. As a result, unconsciousness came as a complete surprise to him when Mannion came up from behind and considerately gave a massive blow to the other side of his head.

'I want the men who came with Jane to turn round and take her back to England, together with Cameron. Take seven of the very best and most loyal men from the troop and one of the sergeants, pay them a King's ransom, and get them to go as well, as extra escort. Tell them to keep an eye on Cameron at all times, as if their life depended on it. I'll explain to Jane what's happening over supper.'

'You believe 'im?' asked Mannion.

'Do you?' asked Gresham.

'No,' said Mannion simply. 'What about you?'

'Me? I'm a happy man!' said Gresham. 'All of a sudden some things are starting to become clear to me.'

A messenger rode up to the castle for Henry Gresham at the same time as a messenger for Essex. Neither recipient was cheered by the news. Sir Clifford Conyers, commanding 1,500 men, was dead when the Irish sawed his head from his shoulders and made a present of it to the fighting Prince of Donegal.

As for Gresham's message, Cameron Johnstone had waited until the ship had docked and he was on the narrow gangplank with a guard before and a guard after him, and turned viciously and without warning and knocked them both off into the foot or so of black water between the grinding hull and the stone wharf. Before anyone else could leap onto the gangplank Cameron had slithered off it, was seen for a moment amid the barrels and the goods piled high on the quay, and then vanished.

CHAPTER 9

August to October, 1599
Ireland

Hugh O'Neill, Earl of Tyrone, and the nearest thing Ireland had to a King of its own, waited silently in mid-stream at the Ford of Bellaclynth, with the waters of the River Lagan lapping at his horse's belly. Small, grey-haired and in his mid-fifties there was little sign that this was the man holding England to ransom.

Tyrone's head was bowed, in an act of submission. Behind him, on the hillside, was a detachment of his own cavalry. Behind them, out of sight, was his army. They had paraded before each other, the Irish and the English forces, two days earlier, Essex challenging Tyrone to a pitched battle. Tyrone had refused. What need had he to fight, with eight thousand men to Essex's four thousand? All he had to do was block the way.

From the middle of the small English detachment on the opposite hill a figure broke away and rode steadily forward on a magnificent grey to the water's edge. It was Essex. He was dressed in gleaming half armour, and the sunlight glittering on the water glittered on the gleaming metal that encased him.

Two armies held their breath.

With the exception of one soldier, who belched.

'Bloody awful stuff, this meat,' he said, in the way of an apology.

He was chewing at a strip of dried, salted beef, of the type an army lived off when on the march. Mannion was the only person in the English army who seemed to enjoy the stuff or eat it by choice.

'So what's 'e goin' to do?' asked Mannion. He and Gresham were a part of the mounted English detachment that had crested the hill and escorted Essex to the parley.

'I've a terrible fear that he's going to make a complete fool of himself and of us,' said Gresham. 'It's increasingly been his response to a crisis.'

Essex had been in an awful state when Gresham had last seen him. This time his illness was real, and despite all the precautions dysentry had ravaged him, drained him of energy, drained him almost of the will to live. He was in the recovery phase now, which meant that he had time and just about enough energy to realise how truly awful he felt, though the damned illness never seemed really to leave a person, returning when least expected.

Gresham had taken some wine with him. It was the very last of the stores he had brought over from England, carefully preserved from Mannion, and reserved for the first great English victory. It would be a very long wait for that moment. It might be better spent on doing something for the man meant to be the architect of that victory.

'Thank you,' said Gresham. 'I think I owe you my life.' He poured the wine. 'This comes from England. From my own cellars. It was simpler when all we used to do was chase women,' said Gresham, 'and get drunk.'

'I'm a married man,' said Essex, with the faintest glimmer of the mad young man Gresham had known in what now seemed a different age. Essex was propped up in bed for all the world like an old woman. 'I deny that I ever chased women.'

'All right,' said Gresham, 'they chased you. Can your noble stomach take a drink?'

'It can try,' Essex said, and they settled into a desultory conversation, leading nowhere, saying and proving nothing.

If only the damned Queen would stop sending him vicious letters! The Queen was Essex's Achilles heel. At criticism from her he either became unspeakably angry, or descended into lacrimonious self-pity, collapsing in on himself.

Essex had ridden out to meet Tyrone as if he, Essex, were the conquering hero with Ireland at his feet, not the defeated invader clinging by his finger ends to what he held. His mood was exalted, almost spiritual, bizarre. It was as if he was seeing things others did not, could not see.

Robert Devereux, 2nd Earl of Essex, was collapsing from within, his private devils eating him up from the inside out, as the dysentry was eating up his body's resistance. The changes that had come over him since he and Gresham had engaged in their mock combat on the Thames were terrifying. The man was a shell, a brittle, fragile shell. And the bravest, most glamorous, most headstrong member of the English aristocracy, the one who might once have taken on the Irish rebel, was now in parley with that rebel, outwardly the same man, inwardly a broken reed, saying God knows what.

He and Tyrone had been talking for an hour, and the men on the opposing hillsides had all got off their horses to stretch tired muscles. Every now and again they looked down to the ford. Tyrone was gesticulating gently, for all the world like a street trader trying to sell dodgy vegetables to a dim housewife.

Suddenly, the two men broke apart and rode back to their respective forces. There was a sudden bite in the air, the smell of fear, of expectation. The small party of men who had come with Essex, gathered round him, some on horseback, some still on foot, the careful ones looking at the opposite hillside every few seconds in case the Irish were planning to mount a surprise charge.

The Earl had a strange expression on his face, a sort of saintly, tranquil smile that Gresham had never seen before. It was almost a stupid expression, reminding Gresham of a village idiot who had been given an unexpected sweetmeat.

'It is peace!' Essex declared, as Moses might have done on bringing the tablets down for the second time from the mountain.

'Peace?' asked Blount, always the most bluff and forward of men. 'On what terms is it peace, my Lord?' He looked round him, brow furrowed and dark, seeking support from the others. He gained none. All looked as worried as he did.

'Tyrone is a gentleman, a true noble,' said Essex dreamily. 'He is not as others have represented him.'

An inkling of what had happened began to dawn on Gresham. His heart sank.

'He knows that my valour and the size of this army will mean inevitable defeat for him if he persists.'

The Earl's valour? His personal courage had never been in doubt, though it had been savaged in several of the Queen's letters in which she had accused him of cowardice. The size of the army? The army that illness and desertion and losses in hopeless battles had reduced by two thirds?

'My Lord . . .' One of the younger men was trying to interrupt, his expression almost comic had it not been so sad. What had the Earl said to Tyrone? What had he agreed to in the name of his Queen?

'No!' Essex raised an imperious hand, stilling the voice. There was still that same dreamy expression on his face. 'The Irish rebels are fearful of our courage. Their army is ill-trained, its outer strength a lie. They sue for peace because they know that if they do not do so, they will lose their courage and their lives. We have won peace without the great battle we were all expecting.' A slight, pathetic note of pleading came into Essex's voice. Something was starting to chip away at his self-confidence as he got further and further away from Tyrone and his dissembling, flattering tongue. 'Of course, there should have been a great battle, a trial of strength, a feat of arms. But how could I put my thirst for glory before the needs of my men? How could I order such a battle knowing that it was not necessary, that I had the subservience of the rebels? Surely a good commander rests his reputation on the outcome of what he

270

has done, not on the means by which he achieves it? Surely that is so?'

'What is the outcome, my Lord? What are the terms of our peace?'

'Why . . . I can remember, of course, I must remember . . .' A wild, hunted look came across Essex's face, but from somewhere he found some certainty again. 'We shall have a truce, a real truce. Tyrone has sworn an oath to it. Peace in Ireland. A glorious thing.'

'And what territories will the Irish give up? Which of their strongholds will they release to us? Which of our captured castles?' It was Blount who asked, almost gently.

Essex's horse moved restlessly, and the emblazoned hilt of his sword clanged against his finely polished breast armour.

'Why, none of course. Of course, none. There has to be concessions for any truce, reason on both sides, some give and take . . .'

A collective sigh went round the assembled group.

'I have agreed . . .' Essex began to gabble. 'I have agreed that we shall establish no new garrisons or forts to allow the truce to take root. But we have insurance! Yes, of course! Insurance!'

'What "insurance", my Lord?'

'The truce will last six weeks in the first instance. Then be renewable, so we can test it, every six weeks. Renewable every six weeks. For a year. Yes, for a year. With fourteen days' notice if we decide to commence hostilities again. In case we are not happy with the truce.'

There was silence on the hillside, except for noise of the wind blowing through the wet grass, the occasional snort and shuffle of horses and the faint, babbling noise of river down in the valley.

Essex had gained nothing from the Irish. They had kept their advantage: they kept what they had and what they had won, and with so few weeks of the summer remaining the truce guaranteed no attack until winter closed in and the campaigning season ended. It was widely expected that a force from Spain would arrive in Ireland before the next fighting season.

Essex looked round the gathered men. He saw the truth in their

271

eyes, though none spoke a word. Perhaps he sensed what this news would do to his reputation in England. His face crumpled, the dreaming expression leaving it to be replaced by the face of a frightened child.

'I am ill,' he said. 'Grievously ill. Get me back to Drogheda.'

The Queen refused to accept the terms of the truce. There was no truce. It did not exist, had never existed. Would the light of royal favour ever shine on Essex again?

Gresham waited until midnight to visit. By then Essex's cronies would have drunk themselves into a stupor.

Essex was in his nightgown, a rich cloak thrown carelessly round his shoulders, a half-empty wine jug on the table before the flickering fire.

'I've lost my senses, haven't I?' he said to the fire as Gresham entered the room. 'Bewitched . . .' He turned to Gresham. The red ring was in his eyes.

'Tyrone is a powerful man,' said Gresham.

'Not Tyrone,' said Essex. 'Lucifer.'

'Lucifer?' asked Gresham, confused.

'Will you swear on your most sacred oath never to reveal what I am about to tell you to any other human being?' There was no excitement in Essex's voice, rather a flat resignation.

'Yes,' said Gresham simply.

'It matters little how I met him,' said Essex, as if discussing the weather. 'Suffice it that I did so. He claimed to be a doctor, to have cured the pox. I was desperate. I believed him. And for a time his filthy cures seemed to have an effect.'

So Essex *had* contracted the pox!

'But then the early symptoms returned. I panicked. I went back to him. Yes, he said, there was a cure. Of a different kind. But it would require . . . commitment. He asked me to come to a gathering. I was almost insane with worry. I said yes. Took Southampton with me. I know what you think about him. But he was the only

272

one of my rank I could trust.' Essex fell silent, staring into the heart of the fire. The silence dragged on. A log collapsed into its own ashes.

'And?' asked Gresham quietly.

'They were dressed in gowns and hoods. Thirteen of them. White gowns. Strange. You would think it would be black, would-n't you? And the doctor, or whatever he was, myself and Southampton, we had to kneel while their leader talked to us. I never even saw his face.'

Gresham held his breath, frightened to interrupt in case he broke the fragile thread linking Essex to speech

'And he told me . . . told me that I had the Devil's illness, that Satan had claimed me for his own by the mark of this disease, that only those who sinned against . . . God's word fell victim, that lechery was one of the seven deadly sins and I must die for it. I owed Satan a death.' The Earl paused. It was as if there was a constriction in his throat. 'But he said his Master was merciful, unlike Him who men called God. He would allow a life to be bought back.'

'The price?' whispered Gresham.

'My soul,' said Essex. 'And a life to take if mine was to be saved. A life for a life.'

More silence. Then the Earl's voice again, devoid of life or emotion.

'They made me sign a deed. In blood, of course. They made the cut by my male organ, so it was hidden in the mass of hair. It's true what they say about the Devil's mark: it never heals, just weeps a little all the time. Like my soul.'

'And after the signing?' asked Gresham. There was dullness in his heart, as if he already knew the answer.

'They brought in the child. Seven, eight years old. Blue eyes, blond hair – a street urchin. Drugged, I suppose. But his eyes were open. And he knew when they plunged the dagger into his stomach and twisted it to draw more blood. By his screaming, I knew he knew. And I drank his blood. I drank his blood. A life for a life.'

'When?' asked Gresham.

'Does it matter?' asked Essex blankly. His shoulders and then his whole body began to shake uncontrollably. He turned, his face distorted in agony like the thief on the cross. 'Help me, Henry. *Help me!*'

Henry Gresham clasped the quivering body of the Earl of Essex to him, like a mother with child, stroking the broad back, running his hand through the long hair.

Was there any way back for a man who had drunk a child's blood?

PART 3

The Road Back to England

Chapter 10

September, 1599
England

Essex's ride. The ride to hell.

It could, perhaps should, have gone down in folklore, become a tale told to children by the fireside, a tale of heroism, of rash courage, of fighting for justice. Instead it became a symbol of folly, of selfishness, of time and talent wasted.

It was morning. Essex had finally fallen into a fitful sleep. Gresham had laid him carefully on the bed, covered him up and sat up all night, sleepless, pondering. Now Essex was awake and feverish. His eyes darted round the room.

'I ride for England,' he said to Gresham. 'Now. Without warning.'

'To meet the Queen?' said Gresham. 'Or to take her throne?'

Essex gave a harsh, brittle laugh. 'Her Majesty is surrounded by evil men, advisers who advise only evil and her own destruction. I have three hundred men, here, swordsmen all, who will ride with me. Ride with me to force Her Majesty to listen to the truth.'

'You haven't answered my question,' said Gresham. 'Do you ride to meet or to rebel?'

'Do you wish to know before deciding whether or not to ride with me?'

So it had come to this. A half-maddened Earl riding in thunderous haste half across England, dragging three hundred wild, excited hot-heads along with him. If word got ahead, it would be seen as an invasion, troops would be mustered. At the very least there would be a pitched battle in London. Essex could not be King. But should he be allowed to ride like a lamb to his own slaughter, or be allowed to bring peace and good order crashing down around his ears in England?

And someone out there was wanting to murder Henry Gresham! There was a truth out there still waiting to be discovered. A truth important enough for someone to want him dead in order for it to remain buried. Someone who believed he knew something of crucial importance. His every instinct shrieked at him not to believe Cameron Johnstone. His accusation of Cecil was too clever, too convenient for it to be true.

'My Lord,' said Gresham softly, approaching Essex as one approaches a wild, slavering dog, 'three hundred men won't wrest the Crown from Elizabeth. Ride with fifty if you will. Ride with fifty, and ride into London as the Earl of Essex returned to right a wrong. Ride with any more, and you ride as the man who wants to be King Robert of England. And they'll destroy you – the Cecils, the Raleighs, the Howards, the other noble families. They'll not permit one of their kind to have precedence over them, and they'll fight you and yours to the death. Their death, your death and the death of England.' Gresham looked pityingly at Essex, whose eyes had shrunk to pinpoints. 'Don't unleash civil war in England.'

But if one was a true servant of the Devil, was not that precisely what one should do?

Essex looked long and hard at Gresham. He seemed a little calmer.

'You might not need to rebel, my Lord,' said Gresham, even more gently. 'Win over the Queen, persuade her of the rightness of your cause, and all you wish will be yours anyway.'

'Will you ride with the Devil?' asked Essex.

'I've done so all my life,' said Gresham.

*

278

And so the ride began that evening as the sun was setting over the battlements of Dublin Castle. Fifty men, Essex ordered, though seventy-five were there shouting and yelling at grooms, falling over each other. That was all right, Gresham thought. Only half that number would survive the mad dash to London.

The horses whinnied, clattered round the courtyard, rose up on their hind legs, their riders cursing and reining back hard. Last-minute orders were given to servants, too few baggage horses were loaded with too many stores. Young men were stuffing shirts, bits of food, leather water bottles and flagons into saddlebags. A servant ran to bring his young master his sword, scabbard and belt, put his foot in a pile of steaming horse dung and piss, slipped and fell head-long. The sword fell out of the scabbard, rattled along the cobblestones. The young man leant impossibly low out of his saddle, like an Irish horseboy performing tricks, scooped up the sword, left the inlaid leather belt and scabbard on the ground where another horse trampled on it, splintering it into two halves. Shouting. Everyone shouting. Yells and shrieks, tears and whoops of joy. With a rattling, groaning crash the great gates were opened, the flood of men piling out on the road to the harbour.

'You *quite* sure you want to be on this ride? You do want your 'ead on a pike on London Bridge, don't you?' said Mannion.

'If I can keep up with him and talk sense to him, it won't come to that,' said Gresham. 'And I'm the only one of this lot who *can* talk sense to him. Are you coming?'

He had not told Mannion about the child.

'Of course I'm bleedin' well coming!' said Mannion, outraged. 'I allus comes, don't I? *Particularly* when I think it's bleedin' madness!'

Strange how human life was so often cast in extremes. Light and dark. Heat and cold. Good and evil. Order and chaos. The mass confusion of their departure was met by supreme order at the quayside. With only a few hours to prepare, ships had been paid for, stored, made ready and extra vessels ordered for the horses. The calm of the embarkation did not silence the young men. All night on board ship they laughed, joked and diced, many swigging from jugs, as the sea hissed past. Essex moved among them, clapping backs, sharing jokes, laughing at things that were not funny.

Dawn. The lowest time for men, when the darkness has sapped the life from them, when the thin, cold light seems to offer no hope. More noise, more chatter.

They started to gallop through the North Wales countryside. The pounding hooves threw up huge clods of earth. Birds and animals squawked and fluttered out of their way in panic as the cavalcade rode remorselessly on, peasants and children standing back in the dreary villages of mud and looking in drop-mouthed wonder.

The first the Queen must hear of her general's return was when he walked in to confront her! Anything less and Cecil and his crew would have time to hide the Queen away, marshal troops outside her palace. Speed was essential!

Essex had never seemed braver, more sure of himself, more in command. If only they had seen this in Ireland! Single-handedly he kept up the spirits of his men, as if the force of his personality alone could drive them to London. They laughed and joked, shouted at each other as the wind tore through their hair. The tiredness crept in slowly, the bone-aching, tortured-muscle tiredness, and they talked and joked less, hunched down over their mounts more, rode on even into the darkness. Essex seemed as if he was not of this world, not possessed of muscles and sinews like ordinary men. They grabbed an hour, two hours' sleep in wayside inns, in hovels where they threw gold at the occupants, through the North Wales valleys, past the Earl's estates at Chartley without thinking of stopping. Pain, the whole journey now becoming a matter of simple endurance. They rode, savagely hard, through a history of England – the Vale of Evesham, the northern Cotswolds, the Vale of the White Horse. As their horses faded and faltered, they threw more gold in the air and took nags, anything that could bear them and had breath in its body. Through the Chilterns, London almost in their sights.

Four days and nights. Four days and nights with hardly any sleep, four days and nights of a breathless, mindless race through England, four days and nights where Gresham wondered if they had the Devil behind them or the Devil as their leader.

Dawn on Friday. They had left Dublin on Monday. The last few days of September, the nights drawing in, the sun losing its heat. Already the smoke from the early morning fires was gathering over London, its wooden buildings creaking with the change in temperature, a thin line of condensation on the cobbles at Westminster. The Court was at Nonsuch Palace, eleven miles south of London. They had to cross the river using the Lambeth ferry. Someone saw a group of horses tethered on the other side of the river. God was on their side! They could get all of those who had survived the ride, some thirty or forty, onto the ferry, commandeer the other horses, then send it back to bring their horses along in the rear. Gresham and Mannion piled in with the others. No one looked at them with hostility. Simply by being there at the end they had proved something.

The cold and damp morning gave no relief to their aching limbs. It had rained in London overnight. The man in charge of the horses was reluctant to release them. Even gold did not sway him. One of Essex's acolytes, Tom Gerard, hit the man a sharp blow to the side of his head, knocking him over. Had anyone else passed this way? Anyone in a hurry?

Yes, the man stuttered. The great Lord Grey had ridden by only moments ago, in a great hurry.

Grey. One of Cecil's men. Had he heard of Essex's return? Was he even now riding to tell the Queen? This was no time to relax!

They piled onto the horses, Essex shouting instructions for Gerard to wait behind and bring up their other horses after them. But the road was slippery. Autumn leaves covered it, and fell on the men. Dead things, Gresham thought. Dead leaves. An omen? Mud was everywhere, the clods of earth they had thrown up in Wales matched by lumps of sodden clay and earth, besmirching them, marking their faces. A man took his hat off, wiped his brow, showing the line on his forehead where the mud had not penetrated beneath the hat. There was a clatter behind them. Troops? They swung round. It was Gerard, bringing the spare horses. He had ignored the treacherous road and the state of his mount, had ridden at full pelt to catch up. Throwing the reins to another man, he galloped on ahead. Minutes later, he was back.

'I caught up with Grey!' he spluttered, spitting mud out of his mouth. 'Asked him to parley with you – to wait for you. He rode on even harder. My horse is blown or I would have knocked him off his mount.'

'My Lord!' shouted another man, 'I'll ride ahead, kill Grey, get to Cecil before he can be warned!' There was a roar of approval from the others.

Suddenly Essex was aware of a figure by his side. Through the caked mud he could just make out the features of Henry Gresham, calmly taking a swig from a water bottle. He offered it to Essex, who shook his head.

'Who will rid me of this turbulent priest?' muttered Gresham, and let his horse fall back.

It was a gamble; Essex was an educated man and knew the story of how rash words from King Henry had sent rough knights off to murder Thomas à Becket, the crime from which Henry's reign had never quite recovered.

'Hold!' said Essex, the old Essex now, flamboyant, alive, radiating energy and command. 'Let the old man warn the little man! My business is with the Queen!' He dug his spurs into his horse, and the exhausted beast picked up its feet and lumbered into an apology for a gallop.

They thundered into the courtyard of Nonsuch. There was no sign of Sir Edward Grey. Essex jumped off his horse, threw the reins to an astonished soldier and barked at him, 'Show proper respect to an Earl!'

The pikeman drew up his pike, stood to attention, his other hand holding the reins.

Essex half walked, half ran into the Palace. He simply walked through two startled guards on the main gate who were unsure whether to cross their pikes to bar the intruder or bring them to attention. Everyone who served in a royal palace, and most of London, knew the Earl of Essex. Sweat had drawn little rivulets of white through the mud caking his forehead, and patches of mud marked his path through the Palace.

On he went without halting, his spurs jangling, sword scabbard flapping against his thigh. He stormed through the Presence Chamber, a dark expression of determination on his face. Again he brushed the guards aside. He grasped the rough wooden handle of the door at the end of the Presence Chamber, swung it down and to one side. The double doors crashed open. He was in the Privy Chamber. Facing the Earl was the door to the royal bedchamber. If any man had ever been invited in there, the world had never been told.

'Stand aside!' roared the Earl of Essex, and the two guards fell back. Essex raised his foot, with its mud-stained and blackened fine leather boot, and kicked at the door. It flew open with a great crash and rending of wood.

The Queen was standing by her bed, looking as if she had just got up. Without her wig, her head was nearly bald, some thin, wispy strands of grey marking all that was left of her once pride and joy. With no make-up, her face was like a sand beach across which the wind has blown, ridged and wrinkled with the scars of time. Her neck was like a plucked chicken's, and her breasts hung down inside her nightdress like the drooping dugs of a worn-out sow.

Essex advanced towards her. She could not know his intentions, must have assumed that a man who broke into her room might easily be there to kill her. Yet to her credit, she did not flinch.

Essex flung himself to his knees before her, bowed his head, and reached out for her hand. He smelt foully of the road, of mud and sweat and of horse. His clothes were dank, dripping, and like a slug he had left a trail across the floor where he had advanced towards her.

'Welcome, my Lord,' she said without a trace of irony. Essex

283

started to babble, some speech of mixed excuse and self-justification that could hardly be heard as he sought to cover his Queen's hand with kisses.

Incredibly, Essex had not realised there was a man standing in the doorway. Henry Gresham, the colour of earth, stood there, outstretched sword in one hand, the other hand clutching a dagger with which he was warding off the guards.

If there is a noise, if he thinks he is being attacked, I do not know what he will do. Could he kill the Queen? Yes, in extremis. Best by far if he was not given an excuse.

The Queen looked up at Gresham. Still unflinching, she raised the poor ruin of what had once been an eyebrow at him. 'Am I safe?' she said wordlessly to Gresham.

He nodded twice, very carefully. Glancing quickly behind him, he saw the two guards being bundled off by Essex's men, who had gathered now in the Privy Chamber. Gresham carefully eased the door shut as best he could. Half the Court would be here in minutes. They should not see the Queen in this state, for the sake of her dignity and that of the country. Gresham touched his sword to his forehead, and stood back, half shrouded by a tapestry.

The Queen was cradling Essex's head in her hands, with him still kneeling at her feet. Minutes, was it? Gresham was keeping no count of time. He heard the Queen speaking softly to Essex, overriding his protestations, like a mother gently chiding a child. He heard her suggest they might meet 'at a better time', when they had both washed and dressed. Stumblingly, almost in tears, Essex agreed, rose to his feet and bowed low to Elizabeth, retreating backwards. Hurriedly, Gresham realised that if Essex banged his arse on the door Gresham had just shut, it might reduce the poignancy of the event. He moved over to ease the door open. There was an expectant hush in the chamber outside. As soon as Essex had gone, Gresham closed the door again, and bowed to his Queen.

'Does he have an army with him?' The tone was clipped, almost ferocious, so totally at odds with the soft, cooing tones she had used a few seconds earlier that Gresham wondered if it was the same woman speaking.

'No,' said Gresham not raising his eyes from the floor, head still bowed in respect, 'he has no army. Just the usual suspects – Southampton, Rich, Rutland, Mountjoy – who have ridden with him. In four days. My Lord of Essex is . . . exhausted, Majesty.'

'You make excuses for this man?' The tone was peremptory, sharp. 'You encouraged him in this . . . this extraordinary intrusion? You were responsible for it, perhaps?'

Gresham was very, very tired, and his body ached ferociously in parts he never knew it had.

'I hope I'm in part responsible for the fact there's no army outside, Your Majesty, only a weeping Earl and some of his sycophants. And I entered after the Earl simply to protect you. I keep my word.'

'I think you do,' said the Queen. 'And, by God, I will keep mine. As you will keep your counsel over what you saw this early morning, if you wish similarly to keep a head on your shoulders. Here, there is a private door at the back. It leads to the dressing room, and thence out into more public areas. It will do neither of us good if you are seen to leave my room.'

So there was a secret door into the Queen's bedchamber at Nonsuch.

'Two guards saw me enter, Your Majesty.'

'Two guards who will not speak of the matter.' She paused. 'Would the Earl of Essex have come with an army? If you had not spoken to him?'

'It is easy to overrate one's influence, Your Majesty. The honest answer is, I do not know. Yet I think it was never his intention to rebel against you. To win your favour, yes. I do not think the Earl is your enemy. I think he needs you too much as his friend.'

He could not tell the Queen that Essex loved her. Not as a man loves a woman who excites him. As a man loves his mother.

'Leave now. Leave the Court.' Gresham's shoulders must have sagged. Damn! How dare his body disobey his mind! 'You are not banished. By your absence I need to make it clear that you are not part of Essex's clan. You lose usefulness for me if you are seen that way. We shall talk again when I have decided what to do with my turbulent Earl.'

Essex was outside, holding Court. His men were smiling, laughing. Their Lord had been well received by the Queen. They had talked. All would be well. The liars and the slanderers would be put in place. The true significance of the Irish treaty would be realised, the appalling difficulties of any Irish campaign understood. Essex cut a dramatic figure, still dripping and covered in mud from his four day journey.

'I have suffered much trouble and many storms abroad,' he announced to the mass of people who had now gathered in chattering excitement. 'But I find a sweet calm at home.'

With that he left to spruce himself up and prepare for the meeting at eleven o' clock he had arranged with the Queen. Clearly he had a store of clothes at Nonsuch as well as at other palaces. His audience lasted for over an hour and a half. His followers were elated, all the more so when the Earl came out smiling, happier than many of his men had seen him for months, if not years. At the meal which followed, men and women crowded round Essex. It was as it had always been – the Earl the candle around which the others flocked, the centre of attention.

Cecil attended the meal. The babble of talk dropped in volume as he appeared, then picked up again. There were a few derisory cheers and groans. Cecil was impervious. He nodded courteously enough to Essex, but seated himself as far away as the table arrangement allowed. Soon he was joined by Raleigh, Grey, Cobham, Howard and Shrewsbury.

And then the Queen asked for a second audience, later that afternoon.

'We got a new neighbour.' Mannion had burst into where Gresham was seeing if stretching his limbs increased or decreased the pain of his recent ride. It had seemed to leave Mannion unaffected.

286

'And who might that be?'

'The Earl of Essex. 'E comes out of his meeting with the Queen, the one in the afternoon, looking like thunder. Before anyone can think, the order comes out that 'e's confined to his chamber. Then the Queen calls the whole of the Privy Council to Nonsuch. They 'old an 'earing. Six charges against 'im, from busting into the Queen's bedchamber to makin' a right mess o' things in Ireland. Next thing is 'e's banished from Court and 'e's in the custody of the Lord Keeper – kept in the Lord Keeper's house, in fact, right 'ere in the Strand. Two servants, that's all 'e's allowed. No visitors, not even his wife. Can't even walk in the garden. I reckon 'e's done for this time.'

'I've got an awful feeling,' said Gresham, 'that this isn't the end of anything. In fact, I wonder if things aren't just starting.'

CHAPTER 11

December, 1599 to January, 1601
London

London was in uproar. Huge, exaggerated versions of Essex's ride from Ireland, of his meeting with a naked Queen circulated and grew even more outrageous in the telling. Essex was banished, imprisoned in the Lord Keeper's house on the Strand, allowed only a handful of servants. No visitors were permitted. But the strain of keeping a tight rein on a man such as Essex defeated Sir Thomas Egerton, the kindly old Lord Keeper. Passers-by hurled abuse against the Queen, cries of support for Essex, then ran on, their faces hidden.

'Yet there's a strange load o' people still goin' in there,' said Mannion. 'All 'is old cronies, the ones with no money and even less sense.'

Gresham tried to visit. He was turned away. He resisted the urge to break the guard's head for him. The last thing Essex needed was a brawl on his doorstep. He smuggled a letter in. The reply was depressing.

'He's got religion again.' In courteous yet formal terms Essex's letter rejected Gresham's request for a visit. It suggested that in their wilder days they had forgotten God and Jesus, and that Gresham would need to refer to both before they could properly meet again. Even more worryingly, it was in the Earl's own hand, and sermonised Gresham for two close-written sides. It was as if the child had never existed. Perhaps Essex had made himself forget that it had.

The inns were rife with rebel talk. Essex could do no wrong. Hundreds of men from Ireland had returned to London, were swaggering and fighting in its streets and taverns, all the time professing their loyalty for the Earl, whipping up the already frothing sense of resentment and fear. Gresham had known nothing like it before, this unreasoning sense of anger centred on Essex and the perceived wrong done to him.

No call from Cecil. No call from the Queen. No ghosts from his past rising up to haunt him. Nothing to do, except try to stop Granville College, Cambridge, from self-destructing, manage his finances and do the minimum to keep in at Court. The Christmas festivities were dire, the light gone from them, the Queen surly and flat. Gresham was haunted by the image of the gilded Earl, once the life and soul of these celebrations, banished with a handful of servants to a cold house on the Strand. So near and yet so very far away. What must it be like for the life and soul of the party suddenly to find himself banned from it, reduced to imagining the pleasures of others more privileged, left with only the anger and resentment of his servants and so-called friends?

Gresham felt the black waves of depression starting to advance again on the shifting sands of his brain.

'You're too used to being at the centre of things, my Lord,' said Jane at supper. 'You only know how to run at full speed, and you falter if you're asked to walk.'

He had invited Jane to their first supper together in The House on his return from Ireland. She had asked for the story of the Ride from Ireland, and for some reason he had not finished it until long after the food was cold. It had only been courteous to ask her to attend the next evening, to finish his story. She had asked him to elaborate on some of the opinions he had voiced, and so she had been asked back a third time. So it had gone on, and now she was a regular attender at supper, voicing an opinion occasionally, but for the most part just listening. He was becoming accustomed to her and he was alone in failing to notice how, in the face of his goodwill, more and more power over the running of The House passed to her. And she was very beautiful.

'She's at her worst with Essex,' said Gresham, talking about the Queen. 'You stick the knife in, or you take it out. You don't leave it half in and half out unless you want to enrage the victim.'

'What's she done, my Lord?' asked Jane.

'Dismissed all his servants from Essex House – including those who served him and his father all their lives – and let him go back there with a handful of new servants. He's a prisoner in his old house, reminded every time he opens his eyes of past glories. And she won't try him, just keeps holding these inconclusive hearings.'

'They was 'avin' fun down the road this morning,' said Mannion, helping himself to a third plate of meat and fish.

There had been a near-riot in Cheapside, when an Irish adventurer had sought to stir up the apprentice boys on Essex's behalf. The man had been whipped soundly enough to make him regret his rashness, but the populace took note.

Essex still refused to receive Gresham although he wrote once a week.

Gresham was deeply in need of a visit from George. Letters to him had received an altogether warmer response than their equivalent to Essex, but the answer was the same. Lord Willoughby, for whatever reason, was keeping to his country estates.

Cecil, on the other hand, was charming to him. It worried Gresham more than anything else. A charming Cecil was a Cecil who thought Gresham no longer mattered. And had Cecil been behind the attempt to kill him in Ireland?

Though Gresham would have fiercely denied it, campaigning in Ireland had wakened instincts in him that he was finding it hard to douse down. He had left parts of both his soul and his body in the

Low Countries, had grown up there, received his real education in life there despite everything St Paul's and Cambridge could offer. The bleak risks of soldiering, the stark simplicity and the simple pleasures of a fighting man and above all the comradeship, the sense of a clear and shared danger, were a heady mix that once inserted into a man's brain never left him. It was a restless, almost hunted figure that attended the minimum of Court functions, and joined high table at Cambridge. He was made even more restless by the news of success in Ireland. Forced to be parsimonious in their use of men, the English commanders had reinforced their strongholds, made Tyrone come to them. There had been no more defeats and growing signs of fatigue among those who supplied Tyrone with troops.

And then the world changed disastrously for the Earl of Essex, and also for Henry Gresham.

In June there was a hearing by the Privy Council, of which Essex had once been so proud a member, confirming that he had offended the Queen and failed in Ireland despite every possible advantage. In August Essex was banished from Court. The highest nobleman in the land was now little more than a country squire, permanently separated from the gold mine that was the Court, savagely separated from all patronage.

In October the Queen dealt the most crushing blow of all, deciding not to renew the ten-year lease the Earl of Essex held on the import of sweet wines, but rather to reserve the income to herself. It was one of the richest monopolies in her power. It had funded all Essex's ambition, most of his excesses and the lifestyle of an aristocrat whose parents had left him so little. Its withdrawal did not mean only that he was now yesterday's man. It meant he was bankrupt. The creditors for the thousands of pounds he owed who had held off for fear of offending someone in the Queen's favour or because the grand Earl had a guarantee to fund his debts, all those would now descend on him like vultures determined to be the first to pick the flesh off his bones.

'Is she trying to force him to rebellion?' whispered Gresham, almost to himself. 'Is this her final challenge to him?'

He wrote again to Essex. The rejection came by return.

So Gresham did what he should probably have done in the first place, and went with Mannion and knocked at the door of Essex House. The surly servant seemed willing enough to let him or anyone else in, and after that it took only a very little money indeed to be admitted into Essex's presence.

Gresham's alarm bells sounded from the moment he stood at the door. The yard was full of carousing men, the worst type of soldier, and there was no shortage of beer, though precious little bread and cheese. The story was repeated as Gresham mounted to Essex's private rooms: drunken men, filthy corridors, Essex House stinking of piss, vomit and worse.

'Stay out here and guard me,' said Gresham to Mannion, as a man with a raddled whore in tow ran past them in the narrow corridor, the woman shrieking in mock terror.

'From the whores or from the dirt?' asked Mannion.

Essex was still gloriously good-looking, thin, but not disastrously so. He did not seem at all surprised to see Gresham, and ignored all formal greetings, his face strangely vacant and empty.

'You represent my past,' said Essex, rudely, in high aristocratic mood. It clashed awkwardly with the bare floor and lack of furnishings. The sombre, unadorned black of his dress. 'It is a past I truly repent of. All of it.' He did not mention the child. Perhaps he was regretting his confession.

There was a Bible on the small desk, and a crucifix on the wall. This was a darker person now, one whom Gresham had only ever half known.

'Yet in my prayers I heard a voice telling me that if you came, despite my refusals, it would be a sign. A sign that God has chosen even a weak vessel such as you. To know the truth and to prove it.'

Gresham was deeply regretting coming. Was Essex about to tell him some great religious truth? The man who had sold his soul to Satan?

'If the truth concerns God, I doubt I'm the right person to tell about it,' said Gresham.

There was no hint of humour in Essex's eyes.

'The truth concerns Robert Cecil. And the clear proof I have of his plot to place the Spanish Infanta on the throne of England.'

Gresham's brain reeled for a moment. Was he going to believe the Earl, fascinating drinking companion that he had been, but also a man blessed with the worst judgement of anyone Gresham had known?

'Are you sure confinement and recent disappointments haven't turned your head?' asked Gresham.

'Quite possibly,' said Essex. 'Or possibly God's taken the time to talk to me at last. You concede that the Infanta has a blood link with the Tudors that goes back to John of Gaunt? I have it on direct evidence that Cecil was heard saying to William Knollys that the Infanta of Spain had the best claim to the throne of England.'

'Evidence?' asked Gresham. There was a stark certainty in Essex's voice.

'Categorical evidence,' said Essex. 'The conversation was overheard. And you know, as does any member of the Court, how persistent the rumours have been that Cecil was taking Spanish money.'

Well, that was true. As were the rumours about half the Court taking Spanish money.

'I have done many things,' said the Earl, 'many evil and selfish things. But I have never sold my country to a foreign power.'

'Apart from one overheard conversation, what other evidence do you have?'

'The evidence that stares you and everyone else in the face. I am ruined because I allowed Cecil the ear of the Queen. And now he is so firmly in command, Elizabeth asks for leniency towards Jesuits and Catholics.'

'That in itself proves nothing. She's never liked burning people.'

'No? But how is it that Raleigh is appointed Governor of

Jersey? I detest Raleigh as much as you admire him. How convenient to rid the Court of a hothead and put a professed member of the Spanish faction in charge of England's western defences? One of Cecil's cronies is appointed Warden of the Cinque ports. Nottingham and Buckhurst control the Treasury and the navy between them – two more of Cecil's sycophants. Cecil has made sure his men control the access to England, and its gold. Lord Burghley, Cecil's brother, is now Lord President of the North, suitably poised to cut off any intervention from Scotland. My friend Mountjoy is to be called back from Ireland, and Carew put there in charge of the largest group of armed men in the country's control.' The Earl paused for breath. Despite an outwardly healthy appearance, Gresham saw the weakness and weariness underneath it.

'And the only man with the standing among the people to resist Cecil is ruined and locked up in his own house!'

'My Lord, I'm deeply sorry to see you reduced to your present state.'

You have no money, no prospects, and the Queen who was your sun has put impenetrable clouds between you and her, he thought. What an appalling end for such a man, like locking him in a deep, dark hole but allowing him just enough dried bread and stale water to survive.

'But all that you list can be denied. Witnesses can change their stories, depending on what the listener wishes to hear. Raleigh is a hothead indeed, but many see his new post as banishment from a Queen who tires of him. The other appointments are all in the way of patronage, not abnormal. When men are in the ascendant at Court, it is their friends who gain promotion.'

What Gresham could not say was that Mountjoy had made the success of taming the rebels in Ireland that Essex should have achieved, and being replaced was widely seen as reward for a job well done.

But what if Essex was right? Who would be easier for Cecil to control? The Infanta? Or an older, male King of Scotland who had already proved himself a consummate survivor? And what power and wealth would come to Cecil from Spain if it was he who set up its heir as Queen of England?

Cecil's smell had hung over London for months. What if Cecil had set up Essex for his fall, for no other reason than to divert attention away from his plan to get the Spanish Infanta on the throne of England? Not only had he rid himself of Essex for the summer Essex was in Ireland, and allowed his poison to seep into the heart of the Queen, but he had also rid himself of Gresham, the one man who might have seen through his plottings. Had Gresham allowed himself to be out-manoeuvred again? He made a sudden resolution.

'I'll research your fears,' said Gresham. 'I'll do it as loyally and as committedly as I would if tasked by the Queen – or by Cecil. If there's truth in what you allege, I'll find it out. It's all I can promise.'

'God tells me to give you something in exchange. A measure of my trust in you. You see this, round my neck?'

Gresham was getting rather tired of God telling them what to do. A small, black bag lay almost invisible against the black velvet of Essex's doublet.

'I have been in communication with King James of Scotland,' said Essex. Is there anyone in this forsaken country who has not been in touch with the King of Scotland, thought Gresham? 'He has written to me. He believes that Cecil is intriguing against him. He will send an embassy to the Queen to ask her intentions regarding her heir, but the real reason for that embassy will be to meet me and hear the truth of who England has allowed to rule it in reality. The letter is here. Around my neck.'

'Precisely where the axe will fall if you let anyone else know what's in that purse!' said Gresham. 'You never did believe in prudence as a virtue, did you?' He sighed. He not only hated it when people claimed that God was speaking to them. He hated when he felt incomparably older and wiser than one of his friends. Gresham much preferred being the young and foolish one.

*

A number of suspicious glances were directed at them by the men carousing in Essex House as they left, the wild groups in stark contrast to the saintly manner being adopted by Essex.

'They're forcing him to rebellion,' Gresham said to Mannion. 'I'm told that he's been incited more and more by his closest friends. I believe him when he says he's communicating with James. James and Elizabeth are a real match for each other – they juggle people like balls in the air.' They were walking in the bitter winter air away from Essex House, their boots crunching through frozen puddles. Two more pamphlets had been pinned on the wall since they had come, Gresham saw. 'They tried it once before in Ireland, and they failed. Now they're doing it again. But who are they?'

' 'E could be right,' muttered Mannion, eyeing two figures who slunk away to the other side of the road under his gaze. 'Typical o' Cecil to put all the attention on someone like Essex, while 'e's doin' the dirty work all the time in the background.'

'I must know what Essex is doing,' said Gresham. 'I need to know if he's actually got the strength to mount a rebellion and make it succeed.'

No one living in London could be ignorant of the popular discontent running through the streets like storm water.

'But I need to know what others are doing as well. I want letters to Spain, to France and to Rome, and the best men to take them. Every contact we have. We must ferret out if Cecil is doing as Essex says. But there's so little time!'

It was winter now, slowing travel down appallingly. It could take many weeks for letters to return from Spain and Rome, even France. It would be January or February before Gresham could be certain of having contacted all his sources. 'Perhaps he's left enough trace of himself here in England, if the worst is true. Let's hope England can give us an answer.'

Gresham could not know in how terrible a manner his prayer would be answered.

Gresham could burn with impatience, but when he had

decided on a course of action Mannion noted that he acquired an almost frightening patience. Half the rogues in London were activated to dig and dig and dig until they hit bedrock, but the results of their enquiries, and a staggering expenditure of cash, crept in with agonising slowness. Now that he was doing something, Gresham's inertia left him, and he flung himself into festivities at Court with all his old enthusiasm, moving easily between the world of Court and the even wilder world of London's writers and artists.

He and Mannion were holding weekly reviews of the information they had gathered. It was late in January that Mannion made his most surprising suggestion.

'You ever thought about bringing that girl in on these chats we 'as?'

'The girl?' Gresham was more startled than offended. 'Why? She's seemed a lot happier recently, she's out of my hair at least. Why should I want to bring her back into it? We're bound to argue again if we talk business. And why her? She just a country girl with an untrained brain and looks to die for – and a personality that can kill.'

'She's got brains, all right,' said Mannion, 'and it's the untrained bit that's good. Means she don't think in channels. And she's a woman. Women see these thing different from men. Witches, they are. Got this intuition about people. And we knows we can trust 'er. She's bin to Scotland, ain't she? And she made her own way over to Ireland – could've been that she saved your life.'

Gresham eyed Mannion with malice.

'Has she put you up to this? I know you're thick as thieves.'

'No, she ain't,' said Mannion firmly. 'If she'd been pressin' me for it, that'd be best reason for not lettin' 'er in on any secrets. She ain't pressin'. I am.'

'Will you talk to her first? Tell her she might hear stuff that could get her hung? Tell her she could get all of us hung if she tells anyone else?'

'I'll do more than that,' said Mannion. 'I'll tell 'er not to be impertinent.'

Gresham was far more nervous when he held his first Council of War with Jane present than was usual, until he realised that Jane was even more nervous than he was. He caught sight of her hand trembling an instant before she drew it into her sleeve. In some way it made things easier for Gresham. The girl was strangely withdrawn, tense, holding back.

'Right,' he said firmly, 'let's go through what we've got.'

'Well,' said Mannion, 'the bad news is that the Earl might 'ave got a real little army, if he wants to use it. Word is that 'e's fallen out with Mountjoy, who won't bring the Irish army back to fight for 'im.'

'So who has he got on his side?' asked Gresham.

'Well, five Earls and three Lords for starters – Southampton, Rutland, Sussex and Bedford, wi' Mounteagle, Cromwell and Sandys just behind.'

'Rutland, Southampton and Bedford ... weren't they all wards of old Lord Burghley, like Essex?' asked Gresham.

'True enough,' said Mannion. 'And most of 'em are thousands in debt. An' I mean thousands.'

'Which means on the one hand they can't muster many men, but at the same time they're desperate,' said Gresham.

'And that's the picture with a real ol' wild bunch he's got with 'im as well. You want the names? You knows most of them.' Gresham nodded, including Jane in the gesture. She would not necessarily know who Essex's lesser supporters were, and there was no point in her joining them unless she was fully briefed.

'Blount, o' course. Then there's that Sir John Davies: bad 'un, that one – acts like a sort of chief of staff, wily bugger. He and that Gelli Meyrick are thick as thieves. Both Essex's creatures: ain't got nothing if they ain't got 'im. Sir William Constable; Sir George Devereux, Essex's uncle; Sir Ferdinando Gorges; Sir Tom Heydon; Sir Robert Cross; Sir Griffin Markham; Richard Chomley; Tom

West; Robert Catesby; Francis Tresham ... there's about ten or twenty more of 'em – gentry.'

'Christ Almighty!' said Gresham, and Jane recoiled slightly at the blasphemy. 'What a list of ... of incompetent, ne'er do wells! It's about everyone who ever missed out on favour at Court.'

'Well, that's it, isn't it?' said Mannion. ''Is supporters are the ones 'o got pushed aside at the feeding trough. They're 'ungry, they feels left out, and they're mad.'

'They're also stupid!' said Gresham. 'There's hardly a brain to share between them.'

'Wait till you 'ear the list of the military men,' said Mannion. He reeled off a list of adventurers, many of whom had sailed with Essex to Cadiz on the Azores expedition and gone with him to Ireland.

'Firebrands,' said Gresham, 'drunkards, braggards and loud mouths. Out of work soldiers whose only hope for preferment – or employment – is Essex. What a mixture!'

'Well,' said Mannion, 'mixture they might be, but there's a fair number of them. And all of 'em with a real capacity to raise 'ell. But that's not the worst of it.'

'Go on,' said Gresham. 'Make me happy.'

'The people we sent out into the Marches. They all report one thing. That Gelli Meyrick's been riding round all summer like a lunatic on Essex's lands. Loads o' people there promised 'orsemen, support. Apparently half the borders is willin' to march to London for Essex.'

Jane spoke, softly and obviously nervous.

'Bolingbroke landed in Wales and gathered his army there when he usurped Richard II, didn't he? He took over the Crown with Welsh peasants.'

'Yes, he did,' said Gresham. 'And the link between them's been noticed in a score of pamphlets. Both Welshmen. Both men who seem to have been wronged by the reigning monarch. Both men with massive public support; both men who ended up King when they swore all they wanted was justice, because the King himself was so unpopular.'

There was silence. Mannion had a list in his hand of those who might be presumed to support Essex in a rebellion, a very long list. It seemed as if every bankrupt, every wastrel in the country, almost every man who had fallen foul of Court patronage was there.

'So can he do it?' Jane ventured. Her voice cracked as she spoke. How nervous was the girl? Surely by now she should be getting used to being there? 'The Earl, I mean? Do you think he could overthrow the Queen?'

Gresham thought for a long minute.

'Yes,' he said. 'If he planned it, if the wind was in the right direction, if luck was on his side – rebellions never go according to plan. But the Queen's in decline, Cecil's unpopular, Essex still has hero status with the people – yes, he could do it. Perhaps.'

'Would it be the right thing?' asked Jane. 'For England? For the people?'

Maybe that was why Mannion had asked her to join them. Who else could ask such a treasonable question with such genuine innocence?

Gresham had to think about that one too.

'No. Probably not.' He thought for a moment longer. 'Definitely not. Essex is unstable. He's a spoilt child really, someone who's never grown up. Elizabeth is a mother figure for him. He craves her authority as much as he resents and fights against it. All he really wants is for people to accept him, to see him as the hero he would desperately love to be. He's also got a death wish. He's like the child who wants to attend his own funeral, to see how sorry people will be when he dies. He's got many virtues, actually. But if he became King, his supporters would call in their debts. They'd descend on this country like vultures denied food for years. Good government would stop.'

And he has drunk a child's blood, thought Gresham, a fact he had sworn never to reveal.

'So is Cecil provoking Essex to rebel? Why would he do that? Particularly if Essex might win.'

300

Gresham was finding this more interesting than he had imagined; Jane's questions were forcing him to put his thoughts in order.

'It's as if the Queen is taunting Essex as well as punishing him – not killing him, but denying him the contact, the favour and the money he needs. That's her instinct – has been all her life – defer the decision until the last moment, change your mind all the time, never put in the killer blow. It's what she did with Mary of Scots. Yet it's wrong with Essex, as it was wrong with Mary. All you do is provoke rebellion. Cecil must know that, and if Cecil told her either to take Essex back into the fold or get rid of him for good on a treason charge, I think she'd do it. So, logically, we've got to deduce that Cecil's holding back, letting the Queen go her own, sweet and thoroughly misguided way. That means he sees profit for himself in Essex rebelling.'

'But how could he profit?'

'He's always seen Essex as a playboy. He's always underestimated the power and strength of popularity. He's always opposed Essex.'

'Why didn't Cecil 'ave Essex killed in Ireland?'

'Perhaps he tried,' said Gresham. 'Perhaps Essex jumped the gun by running home.'

A sudden thought crossed Gresham's mind, a new and blazing insight.

'What if Essex *has* made a friend and an ally of James? What if he's won with James?' he asked excitedly. 'What if James really does believe Essex is his man, and that Cecil is a sodomite and a creation of black magic? What if the letter I carried up to Scotland failed to do its job? Perhaps Essex was more persuasive and won James round? My God! Essex can be persuasive right enough, and he can write like an angel when he's in the mood. He knows how to flatter as well – he's had a lifetime of practice with the Queen. If he's actually won with James, that would mean Cecil would have to produce an absolute thunderbolt to dislodge Essex from James's favour. James is a devout believer in the divine right of Kings – that monarchs hold their power from God, not man. If Essex rises up against Elizabeth, he damns himself in James's eyes!

301

It's about the only thing that would wipe Essex out of James's favour! James will never support someone who rises up against their lawful ruler. If Essex rebels, it proves Cecil right all along. It gifts him power with the King-elect, clears his greatest rival out of the way so he can get on with cosying up to James and securing his accession when the time comes. So perhaps Cecil is provoking a rebellion by Essex because he believes it'll fail and deliver final power to him?'

Mannion interrupted. 'But half the Court and even some of our men, and our two contacts in Spain reckon Cecil's been takin' money from Spain for years, to get the Infanta on the throne.'

'He probably has,' said Gresham, 'but he's bound to smarmy up to all contenders while there's any doubt over the issue. He's like the Queen in that. Keep everyone happy until the last minute. I admit I was tempted to see him favouring Spain and the Infanta for a while. She'll be putty in his hands, after all, while James is a tried and tested monarch, and no one's fool. Then I thought again. James would come to England as the King of a terribly poor nation, someone thanking God and anyone who had got him the throne for what he was about to inherit. Far better that than have King Philip II of Spain pulling all the strings, and having to keep the Queen in control and her father as well.'

'So you're saying that all this trouble with Essex,' said Jane, her eyes wide, 'is because Cecil thinks he will self-destruct. And if he does, Cecil has rid himself of one of his greatest enemies, and built up his reputation for prudence and for being right with both the Queen and James.'

'Then it must 'ave been that bastard Cecil who tried so 'ard to get you killed, first on the Channel and then by that other bastard Cameron fuckin' Johnstone – beggin' your pardon,' said Mannion with a nod to Jane. 'He knew you were a friend o' Essex, knew you'd probably put 'im off rebellion. Must 'ave bin eatin' nails when you stopped him from bringing an army back from Ireland.'

'I suppose so,' said Gresham, 'but somehow it doesn't seem right. Cecil really wanted me to take that letter to James. And hiring

302

twenty men to kill us before the letter was delivered – it doesn't make sense for Cecil, and it's just not his style to kill someone so . . . so *lavishly*. Cecil's a back-of-an-alley man if ever there was one.'

'Well, me, I'm stickin' with Cecil trying to set up Essex and stick you one while 'e's at it,' said Mannion, with the strong sense of a man whose journey had ended.

'I'm sticking with something else,' said Gresham. 'I'm sticking with the fact that whoever's been trying to kill me is doing it because I'm one of the few people who might, just might, talk sense into Essex and stop him from rebelling. So someone wants Essex to rebel. But the style of the murder attempts – they haven't been Cecil's style.'

Jane looked at Gresham, and said in a very small voice. 'I think there's something else you ought to know.'

'What's that?' said Gresham, mildly. His mind was on Essex and Cecil. Was it really that simple?

'Lord Willoughby. George,' said Jane.

'What about him?' Dammit! Why, when things were going so well, did the girl have to bring in one of his oldest friends. Willoughby was off territory for her, off limits.

'I know George – he's said I can call him that – is one of your oldest friends, and I know I've no business commenting on him. And I like him a lot. He was always so nice to me when I first came here, when I was an orphan in this terrifying house and seemed to belong to no one. And when I grew up he never dribbled over me or made a pass at me or thought it was clever to be lewd and suggestive.'

'So?' Gresham's tone was cold.

'So Mannion said women were like witches and had intuition. And George – Lord Willoughby – he's changed so much this past eighteen months, ever since the Essex affair started. Changed when we saw him, and now changed because he won't see you.'

'So?' said Gresham again. 'People change. People have moods.' He had decency enough not to refer to the several hundred changes of personality her adolescence had inflicted on him.

'But down at St Paul's,' said Jane, more nervous by the second, 'they talk of all sorts of things. Not just books. Not books at all most of the time. And they've mentioned all the people you've mentioned – Southampton, Rutland and all the lesser people. And – and – and they've talked of George. Lord Willoughby.'

Gresham gave a caustic laugh.

'George has never been at the centre of any events, now or ever. What are they saying of George at St Paul's? That he watched an ear of wheat turn ripe in the country? That he yawned in his dreadful wife's face?'

'No,' said Jane, raising her eyes to look into his. 'They say he's in the pay of Spain. They say he's working for the downfall of Essex.'

Gresham burst out laughing this time, genuine laughter. 'George! You must be joking! George couldn't conspire to swat a fly. Oh, certainly, he hates Essex, always has. But dear, clumsy old George as a spy! It's simply a joke. St Paul's gossip.'

Jane was holding back tears. 'I'm sorry, truly sorry. I knew you'd hate me for saying this. I've tried so hard not to. But you see, the gossip was that he was in London at times when I was sure if he'd been here he'd have come to see you. Except he hadn't. So I didn't believe the gossip. And then I saw him.'

'You saw him?' asked an incredulous Gresham.

'After I've been to see the booksellers, I like to walk through the cathedral. With Mary, of course, and my escort. You know how many people gather there, people who have nothing to do with religion.'

The fact that the nave of St Paul's was used by every criminal in London had given numerous poets the chance to play upon the difference between 'nave' and 'knave'.

'I saw him – George, that is – talking to a man in a corner. They looked like they were arguing, and then George threw up his hands, like this' – she imitated a gesture of mixed anger and frustration – 'looked round and stalked off, pulling his hat low down over his face. He didn't see me, I'm sure.'

'That proves nothing,' said Gresham. 'Even if it was him he could have been talking to anyone.'

'It *was* him,' said Jane more firmly. 'And I spent the next two or three days waiting for him to visit, because I couldn't conceive of his being in London and not coming to see you. But there was nothing. No visit. No letter, even.'

'And that,' said Gresham, 'was enough to make you believe that George Willoughby – my oldest and beyond any shadow of doubt my most naive friend – was spying for Spain?'

'No,' said Jane; and there was a terrible finality in her voice. 'Like you, I thought life would be much easier if it hadn't been George, if it was someone else who looked and walked like him. And I think I'd half persuaded myself that I'd been mistaken, that it wasn't really him, until that dreadful night on the boat. The *Anna*.'

Why did it cut him to hear her speak the name of the one woman he had loved with all his heart as well as with his body? Jane waited for Gresham to comment. Something in her voice had stayed him, hooked him onto her story. He remained silent.

'I heard the other boat coming alongside!' she said, the memory clear as if it were happening now. 'I don't know how and I don't know why, but locked down in that dreadful cabin I heard the waves in a different way, and I heard a change. I just knew it was another boat. You'd warned us things might happen, but not shared your plans. I expected shouting, alarms. There was just silence. So I worried that no one else had seen this other boat, that you hadn't spotted it, so I tried to come on deck to warn you. I had my hand on the latch of the door when you fired the cannons. The light was like little, red-hot iron bars showing through where the caulking had gone between the planks of the door.'

'What did you do then?' asked Gresham.

'I pushed the door open,' said Jane. 'I don't know why. I've never been so scared in my life, but for some reason I wanted to see what was happening on deck. And I saw him.'

'Him?' asked Gresham, confused. 'You mean George?'

'No,' said Jane. 'Not George. Not Lord Willoughby. On the other boat. Directing the enemy men. The man he'd been talking to in St Paul's. The small man, with the goatee beard. I swear to you, it was the same person.'

A chasm opened up under Henry Gresham. And he felt himself falling, screaming, down into the abyss. It would be so easy not to believe her. So less hurtful.

'So why have you waited this long to tell me?' His outward manner continued urbane, controlled. Inside, every nerve ending had flames licking at it.

'Because my heart wanted it not to be true, not to acknowledge what my head told me I had seen.' Her tone was frantic now, pleading. 'If those men were the same, it must mean that George was a traitor to you, had conspired against his greatest, his oldest friend. And I was scared, of what it would do to you, and I suppose to me as well.'

Gresham turned to Mannion.

'Was this why you wanted her here, at our meeting? Did she tell you before she told me?'

'Just for once,' said Mannion, glaring at him as he had not done since Gresham was a youth, 'as you're the one who's meant to 'ave the brains, use 'em, will you? Of course she bloody well told me! Or rather, she didn't. She said she 'ad something to say about George that only you could hear, but she was frightened to tell you.' Mannion seemed to be having difficulty getting the words out. 'If you want to know the truth, I thought 'e'd made a pass at 'er. After all, all 'e gets from that wife of 'is is the sharp side of her tongue. Shows 'ow much I know.' Mannion paused. 'You know why this 'as 'appened, don't yer? Why we've had to wait so bloody long to hear somethin' we ought to 'ave 'eard ages ago? It's 'cos you're so pig 'eaded! Every time she's told you the truth you've told 'er she's bein' bloody impertinent, 'aven't you? It's a bloody wonderful recipe for getting someone to tell you what you needs to hear.'

An old Fellow of Granville College, a rather lovely man who

had died a year after Gresham had joined as a poverty-stricken undergraduate, had once confided in him and said that friendship was like a loaf: the more thinly you carved it and handed it round, the less sustenance it gave and the less it was worth. You gave a part of yourself to a true friend. The smaller the part, the lesser the friendship. Gresham had only had three real friends in all his life: George, Mannion and, for a brief moment, Anna. And of course there was Jane. Not a friend, but someone whose life had become inextricably woven with his, by accident.

Anna he would never see again. Now the girl, who for all her irritating ways had become part of the fabric of his existence, had proved his greatest friend a traitor to him. And Mannion, who was friend and father, was agreeing with her, and telling him that it was his manner and attitude that was at fault for him not finding out the truth earlier.

At one stroke, Jane had cut through one of the certainties in Gresham's life. He felt sick, physically sick, as if at any moment his stomach would hurl out its contents, as his mind wished it could hurl out what it had been told.

'I must talk to George,' said Gresham flatly.

'He's in London now,' said Jane in a tiny voice, 'or at least, it's rumoured so very strongly in St Paul's.'

'Well,' said Gresham with an irony that would have cut through iron, 'if it's rumoured so in St Paul's, it has to be true.' Despair was a deadly sin, because by its nature it meant one gave up on the prospect of redemption

'You go to 'im?' asked Mannion. 'Or we bring 'im to you?'

'Bring him here!' said Gresham explosively. And in issuing the order for his old friend to be brought to him, Gresham knew that he had accepted the truth of what Jane said. Too many things, too many small gestures had fallen into place as she had spoken. The clinical part of Gresham's brain had seen the truth long before his heart would ever accept it.

'No!' he said suddenly, jumping to his feet, making Jane nearly fall off her stool. 'I'll not have my oldest friend dragged here like a felon, even if he is one! Does St Paul's say where George is to be found?'

Jane whispered something, looking down at the floor. She was crying.

'Speak up.'

'The Duck and Drake. In Cheapside.'

Gresham and Mannion looked at each other. It was a highly respectable inn, so respectable that very few of the informers on Gresham's payroll would ever dream of going there, and hence excellent cover. But why would any of those Gresham paid to spy on London deem it worth reporting to him that his best friend was in town?

'My Lord,' Jane was still looking down, great tears dropping to the floor, 'I am ... I am sorry ... I ...'

There was an icy calm in his heart now. He touched her on her shoulder, and felt the flesh jump under his fingers.

'Look at me,' he said. Two huge, tear-rimmed eyes raised themselves up to his gaze. 'Whatever arguments we might have had, this isn't your fault.' There was no emotion in his voice, no sympathy, not the warmth of a guttering candle. 'It's his fault, and to a far lesser extent my fault for not seeing what should have been clear to me. You ... you're just the agent of tragedy. Not its cause.'

January was at its coldest, and the thin, fashionable gloves Gresham had donned did little to keep him feeling the ends of his fingers. What small warmth the sun had given died with the sunset. Decent people were hurrying home. London handed itself over to a different breed of citizens when darkness fell. The cold seemed to freeze Gresham and Mannion's cheeks, forced water into their eyes. A blast of hot, fetid air hit them as they pushed open the door to the Duck and Drake. The babble of noise dropped slightly as Gresham's saturnine, elegant figure and that of his bulky manservant entered, but only for a moment. This was a respectable inn. So what if one of the gentry had decided to come slumming, to take their drink undiluted before summoning up courage to cross the city to the stews of Shoreditch?

There was no sign of George.

'What we do now? Ask if he's staying?' said Mannion.

'He'll have taken another name,' said Gresham. His calmness was more unsettling than a full-scale rage. A thought came to him. 'Go and ask the landlord if there's an Andrew Golightly staying.' Mannion raised an eyebrow, but did as he was bid. At school George and Gresham had fooled a young and permanently drunk usher that there was a boy called Andrew Golightly in the class, blaming everything they did on him. It had taken weeks for the deception to be revealed, to the huge amusement of the other boys; the whipping he and George received had been deemed well worth the fun.

Mannion returned. 'Sir Andrew Golightly is staying for two nights. He's booked supper for one in a private room. Up there. Servants took it to 'im ten minutes ago.'

They mounted the creaking stairs, ingrained with the smoke from lamps and candles and the cheap coal on the blazing fire, which periodically belched fume, smoke and sparks out into the main room as the wind started to get up outside.

Gresham lifted the simple latch on the door, and walked in. George was coming to the end of his meal, hacking at some hard cheese with his knife as the door opened. He hardly looked up.

'Ten minutes more,' he said, 'and bring me another flagon while—' He looked up. The colour drained instantly from his face, and he stood up.

'Henry! I was just about to come and see you . . . sudden call to London . . . business . . .'

He looked at Gresham, who gazed back expressionless. Slowly his words slowed, and stopped. The two men stood staring at each other in silence.

'When did you first start to spy for Cecil?' asked Gresham finally. 'And did you think that spying on me for him was all in the way of friendship? And how did it feel when you saw your contact on board another ship full of men trying to kill me?'

'I – I never – I—'

'George,' said Gresham with intense pity, 'I can read you like a book. You've not only betrayed me and everything I thought we meant to each other, you've betrayed yourself, got yourself in way over your head, you poor, idiot booby.' Gresham shook his head, partly in disbelief, partly to rid himself of a terrible pain. George looked as if he was about to be sick. He made a sudden movement. Without anyone quite knowing how it got there, a dagger was cleaving into the wood inches in front of George's face, handle shaking gently with the force of impact.

'I won't kill you now, as I've killed everyone else who's betrayed me, simply for the sake of our friendship. But if you make even the slightest move for a weapon, or any sudden move, I will kill you. Do you understand?'

George cleared his throat, made a noise, cleared it again, swallowed and finally got words out, 'I understand. And I believe you.'

'Now,' said Gresham, his voice cold as a frozen sea, 'you'll tell me everything. Mannion!' Even Gresham's tone to Mannion was grim, clipped, short. 'My old friend here's been turning to the bottle increasingly often. Fetch two flagons from the landlord to oil his tongue.'

Mannion left, and took five minutes to return clutching two black large jugs of wine. The two men were still staring silently at each other. Neither had said a word.

'Now, damn you!' and for the first time some of the intensity of Gresham's feelings crept through into his voice. 'Tell me the truth!'

'Mortgaged,' said George.

'Speak up!' said Gresham.

'Mortgaged!' George nearly shouted. 'Mortgaged to the hilt! All my estate. Mortgaged by my worthless father. Debts everywhere, and the estate collapsing. Walls not mended, wells running foul, corrupt stewards, the wrong crops sown in the wrong fields – and then three bad years, what grain there was rotting in the fields. Men and their families – my men, people I'd grown up with, men and women I knew by name – facing starvation. And marriage to a wife whose fortune turned out to exist more in the imagination of my father than in any reality, and whose mother insists on living like a Queen.'

'So someone came . . .' prompted Gresham.

'I borrowed as much money as I could. Tried for positions at Court, was rejected all the time. No powerful relations, no contacts; just friendship with the wildest member of the Court, which did me no good at all. I was about to be bankrupted. Then a man came to me. Offered me enough money to bail me out, see off the most pressing debtors for six months or so.'

'And what did this man ask for in exchange for his money?'

'He wanted me to spy on Essex!' There was anger in George's voice. At least he had some spirit left. 'Not you! He said he was working for the government, and I assumed that meant Cecil, and that Cecil and Elizabeth feared Essex above all others as an enemy and future King of England. Well, I hated Essex – you've always known I hate Essex – so I didn't see that as a betrayal. You only came into it because I could use my friendship with you to get closer to Essex, get inside his social circle.'

'But it didn't stop there, did it?' said Gresham. 'And before he gave you the gold, he made you sign a paper, didn't he?'

'How did you know?' said George, shocked.

'Just tell me,' said Gresham.

'Well, yes, he did make me sign something. It was that or ruin, and everyone knows that half the Court's taking money from Spain! I thought it's what they made everyone do. I thought if everyone else at Court was getting their slice of the pie, why shouldn't I? And then—'

'And then,' said Gresham, 'your little tame man paid you even more money to spy on me. To tell him what I was saying to Essex. He said of course that he knew I was going to Scotland for Cecil, but that you had to tell him if I was about to be sent on any secret missions for anyone else, or carry any secret messages. And where I was to go.'

'Well, yes,' spluttered George, going a deep red, 'but he assured me—'

'That I wouldn't come to harm,' said Gresham. 'Indeed, you would be helping me. Your little man, who spoke perfect English and could so easily have been Cecil's man, who knew so much more about what was going on than you could ever hope to know, told you that if any mission you reported on was going to be dangerous for me he would warn you, and you could warn me. Knowledge, that was all he was after. Pure knowledge. And of course you told him, you poor fool, that I was carrying a message from Elizabeth as well, didn't you? And he thanked you and said that if you carried on simply watching and reporting, not only would no harm come to me but you would find yourself in receipt of a Court pension, or perhaps even a share in one of the lesser monopolies—'

'But how do you know all this? You've used almost his exact words—'

'Because it's how I would have played you, like a fish on a line, how any professional would play a poor, bumbling idiot who stumbled into their trap.'

The words were tumbling out of George now. 'And then you told me about the man. On the boat. With the goatee beard. You told me he was the leader of a brutal bunch of thugs who tried to kill all three of you.'

'And your little world fell apart, didn't it?' said Gresham pityingly. Except there was a harsh undercurrent in his tone. 'All of a sudden you started to realise that you'd been betrayed, that your little man would as like kill me and you if it suited him, and that you'd been used. Used by Cecil. And you probably thought it was about the Queen's message, that in some way Cecil feared it and wanted it stopped, and me stopped in case she'd told me what it was. And you realised what you'd become. Judas.'

'I never meant to—'

'It's the most pathetic excuse people like me hear all the time. If your panic over money hadn't totally clouded any judgement you

312

might have had, you'd have seen that the only thing in the interests of Cecil and others is Essex's total destruction. Either by a rebellion that brings him down, or by his making a total fool of himself. And I'm one of the few people who every now and again has been known to talk sense into him, so I pose a threat to all those who want Essex dead.'

'But you've never faced the loss of everything you own and love!' It was almost a howl from George.

'I owned nothing for a large part of my life,' said Gresham witheringly. 'And I can assure you, I value my honour and my friends more than my possessions.'

In the silence that followed, the talk from the crowded inn filtered through the door. Someone walked heavily across the floor in the room above, and a few tiny particles of dust fell from the thick, dark beams on the ceiling.

'There's one other thing you haven't told me,' said Gresham.

'I can't think of anything—' George started to reply.

'Cameron Johnstone's taken over from your original contact. The little man on the boat.'

George's shoulders sagged even more.

'You know everything,' he said. 'I was a fool to think I could match you.'

'Match me?' said Gresham. It was his turn for confusion now.

'Oh,' said George with a harsh laugh, 'so there *is* something you don't know. Of course I wanted to match you. All my life you've moved effortlessly through plot after plot, intrigue after intrigue. You've gambled with kingdoms, walked through high and low life with equal ease, always seemed to be in charge whoever it was asking you for your favours. You made it all look so easy, and I was jealous. Jealous to the core of my being.'

'How dreadful for you,' said Gresham. 'Well, just to show my effortless ease, let me predict what Cameron said to you when he reintroduced himself to you in Ireland. I imagine he said that he was replacing Mr Little Beard of boating fame, and that you'd better damn well listen because what you'd signed in receipt of

313

your first bribe and hadn't really read because you were so hungry for the money, wasn't a receipt but a contract with the Pope to take *his* money. A contract that could have you hung. And then he left you alone for a bit, but with quite a lot of money to soften the blow to show you the deal was still on. And I bet he's been to see you recently and come clean, and said that at all costs Essex must be made to rebel. If I looked as if I was going to do anything to stop it, you needn't kill me so long as you knocked me out or drugged me. And if you didn't, Cecil would have me killed.'

'Yes,' said George. 'You are right.' There was a dignity to him, despite all the odds. Stripped of his pathetic attempts at intrigue, caught out for what he was, he stood exposed and shivering. He appeared a simple but a genuine man. He was not trying to fight Gresham's rapier thrusts, had not sought to do so: it takes strength to face up to one's total foolishness.

'So what you said when I first made an appearance here was true,' said Gresham. 'You *were* coming to see me. You were going to stick to me like glue, and I bet you've wasted days and a lot of money buying powders to put in my drink from every quack in London.'

'What happens now?' asked George. 'To you and me, I mean.'

'What happens to you? That's your business. If you don't fulfil your obligation, Cameron will crawl out of some rotten woodwork and demand repayment. You'll have to explain to him that unfortunately you can't repay him, at least in terms of any contact with me. Because there won't be any contact. We no longer know each other. Don't bother to call, here or in Cambridge because you won't be let in. Ever again.'

Gresham stood up, yanked his dagger out from the table, and turned away. There was a chasm where his heart used to be, and an aching blackness.

'Henry.'

Gresham did not want to stop. He did so, for a moment, in the doorway, his back to George.

314

'I'm truly sorry, for the insignificance that's worth.'

Gresham said nothing, but nodded briefly as if acknowledging a passing comment. The door closed behind him.

Mannion had always had the knack of knowing when to say nothing, and he exercised it now. He was the only silent person, apart from Gresham in the inn. Something had obviously excited the clientele, and groups of them were gathered in huddles of heated discussion. As they reached the door to the street, Mannion halted, and said to Gresham, 'I knows as you don't want to stay 'ere any longer than you 'as to. But 'ave you 'eard what they're talkin' about? I think we ought to get the story.'

Gresham turned and gave a nod to Mannion as brief as that he had given to George. Mannion looked for a moment round the room, and picked on an elderly man who looked as if his tankard might be permanently wedged to his face judging by the ferocity with which he was ramming it there to drain the last dregs. As the tankard finally dropped it was to reveal Mannion beckoning him, a coin held between his finger and thumb.

The man came over, and Mannion flipped him the coin.

'What's the news then?' he asked, as the man raised the coin in the air and a tap boy came over to take the order.

'Ain't you 'eard?' said the old man. 'Southampton – Earl of Southampton, that is – were riding by Raleigh's house this afternoon, and Grey, Lord Grey, rode at him wi' 'is sword, tried to kill 'im, 'e did. One o' Southampton's pages, 'e 'ad 'is 'and lopped right orf, he did. Cut off clean as a whistle.'

Grey and Southampton had a long-standing hatred for each other, and the Privy Council had been spending much of its time forbidding them to have a duel. Grey was Cecil's man.

'Well,' said Mannion, 'that'll put the cat among the pigeons.' There was no answer from Gresham. 'Look,' said Mannion, 'I don't want to intrude—'

'I wouldn't,' said Gresham, still locked in his own world. How could George have betrayed him? How could he have been so stupid?

'About all it needs,' said Mannion remorselessly, 'for your friend the Earl to go pop is for one of Cecil's cronies to ride full pelt at 'is closest friend. Which, 'as it 'appens, is exactly what *as* 'appened. I'm sorry about George, I really am. I thought 'e were a good man. But get your arse in order, will you? 'Cos if Essex takes off, we could 'ave your pal as King by mornin'!'

CHAPTER 12

February, 1601
London

The scenes at Essex House were ugly. Half an army was camped in the yard, but there were no orderly lines, no bread and cheese. Instead, there was vomit over the cobbles, half-drunk men shouting and cheering, at least two men lying unconscious in a corner, heeded by no one.

It was harder to get in to see Essex. There were guards at the entrance to the house, and armed men outside the room he was in. A group of men emerged from it as Gresham and Mannion mounted the stairs, including Gelli Meyrick and the small, wiry figure of John Davies. Both men drew back, hands on their swords. Before either of them could get their swords more than half out of their scabbards Gresham's blade was in the air between them. Mannion had turned round instantly and was back to back with him, having drawn from somewhere on his person a strange, flat, heavy blade like a Roman sword.

Gresham appeared entirely calm, his sword blade rock steady at eye height.

'I'm rather tired of people trying to stop me seeing my friend,' he said, and despite the quietness of his tone, his voice carried down the stairwell. 'And I do so tend to lose control when I'm tired. Now let me through.'

Suddenly his blade was resting on the side of Davies's neck, right where the vein pulsed.

'What if your friend doesn't want to see you?' asked Davies, tense but not cowed.

'Well, let's find out, shall we? If you and the rest of the crew back into the hallway there, you can let us through, can't you?' Essex's room was at the top of the stairs, with a small corridor outside, a corridor that led to a hallway with a view over the yard.

'You've drawn your sword on me,' hissed Davies, motioning the others behind him to move back. Southampton was there, Gresham could now see, standing on tip-toe to peer over the shoulders of those in front.

'I had noticed,' said Gresham mildly.

'You'll pay!' said Davies.

'One of us might,' said Gresham. His reputation as a swordsman was fearsome. Davies dropped his gaze for a moment.

Essex was agitated, the quasi-religious calm of their previous meeting gone. He was sweating, in his shirt despite the cold weather, tugging at the fine lace on his sleeves. His beard was straggly, untrimmed, his eyes red-rimmed and his pupils pin-points. An awful thought crossed Gresham's mind. Had Essex drunk human blood more than once?

'Has Cecil sent you to attack me? He seems willing enough to order one of his closest allies to attack my friend, in public, in full view of the world?'

'If Cecil is the biggest shit in the land, then Grey is certainly a major and steaming turd. In that sense at least I'm smelling rather clean at present.'

'Who sent you this time? Which of my enemies?'

'Your biggest enemy is yourself,' said Gresham brutally. 'You're being set up, you idiot, and you can't see it. And as for who I'm working for, I've just uncovered a spy who has tried to have me killed, all because I try to keep an eye on you. If you want to kill

318

yourself, go ahead. You always were a pig-headed fool who listened either to himself or to the wrong people. But this is personal. You're in danger of getting me killed, and that takes friendship too far.'

'You spin a fine tale, but what value is there in friendship that comes out of a glass?' Essex was speaking fast, as if he had somewhere else to go in a hurry. 'Do you think I don't know how much I'm being pushed into a situation I don't want! It's like Ireland all over again, in case you hadn't noticed. I had to go over to that God-forsaken country because my reputation and my honour gave me no option. The worst mistake of my life! I've lost access to the Court, I'm ruined – a passive victim for the next time Cecil wants to set me up in some invented plot against the Queen. Do you think I don't know what happens to disgraced nobles? Even if they don't plot themselves, they become a centre for everyone who does. Look in that yard if you want to know how many unhappy sword-bearers there are in England!'

'Are you really telling me you've no option but to rebel?' asked Gresham, incredulous. 'Or is that what that bunch of brainless hot-heads I just met coming out of your room tell you?'

Essex looked Gresham full in the face for the first time since they had met.

'I have friends other than you. Other advisers. Men who have contact with my future, not my past.'

As if on cue, the door opened.

Cameron Johnstone had dyed his hair black, grown a full beard and a moustache of similar colour, and must have eaten himself silly to put on two or more stone. The coal-black hair clashed with the wrinkled face and neck of a man nearing forty, but the combination of appearance change would have been enough to fool most onlookers who had never met or spent time with him. He had also changed his clothing. Gone was the sober attire of the Scottish advocate, to be replaced by double- and treble-slashed doublet and hose, in emerald green, pinched in at the waist, ballooning out until captured again just below the knee. The whole array was just this side of fashionable.

Cameron came unsuspecting into the room without knocking, Gresham noted, saw Gresham and turned to run, only to meet the vast bulk of Mannion who had stepped out from behind the door and closed it. He stood four-square in front of it, short sword clutched firmly in his hand. Cameron flicked a glance towards the window, sized Gresham up.

'We're on the second storey,' said Gresham quietly, 'and there's no balcony, no other door. Quite a fire risk, actually. And if you attack me I'll have my sword through your traitorous, stinking heart before you can even reach your dagger.'

'Kill him,' said Essex, 'and you'll have to kill me. And you'll never leave this house alive.'

Gresham weighed up the odds. Essex was lying. Mannion could kill Cameron in the blink of an eye, and Essex, good as he was, was no match for Gresham. If both jobs were done quickly enough, the noise in the house would cover them. They could probably make it down the stairs and out through the yard.

But he didn't want to kill Essex! And was Cameron worth it?

'You're wrong,' Gresham said easily. 'As you usually have been these past two years or so. If we killed you both, the odds are on our side. Which is more than can be said for you if you're listening to this turncoat little animal.'

'You think he works for Cecil,' said Essex. 'I know. There are others who think he works for the Pope, for France and even for Spain. But I know the truth. I know that he works for King James the First of England, or the man who will become so soon enough; he has done so all along.'

'And therefore is your only hope,' said Gresham, sadly.

Essex looked up sharply. Cameron simply stood there, half crouching, eyes darting from one speaker to the other.

'How say you?' asked Essex.

'You've lost the favour of the Queen, Cecil controls the Court and Raleigh will kill you if you ever get back into favour. You hate the Spanish and they hate you, Henry of France distrusts you and you're too proud to contemplate divorcing your wife, even if you could, and too honourable simply to push her down some stairs, so you can't marry the dreaded Arbella Stuart. King James is your only hope of getting back into royal favour. Oh, I can write this little toad's speech for you,' said Gresham motioning towards Cameron who jumped slightly, as if worried there might be a knife in Gresham's fingers. 'And of course,' he continued, 'James doesn't want you to rebel as such, just keep the Queen in your custody for a while, so you can talk sense to her, perhaps even arrange an abdication. Or at least a sworn document in front of every bloody Bishop in the country stating that James will be the next King.'

Gresham could see he had got it right from the expression in Essex's eyes.

'Get out of here, please,' said Essex, after a long pause. 'I can no longer trust you. I'm sorry. I acknowledge the friendship we've had in happier times, but it must end now. It was a different friendship, for different, more innocent times. We won't see each other again.'

What Essex was saying was so extraordinarily similar to what Gresham had said to George a short time earlier that he had a fit of déjà vu.

'That choice is yours. But if these are to be my last words to you as a friend, they're the most important I've ever said to you in my whole life. *Don't trust this man.* Like the Devil who seems to speak true, he'll only lead to your destruction. There's nothing good for you in this man. Nothing.'

He did not say goodbye. He motioned to Cameron to move aside, waiting for the rush with the dagger that did not come. They made it out to the yard and into the street without incident, slightly to Gresham's surprise.

'Now I am confused,' said Mannion.

'You're always confused,' said Gresham absent-mindedly. 'It's not your fault. It comes from not having a brain.'

'This is serious,' said Mannion. 'George thought Cameron was working direct for Cecil, which means it was Cecil who tried to kill you. Essex thinks Cameron's working for James, which means it's James 'oo tried to knock you off. Can't both be right, can they?'

'No,' said Gresham, 'but they can both be wrong. Horribly wrong.'

All the time he was thinking how extraordinarily clever someone had been. George was an ideal recruit. Right under Gresham's nose and beyond suspicion of spying on him. Out of the London circle of spies, informers, cut-purses, rogues and rascals, and as far distant from the roistering drunkards who made up Essex's crowd, George could be seen near them without arousing the least suspicion. Another country bumpkin on the edge of the charismatic leader's life, looking on in wonder and innocent admiration, probably never going to exchange even a word with the Earl in his life.

'You goin' to tell me?' said Mannion. 'I mean, tell me who Cameron is actually working for?' There was little sign of hope in his voice. He had met Gresham in this mood before, when he closed up like a castle with portcullis and drawbridge firmly shut, and not a light on in any of the towers.

'No,' said Gresham, 'not yet. Not until I'm certain. But I want you to do something. I want all those men we've had working for us given new instructions. I want to know who George's been seeing. Everyone. I said I could read him like a book. There's a page he hasn't shown me. He's keeping something from me. I must know what it is.'

'Then fer Christ's sake tell the girl she was right about George. It's bad enough she's shopped your best mate to you. The thought she might have got it wrong'll be driving her mad.'

It was as reasonable a request as it was unpalatable. Gresham wanted to banish the thought of George from his mind for twenty-four hours, to come to terms with what had happened, not raise the scab on the new wound so shortly after it had been inflicted.

Jane's room was up in the attic, sparsely furnished, he noted, her books neatly stacked on rough planks resting on house bricks. She had not stopped crying, the red rims round her eyes burning and fierce, her expression lost. Red eyes, but very different from Essex. Mannion had refused to go with him.

'You go to 'er,' he had said firmly. 'She's got a tongue in 'er 'ead, and an 'alf, and so 'ave you. Time you started goin' at each other direct, this workin' through me on the important things, it just won't do any more. We've all grown out of it.'

'But why do I have to go and see her in her room? And alone? Won't the servants talk?'

'Not if I 'ears 'em, they won't,' said Mannion grimly. 'And you gotta see 'er in 'er place because the minute you demands to see 'er, it's Lord and Master talks to servant. It ain't what this is about. She'll be shit-scared you'll 'ate 'er for tellin' you a truth you didn't want to 'ear. After all, it's what she's bin' doin' most of her life. Only difference is, the truths 'ave got a lot more important.'

'You were right,' said Gresham. He felt extremely awkward, standing with his head bowed under the sloping roof. The bed had a heavy cover on it. If he concentrated enough he could persuade himself it was not a bed, simply a large chest with a huge counterpane over it. 'About George. I can't say thank you, not without it sticking in my throat. What you said lost me a friend. And I happen to think friendship, true friendship, is the most precious commodity of all. Stronger than sex, stronger even than blood, and so very hard to find. And you can't replace a friend. It's a special place a friend lives in, and once they leave no one ever inhabits that same room again. So there'll be an empty room in my life for evermore.'

'I am so sorry,' she said. There was a sniffle in her voice. She was standing too, her head slightly bowed, and her nose was running. She desperately wanted to wipe it, but was afraid to do so in case it made her look ridiculous. Suddenly, against all his mood and feelings, he wanted to laugh. Laugh as he had laughed so often with Essex, and with George. Laugh at how ludicrous it all was. Muscles he had forgotten he had tugged at the corner of his lips, a smile desperate to break out.

He gave in.

'I think you'd better wipe your nose,' he said. 'I don't know what it's doing to you, but it's hell to watch.' He proffered a fine linen handkerchief, hanging fashionably loose from his wrist. 'It's a pity we can't stop bowing to each other as well. You must move to another room. One with a proper ceiling.'

You did not need to say it twice with Jane. The gratitude for forgiveness was as clear in her sparkling eyes as it was absent from her words.

'Another version of me,' she said, 'would point out that a fine handkerchief like this was never meant to be used at all, never mind on a snot-nosed girl.'

'How many versions of you are there?' asked Gresham.

'Rather too many for comfort,' Jane replied. 'But isn't that true of everyone?'

It was certainly true of Essex, and of George, now Gresham came to think of it. And perhaps of Gresham himself.

'Well,' he said after a moment, 'let that stupid piece of cloth be in place of my thanks, the words I can't speak.'

She smiled at him and held the handkerchief tight.

'One of the other versions – the one who fights and argues a lot – ought to point out that it isn't usually this way round,' she said, still feeling her way. He was seeing a vivacious, fun creature now, someone who could enjoy the fencing dalliance of witty conversation, someone whose brain moved as quickly as her words. 'The lady gives her knight her favour, which he then wears in his helmet.'

'I see what you mean,' said Gresham. 'It does bring it down to earth a bit if the knight gives his lady a soiled handkerchief to wear in her nose.'

'Which I shall treasure,' she said, and he found himself strangely touched. 'As well as use to wipe my nose on.' And, as elegantly as one can in the confines of a small room, she did so.

Suddenly he made his mind up. For the first time in months he felt a real certainty in his head. He took one of the rings off his finger, an exquisite ruby set in a cluster of small but perfect diamonds.

'Please take this,' he said. 'You risked your life to come to Scotland. You saved my life in Ireland, and may have saved it again by having the courage to tell me what I didn't want to hear, and

324

still don't. I would like you to accept this, as my gift, in place of the words I can't find.' He held out his hand. The ring glittered in his fingers, catching the shaft of light that came in through the unshuttered window.

The girl became very still.

'It's too much,' she said finally. 'I'd feel a traitor myself if I took something so valuable in exchange for doing what I wanted to do, what I decided to do freely and of my own will.'

Gresham was not discomfited. 'It's a thing of rare beauty, isn't it?' he said. 'Let me tell you its history. It was given to me by a very great Court lady, a widow as it happens. We comforted each other after her husband died, and I was still recovering from wounds. In a stupid way I thought there was something real and true between us. She gave me that ring one night, and the next day wrote to say our relationship was ended. She used it to buy me off. It was her gesture to her own conscience. And before you ask,' he went on, 'I don't want you to have it because I wish to salve my own conscience, or because I'm hurling you out onto the street, or to buy you off. I want you to have it because it's a thing of rare beauty. Forgive me for a terrible cliché, but it deserves to be paired with another thing of rare beauty. And because I've kept it all these years as a reminder of human perfidy and betrayal, it needs to be cleansed by being given to someone who's stayed loyal, and instead of betraying me shown me the others who wished to do so. Please take it.'

Hesitantly she reached forward. He felt the momentary warm brush of her fingers against his.

'You know I won't wear it,' she said, 'but you won't be offended?'

'Not offended,' he said, 'but tell me why you won't wear it?'

'Emeralds are for sadness,' she said, 'pearls are for death, and sapphires are the lazy stones, the easy ones. Blue matches eyes and dresses. Diamonds are for show. But a ruby . . . a ruby is for confidence. A ruby is a great, red, warm glow that says here I am and this is what I am. It's alive. It's the blood, it's the heartbeat. You know someone's alive when they bleed. A ruby shows life. A ruby matches what people feel. You started wearing that ring soon after you took me in. It summed up your confidence to me. Will it mind being wrapped in a handkerchief and hidden under a floorboard?'

Gresham smiled. 'I shouldn't think it'll mind. But not the floorboard in this room. The floorboard in the red room. I'd like you to move there.'

'But the red room is one of the grandest bedchambers in the house.' There was a challenge in her eyes.

He felt slightly offended.

'I won't charge you for the room,' he said. 'It has a key and a lock. I'm not asking for – favours. You run this House. You're its mistress. It's only fitting I should recognise that fact and give you a room that's in keeping with what you do.'

'Why aren't you asking for favours?' she said, her chin up. He could see a pulse beating in the long sweep of her neck. It was a rather beautiful neck, he could not help but notice. Smooth, clean, clear skin. He began to wish Mannion was there. Damn the man for sending him alone! It was suddenly warm in the room. Didn't the window work?

'Because you're my ward!' he said. 'I took you in as a child. I'm like a parent! I have a duty towards you, a responsibility. What sort of man is it who has a power over a woman that has nothing to do with mutual attraction or consent, and uses – abuses – that power to lure her into bed? It'd be like a father bedding his daughter!'

'Parents realise when their child has grown up,' she answered vehemently. 'Do you think you're the only one with power? I've got power too, haven't I? The power to decide who I love. What if instead of you taking, I choose to give? What if as a wild little girl I fell in love with you for all the wrong reasons, because you were so brave and so handsome and you came out of nowhere like the knight in shining armour in the fairy tale and took me off to a magic land? Then ignored me? Ignored me so I started to hate you, thought you hated me, but found after all that I still loved you? And fended off awful men with greasy hands and fat promises and leery eyes because I'd decided long ago that if I couldn't have you I didn't want anybody? That I had to give in to the inevitable?'

'The inevitable?' answered Gresham. He felt like a sailor surrounded by a storm that had come suddenly and with incredible violence, but which in some way was not sinking the ship.

'That I was in love with this irritating, distant, impossible, patronising, stupid, infuriating man, whether I liked it or not. You're not abusing your power! If you did what I want you to do, you'd be listening to me for the first time in your life!'

She moved forward, until there was less than an inch between them. He felt her breath on his face, warm, sweet-smelling.

'I'll take and treasure your ring. But will you give me something I need? Will you see me as a woman and not as a child?'

The world seemed to implode on him. They fell onto the bed in a tangle of limbs and he gave up any sense of control.

Afterwards, when all was quiet and even their breathing had returned to normal, she turned her head towards him.

'My Lord,' she said, 'please. No torturings or agonising. I gave to you and took from you nothing I didn't wish to give and to receive. Nothing will change. I'll move into any chamber you wish except your own. I'll visit you at night, but leave by morning, if you so wish, or not visit at all if that's your choice.'

She had been a virgin. How much had he hurt her? He did not wish to hurt her.

'Marriage,' he mumbled. 'I must marry you.'

'Nonsense,' she said. Deftly she climbed off the bed, rearranged her clothing, put on the items they had torn off so recently. 'No true friend of yours, no one who knows you at all, would imagine you were ready for that. Did you think I wanted to trap you?'

He recognised that at the back of his mind, even as he had fallen on the bed with her, there had been exactly that fear.

'My Lord,' she said, and was prim and courteous now, 'what's happened is between us. And only us. With your permission, I propose to make it both secret and private.'

He sat on the edge of the bed.

'Keep anything from the servants?' he said. He was not at his most articulate.

'My Lord,' she said almost pityingly. 'The servants have had us sharing a bed these two years past, whatever the truth might have been. And been loyal enough to keep the news to themselves. It would be better if you left first,' she said, matter-of-factly. 'And if the right buttons were in the right loops on your doublet.'

He started and, rather guiltily, buttoned up his doublet correctly.

'Look,' he said, 'I know where we've been, but I don't quite know where I am yet. One thing only: no more "My Lord". If you have to use something, make it . . . oh, I don't know . . . sir?'

'Why, yes, sir,' she said, bobbing a curtsy like a simpering little parlour maid, with a wicked smile lurking at the corner of her mouth.

What did it mean when you left a girl you had just slept with, and found her even more beautiful after the event than you had beforehand? He had not wanted this to happen, or at least had persuaded himself so, but like her something in him had recognised a strange inevitability about the whole thing.

He spent the rest of the day in a daze. Mannion kept an impassive face and said nothing. That night, when he had gone to bed and the embers of the fire were flickering, there was the merest whisper of a door opening, and she stood by the bed. Hesitant, confused as he had never been before in his life since the night he had lost his own virginity, he drew back the cover. Jane slipped in.

Next morning when he woke she was gone, leaving no trace of her presence except for the slightest indent in the pillow and a lingering perfume. When Mannion came, they started the ritual of dressing as first light was coming up over the rooftops. If Mannion smelt a slight fragrance in the air, he said nothing.

He remembered these days as a strange interlude in his life. Outwardly, nothing changed with Jane, except they rarely argued. Once, when she had complained that the cook was paying too much for fish and she suspected the relationship between her and the fishmonger was not entirely restricted to fish he had responded by saying that as far as he was concerned the fishmonger could be going to bed with a school of whales. She had said that he ought to care more where his money went, and he had said it was his money . . . all like the old times. Just when they were about to start going at each other she giggled, and he stopped in his tracks.

'What is it?' he said.

'It's your image,' she had said. 'Cook does look very like a whale! And she puts her lips together and blows out with a sort of – "Harumph!" noise. Just like the books say a whale does. And,' she said, getting carried away, 'the books also say that the breath the whale expels smells awful, and cook can smell awful at times.' Looking at her for the first time with the scales pulled from his eyes, he saw her life force, her exuberant energy. Ruby was the right jewel for her.

At night she came to his bed, and it was strange and new and unlike anything he had ever experienced. Sometimes it was gentle, sometimes almost violent and at other times they did nothing except talk to each other, in stage whispers as if Mannion who slept outside the door did not know what was going on inside. And for the first time in his life he talked to someone other than Mannion about his childhood.

London was convinced that rebellion was imminent the day after Grey assaulted Southampton. As it so often was, London was wrong. The apprentice boys, so frequently the source of riot in the crowded streets, slowly stopped working with half an ear cocked for disturbances, ready to down tools at a moment's notice and start to break some heads. The guards at Whitehall went back to normal manning levels, and it was rumoured that late one night cartloads of muskets and small arms rumbled and rattled their way back into the armoury in the Tower of London, whence they had been summoned to reinforce the guards at Whitehall.

And then the storm broke, one Saturday after what George

would undoubtedly have described as Gresham's revelation in an attic.

Gresham was in deep thought when Jane came to see him. There was a purse on the table in front of him, open where he had just taken money out to give to an informer who had skulked in through the back door of The House. It was early morning, and the man had given Gresham much food for thought.

'Sir!' she said, breathless and flushed, 'there's something very strange happening at the Globe. One of the delivery boys was full of it this morning, and I've checked and it's true. Something I think you ought to know.'

'Tell me,' he said, only half interested, his mind churning over what he had just heard. News from a delivery boy did not seem likely to change the world.

'A group of Lord Essex's men were at the Globe yesterday. They saw the play, and then apparently one of them, Lord Mounteagle I think, offered the players forty shillings – forty shillings! – to put on a performance of *Richard the Second*. You know – the old play by Shakespeare!'

'I should think the players'll have forgotten the lines by now,' said Gresham. 'It hasn't been performed for years now, has it? It's hardly the height of fashion.'

'That's what the players said, apparently. But the money was too good, and they've agreed to stage it. Tonight. You know what it means, don't you? The play, I mean.'

'It's the story of the rebellion by the Welshman Bolingbroke, who's shown as a loyal and good servant to a fickle monarch. He's banished, returns to England and, with the help of Welsh support, overthrows and imprisons Richard, eventually becoming King himself,' said Gresham.

An incitement to rebellion? A signal to London of what was going to happen? He jumped up to his feet.

'Are we going to the play?' Jane wanted to be in the action.

'Yes. Perhaps. Why not? But first I have to see someone.'

Plays were performed in the early afternoon, after the main meal of the day which, for most people, was at noon. There was time for Gresham to do what he had to do and see the play.

'Who?' asked Jane.

'I have to see a man called Smith,' answered Gresham grimly.

He took Mannion and four men with him and returned in time for their dinner. There was a sense of suppressed tension in him.

'Are we going to the play?' asked Jane.

'Yes,' said Gresham. 'But I warn you it could be dangerous. I'm gambling that Essex will be there, so that I can talk to him. I must talk to him! If he is there, you'll be safe. He won't attack me if there's a woman in the party, I know it. If he's not, it could get nasty. Very much so. So if you come it's as our insurance, but at great risk.'

He could see the fear in her eyes, but also the excitement.

'Will I need a pistol?' she asked.

'Can you stuff one in your dress?'

'I'd rather you carried it for me.'

They ordered the boat. Unusually, Gresham chose the crew.

The playhouses were on the south side of the river, outside the strict boundaries of the City of London and thereby granted a little more freedom to do what the City Fathers so hated them for doing. Plays were seditious, evil things in the opinion of many, inflaming the popular imagination and corrupting it, hotbeds of riot, breeding centres for plagues of the body and plagues of the mind. It was a damp, cold day, though not wet enough to cancel the perform-ance. The actors had an awning over the stage, and those who could pay sat in the tiered ranks and boxes of the wooden 'O' that was the Globe theatre. Only the groundling stood and caroused in the open area of the pit, and they were used to being soused.

It was a smaller crowd than usual flitting across the river, and the Globe was only half full, some put off by the damp, some by the unfashionable play and others fearful of what this revival might mean. Some people came onto the streets when rebellion was in the air but more locked and bolted their doors. Yet it seemed as if every rabble-rouser, Welsh peasant and unemployed soldier who had ever walked London's streets was packed in the theatre. Half an hour before the play was due to begin the noise level was rattling the timbers and shaking dust out of the thatch.

'Is this safe?' asked Mannion, not usually prone to feeling nervous.

'For us? For London? Or for the Queen? I don't know,' answered Gresham. Southampton was there, he saw, Mounteagle and the vulture-like Gelli Meyrick, plus a host of the others Essex had gathered round him like a graveyard gathers corpses. And Davies, of course. Would Essex come? Surely he would. For months now he had refused to leave Essex House, citing the danger he believed he was in from his enemies. The attack on Southampton by Grey, when for once the odious little toad was apparently doing nothing more than riding about his own business, had confirmed Essex in his opinion, and produced a host more pamphlets. Even without their master, the mood of the assembly was dark, violent, poisonous.

They had been spotted by the Essex crowd – Gresham, Mannion and Jane, together with the eight men who had rowed them there. There was a strict order among them for who rowed to the play, and such trips were a zealously guarded perk of working for Gresham. Gresham had ordered the rota to be thrown out of the window this time, and had chosen the men himself. Jack, Dick and Edward were there, and five others whose qualifications for the trip seemed to be in the broadness of their backs rather than in their love of poetry. They were on open seats on the first tier, just to the side of the stage. Essex's major cronies were in the same tier, taking the middle seats as befitted the patrons of the performance. Meyrick nudged Davies, and both men looked up to gaze calmly at Gresham. He gazed back. The two men looked impassively at him for a moment, whispered a few more words and turned away.

'We could 'ave trouble gettin' out of 'ere,' said Mannion.

'We could,' said Gresham. 'Give the nod to Tom.'

Jane had not understood why three of the men were carrying bulky leather sacks on their backs, with a flap of leather over the top to protect their contents from the rain.

'It's to carry your pistol,' said Gresham.

Nor did she understand why a ninth man, the rather nondescript-looking Tom, very different from the man who had died on the *Anna*, had been parked as an extra in the boat, between the oarsmen, and confined to the pit, and banned from wearing the black and silver of Gresham's livery. Jane had heard him being told to lose himself, but to keep in touch. He kept turning round and staring up at the gallery with a fixed, white look, his hair plastered down on top of his head by the thin drizzle. Mannion waited until none of the Essex men seemed to be looking in their direction, stood up and snapped his fingers at a boy selling nuts and ale. As he bought them, he looked down at Tom, and gave a slight nod. Tom nodded back, and quietly and without fuss began to edge to the exit door nearest to him. No one paid any attention to him. Mannion's eyes followed him to the door. So far so good.

The cannon roared its blank shot from the roof, and the trumpet blast sounded for the last time to announce the start of the play.

They were rusty in the parts, the actors, but they were professionals and they warmed to their material. King Richard was a pathetic figure, a man more destined for a College than for a Court, while the powerful figure of Bolingbroke was shown reluctantly wresting a Crown he did not want. It did not take long to see why Essex's men had chosen the play. Bolingbroke talked of his, 'Eating the bitter bread of banishment.'

In Gresham's mind Essex kept recurring not in the figure of Bolingbroke, but in the doomed figure of Richard II. All the huge melancholia of the man, his vast capacity for self-pity, was there in Richard's lines:

> 'Of comfort no man speak:
> Let's talk of graves, of worms, of epitaphs;
> Make dust our paper, and with rainy eyes
> Write sorrow on the bosom of the earth;
> Let's choose executors, and talk of wills.'

Gresham felt a chill in his heart as the actor recited the words:

> 'A brittle glory shineth in this face:
> As brittle as the glory is the face.'

It was Essex's face he saw, and Essex's voice as the actor intoned:

> 'I wasted time, and now doth time waste me.'

The stamping and cheering at the end seemed to last for ever, and while it was at its height Gresham gave the signal and he and his men, gathered protectively round Jane, made their way to the door and the thin, narrow wooden passageway that led downstairs. It smelt of piss and worse, where men and women had used it to answer nature's call. Two men brought up the rear, facing backwards, in case of a rush from behind. They emerged into the open, muddy courtyard, the sound and smell of the river just before them.

A line of men, in the tangerine livery of Essex, stood before them. How ironic. There were twenty of them, about the same number as had attacked them on the boat. They were armed with knives and clubs, were soaked through, had clearly been waiting for an hour or more. Meyrick and Davies must have sent for them before the play had even started. The startling Essex livery had not been seen since the Irish campaign, its appearance on the streets enough to cause a riot and have the fortunate man wearing it feted and taken to every tavern within sight. Well, well, well, thought Gresham. How interesting that on this Saturday night of all nights so many men in the Essex livery were armed and ready.

His own eight men had drawn into a protective circle. There was a rustle from behind him, and he sensed rather than saw Meyrick and Davies come out from the same exit and into the fading light.

Gresham's gamble had failed: Essex had not come. Now on the eve of rebellion his cronies had seen the man who had argued against them, the man whose influence on their master they most hated and resented, infiltrating their clarion call to rebellion. Now, with their master absent, was the time for them to wreak their revenge on Gresham.

'Can you turn to look at me?' shouted Davies. 'Or are you too much of a coward?'

'I'll stay facing the greater threat, thank you,' shouted Gresham over his shoulder. Other playgoers had melted into the gathering gloom, sensing that something terrible and dangerous might happen any moment. 'But I've something I want to show you.' He clicked his finger.

Effortlessly, and as they had been trained, the men on either side of those with the strange leather bags took a step back, flipped a brass catch, lifted up the leather flap and drew heavy items out. One was tossed to Mannion, the others handed to the eight men.

Blunderbusses: a short-barrelled musket, its end opening out like a trumpet. Usually a cheap weapon, these had hardwood stocks and glinting muzzles, their firing mechanism a state of the art combination of flint and matchlock, the cover over the mechanism, waiting to be torn off in an instant by the men. Loaded with old nails and bits of scrap metal, it was a lethal short-range weapon. A weapon for when a body of men were rushing at you.

There was a mutter from the men in front of the Essex mob, and two or three took a step back. Mannion took advantage to reach into one of the bags, and draw out three pistols. He kept one and handed two to Gresham, who took one and stuck one in his belt, and, grinning, handed the other to Jane. She did not grin back but, pointing the gun up into the air, pulled back the hammer to half cock and checked the firing mechanism. Something in the cold, calculated professional way she did this seemed to unsettle the men facing them even more. They muttered among themselves.

Davies and Meyrick walked round the circle of men. Gresham risked a brief look behind him. Another thirty or forty men, the so-called gentlemen, had fanned out from the door. All were armed with swords and daggers. One or two even had pistols in their hands, though to walk through London armed with such was to risk attack rather than prevent it.

335

'There are fifty men here!' barked Davies, 'and for all your farmer's guns, we will overwhelm you.'

'Fifty-four, to be precise,' shouted Gresham. 'Not including yourself and jelly brain there with you.'

There was a rustle from the men, and a roar from Gelli Meyrick, 'You bastard, Gresham!'

Gresham had achieved his reputation as a swordsman by answering insults such as that. He smiled. 'True,' he said, managing to sound almost cheerful. 'But that means this ball is for your stomach and not your head.' There was a moment's silence. Gresham knew these moments. Any second a man would leap forward, or one tiny imagined shout or movement would start the action. He spoke again. 'I reckon on two of your men taken out as a minimum by each blunderbuss. My men are trained to aim alternately. One fires at the eyes, the other at the balls. It'll be those in the front rank who get it, of course. Then there's three pistol balls before you can reach us. That's you in the stomach, Hay Rick and Davies there in the head. And whoever my ward chooses. That's nineteen at least on the ground, dead or screaming, and maybe more.'

'It's worth it to rid the world of one of Cecil's spawn!' said Meyrick, almost out of control.

Gresham didn't bother to deny it. He had something else to say, 'Your men might not think so. The ones who get killed or have their balls blown off, at any rate. But there is one other thing.'

'What other thing?' asked Davies. Gresham could sense that at any moment the man would make a rush forward. Davies did not lack courage, merely charm or any sense of humanity.

'The rather large number of men just emerging from the shadows behind you,' said Gresham. 'My men, actually.'

Davies turned. The houses round the Globe were mean things, low drinking houses or brothels with mud-filled jennels between them. Like ghosts or Irish soldiers emerging from the woods, thirty or so men had drifted out. Ten of them had been in Gresham's squad in Ireland, men who had come back and asked if they could serve him. Some instinct had told Gresham that in these of all times such men at his disposal in London might be useful. They stood a yard in front of the other men, the porters, grooms and servants, in a straight line, with the muskets Gresham had bought them held across their chests. They were impassive, staring ahead. Gresham had taught them to never see their enemy as human. As a result, they looked like statues, staring through the ranks of Essex's men. It had a chilling effect.

Essex's men began to shuffle, look to one side. Davies glanced at them scornfully, and moved towards Gresham. There was a click of a pistol being pulled back to full cock. It was Jane's. He stopped, spat on the ground, and whirled around. Grumbling and muttering, his men started to move away to the left, in the gap between the theatre and the ranks of Gresham's men.

The Gresham crowd burst out cheering, rushed forward and clapped the boat crew on the shoulders. The ten soldiers, still grim-faced, walked in and faced outwards, guarding against a surprise attack.

'Silence!' shouted Gresham, and there was a sudden hush. 'For God's sake, uncock those blunderbusses before we blow down the Globe or our own backsides off!' There was a ribald cheer. 'But keep them on half cock. We've got to get home.'

'Tom,' said Gresham to the man he had sent for the reinforcements. 'Well done. Any troubles?'

'Nearly fuckin' messed it up, sir, beggin' your pardon. First time I've 'ad unlimited money to get a ferry across, and the first bloody time there's not been a boat in sight. Got one in the end, though. Thank God. And 'e 'ardly charged. 'Ere's your money, sir.'

'Keep it,' said Gresham.

They marched rather than walked to the jetty. Gresham was half expecting to see his boat and the others that had brought the extra men from The House holed and smashed, half sunk in the mud, but to his surprise they were in one piece.

'What do you think that proves?' he asked Mannion.

'They were wild. Up for anything,' said Mannion. 'It's Sunday tomorrow. Apprentice boys ain't at work, free to cause any trouble they wants. Nothin' on at Court tomorrow. Lots o' the good and grand gone 'ome for the weekend. Fine time for a rebellion, if you asks me. That play. It's got to be a signal, ain't it?'

'Great strategist, my friend the Earl,' said Gresham. 'Don't just mount a rebellion; tell everyone you're doing it beforehand.'

'Hang on,' said Mannion. 'It ain't that stupid. Town's full o' stories of wild Welshmen comin' in at every gate, sleeping in alleys and in attics. Not easy to get the word to that lot. But if you makes your signal *Richard the Second* on at the Globe – well, London only ever knows two things for sure: if the Queen's in town, and what's on at the Globe. And the other theatres, o' course.'

Jane had been silent until now. She was wrapped in a vast cloak, and had seemed wrapped in her own thoughts.

'There's been talk of a thousand men at Essex's command, for months now. In St Paul's, that is.'

Gresham looked at her, and for a moment his astonishment defeated his self-control.

'You've known about this rumour? Why didn't you tell me?'

'Because I assumed if a stupid girl hanging round the bookstalls heard it, you, who've made it your job to pick up these rumours, were bound to have heard it too. And I didn't want to look a fool.'

'What else have you heard?' There was real urgency in his tone. 'This could be really important. This isn't a time for dignity, yours or mine. London's going to blow up any minute, and we're on the edge of civil war. I do know about the rumours. But what else had you heard?'

She was frightened by the intensity in his voice, the tension in his body.

'Only that people keep mentioning a man called Smith. A sheriff, someone meant to be very friendly with Essex. Is it militia he's meant to control? Something like that?'

'Sheriff Smith,' said Gresham. 'In theory he can call out a thousand militia men, though it's doubtful if the real figure he can call on is more than five hundred. And, yes, he's been seen visiting Essex House by night, and so people assume secretly. Though how

338

anyone can think anything taking place in that house is a secret is beyond me.'

'And Essex will make him call out these men?'

'I think Essex will think he can call out these men. It's not quite the same thing.'

'This makes my head ache,' said Jane rather pathetically. 'Is nothing as it seems in your world? Is nothing ever what it seems to be on the surface? Is there always a double or a treble meaning?'

'It's usually not that simple,' said Gresham, looking at her fondly. Welcome to the real world, he thought. A world where after a time you may well yearn for the safety, security and above all the pre-dictability of making preserves that need to be stored for winter and the supply of sheets and linen.

'So why won't you tell us?' They were within sight of the private jetty at The House. One of the other boats would go in first to land men to act as a guard if The House had been infiltrated or taken over.

'Because I believe Essex is about to be forced into a rebellion. And I believe he thinks he may have an extra thousand men to call on. But I don't believe, never have believed it's as simple as that. Yet what I believe is so fantastical, so much in the face of any evi-dence, so much my own invention based simply on a feeling I have ... Do you know,' he said in the tone of a man facing a sudden revelation, 'I think I can't tell you for the same reason you didn't tell me about the thousand men. For fear of being laughed at. For fear of being proven wrong. Now isn't that strange?'

'I'd call it normal,' muttered Mannion. ' 'Bout the only normal thing there is with you, I 'ave to say. Ever considered bein' normal? Might make a change for all of us.'

'So,' said Jane, snuggling down rather fearfully into the depths of her cloak, like a mouse burrowing down in cut straw and hoping the hawk had not seen her, 'civil war's about to be unleashed from a house a few yards along our street. We're facing pandemonium, chaos, a collapse of all civil order, bloodshed on the streets and probably rape, loot and pillage for those stupid enough to be caught out in it, and some of those trying to hide from it. What are you going to do about it?'

'I'm going to get captured by Essex, probably,' said Gresham.

'No you fuckin' ain't – beggin' your pardon, miss!' exploded Mannion.

'Essex is like a lit fuse. I can't stop that. I've just got this sense that he's finally going to blow. If that fuse reaches the powder, the country could be blown apart. And if my theory is correct, something even more shameful may happen. And it'll mean I'll have broken my word. I have to see Essex! Even if I can't stop him, I have to try and limit the damage. To him, and to everyone.'

'You can't do that!' said Jane aghast. 'They'll kill you before you get to Essex! You saw them tonight. They'd have cheerfully ripped the flesh from our bones and eaten it as talk to us if you hadn't out-thought them!'

'She's right,' said Mannion. 'Least they'll do is rough you up, mebbe bad. Might get to Essex and find you ain't got a mouth or a tongue to speak to him with.'

'I know,' said Gresham. 'But sometimes you don't get choices.'

CHAPTER 13

February, 1601
London

Gresham had chosen to wear a nondescript cloak, and ride on a nag that was like countless hundreds of others in London. His hat was pulled low down over his brow.

Essex House was lit up like the Court on Twelfth Night, and among the noise and turmoil emanating from it there was the occasional ominous clang of metal on metal. The front entrance was heavily guarded, the back one as well and the river gate sealed.

On a whim, Gresham made Mannion ride with him west up the Strand. The Queen was at Whitehall, the proximity of the Palace as much a feature in the popularity of the Strand as London's prevailing wind direction.

'Nothing,' said Gresham. There were no extra guards, no sign in the far distance of any extra activity in the Palace. As they were turning round, there was a clatter of hooves behind them. The rider was in a hurry, four men in the Queen's livery with him. He had lost his hat, and his face was covered in mud.

'John! John Herbert!' Gresham called into the darkness. The man reined in, peering through the gloom. Secretary John Herbert was a prime administrator for the Privy Council. A decent man, he was typical of the hundreds who slaved away quietly and without

341

much evident ambition to service the workings of government. Why was Secretary Herbert riding out at this time of night, when all decent men were tucked up in bed? It must be approaching midnight.

'Sir Henry!' Herbert was nervous, and his escort drew round him. 'What business have you riding in town on this of all nights?'

'I might ask the same of you,' said Gresham, 'except to say that I serve the Queen to whom I remain loyal. And you have nothing to fear from me.'

'I have never thought I had,' the man answered simply, 'unlike many others. But excuse me, I must about my business.'

'I would caution you against Essex House this night,' said Gresham. 'It's a wild place.'

'I have no option, Sir Henry,' said Herbert. 'There is no reason why you should not know. The Privy Council summoned the Earl of Essex to their presence late this afternoon. He returned no answer. I am sent to demand his presence. Now.'

'He won't come,' said Gresham. 'You know that.'

'On a night when my family are on their knees praying for my safety, I know only that I have my duty to do. Will you let me pass?'

'Of course. I'm not your enemy.'

Strange how bravery and courage showed themselves. There was the bravery of the great general, the great leader. And there was the bravery of the ordinary man, the man with just a little courage and a sense of duty, the man who would go where duty drove him, quietly and without fuss. History would discard him and his name without a moment's thought if he fell foul of a drunken rebel or Gelli Meyrick's knife, something John Herbert knew as well as history.

The two men let Herbert have a decent start, and then followed after him to where a glow in the sky showed London and the burning lights of Essex House. They had lit a vast fire in the courtyard to warm the men who were gathered there. Two hundred? Three hundred? It was difficult to say.

They stopped in the darkness that lay like a cloak around the great house, and Gresham dismounted, handing the reins of his nag to Mannion. Mannion was awkward, troubled. 'You shouldn't be doin' this,' he said.

'You're probably right,' said Gresham.

'I should come with you,' said Mannion.

'It wouldn't work. Even you can't fight off all Essex's men, and they'd separate us immediately. Probably torture you to find out if you knew anything. Or just for the fun of it. You know it's got to be me. And why.'

Gresham had told Mannion what he thought was the truth as they had ridden down towards Essex House. To his relief, Mannion had not laughed, but had agreed.

'Yeah,' he said with a vast sigh. 'That figures. It's just what them bastards would do, isn't it? Clever, though. You got to give them that. Well, that's it then,' he said. Then he did something extraordinary. He got off his horse, came up to Gresham and enveloped him in a vast bear hug. Gresham gasped. It was like being clutched by a large hairy carpet. Mannion let go, and the breath returned to Gresham's chest.

'You bloody well survive!' said Mannion, 'or I'll never forgive you.' He rode away with both horses into the dark. It was, of course, a trick of the light that suggested the phlegmatic Mannion had tears in his eyes.

Some soothing influence must have been released into Gresham's blood as he walked up to the gates of Essex House. He felt nothing, no fear, no tension. Calmly he said to the man on the gate, 'My name is Sir Henry Gresham. I am an ex-friend of the Earl's and I have vital news for him.'

A startled look came over the man's face, but he opened the small gate cut into the huge wooden one, ushered Gresham in and shut it quickly behind him. The scene in the yard was like a vision of hell. A furious fire was blazing, sparks flying up into the night air, and all around men were walking, talking, doing exercises, oiling weapons or sitting silently in corners, guns and swords laid carefully on their laps. The guard whispered to another man, who waved a hand and called two others over.

Now it begins, thought Gresham, tensing himself for the first blow. Instead, the three men took him across the yard, spoke briefly to the man acting as a sergeant, handed him over and went back to their stations. The sergeant listened politely to his story, motioned him to sit on one of the crude boxes littering the yard, and called to a man whose long cloak concealed the dress of a gentleman.

It was Gervase Markham, the young officer Gresham had struck up a friendship with in Ireland. He did not look nearly so happy to see him now.

'Are you mad?' he hissed. 'Meyrick and the rest of them are saying you're Cecil's creature, one of the causes of the Earl's disfavour. The rumour is you outwitted them at the theatre, and they're spitting. Get out while you can! You're only still alive because I've got my men on duty, and they still have some semblance of training.'

For the first time in this awful business was God smiling on him?

'Firstly, can you get me in to see Essex? Or at least into the room he's in? I promise I won't harm him, or cause harm to him in any way. Secondly, get out of here, Gervase. This is no place for a real soldier. You're being used, all of you, used in a foul plot. It's you who should get out while you can. You can't win. And even if you seem to have won, you'll have lost. Believe me.'

Markham looked at him for a moment, gave a brief nod and said, 'Keep your hat low down over your brow. They're having a Council of War. All the good men and true.' Markham's sense of irony had not left him. 'I'll open the door for you. I doubt you'll ever get out.'

'That's my choice, isn't it? And thank you.'

'It's a pleasure,' said Markham lightly. 'Things are always more fun when you're around. More dangerous, but more fun.'

Another strange echo, this time of what Gresham had always said of Essex.

They skirted the edge of the yard, hiding in the gargantuan shadows thrown up by the fire, and climbed two sets of stairs. Men hurried past them, all heavily armed, but set on their own business.

Markham opened the door, and suddenly they were in the dining hall of Essex House, a long, imposing room with a vaulted ceiling and portraits along each wall. The fire was piled high with huge logs, so high that flames must almost be pouring out of the chimney. Huge, flickering shadows were being thrown round the room with ten or twelve candles in one spot, then yards where there was no light at all. A sudden silence descended.

Davies stood up, knocking his stool back with the force of the movement.

'Kill him!' he said.

'No!' said another voice. It was Essex. He was wild-eyed, seemed to have lost weight since Gresham had last seen him, and was dressed in full Court rig. Was he planning to break in on the Queen again? Or did he simply feel one ought to be properly dressed to ride to one's death?

'My Lord,' said Gresham, hoping these would not be his last words, 'I have something you must know. Something that affects this enterprise and yourself most crucially.'

The silence lengthened, unbearably.

'Tell me,' said Essex finally, his voice thin.

'The thousand men. The militia. The men summoned by Sheriff Smith – the men you are counting on for tomorrow – they do not exist. They have been disbanded. Sheriff Smith has been warned off and told that the Crown knows of his disloyalty.'

'And who has done this?'

'I have,' said Gresham. A rumble as of thunder swept round the room. Two or three of the twenty or so men gathered there reached for their swords. Essex held out his hand to stay them.

'And why did you do so?'

'To save you and your honour. Because I know who is behind those thousand men, know now who is forcing you into rebellion. My Lord, you—'

345

The blow to the back of his head was savage. He had heard nothing. As his conscience splintered and then broke, he had just one glimpse of his attacker as he slumped to the floor.

Cameron. Cameron Johnstone.

It was dark when he came to, his head split by pain, his doublet sticky with blood. He was being cradled by someone, a damp cloth wiping his face and head. He reached for his sword and the hidden dagger. Both gone. He had been disarmed. His feet were tied together, cruelly tight. There were fragments of rope round his wrists.

'Your hands were blue,' said George, holding him like a baby. 'So I cut through the rope when they stopped talking before your hands fell off.'

Gresham tried to struggle up, but pain lanced through his head, pierced his eyes, and he fell back into George's arms.

'And for once, you've got it wrong,' said George, continuing to sponge gently, ever so gently, at his wound. 'The great Henry Gresham, master spy and master of all intrigue got it wrong. Completely wrong. Those thousand men, Smith's militia. They weren't designed to win Essex the rebellion. They were designed to make him lose it.'

'Were they?' said Gresham wondering if this was a dream. They seemed to be in the dining hall still, the fire half banked up and flickering, candles and lamps around the room, some of them out. There were men asleep, snoring, round the walls. That would be why George was whispering, so as not to wake the men. Gresham had not lost his hearing after all. 'How is that so?' he managed to mumble.

'Cameron made me the go-between with Smith. Oh, don't worry. Cameron's working for Cecil still. Actually, he's working for James, but Cecil wants James as King, so it's the same thing. But Cameron's clever enough to make Essex think that James is on his side. I wasn't tarnished, you see, with any of the Court intrigue. People thought I hated Essex so I could see Smith without any suspicion being raised. Cameron told Essex I was a double agent – that he'd cultivated me for years. That's why I'm here. Essex thinks I'm one of *his* men! Cameron hates Essex as well. So does James. Essex thinks Cameron and James love him. Do you understand?'

Gresham managed to move a little this time, and get his head above his chest. Maybe if there was a little less blood going to his head it might hurt just a little less.

'I'd have difficulty understanding that even if my head were unbroken,' said Gresham.

'Look, it's simple,' said George, continuing to cradle Gresham, 'Cecil hates Essex. James of Scotland hates Essex. Cameron hates Essex, and I hate Essex. All of us have been working against him, except that James and Cameron and myself have made it look as if we were on his side.'

'I see,' Gresham managed to say. The pain went through his head and into his jaw, making it extraordinarily painful to speak. 'It's simple. James sees Essex as a threat. Cameron works for James. The best way to deal with a threat is to get it to trust you, rely on you even. Essex is so desperate for the approval of the next King, for influence with the next King, that he'll believe anything of Cameron. All the time Cameron seems to be working for Essex he's working *against* him.'

'That's it!' said George, so happy that Gresham had got the message at last that his voice became dangerously loud. A man muttered in his sleep, turned over, reached out for his sword then fell back into a disturbed slumber. 'You've got it! Except you've gone and spoilt it! That was why Cameron was so angry. Why he laid you out. He told me so. I'd already told Sheriff Smith not to call the men out. I'd already ensured there'd be no men at Essex's call tomorrow. But Essex needed to think there would be – to make him rebel, so he could destroy himself. And you nearly spoilt it.'

'Nearly?' croaked Gresham. 'And as you've been rubbing at the same spot for five minutes, do you think I could suck on the cloth, even if half the liquid's my own blood?'

347

George reached for a pitcher of water on the floor, and offered it to Gresham.

'Just pour it over my bloody head.'

It was water in the desert. Cold snow on the burn from the fire for a few seconds. Then the pain returned.

'Yes, nearly,' said George. 'Cameron explained to Essex that you'd be bound to say what you did, that you must have found out about the thousand men and decided the only way to stop the rebellion, the only way for Cecil to preserve his power, was to persuade you that the thousand men didn't exist. Cameron said he'd had direct word from Smith that the men were still there. So it's all right. It really is! Essex *will* go to the City tomorrow, expecting a thousand armed men to turn out for him. And they won't be there! And Essex's followers will lose heart, lose faith in him and evaporate. The rebellion'll be over! And no one will die except Essex and some of his foul cronies.'

'Why am I alive?' asked Gresham. He had just enough strength to reach out for the pitcher, drink, roll the stale fluid round his mouth and dried-out lips.

'Because of me,' said George. 'They were going to kill you. I said I'd done good service for the Earl, and that you and I'd been good friends, and that I only asked for one thing from him: your life. I said he could decide what to do with you when he was King, but that all great Kings started their reigns by acts of mercy. I gave him my word you'd stay tied up here, and I'd guarantee you wouldn't be released. I think Cameron wanted you dead. Essex wouldn't have it, though I think he was tempted.'

Cameron would have hated seeing Gresham live. Essex probably had enough shreds of decency left in him to respond to George's plea. Gresham probably did owe his life to George. How ironic.

'What's their plan for tomorrow?' asked Gresham. He was strong enough to inch himself up a little more now. He only saw two images of George instead of three.

'They had a terrible argument,' whispered George. 'Davies had a brilliant plan to take over the Court, capture the Queen and go from there. Then that terrible man Gorges poured cold water over it, said that unless we captured the Tower and the City first we'd simply be besieged in Whitehall, particularly as we don't even know if Cecil and Nottingham and all the rest of the power brokers are actually at Whitehall. All we know is that we march at dawn. Cameron's doing everything he can to make Essex march to the City. He says if Essex goes to Whitehall – Essex has nearly four hundred men here already, you know – he might actually capture the Queen and the Court, that the rebellion might succeed.' George looked down at Gresham. 'Look, I'm really sorry. Sorry for all of it. I didn't mean to get you in danger. Cameron swears you'd have been spared on the boat. But I did save your life, tonight, here. They'd have killed you if I hadn't stood up. Now I can untie your legs, but only if you give me your word you won't run off. You see, if you're not here tomorrow, I'm well and truly dead.'

Gresham looked at George, and wondered if he could tell him the truth. He had to. He had no option.

'George,' he said, 'you've been fooled. You've been sold a line.'

'Oh, not that again!' said George. 'You just can't bear it that for once I've been cleverer than you.'

'George,' said Gresham, 'those thousand men exist. Or five hundred of them at least, and about fifty others who arrived in a merchant ship last week, moored up-river. They're there now. They're battened down below in the day, but they take them ashore to walk and breathe a bit at night, when no one can see them.'

No one except the father of one of Gresham's men, who was a poacher, and had seen strange men exercising on the shore at a time when no law-abiding man was about. That had been the message which had been causing him so much thought, just before Jane had told him about *Richard the Second* being performed at the Globe.

'Men? On a boat? But I don't understand!'

'Nor does the poacher who heard those dozen men talking on the shore in Spanish. Nor did anyone else when a man with a goatee beard yelled at two of his men not to kill me on board the

Anna. Or perhaps only I heard. When he called out first of all, he shouted Spanish for "Hold off!" Then he shouted in perfect English. It happens to people in the heat of battle. They revert to type.'

'But I still don't understand—'

'No, you don't. That's the whole point. Cameron doesn't work for Essex, or for Cecil, or even for James.'

A wave of nausea hit Gresham. He recognised it as a result of minor concussion, the almost inevitable result of a bad blow to the head.

'Cameron works for Spain. Has done all along.'

'Spain? *Spain?*' George's brow was furrowed. 'But that's impossible! I don't see—'

'Keep your voice down! Can't you see it's the only explanation? Do you think Spain's given up its ambition for the English throne when it has a perfectly good claim to it, one that stands up in any court? One that even Cecil has to acknowledge? When countless thousands of its men and countless millions of its gold have been poured into a string of Armadas, only one of which ever got within sight of our shores? When it's funded ten or more assassination attempts on the Queen? When it pays a "pension" to half the influential people in the Court, including Cecil? When the Queen, and Cecil, and Essex, and Raleigh, and for all I know even bloody James himself, have seen James as the heir apparent, thought the threat from Spain was only from Spanish invasion and dismissed it, been lulled into a sense of false security? And all the while Spain's been working on the real plot, the one way it can guarantee to get the Infanta on the throne of England.'

'But how? I just don't see—'

'Think!' said Gresham. 'For years Spain's been working on Cecil to isolate Essex, to get rid of him. Essex – the only one who wouldn't take a Spanish pension. And Cecil does their job for them, because he thinks he can play them and King James off against each other, and he wants rid of Essex – the only man with more influence with the Queen than he has – as much as they do. So Essex is first of all put in a position where he can't refuse to go to Ireland, and as a direct result is forced into rebellion. After that, it's simple. It only takes two men to get Spain on the throne of England: Grey is one. Bastard that he is, I'll bet my inheritance he's been in the pay of Spain for years. So he launches an attack on Essex's closest friend, Southampton, guaranteed to provoke Essex, be the last straw, act like a glove slapped across his face. The famous Sheriff Smith is the second man. Pay him to be on Essex's side, raise these men. And pay him to look the other way when his militia are reinforced in the morning by fifty extra men, dressed like militia but Spanish. Trained marksmen.'

'How can so few men make a difference?' asked George in desperation.

'You still can't see it, can you?' said Gresham. 'If Essex has any sense, he'll take Smith's men straight to Whitehall. He secures the Queen, takes her prisoner, calls Parliament together and declares a protectorate. London's fed up enough with the Queen and Cecil to rise up in support of him. Particularly if the Queen's kept alive.'

'So . . . so how does Spain come into all this?'

'So unbeknown to Essex, to Cecil and to anyone else except King Philip of Spain, there's fifty trained marksmen in that troop of bloody militia. Fifty *Spanish* marksmen smuggled in by bloody Cameron. Fifty trained marksmen who'll make sure they're in the forefront of those who go to drag the Queen from her bedchamber, who'll then calmly put a musket ball in her head or in her breast.'

'Oh God,' said George in a quiet voice, the enormity of it all suddenly dawning on him.

'Oh God, indeed,' said Gresham. He was sitting with his back to a wall. 'Are you starting to see it now? I'll bet half the Spaniards are English speakers, renegade Catholics who think they'll get to heaven by killing the heretic Queen. A few of them might be Scots too. No shortage of Scotsmen in the mercenary trade. When they've shot the Queen, they'll find and kill Cecil. He never leaves any Palace where the Queen is staying. Then they'll shoot Essex, and probably Meyrick and Davies if they get a chance.'

'And Cameron Johnstone will stand up with his Scottish accent,' said George, 'and declare the rebellion is in the name of King James of Scotland, soon to be King James of England.'

'And for good measure probably say as well that James is poised with an army just north of the border, poised to invade England to reinforce his point that he's our next King. It's very clever, isn't it?' said Gresham who was tiring of saying important things in a whisper. George's head was bowed. 'Both of James's greatest supporters, Cecil and Essex, are dead. A Scots King has not only killed his allies in Court, but has also killed our Queen. The English have gone off Elizabeth recently, but if anyone's going to kill her the average Englishman wants it to be one of us, not some hunchbacked sodomite from Scotland. And he's killed Essex as well, who they really do like. They're going to love James, aren't they? Raleigh will be the only survivor with any real clout. And guess what? For some strange reason they won't seek him out and kill him. He'll be the only figure with power in Court who's allowed to escape. He'll go berserk if he thinks James killed Elizabeth, he'll be galvanised into action. He'll have ambassadors off to Spain pleading for the Infanta to take over the throne before dawn's risen, and by evening he'll have an army marching to block the border. For once, everyone in England'll be on his side. And dear old James, who thought he had it all sewn up – Elizabeth seeing him as the least worse choice, Cecil gunning for him, Cameron Johnstone orchestrating it all beautifully, even Essex on his side – suddenly finds himself high and dry, the most hated man in England, his greatest ally proving to be a traitor, his other so-called allies all dead.'

'How could Cameron do that?' asked George, needing no concentration now to speak in a whisper. 'And how could I have been such a fool?'

'Same answer,' said Gresham. 'You see, a fox doesn't worry about killing a chicken. It doesn't invent a God, or morality, to tell it what to do. It doesn't give meaning to things, try to work out reasons. It just goes for the kill, because that's how it survives. Most humans aren't like that. They aren't animals, they have all these weaknesses: goodness, morality, feelings, a conscience, all that rubbish on the road to survival. Sometimes you meet people who've none of it: Cecil's one; Cameron's another. They have one, simple instinct, and no morality. Used in the right way, it gives you tremendous strength. And a huge advantage over the rest of us. By the way, he'll be here to kill me before long.'

'What?' said George.

'Think about it,' said Gresham. 'Cameron laid me out because I was about to tell Essex the truth. He'd have shot or stabbed me if he'd had the chance, but he didn't have a pistol and Essex had stopped everyone drawing their swords. What did he lay me out with? A stool? Or was it a complete table?' Gresham felt gingerly at the edges of his wound. 'Anyway, he can't let me live.'

'So what do we do?' asked George desperately.

'If I vanish and he comes in, he'll simply raise a hue and cry. You stay awake,' said Gresham, 'and keep my arms free, and lay your sword down here, by me where it won't alarm one of these men if they wake, but where Cameron can see it. And if you can grab a pistol, and point it at him, so much the better. But resist him because you're a friend of mine. Don't let him know what I've told you.'

'I thought we weren't friends any more,' said George.

'Irony comes back before friendship,' said Gresham. 'Stay awake.'

'But what about the fifty men?' asked George.

'As it happens,' said Gresham tiredly. It was going to be a real struggle to stay awake, never mind what dawn brought. 'High tide was about half an hour before sunset today. They can't land the men until nightfall. Take an hour, maybe a bit less to get them to the City. So by night the ebb tide would be positively ripping along. My men should have cut the mooring ropes just after dark. If it was windy they'll have had to board. But I don't think there's been any wind, so simply cutting the ropes should be enough. They'll only have one spare anchor at most, and it won't hold on that bottom, not with a full tide. There's no point in trying to sail up against the tide, not without wind. My men'll follow them down, give them a shooting party if they try to leave the ship. It'll be enough to make sure they're not where they need to be when they're needed. And Smith won't be there either. I saw to him this morning. It's amazing what an intimate description of what it's like to be hung, drawn and quartered does to a man.'

Cameron came in the hour before dawn. Gresham was still propped up against the wall, one arm conveniently near George's sword. George stared at Cameron, unblinking, a pistol surprisingly steady in his hand.

There was nothing in Cameron's eyes. No expression. No feeling. He looked directly at George.

'Your lands and your life, or your so-called friend? The choice is yours. But don't think you can have both! If I leave here with Gresham, you're safe. If I leave here without him, I'll make sure you're one of the first to be hung, drawn and quartered when Spain takes over the Crown!'

Gresham looked at George, not seeing a man worn down by failure, jealousy and bad decisions. Instead he saw the burly figure who had waded into the boys in the playground when Gresham was being beaten to a pulp, losing his senses and his dignity when a group of boys who had decided that to be a bastard was a crime had set on him.

'My so-called friend has scuppered your and Spain's chances. I hope even if I didn't know that, I'd choose my friend.'

Cameron was weighing up his chances, Gresham could see. Yet the pistol did not waver, and Gresham's capacity to resist was an unknown quantity. Cameron looked straight into Gresham's eyes.

'Perhaps not now. But later: you and your woman and your servant.'

'You realise the worst of it?' Gresham asked after Cameron had left, radiating malevolent hatred. 'If Essex turns to Whitehall, we might still have him as King. I've no way of knowing if Spain has

354

other men suborned at Whitehall, other men who might kill the Queen. It's possible.' It was the thought that had helped keep him awake through the dreadful night.

'So what's the answer?' asked George.

'I'm thinking,' said Gresham.

Essex House awoke before dawn, the atmosphere as frenzied as it had been the night before. Men were hoping to see their leader. They were disappointed.

'Bundle me in a corner,' said Gresham to George. 'Half hide me in that tapestry! And put some rope loosely round my wrists, so it looks as if I'm tied up still.'

Where was Essex? There were 300 armed men in the yard now, and more men coming in and out of the dining hall, not least because food was being prepared and handed out there. They could hear the noise of men riding out from the yard an hour or more before dawn, calling to Essex's supporters, gathering the clan. The men who came in to feed, gossip and look for their leader talked wildly. Raleigh had called to see his kinsman Sir Ferdinando Gorges at first light. Essex was so suspicious that he demanded the meeting take place on a boat in the middle of the Thames, in full view of Essex House. Discussion had been cut short when Essex had ordered four musketeers to set out from the river gate, and his bitter enemy Raleigh had rowed away. A consignment of arms ordered by Rutland from Europe had not arrived. Too many of the Welsh had not come to London yet. Where was Essex? Every minute that went by allowed the Privy Council to muster its forces.

It was late now, long past dawn, and the sense of frustration in the dining hall was getting greater by the minute. There was a sudden burst of jeering, yells from the yard; then a sudden cheer.

'Go to the window,' said Gresham, 'or better still, help me up so I can see.'

Gresham was convinced that if he appeared unbound he would be killed. Nearly every man who came in cast a wary glance at him. With George's help, he hobbled to the window.

The Privy Council had sent a deputation to Essex. Their arrival had been the source of the jeers. The cheers had been for Essex. He was there with a host of the others – Southampton, Rutland, Mounteagle – standing in the yard.

'Open the bloody window!' urged Gresham, and George fumbled with the catch. 'My God they're trying!' Gresham said.

'Who's trying?' said George.

'The Privy Council, that's who,' replied Gresham. 'Look at who they've sent: Egerton with the seal. He was Essex's jailer when he first fell out with the Queen, and by all accounts tried to be as decent as he could. Then there's Essex's uncle, Sir William Knollys and Worcester – he's a friend of Essex's. Who's the other one?'

'Popham,' said George, 'the Lord Chief Justice. I suppose they had to send him.'

'Hush!' said Gresham. He could only pick out odd words. Egerton raised his voice over the noise of the crowd, asking what the reason for this assembly was. Essex shouted back, speaking to his own men more than to the Lord Keeper, that men had sought to kill him, murder him even in his bed.

The Privy Councillors all tried to speak, but Southampton burst in, shrieking about the assault on him by Grey. The men started to chant, cheer and jeer. Egerton suddenly rammed his hat firmly down on his head. His words were clear enough. Disperse, he said to the crowd, or be found guilty of treason. Now that was guts, thought Gresham. He only hoped the actual guts that had produced the order would not soon be laid out on the cobbles of the yard. There were howls, yells, obscenities. 'Kill them!' was the least violent. Essex swung round, marched into the house. The four Privy Councillors followed him, buffeted by the crowd. The tumult came inside the house. Essex's study was along the corridor, separated from the dining chamber by a vestibule. For a moment Gresham thought the Privy Councillors were going to be marched into the dining hall. There was an increase in the noise, shouted words, raised voices. A door slammed. The Privy Councillors had been locked in Essex's study. The noise advanced to the dining hall. The door was flung open, and Essex was caught in the light from the high windows. He looked ill.

Two of the men they had sent to Essex were his relatives. The third was his erstwhile jailer who he had outwitted on every occasion. This was not the action of a Council with armed soldiers gathered round the Palace of Whitehall. Gresham thought of the fifty fat and pampered men who supposedly guarded the Queen, the edge on their pikes blunted by the gilding applied to the blade. These were the guards who had allowed the Earl, on his own, to burst directly into the Queen's bedchamber. Cecil, who had done so much to allow this rebellion, scorned military men and warfare as the last resort of the incompetent. Perhaps now he was being hoist by his own petard. Had he underestimated the power of the Earl and the 300 armed men Gresham had seen in the yard?

If Essex ordered his men to the Court, he would win the power he had craved for so long. Gresham knew it, felt it. If Cecil had prepared for this, it would have been armed men who came to Essex House not conciliatory Privy Councillors. Gresham was feeling rather sick, and his head was swimming. There were five Georges, where for a brief and merciful period there had been only one. He felt the need to vomit.

Essex burst into the dining hall. George stumbled to his feet. Essex ignored him. Poor old George, thought Gresham irreverently. His greatest skill was to be ignored by important people. Essex stood over Gresham with fifteen or twenty people behind him, every one of whom wished Gresham dead. Cameron, thank God, did not appear to be among them.

'I see you've managed to move in the night,' said Essex.

Damn the man! Someone in his position should not have remembered where he left a prisoner the night before.

'So, *Sir* Henry,' said Essex, laying ironic emphasis on the 'Sir' and getting the laugh he had aimed for from his followers. He drew his sword, and placed it not on Gresham's neck but pointing straight at his crotch. 'I and my men move out now.' He half turned to those behind him. 'They have banished us, they have told lies against us, they have tried to kill us. And now we march to tell them the truth, and to bring back justice to the land.'

A huge cheer rocked the vaulted ceiling of the hall.

'But do I turn to my left as I leave my house? To the Palace of Whitehall, to the Court and to the Queen? Even to Cecil and Raleigh?'

There was a huge cheer at this, even greater than before.

'Or do I turn to my right, to the City where my support lies, to pick up the thousand men you tell me do not exist, the men who will let me take the Tower – to the armoury for London, the fortress that commands it and commands the river – *and* the Palace?'

The red ring was round his eyes now, the flaming mark of the Devil.

'What is your advice, Sir Henry?' Again the ironic cheers, albeit a little confused. This game was going on too long. 'Do I go to the left or to the right? Think carefully before you answer. Kingdoms might depend on it.'

Gresham tried desperately to concentrate on Essex's face, which was going in and out of focus all the time. The right answer was clear. Go to the Court. Turn left. Capture the Queen, kill Cecil. But what if other, undiscovered Spanish marksmen were lurking there to kill Essex as well as the Queen? The fate of a country might depend on this decision, whether to turn to the right or the left.

If Essex turned left, England might have him as its next King. The wild, uncontrolled Earl, less suited to be a King than any man Gresham knew. Or it might find its throne handed over to Spain, its oldest and most bitter enemy, whose last reign over England had, under Queen Mary, produced clouds of greasy smoke smelling of burnt human flesh.

If England was to survive, Essex had to turn right. To the non-existent thousand men of Sheriff Smith, away from the Court.

What to say to Essex?

'Turn left, my Lord,' said Gresham. 'Turn left to the Court. It's your only chance.'

There was the longest pause in Henry Gresham's life.

'We turn right,' said Essex. 'We go to the City.' There was a muttering from the men behind him. 'This man has no love for me. He has tried to deceive me, lied to me about my thousand men. If he tells me to go one way it is to deceive me. We go to enhance our forces. We go so we shall be marching by afternoon on the Court with a thousand men, and the Tower in our hands!'

There was a confused cheer, and Essex swept from the room. That same rather half-hearted noise emerged shortly afterwards from the yard and, after a great clattering of hooves, a sudden silence descended on Essex House.

Time passed.

Gresham was still seated on the floor by the window, his back up against the panelling. George had wandered off to the other end of the room, and Gresham was gazing up, despite the pain in his neck, at the winter sunlight flooding in through the glass. He was entranced by its beauty. There was a faint thud from the other end of the room, and the noise of a pot breaking. Dear old George, clumsy as ever. He never could stop knocking things over. It wasn't worth moving his eyes from the wonderful light. Gresham called out, 'Bring some food, will you? And take this bloody rope off my feet before they fall off!'

There was silence, and a terrible fear crept into Henry Gresham's heart. He turned his head, slowly, painfully.

George's mouth was open in an expression of total surprise, his eyes wide, gaping, empty. He had fallen over a table, and a bowl full of pieces of bread was jammed under his cheek and raised up against his eye at a ludicrous angle. The dagger in his back stuck out like an obscene crucifix.

Cameron Johnstone, sword in hand, looked casually at the body, wiped the hand that had plunged the dagger into George against his side, and advanced towards Gresham. There was nothing in his eyes at all. No feeling, no compassion, not even any regret.

He stood over Gresham, and stuck his sword under Gresham's chin, not caring that the point broke flesh, producing a little stream of warm blood.

'Pleased, are you?' He had grabbed a piece of stale bread on his passage to Gresham and was eating it casually. 'I take it my fifty men won't be there to meet Essex? Or Sheriff Smith, for that matter.'

'Your fifty men won't be there, or so I hope. They'll be spitting nails, careering down into the sea with their mooring ropes cut and fifty of my own men shadowing them. Sheriff Smith'll be there. Briefly. To tell Essex to bugger off. He's been persuaded to change his mind.'

'Well, there's a thing,' said Cameron, and actually flipped a piece of bread in the air, catching it in his mouth as it fell. As he did so the point of his sword sunk further into Gresham's neck producing more warm blood.

Gresham suddenly shouted, 'Well, you're safe now, aren't you? It's only George and me who knew the truth about you and Spain, and George's dead and I'm about to be! Isn't that right?'

'Why are you shouting?' said Cameron, quickly glancing round the empty room. There was no one there, just the tables littered with pots and scraps of food. At least the shock of his shout had made Cameron withdraw the blade an iota, instead of pushing it in even further.

'Because ... because ...' Gresham was forcing himself to remain conscious. He might as well be aware of the moment when Cameron killed him – it would be the last thing he would ever be aware of. 'Because I'm delirious and concussed from where you hit me, and because where there should be one of you there are three or even four sometimes, none of them any more attractive than the others ... my, you have put on weight,' he added inconsequentially, 'shouldn't eat so much bread.'

'Oh, very funny,' said Cameron. He pushed the blade back in a bit, for good measure. 'But I don't want you to die just yet. Very soon, but not just yet. You see, you've caused me more problems than anyone else I've met. If only Essex had turned left and gone to the Court. I tried to persuade him. If only.'

'So you had other men at Whitehall?' asked Gresham.

'And only at Whitehall, as it happens,' said Cameron. 'None at Nonsuch, or Greenwich or Hampton. Only at Whitehall. Three of them. It might have been enough. But Essex wouldn't listen. He thinks you are the cleverest man in England. Was convinced that the cleverest man in England would never give him the right advice, was too loyal to the Queen to do so. You double bluffed him, didn't you?'

'Yes,' said Gresham. There was not much more to say. Elizabeth would never know he had saved her throne, kept his word. In doing so, he had ensured Essex's death. The rebellion would fizzle out without the men Essex was expecting, and by the time he reached Whitehall there would be half an army round it. Was it a fair exchange? Essex for Elizabeth?

It is better for England, he kept saying to himself. Not that England would ever know, or care.

'Well,' said Cameron, 'you may have double bluffed him, but you won't do it to me. There are two more people who know about me, aren't there?' He tweaked the blade a little, to emphasise the point. 'There's that woman of yours. The lovely Jane. I'll have her raped before I kill her. Might even do it myself. Several times. The rape, I mean, as well as the killing. So she knows what she's done by believing in a shit like you.'

The agonising pain in Gresham's head and the different pain in his neck began to spread to the rest of his body.

'And then there's that hulk of a man you call your servant, and who's actually your master. Mannion. We need something special for him. I wonder ... perhaps if I castrate him and cut out his tongue, but let him live?'

'He might surprise you,' said Gresham suddenly.

'You've surprised me,' said Cameron, withdrawing his sword and looking carefully at its bloodied point, 'but not for much longer. And I don't propose to let anyone else surprise me.'

It is a strange sight seeing half a man's head mashed to pulp by a lead pistol ball that enters from the rear and blows out the front of the face. The half of the head that is still recognisable carries the

361

expression formed by the last order the brain was capable of sending it. So as Cameron Johnstone died, the left-hand side of his face retained the look of snarling superiority. His body stood upright for a ludicrous second, and then toppled forward.

Mannion stood by the table from under which he had emerged, a smoking pistol in his hand.

'I don't propose to let anyone else surprise me!' he said, and spat on what was left of Cameron's head. 'Castrate me, would you, you bugger!'

'I shouted when I saw the latch lift up!' said Gresham desperately.

'I know,' said Mannion, cradling him as George had done.

'I tried to keep him talking as you crept up under the table,' said Gresham.

'I know,' said Mannion.

'And he killed George. George saved my life earlier,' said Gresham gabbling. 'Do you think there's any chance he's alive?'

'I didn't know that about George,' said Mannion with infinite compassion. 'And I'm afraid he really is dead.'

'Oh God,' said Gresham, and fainted.

CHAPTER 14

25 February, 1601
London

Gresham and Jane were sitting in the Library. Few households ate breakfast as a formal meal, preferring to grab a crust or a handful of leftovers from supper. Dr Stephen Perse at Cambridge had advised Gresham always to start the day well with food. Gresham's weakness from campaigning days was cremated bacon, burnt to a crisp on an open fire. This morning he had to force the food down his throat. Jane joined him at breakfast if he asked, but never ate.

'Why won't you take breakfast with me? I mean actually eat with me?' he had asked idly one morning.

'Because that is what a wife would do,' she had answered simply. Most men dreaded their mistress demanding marriage. Jane must be the first mistress to have turned the offer down.

The rebellion had fizzled out, of course. Essex had left it too late. If he and his men had been by St Paul's Cross at eight in the morning, in time for the first sermon, they might have started a tidal wave that would have swept through London.

As it was, they marched to the east, turned right, through streets that were increasingly empty. Sheriff Smith, whom Essex had never met, always relying on others, denied any promise of support and had fled through his back door. The City authorities drew a chain over Ludgate where Essex had entered, meaning he would have to fight to get back even to his own house. He lingered in Fenchurch Street, in the house of Sheriff Smith, stealing the supplies the Sheriff kept in his kitchen. Roused to action at last, he fought a minor skirmish at Ludgate, was beaten back and finally made it to the river. In the end Essex retreated to his house, the most dynamic thing he did all day being to ask for a clean shirt, because his own was soaked in sweat. When the Privy Council brought up cannon to demolish the house, they surrendered: Essex, Southampton and the rest.

'Do you wish you had gone to the trial?' asked Jane.

'And rub his face in the fact that I helped destroy his rebellion – a man I'd once claimed as a friend? No. And the trial was a farce, as all such trials are. A show trial.'

In response to a heated accusation from Essex, Robert Cecil admitted that he had said to Sir William Knollys that the Spanish Infanta had a claim to the throne, but in such a context as to make the statement meaningless. Both he and Knollys denied they had fixed up their story beforehand. It had destroyed any case Essex might have had, condemned him.

'But they let Southampton off,' said Jane, 'merely locked him up in the Tower.'

They said it was because of his youth and inexperience. Yet this was a man who had drunk a murdered child's blood. Gresham had talked of Essex's confession to no one. Essex had never said who the men in white with hoods were or where they came from. Were those men so powerful as to be able to protect Southampton, even if they could do nothing for Essex? Was English society corrupted to its core with Devil-worshippers? Or did the Devil really exist, and look after at least some of his own?

'Are you going to . . . the Tower?' asked Jane hesitantly.

'How can I deny a summons to attend the execution from the Queen? I've no option.'

'Why has she asked you?' Jane looked worried.

'They're executing him inside the Tower in case there's a riot. They've made no public announcement.' The order for Gresham to attend had come late the night before, the most strict secrecy enjoined on him. A final test of loyalty? 'They need a few eyewitnesses, and people who won't call out for Essex. I'm an obvious invitee.' The food rose in his throat as he contemplated what he must do and see. A blow struck in anger, a blow struck in the heat of battle, these had a validity, justification. The slow, cruel, methodical process of an execution, its clinical lack of emotion, its reasoned premeditated calm, sickened him to his core.

'And what of us?' he asked gazing fondly at her.

She looked up, startled.

'Are you unhappy with our relationship?'

'No,' he said, 'I'm not. I have everything – a mistress for my bed, a companion when I need one who yet knows when to leave me alone, a steward for my house. You, on the other hand, have very little, not even security. You place no restriction on me, no obligation. It hardly seems fair.'

Jane looked at him levelly, glorious eyelashes framing the unfathomable depths of her eyes.

'It's as I choose and as I wish,' she said simply. And something like a grimace crossed her face. 'The person who tries to tie you down will simply be left with a broken rope in their hands. And ropeburn.' She rose.

'Before you go,' he said, 'you should know I've arranged for an annuity to be paid to George's children.'

Lord Willoughby's estate had proven bankrupt on his innocent death as the result of a stab wound from a wild and drunken supporter of the Earl of Essex.

'Lady Willoughby's also been looked after.' There was distaste in Gresham's voice. He could think of better uses for his money. 'She seemed reluctant to care for the children of a bankrupt – I didn't tell her about the annuities – so they're going to the care of Gervase Markham.'

As far as the public were concerned, Gervase Markham was a

lively young man who had left the service of the Earl of Essex when it became clear that the Earl was headed towards rebellion.

'May I ask you something?' said Jane. 'Was it Spain who tried to kill you, on the boat and in Ireland? And when Cameron said he killed someone trying to kill the Queen, who was that? Was he telling the truth?''

Gresham sighed. 'Cameron told the truth about the assassination attempt on Elizabeth. It was a fool of a young Scotsman, put up to it by some hotheads in James's Court who thought that if they killed Elizabeth James was bound to inherit, and Christmas would come early to the Scottish Court. James heard about it, and simply wasn't prepared to kill a fellow monarch. He didn't have to; he knows she'll die of natural causes in a few years anyway. So James ordered Cameron to stop the assassination – to Cameron's great annoyance, I imagine. Cameron had been bought by Spain then, and a Scotsman killing Elizabeth might have done wonders for the Spanish claim. But it'd all come about too early, and Cameron daren't disobey James in case he revealed himself.'

'And on the boat?' Jane prompted, 'and in Ireland?'

'It was the Spanish on the boat. I thought they wanted the two messages from Cecil and the Queen. Oh, they'd have used the one from Cecil to blackmail him, and the Queen's message was simply to say thank you – rather grudgingly, I imagine – for stopping the assassin. But the messages would have been a bonus. It was me they wanted. I'm sure they saw me as the only person talking sense to Essex, and all their plans hinged on him leading a rebellion. So I was a real threat, and what better way to dispose of me than out of sight and out of mind at sea? It would have been just another boat that set sail and was never seen again.'

'And Ireland?' she asked.

'That's the funny bit,' said Gresham. 'When they were all set to hang me, at the Council of War, that was Cameron's doing. He and Spain wanted me dead, so what better way than to organise a judicial killing, let Essex's cronies vent their hatred of me as a rival for

Essex's favour? Cameron had been working on them for weeks, and it damn nearly worked.'

'But what about the soldiers you told me about? The ones who fired on you at the Pass of Plumes?'

'Cecil's men,' said Gresham. 'We spent a lot of money and a lot of time tracking them down. We found them eventually. Or Mannion did.'

A shudder passed through Jane's body. She did not want to know whether those two men were still alive.

'So Cecil was trying to kill you as well!'

'No,' said Gresham. 'That's the other funny bit. He was trying to kill Essex. That was what he'd paid the men to do. He'd bribed two men from my company. Why waste a chance to throw muck on my reputation? But someone had told the men it was Essex leading the charge, trying to regain his reputation. Then there's this great clatter, and amid the smoke and dust they see someone vaguely of Essex's build leading the charge on Essex's horse.'

'Essex's horse?' said a bewildered Jane.

'An accident,' said Gresham. 'His war horse and mine could be identical twins. So the soldier only had a split second. He assumed it was Essex and shot, thinking fate had given them a one-off chance to earn their pay.'

'So Cecil didn't try to kill you?' she asked incredulously.

'No,' said Gresham, almost sadly. 'For once he appears to be innocent. He gave me a package for Scotland, in good faith. He really thought I was the best person to take it. The rest of it was Spain trying to get me out of the way.'

They pondered this extraordinary fact in silence for a few minutes. Then Jane left, sensing his need to gather his thoughts alone before leaving on the fell journey to the Tower.

There were only a handful of them there to see Essex die. The Queen had sent two executioners, in case one refused. Essex was calm, dignified, perhaps almost heroic. How often had the Tower seen men who were sworn enemies to the man on the scaffold wipe away surreptitious tears as their enemy spoke his last word? Essex's last words were whipped away on the wind, inaudible to all except the executioner and the priest on the scaffold. Essex had not caught Gresham's eye, preferring to raise his eyes to heaven, if it existed. Where God, if he existed, might forgive him the sacrifice of a child. Or where Lucifer, if he existed, might claim him as his own.

EPILOGUE

Sir Gelli Meyrick was hung, drawn and quartered, his knight-hood being deemed inadequate to protect him from the fate of a common man. Some others were similarly treated or beheaded, but the Earl of Southampton was simply imprisoned in the Tower, on the grounds of his youth and inexperience. Accusations of sodomy and Devil-worship were never proven against the conspir-ators, though Southampton was widely believed to take men and boys to bed. He flourished under the reign of King James. As part of the rewards lavished on the Earl, James granted him the farm of sweet wines. A number of the hotheads who were allowed to sur-vive went on to be leading lights of the Gunpowder Plot.

The rumour was born at this time that several years earlier the Queen had gifted Essex a ring, stating it as a testimony of her love to him, and that if ever he needed true forgiveness, when he had been true to her, he should send her that ring and be forgiven. Various people were deemed to have been given that ring by Essex for safe keeping. It was a ruby, set round by small but perfect dia-monds.

HISTORICAL NOTE

The events in this novel took place in history as described here. As for some of the things that might seem fanciful fiction, the Earl of Essex did wear a black bag round his neck, and its contents were as described. The only fictional characters, apart from minor ones, are Henry Gresham, who is based on two contemporary figures and one living person; Mannion and Jane, who are based on one dead and one living person and, in the latter case, someone I know very well. Cameron Johnstone is also fictional, and I apologise to my Scottish family for using the Johnstone name in his case. The character of Robert Cecil is, unfortunately, based on a living character.

There is great uncertainty about both the author and the date of the crude revenge tragedy *The Revenger's Tragedy*, almost certainly erroneously credited to Cyril ('Cy') Tourneur. A possible author is the ill-fated Thomas Kyd, whose work is largely lost but who we know was heavily plagiarised, and probably wrote an early version of *Hamlet* and *The Taming of the Shrew*. A Swiss tourist recorded seeing a production of a play that might have been Shakespeare's *Julius Caesar* in September 1599. It is entirely possible that Shakespeare's play, or a version of it, could have been performed a year earlier.